the Sweetness of life

KATHRYN ANDREWS

The Sweetness of Life

Published by Kathryn Andrews LLC

www.kandrewsauthor.com

ISBN-13: 978-1975867324

ISBN-10: 1975867327

Cover design by Julie Burke

Formatting by CP Smith

Dedication

For my boys . . .

the Sweetness of life

Chapter 1

kiss my grits

Shelby

"Oh my God, you have to try this, Shelby," Meg says, startling me as she bumps her hip on the kitchen door, forcing it to swing open. Cinnamon and clove floats through the air of the empty restaurant and hits my nose. I watch as she crosses the small dining room to sit at my table.

It's Sunday night, we're closed, and the last of our staff left a while ago. The light from a streetlamp outside pours in the front window, illuminating the partially lit room. I hadn't even realized the sun had set. We've both been here for fifteen hours, and it's true what they say, time does fly when you're having fun.

Closing the lid to my laptop, Meg takes the first bite of the dessert and drops the fork. It clatters to the plate as she leans back in her chair and lets out a low, satisfied moan.

"You're so dramatic," I scold, shaking my head and fighting a smile.

Her eyes snap to mine and sparkle with laughter. I've known

Meg since we were freshmen in college and I swear the older we get, the more theatrical she becomes.

Snatching the fork, I cut off a bite of the dessert for myself, watching as the honey strings between the warm pastry layers and the fork. I'm not gonna lie, it smells divine, and I've been waiting for the last forty-five minutes to taste it.

"Yeah, but you love me anyway." She grins. "Tell me, did I kill that recipe or what?" she asks, waiting for my reaction and watching me chew my bite. Then, as if she can't handle the anticipation of my answer, she wipes her hands across her thighs to smooth down her apron—a light green-and-white gingham apron that once belonged to her grandmother. She wears it every time she's creating something new in the kitchen. It's like her thinking cap, and when she puts it on, I know to let her be.

Focusing on the individual flavors, I sort through each one to see if anything is lacking or overpowering. Swallowing the bite, my eyes find hers, and I smirk, knowing I'm about to set her off. "It needs salt."

Her jaw drops, and a piece of her brown wavy hair escapes from the messy bun on top of her head.

"What! No way." She blows the hair off her face, grabs the fork, and sinks it back into her version of baklava. In the South, we're ruled by pecans, so she's substituted them in place of the walnuts.

"Yes way." I lick my lips. "And the cloves are a bit too strong."

Silence falls between us as she takes another bite and then hands the fork back to me. Together, we finish off the piece, and she swipes her finger across the plate for the last remaining crumb.

"You're crazy. That"—she points to the empty plate—"was delicious."

"I'm not saying it wasn't, but I'm right." I reach for the sweet tea sitting next to my laptop and take a drink while letting her think through the recipe.

The sharpness in her eyes dissolves and the defensiveness in her posture relaxes as she lets out a long, loud sigh. “I hate it when you’re right.”

“No, you don’t. Just like I love you for your brand of crazy, you love me for my awesome, perfect palate.” I grin at her, and she rolls her eyes.

“I can’t argue with you there.” She wraps the fallen piece of hair back up into the knot. That’s what makes us so great together: she’s brilliant at creating, and I’m spot on at tasting.

Meg pushes away from the table, grabs the plate, and heads back to the kitchen, her heels clicking across the wood floor. That’s the other thing that connects us—we love—LOVE—high-heeled designer shoes.

Packing up my laptop, I look around at our two-year-old restaurant that I adore, Orange Blossom Avenue, or OBA for short. OBA isn’t a huge place, but we don’t need it to be. During the week, we’re open for breakfast and lunch. On the weekends, we open for brunch and the occasional special dinner, and we are always open for private events. The ambiance is quaint, clean, and Southern chic, with the color scheme focusing on orange, green, and white—like an orange blossom.

Owning this restaurant is Meg’s dream whereas mine is to have my own show on Food Network. Over the last ten plus years, I’ve spent almost every moment thinking about and working toward that moment when my dreams will finally come true and three weeks ago, I interviewed for a host position of a new show at their headquarters. I’m not ashamed to admit that I’ve lost hours of sleep dreaming about what my life will be like when I get to New York

City.

"So, what are you going to call it?" I ask, walking into the kitchen.

"Southern baklava, of course." Meg flashes a smile at me as she wipes down the prep station. "Who knows, maybe it'll end up on your blog." She eyes me with mischief.

My blog, *Starving for Southern*.

Sometime during our second year of college, I got the bright idea to start a food blog. Every weekend, instead of chasing boys and partying, Meg and I would travel all over and look for the best places to eat. It made sense to record it all. We ate at some amazing places and some not-so-good ones, too. Toss in our own recipes of things we liked, and before I knew it, the blog had a huge following. A huge, *unexpected* following.

Mostly, I've been able to keep my anonymity. Only a handful of people know that one of the owners of OBA and the author of *Starving for Southern* are the same person. After all, a true critic never exposes who they are, even though it was never my intention to be one. I would say that eighty-five percent of the food blog is positive—it really isn't my goal to bash someone's dream—but that other fifteen percent . . . it can't be helped.

"I thought you were going out with that guy Neil tonight?" she asks me, carrying the last of today's dishes to the dishwasher and stacking them on the rack.

"No, I need to finish this next article for *Food Network Magazine*."

"He seems to be really into you . . . and he's cute." She takes my iced tea glass, adds it to the others, and pulls down the cage of the washer. It kicks on and the hum fills the space between us.

I met Neil at an art gallery opening last weekend that Meg and I catered. He was there to support his friend, the artist. "I know, and I thought he had potential until I watched him eat."

Meg's forehead wrinkles with confusion as she glances back over her shoulder at me, unties the apron, and hangs it on a large wrought iron coat rack that houses all the aprons we've collected over the years. "What happened?"

"He dropped in yesterday while you ran to the grocery store. He ordered the fried green tomato BLT and sucked his teeth after every bite."

"Eww!" Meg squeals in horror. "I can't believe you didn't tell me about this yesterday! What is it with you and guys lately? You have the worst track record of anyone ever," she says as we walk out of the kitchen. I head back to my table as she goes into the small office to get today's bank deposit.

"I know! I don't get it at all." Not that I'm interested in dividing my time between work and a guy, I prefer the work hands down, but I do enjoy their company every now and then. Bending over, I unclasp the straps of my heels, slide them off, and toss them in my bag. A groan escapes me as my feet flatten to the floor.

In the last year, I've cooked for a guy here at the restaurant who was vehemently against vegetables, so he wouldn't do, and I found another taking photos of my recipes on his phone when I left the room—thief!

"You know, it all started with that wine guy Lexi tried to set me up with last fall at the Feeding America charity event."

"Oh, that guy was the worst! What was his name again?"

"Zachary Wolff."

Just saying his name heats my blood to a near boil, and my mind drifts back to an image of him and his haughty, disapproving glare. Lexi, who we met at culinary school, set us up on a blind date and had pointed him out to me shortly after we arrived, so I saw him before he saw me, and my breath caught at how incredibly handsome he was. For the first time in a long time, I thought, *maybe, just maybe*. But once introductions were made, he immediately frowned and looked away. Talk about a self-confidence crusher.

"That's right. Too bad, too—he was hot. Wasn't he a football player or something?"

"Yeah, he was hot, and he knew it, too. Lexi did mention that he was ex-NFL. I've never met a man so stuck on himself. How or why she's friends with him, I'll never know. Whatever. He barely gave me a second glance, which was so rude since he was supposed to be my date. Plus, he thought he was God's gift to the wine world, looking down his nose at everyone at that event. And his wines aren't that good!"

"How do you know? We don't stock them here," Meg asks as she emerges from the office.

"Well, technically I don't know. I've never tasted his wines. But don't you remember that article I stumbled across and showed you shortly after the event? The one that talked about the mediocre table wines? That's his winery."

"Now that you mention it, I do remember that. They rated those wines with four wilted grapes. Well, karma's a bitch. Someone needs to remind him that you catch more flies with honey than vinegar."

"Seriously. I almost felt bad for him after reading it. Almost." It's too bad, though. I'd never seen eyes as blue as his—ice blue, that is. Just like his personality. "It's all right, I really don't have time to deal with a guy right now anyway. I want these articles to be so good that the editors of *Food Network Magazine* want to work with me year after year. And between the restaurant and the blog, I'm too busy. Career first, guys later. Remember?" I lift my bag onto my shoulder and tuck it under my arm.

Meg turns to face me with an understanding look. "I know you're worried about the articles, but don't be. They'll be amazing . . . no, they already are." She smiles, and it's so genuine I almost believe her. How crazy different would life be if I'd never met her?

"I hope so," I mumble.

Last year, a representative from the magazine contacted me to see if I was interested in writing for a special edition magazine, *All About the South*, and I about died. Someone had seen my blog and thought I would be perfect given my thorough knowledge of restaurants in the South. Meg and I celebrated for a solid week by eating, drinking, and splurging on some new shoes.

My assignment was simple, they were constructing four magazines for the four regions of the United States, and I was asked to recommend twenty-five different restaurants across the southeast with the theme focusing on seafood: Gulf shrimp, crawfish, crab, grouper, et cetera. Meg and I changed OBA's operational hours to four days a week and we traveled Monday through Wednesday for three months, eating our way to a complete state of bliss.

I mean, why not? Both of us are young, single, the restaurant is ours to open and close when we want . . . and best of all—we got paid. So, when they called again this year, I was over the moon. I now have two consecutive years of work for the magazine to add to my resume, and I know I have to make my contribution super spectacular.

This year the focus is farm-to-table. Each regional issue will highlight restaurants that use locally grown food. They want another twenty-five recommendations where I mention impressive farmers' markets and family farms. Personally, I think it's a great idea. The fresher the better.

"You headed home?" I ask her. Meg and I are also roommates, but occasionally she sleeps at her aunt's just to keep an eye on her.

"Yeah, after I drop this off at the bank." She waves the zippered bank envelope at me and flips the lights off.

Together we walk out the front door, she locks it and hits the remote alarm app on her phone. From inside my bag, my phone starts ringing. I drop it on the sidewalk and start digging until my fingers find it.

"I'll see you in a bit," Meg says, taking a few steps backward. "I'm thinking it's a wine and a hot guy dancing kind of night." She drops her arm and does a bad version of the robot.

A laugh bursts out of me and echoes down the sidewalk.

"Sounds perfect!" I grin at her before turning my attention to my phone. It's my editor from the magazine, Teddy Carothers. Every time his name flashes across the screen, my heart skips a beat—half excitement and half nerves. I've wanted to be a part of the Food Network family for so long, there's always this slight fear that with one phone call it can go away, just like it arrived.

"Hi, Mr. Carothers. How are you?" I stand and grab my bag, trying to keep my voice calm and my hand steady. Ever since I started working for him last year, I have had to remind myself to show no fear. I've worked hard for this, and I deserve it.

"I'm great, Shelby, thanks for asking. Is now a good time?" It's after eight—he never calls this late—and my hand tightens on the phone. Part of me wonders if he was contacted about the studio job, but I'll never ask.

"Yes, now's a great time. We just locked up OBA, and I'm about to head home." I make my way across the street to my car, barely feeling the inconsistencies of the cobblestone and fallen oak pollen under my bare feet.

"Very good. So, I'm curious, how's the assignment coming along?" Last year, he never asked me about the assignment. I had three deadlines—the twenty-five recommendations were broken up into sections: nine, eight, and eight. I submitted on time, he said, "Great job," and that was the end of it.

Sliding into my car, I toss my bag onto the passenger seat and when it tips over, I frown as all my things spill out onto the floor. "I'm almost done with it. Would you like me to send you what I have?" Nerves flit through my stomach and I grip the steering wheel. The article isn't ready yet, I glance to my laptop which is standing on its side, but I could spend all night on it if I had to.

"No, that won't be necessary. You can send it all once it's done." There's a pause in the conversation. I can hear the shuffling of some papers on his end, him swallowing, and a glass hitting the table. Anxiety takes off and my hands start to sweat. "But listen . . . turns out, I have another idea to run by you."

Another idea?

Images of the last two months and all the work I've put in skip through my mind.

"Okay, what idea is that?" I ask as calmly as I can.

"I know this is last minute, and we still want you to finish your current article, but tell me, have you ever heard of Wolff Winery?" Blue eyes and a condescending scowl flash before my eyes for the second time tonight. I shake my head to clear the image and find the road in front of me cloaked in shadows and empty.

"Yes. In fact, I met Mr. Wolff last year." I grit my teeth at his name. *Arrogant ass.*

"Ah, well, that's great then! We've spoken to Mr. Wolff, and if you agree, we've decided to pair the two of you together for a feature article in the upcoming Southern issue. We would need you at his winery by tomorrow afternoon if possible. I just e-mailed over the details, you'll need to clear your schedule for a bit, and he can fill you in on the rest."

What!

No. No. No. No. No.

The nerves in my stomach instantly flee and dread drops in. They want us to work together? I have to work with him? But I don't want to work with him. He agreed to this? He doesn't like me . . . and that's fine with me!

"Okay, I need to run this by Meg, but it shouldn't be a problem." Meg is going to flip out, and then she's going to laugh at me. Again, these things only happen to me. Of all the wineries in the south, they go and pick his.

"Perfect. We're really excited about this new project for you two. You were our first choice, and we know the article is going to be great. Once you get settled in, give me a call." The creak of his chair comes through the line and more papers shuffle in the background.

"All right, I will," I say, trying my hardest to sound as excited as he is when everything in me is screaming to abort the mission.

"Thanks for being so flexible. Take care, Shelby." Then he hangs up.

There should be silence in the car, but my ears are ringing so loudly my vision blurs.

Oh my God!

Sucking in some air to calm my pounding heart, my head hits the steering wheel, the phone drops to my lap, and I squeeze my eyes shut. What are the odds that Meg and I were just talking about him? What are the odds that of the thousands of wineries out there, his gets picked? And why did his get picked? Per that review, the wines are supposed to be mediocre. Maybe this is karma's way of getting to me somehow. But why? At the event, he was cold and made me feel as if I were nothing more than an unwanted relative he was stuck with. He ignored me most of the night, preferring conversations with every other girl there but me, and he drank too much. It wasn't that he became loud and obnoxious, quite the opposite, he became sullen. He made me feel inadequate, and I don't let anyone make me feel that way, ever. I don't care who you are. After that night, I made a solemn vow to never see him again . . . or drink his wine.

Leaning back in the seat, I take a few deep breaths and let out a resigned sigh before pressing the ignition button. Hopefully, this assignment with him won't be a big one, and we can get it over with as soon as possible.

Shaking my head and rolling my shoulders, I push away the tension weighing me down, and that's when it hits me.

Featured article.

Mr. Carothers, from *Food Network Magazine,* has asked me to pair up for a featured article! *Me.* Not another journalist, but me. And he said I was their first choice!

Elation takes over, and I squeal as if I've won the lottery. My name is going to be printed several times in this new issue, giving me even *more* exposure. Little by little, a little becomes a lot, and step by step, article by article, I'm getting closer to my dream.

My dream.

Flashes of my childhood flip through my mind, and each passing one acts as a stimulant to my already racing heart. That ever-present reminder of the things he said and the things they did, it's the constant spark that keeps my determination blazing, and as my eyes widen and my hands tighten on the wheel, I'd swear the street light's glow is brighter.

"I can do this! I will do this!" I chant to myself. Zachary Wolff is nobody to me, and he can kiss my grits. No one is *ever* going to get in my way.

No one.

Ingredients:

2/3 cup honey
1/2 cup sugar
1/2 cup water
1 teaspoon lemon juice
1 teaspoon ground cinnamon
1/2 teaspoon ground cloves
8 ounces of finely chopped pecans
1/2 teaspoon salt
1 teaspoon ground cinnamon
1 stick of butter
1 16-ounce package of thawed phyllo dough

How to make:

Preheat the oven to 350 degrees. Combine the pecans, cinnamon, and salt in a bowl. Melt the butter in a small sauce over a low heat or in the microwave. Unroll the phyllo dough for a 9×11 glass dish. Cover with waxed paper topped with a damp towel until needed.

Layer 4 to 8 sheets of the phyllo dough, brush with butter, sprinkle some of the pecan mixture across the top. Layer 4 to 8 more sheets on top and repeat the process until all the layers of phyllo have been used and the pecan mixture is gone. Don't forget to brush with butter. Cut diagonally into 1-inch diamond shapes, cutting through all the layers. Bake for 35 minutes or until brown. Remove from the oven.

Combine the honey, sugar, water, lemon juice, cinnamon, and cloves in a medium saucepan. Cook over a medium heat and stir until ingredients are mixed well and dissolved. Reduce heat to low and cook for 10 minutes. Remove from heat and allow to cool.

Pour the honey mixture over the warm baklava. Let stand 45 minutes to 1 hour before serving.

Chapter 2

madder than a wet hen

Zach

A car door slams, and I glance out the window of my office to see a small black BMW parked by the fountain. A girl slips behind the back of the car and she appears to be alone. We usually don't have many guests at eleven on a Monday morning, so my guess is that she's here to sell something.

"Earth to Zach, are you even listening to me?" Kyle, my sales director says grabbing my attention. I turn back to him and find his lips pinched together, frustration evident. Whatever. He'll get over it.

Scrubbing one hand over my face, I squeeze the football resting on my leg with the other and give him an apologetic look. My computer dings twice, alerting me of incoming e-mails and a sigh escapes me. My to-do list grows faster than I can cross things off, and I'm beat.

"Sorry, my head's all over the place and now we have this *Food Network Magazine* project, too." I shove a detailed list of requests and requirements for the next two weeks across the desk to him, grab a piece of bourbon bacon pecan brittle, and contemplate moving the plate so Kyle doesn't eat any. Yeah, I know it's a dick move, but I can't help it—it's one of my favorite things.

"I understand; you don't need to explain it to me." He picks up the list and scans it. "But this is going to be good for us." His look is somber, but his eyes give away the hopefullness he feels. The last few months have been difficult for both of us.

"Well, it's this or you lose your job." I grin to try to lighten the mood, but he just snorts and shakes his head. "This is going to be good for us, and I know it's going to boost sales. This winery has been in my family for over a hundred years, and I won't be the reason it collapses. Short of selling my soul to the devil, I'll do anything."

"So, what time does the circus roll into town?" Kyle asks, pushing the paper aside smirking as he steals a piece of the brittle. I'm on to him, and this is his passive way of getting me back for that comment.

"I'm not sure. There was a message on my office line this morning saying the Charleston chef will be here sometime later today, and the crew isn't showing up until tomorrow morning. We're supposed to help them get settled, and our first interview is at noon." I wish they had left a full name for the chef. After a quick Internet search, I came up empty handed. Apparently, Leigh is a common name in Charleston, and I can't help but wonder if they tried to search the winery.

"Girl? Guy?" Kyle grabs a bottle of water he's placed on my desk and takes a gulp.

"Girl." Palming the football, I toss it into the air and catch it. "All they told me is that her name is Leigh."

"I hope she's hot." My eyes lock on to Kyle's. He raises his eyebrows, nods his head and smiles as if that's the best idea ever. Kyle is five years older than I am, and he gets out even less than I do. He lives and breathes the winery.

A laugh breaks free from me and echoes around the office. "I seriously doubt it. This chick eats for a living. Who do you know that's a hot chef?"

"Come on! There's Katie Lee, Giada, Cat Cora, and besides, what do you have against big love?"

"Okay, I'll give you those three. Three. And nothing—I love them all shapes and sizes, but you know as well as I do that I don't have time for a girl. Plus, a girl brings gossip, bad media, and we need every word to be positive." After Elaine, my ex-girlfriend, and I broke up, I threw myself into taking over the winery. I've been so consumed with running it and trying to keep it afloat, it seems I haven't had time for anything or anyone else. The smile slips from his face, and he pinches his lips together.

Another car door slams, and my look is dragged back out the window to see the woman walking away from the passenger side of the car and toward the tasting room. She appears average height and build, blonde hair, and she's wearing a loose shirt, tight jeans, and heels. Heels. No one wears heels out here unless there's an event—or is a salesperson. Our winery is a farm winery. The girl stumbles as her heels sink into the gravel walkway, and she drops her big fancy bag. I'm immediately annoyed. I don't have time to deal with any solicitors today.

"Do you know who that is?" Kyle asks, following my gaze outside.

"Nope, but whoever she is, she doesn't belong here, not today at least." Together we watch her walk up the stairs and through the door.

"All I'm saying is if you have to spend two weeks with someone, it would be nice if she was hot."

"I can't argue with you there, but still. No girls." People have seen enough of my face. They don't need to see it anymore, and quite honestly, I don't need the headache of it all.

I am a football player, or I should say was. My whole life has been about farming this land and playing football. There was no question—ever—whether I would take over the vineyard; it was just a matter of when. I wish I could have played in the NFL a little longer—it's a sore subject for me, very sore—but my time was up. One injury too many, and I had to graciously accept defeat, hang up my helmet, and say goodbye. At twenty-seven, I bought out my father's ownership of the winery so he and my mother could retire and travel the world, and here I am. I really do love it, which is what makes this all bittersweet.

Kyle frowns at me as my phone rings. A light next to the back bar line flashes.

I punch the button for the speaker and bark out, "Yeah?"

"Zach," Michelle's voice blares across the office. "There's a Ms. Leigh here to see you."

Whoa, fashion queen is the chef? My eyes widen a bit and Kyle's smile shifts to an I-told-you-so smirk.

"Please let her know I'll be right out."

Kyle leans forward and places his bottle back on my desk, grinning, and my eyes narrow at him.

"Will do," she says.

"Thanks." The phone clicks off, and the annoyance I already feel for this girl tightens in my chest and twists to something more like nerves. Getting the phone call that my winery had been chosen for the *All About the South* issue had been an answer to our prayers. It turns out that one of their executives was in town with family over spring break and stopped in. We didn't know it at the time, but it was relayed to us that the executive loved our history, our location, and our wines. This assignment was a last-minute addition, and we've spent the last thirty-six hours preparing for the crew's arrival. The thought of something going wrong has my stomach in knots.

Kyle slaps his hands together and rubs them back and forth as he stands. "Things just got really interesting," he drawls out.

"Why do you say that?" I stand with him and grip the ball in both hands before I fake like I'm going to throw it, rolling my shoulder through the motion.

"Dude, I saw her. Even from here, the girl is hot. Didn't you get a look at those long legs?"

"Actually, I didn't." Well, maybe I did. My eyes dropped right over her lean figure as they landed on her ridiculous shoes. She didn't look awful, but I really don't have one more second in my day to think about her. My focus is on restoring our name and increasing sales.

"Mm-hmm," he mutters as he turns for the door. "It's been a long time, you should think about it."

Whatever, he can talk about the girl all he wants, but there's no way I'm getting involved with her or anyone.

Elaine and I were together for over a year, but as soon as my career ended, so did we. Her sudden departure left an incredibly bitter taste that I haven't been able to wash away, and then last November, a bad review dropped on our wines. Rarely does this happen, so when my father called eight months after I had taken over, yelling at me all what-the-hell-have-you-done, I was shocked and even more pissed.

The wine community is very tight, and in general, we all support each other. A bad review can haunt a winery for years, and that isn't good for any of us. Unfortunately, my past of being photographed with A-list celebrities, Elaine the infamous daughter to our team owner, and the rumors that I would one day be a shoo-in for the hall of fame didn't help. Someone caught wind of my name in connection with the winery, the story caught like wildfire, and the backlash has been near devastating.

"So, what's going on with you and Michelle?" I change the subject and test the waters.

He tenses and his eyes dart to mine before returning to the hallway. "Nothing. Nothing at all." His voice fades off at the end, and I nod, not believing him for a second. Since my point is made, I let it drop. He stays out of my personal life, and I'll stay out of his.

Walking into the tasting room, I smile at Michelle. Her eyes leave mine for a split second to find Kyle and then bounce back to me. Like Kyle, Michelle has been here for years and is a great team member. She's a little too rural for my tastes, and she's an employee, but I can see the appeal. Her brown hair is always kept in a braid, she has adorable dimples, and she always wears short skirts with cowboy boots. A smirk lights up her face, and she shifts her eyes toward the woman standing across from her. What is it with the two of them today?

I follow her glance down the old mahogany bar and freeze.

Holy shit.

It's as if the air is sucked out of the room and I can hardly breathe, catapulting the vision of her straight at me even though she's standing eight feet away. I'm looking at the one girl I never wanted to see again.

I stop breathing.

Speaking of the devil, here's one in the flesh. A she-devil!

Only I will not be selling my soul to her.

Ever.

Her eyes widen a little as my jaw locks tight and my teeth grind together. Flashes waver in front of my eyes as I lower them and trail over her body from head to toe. Her hair is pulled into a messy ponytail, showing off every detail of her perfect face. Her shirt has slipped to the edge of one shoulder, revealing the smooth white skin over her collarbone, and her legs are endlessly long and wrapped in skin-tight denim. I hate to say it, but the shoes are incredibly hot. She's hot . . . even more so than I remember.

Shit.

More flashes follow, and twinges alert me to a headache moving in.

My eyes land back on hers, and she's scowling at me in complete disapproval. What she has to disapprove of, though, I don't know. I'm the one who has to be worried. Fear slides like glacier ice into my veins, only to melt from the anger—anger, which is causing my blood to boil. I know who she is, I know what she does, and she needs to leave—immediately. Although she didn't write the four wilted grapes review, I still despise her and everyone like her. I don't want her to have any ammunition she could fire at us. We've worked too hard building back up our brand and business.

Kyle clears his throat to break the silence, or should I say standoff. Out of the corner of my eye, I see him and Michelle glance at each other.

"Really?" Her voice echoes across the room and sends my heart racing. Damn, I forgot how lovely her voice is. It's all Southern and slightly raspy. Too bad she's the epitome of a snake in sheep's clothing, the devil in disguise. She props one hand on her hip and gives me a disgusted look. "That's all you have? A blank stare and baby owl eyes."

"Baby owl?" My voice is rough with emotion. What's she talking about?

"Oh, he *can* speak. Yeah, you know." And she blinks at me several times in an exaggerated way. Her long eyelashes waving at me.

Kyle chuckles and then turns it into a cough, covering his mouth with his fist as I flash him a warning look.

Turning back to Shelby, I ask her, "What are you doing here?" My hand holding the football squeezes to the point of pain, she sees the movement and her face clouds with confusion.

"What do you mean?" Slowly, her bag begins to slide down her arm. She catches it and places it on the floor next to her feet.

"I didn't realize the question was a difficult one. Let me rephrase then, why are you standing in my tasting room?" The hate I feel for this girl drips off my words, and she takes two steps back.

"You're joking, right?" She crosses her arms under her chest. My eyes drop straight to her rack, which is being pushed up in a very enticing way. Damn. Internally, I curse myself. I cannot find this girl attractive.

I don't answer her, and her frown deepens.

"The magazine did tell you I was coming, right?"

"They told me they were sending a chef from Charleston, a Ms. Leigh from OBA."

OBA! Oh, hell! I was so excited during the call I didn't realize that was the name of the restaurant! I am an idiot.

She throws her arms out in a "here I am" gesture and then drops them down by her sides.

You have got to be kidding me.

Not once in all of the conversations I had with the editor of the magazine, did I ever consider the possibility that Ms. Leigh would be *her*. When Lexi, a close friend who is the sister of a former teammate, first told me she had someone for me to meet, she called her Shelby Leigh, but it sounded more like Shelbyleigh—one word, like KerriAnn. And after the charity benefit, I tried my best to forget her and her name, but her face—a face so beautiful it's haunted my dreams—has stuck with me. But once I agreed to the article, I should have realized. I mean, I don't know a lot of people from Charleston, but I do know one Ms. Leigh, and here she is . . . staring at me as if I've somehow ruined her day.

Shaking my head, the condemnation of this situation I've found myself in leaves a bad taste in my mouth. More flickers of light appear, and the pain above my left ear takes root and increases. I glance at Michelle, and my left eye twitches a little. She sees the movement in my face, frowns, and goes about getting what I need.

Of all the people the magazine could send! Why? Why did they send her? Don't they know she's a critic? A critic! Or should I say dream killer.

Anger surges through me, and my hand grips the football so tight I feel strong enough to pop it.

Wait, shit.

Of course they know! Magazines love to give reviews and recommendations. Hotels, restaurants, equipment, which brand is best, and so on. They all know each other, and they all stick together.

Slowly, I unfold my arms and set the ball on the bar. Kyle, who must have finally realized I am about to lose it, steps up.

"So, I take it you two have met?" Kyle says, waving his finger back and forth between the two of us.

"Unfortunately," she says, shifting her weight to lean against the bar.

"What's that supposed to mean?" I snap at her. What have I ever done to her? She's the one who goes around consorting with the enemy and sucking the life out of people.

"And now he needs a vocabulary lesson. Hmm, let's see . . . unfortunately, as in regrettable, unlucky, or unsuitable."

My jaw tightens.

I stride toward her, and her eyes widen. Usually, I tower over girls, but she's already kind of tall, and in those shoes, any level of intimidation I might have held with my size is nonexistent. "You know, you have a lot of nerve coming in here and talking to me like this." I lean down to get in her face, and her eyes drop to my mouth a split second before mine drop to hers. Her lips are parted as she breathes heavily.

"Trust me, coming *here* wasn't my idea at all." She leans a little closer, leaving us only inches apart, and I'm hit with the sweet scent of honey and vanilla. "I would have *never* picked this winery." She about hisses the words at me.

What the fuck?

Her words are like a slap to the face, and unconsciously, I take a step back. Her chest is rising and falling at a rapid rate, and her skin flushes pink. Pink turns to red. All I see is red. I love this winery more than this girl will ever understand, and I'm officially done with this conversation.

Regret slips across her face and then it disappears. She drops her gaze to the floor and then locks it back on me with renewed defiance. A piece of her hair slips over her shoulder, and I hate that I notice it.

Breaking the stare down between us, I turn to Michelle. Her

eyes are narrowed at Shelby, her lips are pinched together, and she looks madder than a wet hen.

"Michelle." She shifts her attention to me, and her expression softens. "Will you please show Ms. Leigh to her accommodations? We're done here." She nods and slides a hot tea and an ice pack across the counter. Without another glance in Shelby or Kyle's direction, I pick up the items, and walk out, leaving the football on the bar.

How in the hell did I get myself into this situation? Any sliver of hope I was feeling disintegrates, and the wind feels completely knocked out of me.

A chef they said.

A journalist I thought.

A critic . . . *never*.

I settle into my desk chair and press the ice pack over the throbbing spot. God, I hate these headaches. I never thought I'd hate anything or anyone as much as them, but after seeing *her* again, I may be wrong.

What am I going to do with her here for two weeks? Two. Weeks. That's how long the magazine expects her to spend here while she's cooking in one of our kitchens. "Photos. Lots of photos," they said. Damn it. I'm going to have to be in those photos with her.

Part of me wonders if I would have agreed to the assignment if I had known she was the one they were sending, but reality is Wolff Winery needs the exposure. Our assignment is to work together to come up with delicious, easy, Southern farm-to-table food pairings to go with my wines. She's to work the farm, learn all about us, and a crew from the magazine will be following and documenting it all. At the end, she will be the one who writes the featured article.

She's to write the article.

Shit. Maybe I should have been a little nicer.

Ingredients:

1 cup of cooked bacon, crumbled/chopped
1 8-ounce package of pecans, chopped
1 cup of maple syrup
3/4 cup of sugar
1/4 cup of corn syrup
1/2 cup of water
1 teaspoon of salt

How to make:

Line a baking sheet with parchment paper and set aside.

In a large sauce pan, combine maple syrup, sugar, corn syrup, water and salt, and cook over medium heat until all of the sugar is dissolved. Using a candy thermometer continue cooking, stirring frequently, until it reaches 255 degrees.

Increase the heat to medium high, add bacon, and stir until well blended.

When the candy thermometer reaches 265 degrees, add the pecans and stir until well blended.

Continue stirring until mixture reaches 285 degrees.

Turn off the stove, remove the pot, and pour mixture onto baking sheet. Spread evenly with a spatula. Allow brittle to cool. Break into pieces and serve.

Chapter 3

catch more flies with honey

Shelby

I hate him.

And I don't hate anyone.

Watching him walk away without even so much as a nod goodbye causes every cell in my body to go up in flames. He's dismissing me as if I'm not even here. I swear I've never met anyone so rude! He's lucky I don't take my very pointy-heeled shoe off and chuck it at his head . . . his gorgeous head. And that's what makes this so much worse—I've also never met a guy as good-looking as he is.

When Zach walked into the room with the other guy, I was struck speechless. At the event, he was wearing a tuxedo, which can make anyone seem more appealing. Here on a regular Monday morning, he's dressed down, wearing dark blue jeans that look worn and soft, a perfectly fitted gray T-shirt with the winery logo stamped across the front, a pair of trendy running shoes, and he was holding a football. In my haste and anxiety on the drive here, I'd briefly forgotten that he was a former football player, but everything about his tall, muscular build screams the part.

Closing my eyes, the excitement over being selected for this project falters and disappointment and embarrassment fill me. I'm so out of my element. I feel stupid even being here, and I don't understand what it is about him that causes this extreme, visceral reaction in me. All it took was one look, and his expression shifted from playful with his friend to a scowl at me. Maybe I should have declined the project.

No.

No, that's ludicrous. I should not have. Aside from my father, he's the only person who has ever made me feel like less than who I am, and I refuse to put up with that—job or no job. Squashing the unwanted feelings, I remind myself that this is my project. My. Project. I was chosen for this and I'm going to write a damn good article.

"Ms. Leigh?"

My back straightens as the girl standing across from me raises her hand in a small wave. I turn to face her, and she's frowning at me.

"Yes?" I frown back, feeling every bit of what that expression means: angry, sad, and disappointed. She has no idea how much he makes me want to run out the door and never look back. But I won't. I won't because this project puts me one step closer to my dream, a dream that means more to me than anything.

"If you're ready, I'll show you to your cottage."

Cottage. Well, at least that sounds nice. I'm extremely relieved to hear that I'm not staying in the same house with him. God, I can't even imagine. The thought of randomly running into him makes my stomach turn sour.

"That would be great. Thank you."

Bending down to pick up my bag, I spot the other guy in the room studying me. It's bad enough that I have to spend two weeks here working with that asshole who hates me, I don't want the rest of the staff to hate me, too. So, after I sling the strap of my bag over my shoulder, I walk over to him and hold out my hand.

"Hi, I'm Shelby." His eyes are unreadable, but he slips his hand into mine and shakes it. He's handsome in a young Harry Connick Jr. kind of way.

"I gathered that. I'm Kyle. I oversee general and wholesale distribution for Mr. Wolff, and that's Michelle. She runs front end operations." I glance at Michelle, and she gives me a strained smile.

I take a step back and release a deep sigh. Flashes of my interaction with Zach and the words I said to him increase my humiliation. I understand their skepticism. I would be wary of me, too. I may always try to be kind and courteous, but I was as bad as Zach was in our little exchange.

"Yeah, I'm sorry about that." I look between him and Michelle. "That must have sounded pretty bad." Heat climbs up my neck and into my cheeks. I really don't know what came over me, and now that the anger has dulled, I'm thoroughly embarrassed.

"I'm not actually sure what *that* really was," he says, pointing between the door Zach left through and me. He looks concerned and confused, but really, I find that hard to believe.

I don't know why I thought Zach would be civil when I got here. Maybe because he agreed to the project knowing I would be his partner on it, or maybe because we have a mutual friend, I don't know, but I was giving him the benefit of the doubt and really hoping that night last fall was a fluke. Apparently, it wasn't.

How is it possible that he didn't know it was me coming today?

He. Didn't. Know. I guess he just thought so little of me before, from the benefit, that he forgot my name.

Forgettable.

"It is what it is," I say, shrugging and trying to release the stress that's built up in my shoulders. "I'm here to do the assignment. I'll stay in the kitchen and out of the way, and then I'll be gone."

I shift my weight from one foot to the other, uncomfortable under their separate gazes, and Kyle's phone dings with an incoming text, breaking the silence.

"All right then. It'll be easiest if you follow me." Michelle tilts her head toward the front door as she walks out from behind the bar and spins a key ring full of keys around her finger.

Michelle is a pretty girl. There's something about her that's very girl next door, the kind everyone wants to be best friends with and secretly envies at the same time. Her smile is bright, and her eyes are kind and unjaded. I can see why she runs the consumer side here, especially if the alternative is Zach. The thought of his name has me grinding my teeth.

"Michelle, text me if you need anything. I'll be in the barn," Kyle says, glancing up from his phone. He smiles at her, winks, and then heads off in the other direction. She blushes, and I feel a pang of jealousy.

Jealousy. My stomach drops—I've officially hit a new low.

I don't even know these people, and I don't want anything to do with the responsibility or obligations that come with a guy; yet, I'm suddenly wishing I had someone who'd look at me with flirty eyes like he just looked at her. I was fine before I came here. I'm independent, driven, successful, and I love what I do. I have rules in place, I don't mix business with pleasure and I never involve the heart. I've also stuck to the plan—career first, guys later—

and I shouldn't care that this guy, a guy who I've met twice, isn't interested in me.

So, why do I?

I don't know.

I hate this. I hate him.

Following Michelle outside, the sun warms my skin and I'm struck with how beautiful it is here. I'd been so focused on getting here and through the first reintroduction with *him* that my mental tunnel vision blocked everything around me.

The winery sits on the outskirts of a town called Dahlonega, in north Georgia at the foothills of the Blue Ridge Mountains. Living in a coastal town, I often forget how close and how remarkable the mountains are. The hills around the winery seem to roll and lush grapevines and orchards are in neatly pruned lines. It's easy to see why the network producers chose this place—it's exquisite and a backdrop dream.

"Have you worked here for a long time?" I ask Michelle as I turn back to take in the essence of the winery.

The building looks like an old stone mansion, or a small castle, and it's made up of polished ivory stone and rocks. Each window is ornately shaped, there are two towers on both sides of the wooden double front door, and an east and a west wing. In many ways, it looks out of place with this part of the country, but at the same time, it doesn't look like it could belong anywhere else.

I look past the large circular drive with an ornate fountain in the middle to the windows of the west wing, which fall in the direction Zach stormed off. Is he staring at me right now? Is he laughing or scowling? Not that it matters in any way, and actually, from what I know of him so far, he's probably forgotten I'm even here.

Forgotten.

My heart sinks. I abhor that his indifference bothers me so much.

"I've worked here for about five years, and I love it." Her answer is short and clipped. She shoots me a look that screams "loyal". Not that I want any gossip about this place, but a friend might have been nice.

"Does it get crowded on a typical weekend?" I ask her.

"It really depends on the weekend. Obviously, harvest season is the most popular, but the surrounding towns often hold festivals throughout the year that bring in tourists as well. Plus, we host a lot of larger events and weddings."

"I do love weddings." I smile at her, and she gives me a genuine smile back.

"Me, too," she says, and her tone is a little warmer. Maybe I'll end up with a friend here after all.

"I love your boots, by the way. My best friend and I have a thing for shoes." I kick up my left foot, showing off my most recent purchase: a pair of strappy, camel-colored Jimmy Choos. "But I'm thinking these might not have been the best choice to wear here."

She laughs. "Thanks, and yeah, if you're going to be working here for two weeks, I'm hoping you brought something a little more . . . flat."

"I did, thank goodness." A few years back, I bought a pair of rainboots and had my initials monogrammed on the front. I love them. They're very Southern, and I figured they'd be perfect for walking around here.

"All right, I'm gonna take a golf cart." She points to designated parking under a tree off to the left where there are three carts. "You follow me. The cottage is behind the main house, but it's far enough that I don't want to walk back."

"Sounds good, thank you." She throws me another smile, this one definitely less guarded and more open.

Driving down the gravel path and through the vineyard, a sense of calm settles over me. The vines, which are full of new grape clusters, are taller than the car, and the sweeping views of the hillside are breathtaking.

Too quickly, we pull up to the cottage, which is far enough away to feel secluded but still close enough that I can see the main house in the distance.

Stepping out of my car, Michelle comes to stand next to me as I stare in awe of my home and studio setting for the next two weeks. "This place is beautiful. I had no idea the property looked like this before I got here."

"It really is. This cottage is the original home to the Wolff family. The main house up the hill was built in the twenties, just before the Great Depression. Of course, the cottage has been updated and modernized over the years, but it still has a quaint charm that everyone loves. Everything is set up for you inside—pretty standard, like a hotel room. I made a peach pound cake for a snack and stocked the kitchen for you since I heard somewhere you like to cook." She grins at me. "Hopefully, you'll have everything you need, but if not, give me a call at the main house. Oh, and there's also an herb garden on the back porch you can help yourself to."

I squeeze my hands into fists to try to contain my excitement. "I really have no words. This is incredible, and I feel a little guilty—it's like work and a vacation all in one."

She laughs at my enthusiasm and holds out a key. I take it from her and roll it over in my hand. It's an ornate key. On one side is the winery's logo and on the other is a vintage-looking bee.

I love bees, and I *love* honey.

Michelle watches me as I collect my bags from the trunk of my car, and I can tell she's waiting to say something.

I turn to face her. "Is there anything else?"

"Actually, there is." She bites down on her lip, as if she's worried, and then walks back to the golf cart, leans against it, and crosses her ankles. "I don't know what your deal is with Zach, but I've never seen him react to anyone like he did to you." She pauses and looks back at the house. "Shelby, he's a really great boss and a great guy, so try to go easy on him while you're here."

She may not have ever seen him behave this way before, but I have. And the fact that she's insinuating I'm the problem makes me angrier than I'd like to admit. I understand her wanting to defend him; after all, they're probably friends, but this doesn't have anything to do with her, and it doesn't matter what I say, she's team Zach.

Taking a step away from her, I move closer to the door. "Seems to me he can take care of himself."

She frowns at my tone. "Oh, he can without a doubt . . . but . . . well, never mind." Concern flashes across her face and then disappears.

"But what?" I'm curious to know what kind of concessions she feels he needs.

"Nothing." She shakes her head and smiles at me as she slides back into the golf cart. "Call me if you need anything." And with one final wave, she's gone and dust floats through the air in her wake.

Turning back to the cottage door, I unlock it, step inside, and drop my things in the entryway. This is the most tranquil home I've ever seen. The entire downstairs is one large great room, and I'm overwhelmed by all the details. The floors are made of large stones, and there are several huge gray shag rugs. The walls are white and the windows are covered with sheer white curtains. There is a stone fireplace on one wall, and the gray furniture is accented with yellow and lavender pillows and throws. In the back of the room is the kitchen. The cabinets are distressed, there's a large center island, a rustic wooden table, and French doors leading out back.

Twirling around, everything is perfect, and sure enough, there on the kitchen island is a large bouquet of wild flowers, a pound cake wrapped in plastic wrap, and a bottle of white wine chilling next to it. My stomach growls.

If there's one thing a chef never misses, it's a meal. And right now, it's lunchtime.

I hunt down a fork and a plate and then cut off a piece of the cake, which is delicious. Seems to me Michelle has her own culinary skills hidden up her sleeves. Deciding that it's five o'clock somewhere, I uncork the wine and pour myself a glass.

Raising a toast to myself, I repeat Meg's words, "You can catch more flies with honey than you can with vinegar."

I can do these two weeks. It's not as if we'll have to see each other a whole lot. I'm here to learn and cook, and smile for the camera, neither of which have much to do with him. The first sip of wine sets my taste buds tingling. Different flavors burst over my tongue, and I'm delighted by how smooth it is.

Picking up the bottle, I read the label, which declares it a chardonnay reserve, The Queen Bee. It's one of their wines, and it's very good. This confuses me, because if they're all as delicious as this one, I'm not sure why they received four wilted grapes. I've never tasted their wines before, but maybe I was wrong assuming they were below average.

From across the room my cell phone rings. Hoping it's Meg, I race to dig it out of my purse, but see it's a local number instead.

"Hello?"

"Shelby, this is Zach." The timbre of his voice slides over me. He sounds every bit as good over the phone as he does in person. Wait, what? No! Nothing about him is good!

"How did you get my number?" I snap.

"How do you think?" Irritation leaks out between his words.

Silence ticks by.

"Well, what do you want?" If he called to antagonize me, it's working.

He chuckles as if he knows what he's doing to me. "Tomorrow at eleven thirty, someone will pick you up and bring you to the main house. The magazine wants to interview us at the beginning and end of the assignment."

"Together?" Please say no. Please say no.

"Yes."

A sigh escapes me. So much for not having to spend time together. "Fine, I'll be ready."

He snorts, and before he hangs up, he mumbles, "I'm sure you will."

Whatever.

Such an asshole.

I toss my phone onto the counter and reach for the glass of wine, but it doesn't help. The hostility and the rejection from earlier weaves its way back through my muscles and I hate that he made me think of my father. Granted not a day goes by that I don't hear him whispering one of his many slurs in my ear, like I'll never amount to anything and I'm useless just like my mother, but up there at the manor, today, it just felt like more.

Letting out a deep sigh, I take another gulp of the wine and swallow the insecurities that surfaced. I refuse to be weak. I refuse to allow him or anyone make me feel inconsequential. And I will continue to prove him, them wrong. I mean, why does Zach have to be so uncivil? Really, what is his problem?

My eyes drift to the French doors off the kitchen and land on a black crow, which is standing on the patio table. My breath catches as I take the bird in. The crow tilts its head to the side, staring right at me, and my stomach drops. A black crow is a bad omen.

"Yeah, yeah, I get it okay. He and I are like oil and water, but I can do this, I've dealt with someone like him before," I say to the bird. It bobs its head a few times and flies off. I hope that I'm wrong about the bird and that because it left, it thinks I can do this, too.

Tomorrow will definitely be interesting.

One day down, thirteen to go!

Ingredients:

1 cup of butter, softened
2 cups of sugar
4 eggs
1 t vanilla
3 cups of flour
1 t baking powder
2 cups of chopped peaches

How to make:

Preheat the over to 325 degrees.

Grease a 10-inch Bundt pan with cooking spray, or with butter and sprinkle with sugar, shaking out the excess.

In a large mixing bowl, cream the butter and sugar until well blended. Beat in the eggs 1 at a time, and add vanilla. On top of the wet mixture add flour, baking powder, and salt. Gradually mix, beating until batter is well blended. Fold in the peaches.

Spoon into the prepared Bundt pan. Bake for 75 minutes or until a wooden toothpick inserted into the cake comes out clean.

Cool in the pan. Invert to remove. Flip the cake and sprinkle with powdered sugar before serving.

Chapter 4

barking up the wrong tree

Zach

Natural light fills the sunroom, which is the chosen room for the interview. It's my favorite room in the manor, as it gives a sweeping one hundred and eighty degree view of the winery and hillside. The room isn't overly large, but my mother made it cozy by filling it with it with three separate seating sections. Guests are allowed to relax and lounge as long as they want. This morning, two of the sections were removed and ours is set up in the middle.

When they first suggested this location, I figured why not. I love this room, but when Shelby walks in, I wish I chose the cellar instead. Down there, it's dark, whereas here the light makes all her little detailed nuances stand out even more.

I hate it.

Today, she has on a little white dress that's tight through the top, showing off her amazing full chest, and it flares at the waist, stopping right at her knees. She has on pearls, another pair of insanely hot shoes, and her lips are a dark red. At the event last fall, and again yesterday, her hair had been pulled back. But today, it falls in waves down her back, and I'm torn between wanting to drag her around by it and running my fingers through it.

Shelby carries an air about her that screams sophistication and poise. Her back is straight, her feet are crossed at the ankles and off to the side, and her hands are perfectly folded in her lap. With breeding comes training, and knowing that she's fierce in the kitchen, I can see why Lexi is friends with her. They're cut from the same cloth. They're both true Southern girls. And that isn't something you can become, it's something you're born. Only, this one lacks the heart of gold. Hers is empty, like her soul.

Shelby's eyes flick to mine and narrow. She's caught me staring, but she doesn't back down.

That's okay, sweetheart, keep it up. Eventually, I will break you.

"All right, let's get started, shall we?" says Kelly, the reporter conducting our interview. She's sitting to my left and Shelby is to my right. There's a small lounge table in the middle of us, which holds a pitcher of sweet tea and some blueberry muffins. I love muffins. No scratch that . . . I love food.

"Yes, let's." Shelby smiles at Kelly, and my traitorous heart thuds in my chest. Holy shit, her face completely transforms when she smiles, making her even more gorgeous, and that's just wrong on so many levels. I swear this chick reminds of one of those beautiful, but poisonous, flowers. So tempting, but one touch and a painful rash covers your body from head to toe. Both of them turn to look at me, and I have to clear my throat.

"Let's do this." I grit my teeth.

Kelly smiles at me, glances down at her list of questions, and then nods to the camera guy who will be recording this.

"Thank you for sitting down with me today, I appreciate you

both making the time." She smiles at me again, this time her eyes are heavy with interest, and she never even glances to Shelby. It should irritate me that she's being rude, but it doesn't. Instead, I find it humorous and typical. All women love to look at me—all women, that is, except the one sitting to my right. Not that I want her to, because I don't. "This interview will not be printed with the feature article, but it will accompany it on *Food Network*'s All About the South website. All interviews, videos, still pictures, both bios, featured wines, et cetera, will be advertised to act as a link to entice our print readers to view us online, and to encourage our online readers to pick up the magazine. Sound good?"

Shelby smiles and I nod.

"Zach, it's public knowledge that you bought the winery from your father last May. Your father was legendary in this part of the country for the delicious wines he produced over the years. How does it feel to step into shoes so big?"

I watch as Kelly's eyes drop over my body and land briefly on my shoes. I know football, I know wine, and I know women. The look may have been subtle, but that's twice now I've caught her. And I know what she's wondering, big feet, big . . .

This interview started two minutes ago, and that's all it took. It doesn't even matter that she's probably ten years older than I am or that she's barking up the wrong tree. She's still the perfect distraction from the she-devil sitting to my right. Besides, there isn't anything I'd like more than to piss Shelby off. Let her see how nice I can be to everyone but her. In fact, excluding her from this interview would be fine with me. I give Kelly a knowing smirk.

"Feels great, and if you must know"—I lean a little closer to her—"my feet are actually bigger than his, so my shoes are . . . larger." I nod at the reporter, and a nice shade of pink slides into her cheeks. From next to me, Shelby lets out a single laugh, and I turn to glare at her. "What?"

"That's what you have to say about the winery and your father? Didn't they coach you on how speak to the press when you played football? So humble you are about your business and your . . . shoes." She looks at me as if she's disgusted and shakes her head.

"You don't know the first thing about my business." I sneer at her.

"You're right, I don't, and neither do all the readers, but hey, kudos for having *big* feet." She turns away from me and looks back to Kelly.

Damn it.

Heat spreads up my neck into my face. She's right, and I hate it. More importantly, I hate that I've let her get under my skin. All it took was for her to walk into a room for my mind to switch from business mode to conquer and defeat mode. She's throwing me off my game—a game I'm very good at—and I blame her. This assignment is immensely important for us, and that answer was out of character for me. Yeah, I do know women, but there's a time and a place, and this is neither.

Shit.

When I drag my eyes back to Kelly, the confusion on her face matches those of others in the room. Her eyes bounce back and forth between Shelby and me. The tension between us is palpable, and just like that, the crew from the magazine knows we don't get along. My heart sinks.

Behind Kelly, Kyle shifts. He looks furious as he mouths, *What the hell?* I don't think I've ever seen his face this red, and even though his hands are shoved in his pockets, I know they are clenched into fists.

Damage control. Got it.

I look at the guy recording this and pin him with a severe look.

"Delete that." I'm not even nice about it, and he flinches before he starts pressing buttons. Once he's reset, he nods to Kelly and then me. Turning back to Kelly, I launch into a better answer.

"Here's the thing, Kelly. My father was, and is, exceptional. Yes, I understand the role I now play as the new owner, but I'm excited to follow his legacy. He has the ability to know the exact moment a wine is done fermenting and ready to be bottled." Shifting in the leather chair, I peek at Shelby to make sure she's paying attention. She needs to hear this as much as the reporter. "I'd like to believe that instead of filling his shoes, I'm following in his footsteps. This is my home. This is *my* winery. I grew up here, worked part of every harvest, and spent every holiday here. I'm not new to running a winery. I was born for this. Wolff Winery is very excited to be a part of *Food Network*'s Southern issue. We appreciate Shelby coming all this way to stay with us"—my gaze briefly lands on Shelby, who's leaning on the armrest closest to me and listening intently—"and look forward to tasting what she comes up with to pair with our wines."

My eyes trail back to Kyle. His hands are now down by his sides, relaxed, and he's leaning against the wall. He nods in approval, but then he glances to Michelle, and the two of them exchange an unspoken comment. There's something about that look that irritates me, and it leads me to believe they've been discussing me. Not that I blame them, my mood has been off since *she* arrived.

Everyone around me has felt it and steered clear. I don't even know why I let her bother me so much. Maybe it's on principle since she's a critic, and I can't stand critics, or maybe it's because I've spent too much time around people like her: unapologetic, selfish, career climbing workaholics. Her expression is blank—guarded. I have no idea what she's thinking, and this bothers me, too. Everything about her bothers me.

"Shelby, you must have been very excited to be chosen for this. How did you feel when you got the call?" Kelly crosses her legs and shifts them in my direction, pushing her skirt up a little instead of down. The move is blatant, and everyone sees it, including Shelby. Why I thought encouraging Kelly would be fun, I have no idea, and now I'm going to have to deal with her.

"I was very excited. I love *Food Network*, and I love working for them. As you know, Kelly, I've worked with them in the past, and in addition to this assignment I'm writing another article for this special issue on the top twenty-five farm-to-table restaurants across the southeast. We've stumbled across some incredible places."

Huh, I didn't know she was writing that. Come to think of it, I didn't know she had worked with them before either. Great, just great. May as well throw another log onto the fire that's become my living hell. She has an established relationship with the magazine, which means I really can't mess this up—no matter how much I dislike her.

"Wolff Winery is beautiful. I mean, who wouldn't be excited about getting to spend two weeks here?" Shelby smiles at me brightly.

You!

I want to yell at her, the little liar. My hands grip my thighs as I think back to yesterday when she made it abundantly clear that we were not her first choice.

Looking away from us, her eyes sweep over the hillside, *my hillside*, and it feels strangely intimate, as if she's looking at me and I don't want her to be. I want her to look at nothing. I want her to disappear.

"How do you think you'll come up with the pairing ideas?" Kelly's voice breaks through my raging thoughts. I realize I'm staring at Shelby, and she's looking back at me as if she wants to poison me.

Feelings mutual, sweetheart.

She turns away from me and smiles fakely at Kelly.

"Food is best represented when it's like its family. I'm looking forward to spending the next two weeks with the Wolff Winery family and seeing how they cohesively interact. I'm certain they have a few food suggestions that mean something to them, and I can't wait to dive into their garden."

"Have you had a chance to tour the winery yet?" Kelly asks Shelby, but she looks my way with a hopeful expression that I'll extend an invitation to her. No thanks. I'll leave that to Kyle.

"No, I arrived yesterday and took the time to settle in. I did, however, open a bottle of chardonnay that I found in the cottage. I'm not embarrassed to say there is none left. It was delicious." She licks her lips, and my heart involuntarily stutters.

She likes my wine.

This shouldn't surprise me. After all, it's excellent. But coming from her, someone who I expect to be indifferent toward us—toward me—it does. Hearing praise for our wines, no matter whom it's from, never gets old.

Shelby glances my way, and her smile drops when she realizes I'm still watching her.

"So, you're a big drinker?" I ask, my brows rising in amusement. "An entire bottle of wine and here you are looking chipper today." I lean back in my seat, cross one foot over my knee, and smirk at her.

Her jaw drops, and Kyle clears his throat.

Shit. I really have to work on my filter around her.

Recovering quickly, she surprises me when she laughs. Laughs. As if her smile weren't temptation enough to draw my attention to her mouth, her laugh is infectious and hypnotizing. She reminds me of the femme fatale firefly. The females can't fly, so they flash to lure in a mate, and the minute he lands—he's eaten.

The interview continues for about another twenty minutes. Kelly asks questions about the winery, last season's harvest, and the current menu at Shelby's restaurant. I can't remember the last time I was in Charleston, and I chuckle to myself, wondering how she would react if I showed up at her door.

"All right, this has been great. I'd like to go ahead and get a few pictures of the two of you together. Let's get one out back on the patio with the vineyard in the background, I'll have you two toasting each other, and then let's get a few of you down in the cellar." Kelly turns her smile to me, and I inwardly cringe.

Shelby stands and starts walking for the door. Following her seems to be the lesser of two evils, and without thinking, I set my hand on Shelby's lower back to guide her out of the room. She stiffens and shoots me a death glare. I don't know why, but this takes my already irritated mood and pushes me toward the edge. An edge I'd like to push her off. I scowl at the back of her head as we turn down the hall, and I'm certain the entourage behind us saw both of our reactions. *Just a little bit longer*, I chant to myself.

Pride rushes through me as we step out onto the porch. The view here really is one of the best on the property. The vineyard sweeps over the hillside, which slopes down and is surrounded by orchards of fruit and pecan trees. It shows off almost all one hundred and twelve acres, and it doesn't matter how many times I've seen it, it never gets old.

The magazine crew has already staged the area. There's a high-top table with an open bottle of wine and two partially filled glasses. Behind us is the vineyard and in front of us are light diffusers and six people staring at us.

"Okay, you two. I'm going to place you." A guy walks over, pushes me behind the table, and then guides Shelby to stand next to me. She looks at me, flinches, and then takes a step to the side. The guy frowns.

"Shelby, I know it feels like you're standing in his personal space, but we need the shot to be tight. The closer you are together, the more of the winery the readers will see."

She steps back in as a breeze sweeps across the porch, successfully blowing her hair all over my face. It smells even stronger than yesterday, like vanilla and honey. She smells good, real good. To myself, I groan.

The guy moves back in, smooths her hair down, brushes some translucent powder over both of us, and then claps in delight. "I can already tell these are going to turn out beautifully. I appreciate you two coordinating for today. It definitely helps the photos."

Coordinating? I look at her white dress and black shoes, and then I look at my own outfit. I'm wearing a white button down with the sleeves rolled up, gray dress slacks, and black shoes. I wouldn't say we're coordinated, these colors are standard, but we don't clash.

"The white attire will make the color in the wines stand out. Very good choice." He moves out of the way, and the photographer steps in front of us, testing the light.

"All right, folks." He looks through the lens of the camera.

"Zach, take a half step back and move a bit to your left so Shelby's a little in front of you."

A little? Where they've positioned the table has left almost no room between it and the porch railing. I do as he asks, brushing against the backside of her. She tenses and quickly sucks in air, expanding her chest. My eyes are drawn to it, I can't help it, she's beautifully proportioned, and I find I'm squeezing my glass so tight it may shatter. At least it doesn't look as if she's any more comfortable than I am. She kind of has the deer caught in headlights look, which makes me feel better. If I have to suffer, so does she. Though, the way her lips are slightly parted . . .

Shit. I need to stop looking at her.

Click.

Click.

My head pops up and the photographer takes a few more test shots before looking at the screen of his camera.

"Perfect. If you two could take a deep breath and relax your shoulders, it'll look more natural. On the count of three here we go."

We both hold up our glass of wine, and on three, we smile for the camera.

Ingredients:

2 cups of flour
2 t. baking powder
1/2 t. baking soda
1/2 t. salt
3 T. sugar
1 egg
1 cup sour cream
1/3 cup milk
1/4 cup vegetable oil
2 cups of blueberries
1/2 cup of brown sugar, packed
1/4 cup of flour
1 t. cinnamon
3 T. butter

How to make:

Heat oven to 425 degrees.

Grease two muffin pans – roughly two dozen muffins.

Combine and stir flour, baking powder, baking soda, salt and sugar. In a separate bowl beat the egg with sour cream and milk. Stir in the oil. Add liquids all at once to the dry ingredients. Stir only until well blended. Carefully fold in the blueberries. Spoon into greased muffin pans.

Mix brown sugar, flour, and cinnamon. Cut in the butter with a blender until crumbly and sprinkle over the top of the muffin batter.

Bake for 15 minutes or until topping is deep brown.

Remove and cook.

Serve warm or cool.

Chapter 5

bless your heart

Shelby

Two hours have passed since we started taking these photos, and even though I think I'm standing in the most gorgeous wine cellar I've ever been in, I'm officially over it.

Michelle and Kyle are off in their own world, and the camera crew hasn't stopped fussing over the current set of shots. Kelly hasn't talked to me once, not even to ask me a question. All I've done is memorize every detail of this room.

The wine cellar sits beneath the manor. There are several rooms that house the wine, but we are currently in a large great room that could easily hold fifty people. The floors are quartzite, the room is lit by crystal chandeliers, and in the center of the room is a large, wooden table for private dining.

Since no one is paying attention to me, I shoot inconspicuous glares at all of them. Everyone but me is in long sleeves, including Kelly. She has on a suit jacket. I'm in a summer dress. The special issue of the magazine comes out over the summer, so the dress is appropriate, but no one mentioned we would be down here, and I'm freezing.

Letting out a sigh, I rub my arms and then reach over to the snack plate, grab a cracker, and dip it into a pimento cheese dip. I don't think snacks were originally a part of today's schedule, but Michelle did a great job throwing together a few tasty things and an antipasto appetizer board. All of it's delicious, and as I savor the classic Southern dip, I appreciate that she hand-grated the cheese. I wonder what this would taste like as a grilled cheese, and then I frown. I shouldn't be thinking about food; I should be thinking about how awesome this feature article is going to be. Instead, I'm bored, ignored, and feeling very out of place, just like the Feeding America benefit. God, what an awful experience that was. I never should have agreed to be set up with him . . .

"Oh my gosh, Shelby. You are going to love him, I know it." Lexi had squealed as she reached over and squeezed my arm. "He's tall, good-looking, ambitious, and one of the nicest and most genuine guys I've ever met. And trust me, having a twin brother who played football and is in the military, I've met a lot of guys." She rocked up on her toes, grinning at me as excitement poured off of her.

My stomach had tightened with expectancy, and I had known I'd been caught up in her exuberant emotions of introducing us as well as my own of meeting someone for the first time.

"If he's so great, why isn't he your date?" I asked as I turned to face her.

Her smile slipped a little and her shoulders slumped before she shrugged them, shaking off whatever thought saddened her. In all the time I had known Lexi, she had never dated anyone, and for the first time—especially after seeing her respond that way—I wondered why.

"I guess he could be, but only as a friend. It isn't like that between us, it never was. Besides, you two are perfect for each other." I didn't push for a better explanation as we stood there watching the door and chatting with people who passed. I had no idea what the guy looked like, but I still hoped that I would somehow know him when I saw him.

Sure, both Lexi and Meg had encouraged me to look him up online first, but I didn't want to be influenced or intimidated more than I already was. So, I waited and waited. He should have already been there, but Lexi hadn't spotted him, either. With each minute that passed, I became increasingly nervous. It's one thing to go on a blind date set up by a friend, it's another to go on one set up by a best friend.

"There." Lexi finally pointed over toward the bar where he was waiting in line. My eyes followed hers and my heart sputtered a bit. "You can't miss him: tall, blond hair, and a scowl." She giggled, dropping her hand to her side. "He actually looks like he'd rather be anywhere but here."

"I see him." And I did. Every bit of him. Lexi hadn't been kidding, he was incredibly handsome, but he also looked incredibly annoyed. He had one hand deep in his pocket and the other ran over his face and around to the back of his neck. Everyone around him seemed to sense his mood and were all standing a half step away from him, as if they agreed to give him some breathing room.

He moved forward in the line, placed his order, and dropped a few bills in the tip jar. Turning in our direction, he stepped out of the way and took a sip of his drink. Holy moly. He was nice to look at from the side view, but straight on, this guy was gorgeous. Trendy styled hair, strong jaw, broad shoulders, solid arms and legs, and an overall air to him that screamed confidence.

Lexi let out a little squeal next to me. "This is going to be so great, I know it," she said, barely louder than a whisper.

Taking another sip of his drink, his eyes lifted and landed right on Lexi. She grinned at him and waved him over, but he didn't return the smile. Instead, his chest deflated as if he'd let out a deep sigh and he hesitantly moved across the room toward us. His eyes found mine, and my heart plummeted into my stomach. Not because of the anticipation to meet him, but because of the way his eyes narrowed and nostrils flared. The way he was looking at me made me want to shrink back as if I'd done something wrong.

When he gave me a once over, the energy pouring off him felt tangible, almost as if it were pushing me, which was confusing. I glanced at Lexi. She too had calmed her excitement over our introduction and was looking at him questioningly. Lexi's eyes flickered to mine and widened slightly.

Sucking up my nerves, I held my hand out to greet him. "Hi, I'm Shelby." My voice wavered, cluing him in to my nervousness and his eyes narrowed before they dropped to my outstretched hand. Then he actually had the gall to take a step away from me as if I'd offended him.

Lexi squeaked a little next to me in shock at his reaction. My hand lingered in the air and then slowly lowered. The heat already in my cheeks flared to full effect, and I glanced at the ground, humiliated.

"I know," he said with a condescending tone that was rich with a Southern drawl. My eyes flipped back to him as someone near us took a photo and the flash lit up his very blue eyes. He blinked and long thick lashes swept down.

For two weeks, I'd been looking forward to that night. I had gone out, bought a new dress and had gotten my hair and nails done. Deep down, I had truly believed that night would be the beginning of something new and great. I guess I had thought that if he were such a good friend of Lexi's, he would become a friend of mine, too. Maybe even more. Apparently, I had thought wrong.

"Zach?" Lexi threw him an irritated what's-wrong-with-you look.

"What? You said you were going to introduce me to a Shelby tonight." He had looked at me, looked back at her, shrugged, and then walked away.

"So, you two already know each other?" Kelly asks, breaking me from my train of thought. We're standing around an old wine barrel that had been repurposed as a tasting table. She's practically leaning on Zach, and I have to give it to him, he looks uncomfortable, but he's being polite. Then again, I guess he can't actually be the rude prick that he is to a reporter.

"No," I respond at the same time Zach says, "Yes." His eyes lock on to mine, and my world tints blue from the color. It's unfortunate that such a pretty color is wasted on someone like him.

"We met once," I say acrimoniously. A flash from off to my right forces me to blink. I suppose it looks like the three of us are conversing nicely, but nothing would please me more than to take one of these bottles and shove it up his ass.

"But that doesn't mean I don't know you. I learned a lot about you that night." He leans forward, placing his elbows on the table.

"I highly doubt that. I seem to remember your focus being somewhere completely different."

After our initial introduction, he left Lexi and me to head to the bar. Then he spent the next hour walking around the room saying hello to people he already knew and going out of his way to meet new people—or should I say *new women*.

Occasionally, he checked back in with us, bringing over whomever he was charming at that moment, and he always introduced me as his date. The looks that would flash my way were a mixture of pity and jealousy. It was humiliating, and poor Lexi apologized profusely.

I didn't need a date to go to the Feeding America event. I attend functions all the time by myself. In the food industry, it's important for me to keep my name and face recognizable, and I never know who I might meet or run into, but I was led to believe that I was going to be on one, and that changed the entire dynamic of the evening. Any other time, I would have walked off and said forget it, but for some reason, this rejection stung.

"Ah, was the little chef from Charleston jealous?" Zach smirks at me, his eyes dripping with contempt.

"Jealous? No. Your reputation precedes you. You are a known womanizer. That night was supposed to be a fun night out and nothing more. I would never get involved with someone like you, nor would I ever have emotions like jealousy attached to you."

The truth is, I know nothing about his reputation. I did go home and look him up after the event, and other than the bad review on the wines, I didn't see anything negative about him. Sure there were photos of him with girls, but most looked like candid fan shots rather than posed event shots.

"I'm not a womanizer." His eyes dart over to Kelly before flipping back to mine. He hates that I'm speaking ill of him in front of her. People from the media are notorious for spinning off the cuff comments badly all the time, especially in the business setting where appearances mean everything. He pins me with a severe look, but all that does is challenge me.

"Oh really, what is it that women call you? Oh yeah . . . *ten*. I can only imagine how you got that name." I roll my eyes with sarcasm. Along with the candid shots I saw of him, there were several with homemade signs all calling him ten, saying he ranks a ten in their book, stating they only need ten minutes, asking if he's ten inches, et cetera. Yes, I understand that was his jersey number from when he played in Tampa, but still, it had to have gotten started somewhere.

His jaw locks, his neck turns red, and his hands tighten around the wine glass he's holding. Clearly, he doesn't like the nickname as he went from teasing me to pissed in two seconds flat.

A laugh escapes me. "Well, would you look at that? Someone doesn't like hearing the truth. Bless. Your. Heart." My words drip with disdain, but I plaster on the sweetest smile I can.

Zach abandons his wine glass, stands straight, pushes away from the table, and walks straight at me. I back away from him. It separates us from the others, but I still feel a hush fall over the room. All eyes have turned to watch him approach me. Every true Southerner knows the expression "bless your heart" can be meant in one of two ways: the nice heartfelt endearing way or the publicly acceptable go fuck yourself way.

"You are such a bi—"

"All right, everyone!" Kyle claps his hands to gain the group's attention, and Zach stops directly in front of me, barely acknowledging him. "I think we're done here for today." Kyle affixes Zach and me with a harsh look, which we both ignore since we're too focused on each other.

There is animosity between us, and although I'm certain we alluded to it here and there over the last few hours, Zach is seething and making his feelings about me known.

"Thank you, everybody," I say to no one and everyone at the same time, thrilled that the photoshoot is over. Once the people leave, so can I.

One-by-one, they begin to file out of the cellar. Zach says nothing, does nothing, he just stares me down, and I refuse to look away.

"Zach, are you coming?" Kelly asks. I'll never understand some girls. Other than the first five minutes of the interview, he's given zero reasons for her to think he's into her, and yet, she's still vying for his attention.

"In a few." His answer is short, and his impatience for privacy is evident. He wants everyone gone, and very quickly, they all disappear, leaving the two of us. I don't budge and neither does he.

Raising my chin, I match the inimical energy surrounding him. I've dealt with guys worse than him before, and I'm certain he won't be the last. I'm not easy to push over, and the sooner he realizes this, the better.

Crossing my arms over my chest, I know some would say it's a defensive move, but really, it's more out of intolerance. "Why don't you tell me what your problem is. Maybe then you can take the hostility down a notch."

His eyes narrow at me. "The only problem I have is you," he says, taking a step closer and invading my personal space. "You here at my home." He takes another step, and my arms drop. "You drinking my wine." Another step. "You breathing my air."

He's standing so close I have to tilt my head to look at him, the depth of his voice resonates across my skin, and a tremor runs through me.

"You are such a dick," I snarl up at him, but it just makes him sway closer to me. I can see a storm brewing in his eyes as the blue shifts between irritation and distaste for me, but all are overpowered by something else. Something else that's pulling us together like magnets.

A hand lands on my hip. The warmth from it burns through my dress, and slowly, he pushes me back against the custom built-in shelving that houses thousands of bottles of his wine. Individual bottle heads push into my back, they're cool and although the temperature of them slowly seeps through the fabric of my dress, the heat from him standing so close sets me on fire.

"Funny," he pauses and tilts his head to the side, "I've never had *anyone* complain about my dick before." His voice is rough and deeper than normal.

A sharp intake of air chills my lungs, and I shiver again. His eyes drop to my mouth and stay there. They've darkened even more, and his chest begins to lift and fall a little faster.

"You can't speak to me like that." My words are breathy, giving away how affected by him I am, which I hate. I hate him. He's rude, arrogant, and mean.

"I just did." He licks his lips and sets his free hand next to my head, leaving only inches between us.

"Fine. Really doesn't surprise me. I've known from the first moment I met you that you were an asshole, didn't your mother teach you any manners?" I grit through my teeth.

He smirks. "Keep running your mouth, and I'll show you how big of an asshole I can be." His breath hits my face. It's warm and smells like the delicious wines we used for the photographs. My mouth waters. Why does he have to be so incredibly attractive?

"Funny, I've never had *anyone* complain about my mouth before," I counter. An instant blush bursts and heats against my skin.

Oh, God. Did I say that aloud?

His eyes widen and his forearm drops next to me, bringing us so close that when he breathes his chest rises and falls pressing into mine. I've never hated or wanted anything more. My brain is screaming at me to push him away, but my traitorous body wants to climb into his and stay there indefinitely.

With both hands, I grab on to my skirt. There's no way I'm giving him the satisfaction of a reaction. As tempting as he is to reach out to, I can't have any slip-ups. There needs to be no misunderstanding about how I feel about him . . . and that I *hate* him.

His eyes scan my face and find their way back to my mouth. Silence falls between us, and my tongue slips out and wets my bottom lip. He watches the tiny movement, gauging my reaction as he slowly leans forward until his lips are a breath away from mine. Everything about this moment feels forbidden but so damn hot.

His fingers on my hip tighten and then flex. His hand slides around to my lower back and he pulls me into him, connecting us now from chest to thigh. Every hard plane of him pushes into me, every single one, but I'll be damned if I let him know how much I like his body next to mine. I stiffen under his touch to show a bit of defiance instead of melting into him like I so desperately want to do.

Looking up at his ridiculously handsome face, I whisper, "What are you doing?"

His eyes narrow, his lips pinch together, and he sucks in a breath of air through his nose. My heart is beating so hard in my chest, I'm certain he can feel my body vibrating against his.

He swallows and then lets out an annoyed sigh. "I don't know," he mumbles, pushing off the wine rack and taking a step backward.

His arms drop to his side, and I shiver but refuse to acknowledge that I miss his body heat.

Seconds tick by as the turmoil in his eyes clears only to be replaced by the complete loathing he's carried around with him since I arrived. His hands clench, and his gaze drags over me one more time. If there were a photo to define the word repulsed, his face would be it, and this makes me angrier than I have ever been in my whole life.

Who does he think he is?

He's certainly no one to me. So, why is he trying to make me feel like the dirt on the bottom of his shoe? I'll never understand.

It's then that he notices that I have my hands clenched into fists and am grasping my skirt so hard my fingers ache. As if sensing that I'd like to take one of these fists and ram it into his stomach, he takes another step back.

"You know how to find your way out." His voice is coarse, and he gives me one last glare before he turns and stalks out. The only sound being his shoes as they strike the floor and echo off the stone walls. It takes me a few minutes to relax after he leaves, but eventually, I let go of the fabric and wrap my arms around my middle.

What the hell just happened?

Ingredients:

1 cup shredded extra sharp cheddar cheese
1 cup shredded sharp cheddar cheese or Gouda
1/2 cup mayonnaise
1/2 block of cream cheese
1 small jar of pimentos
1/2 teaspoon of onion powder
1/2 teaspoon of cayenne pepper
salt and pepper to taste

How to make:

Mix all ingredients and pair with crackers, chips, toasted baguette slices, or vegetables.

Refrigerate when not eating.

Chapter 6

tackle the quarterback

Zach

Seriously, what is happening to me?

Football, wine, and women. Those are what I'm best at. Yet, with her, I feel completely out of my element, and that's so wrong. She's the one who's the critic, and she's the one who needs to worry about her deceitful character being exposed to the unaware unsuspecting followers of her blog. So, why am I the one who's so flustered? I feel like I'm wandering into an unprotected area, and I'm about to be blindsided.

Slipping through the employee access hallway, I head straight for my office. Slamming the door, I turn and drop my forehead to the cool wood before my eyes drift shut and I force air into my lungs. There's no way I can be social right now. I know the camera crew and a few others are lingering in the tasting room, but I need to escape from them, escape from all of it, escape from her.

What is it about this girl that makes me utterly insane? I've been around plenty of women I don't particularly care for. I've never had a problem controlling myself. She's smart-mouthed, which only draws attention to her full, inviting lips. She has this all-knowing look in her eyes, which makes it clear she's into me and drives me insane, and she carries herself as if she's better than everyone here. It's unnerving and makes me feel crazed. It has to be because of the magazine assignment and what she does. I've been so restless over the potential outcome of the article and what it can do for the winery's sales that I can't think of anything else. And now, with her here, her lack of enthusiasm about our winery in her article could potentially be the difference between a small jump in revenue and a large one.

Ever since that shitty review about us went live last year, I've been in defensive mode, and nothing I've done over the last two days has helped all our efforts in the restoration of the winery's name. Yes, there have been dozens of great reviews over the years, but that one four wilted grapes haunts me at every turn.

Pushing away from the door, I pull in a deep breath and then scrub my hand over my face. What was I thinking trapping her against the wall like that? It's one thing to think she's beautiful and to let my mind wander with the what-ifs, but it's something different to act on it. Especially when I have zero interest in her. Come to think of it, she's made it pretty clear that she hates me as much as I hate her, but it was also clear how much her body wanted mine.

My hand wraps around the back of my neck to try to rub out some of the tension while I will my body to forget the way she felt pressed up against mine.

She could have pushed me off at any time. Instead, when my hand wrapped around her, she arched her back to get even closer. From what I know of her and her stubborn personality, I understand her not backing down, but I felt the way her heart beat through her chest and her breath quickened. She may not have acted on my advance toward her, but she was as caught up as I was.

Shit.

The memory of her body is the last thing I need.

The door flies open and bangs against the wall. Kyle's jaw is locked tight, his eyes are narrowed, and the vein on his forehead is bulging.

"Do you mind telling me what the hell that was?" he snaps, pointing toward the hallway. "Need I remind you that regardless of whatever your relationship is or isn't with her, she works for Food Network. The same Food Network we need to help save our asses."

Letting out a sigh, I walk behind the desk and fall into my seat. I hate the thought of not being the business owner that I know I am. "She doesn't work only for Food Network." I lean forward, rest my arms on the desk, and unconsciously pick up and twirl a pen.

"I know that. She's a chef and co-owns a restaurant in Charleston. A very successful one," he says. Funny, over the last two days, I haven't once thought about her restaurant. It never occurred to me how successful it may or may not be, but this reminds me again of how career climbing and driven she is. There's no telling how many she's run over or backstabbed along the way.

"That isn't all she does."

"What do you mean?" He moves to sit in the chair in front of me.

Leaning back in my chair, I spot the sandwich in his hand. Kyle loves food as much as I do, so I'm not surprised he grabbed something on his way in here to berate me.

"She's a critic, but I'm pretty sure she doesn't know I know." I nod my head toward his hand. "Sandwich good?"

He looks down at the sandwich as if he'd forgotten about it and then takes a huge bite while somehow managing to smirk at me.

"What makes you think she's a critic?" he mumbles between bites.

"Remember that event Lexi talked me into going to for Feeding America last fall?"

"Yeah?"

"Well, she set me up on a blind date, saying I'd *love* this girl, and sure enough . . ." I wave my hand toward the showroom.

"You're kidding?" He finishes the sandwich in two more bites and wipes the back of his hand across his face.

"Nope."

"But why do you think she's a critic?"

"Because, right after I got there, I spotted Lexi across the room and I made my way toward her and her friend. I was standing behind them, neither one of them noticed me, and they were discussing her last critique on her blog."

In my mind, I can see her like it was yesterday. It was her legs that first caught my attention: long, lean, and toned. Killer shoes that made them stretch on for days. Next was the tight little short silver dress, followed by a smile so stunning time stopped. It snapped back into motion seconds later when I heard what the two girls were talking about. Apparently, Shelby was telling Lexi about some guy who had the "gall" to serve her raw food. At first, I thought she was talking about some date gone bad, which almost made me laugh. Some guys didn't have any luck. I kept listening. A small seed of doubt settled inside me, and with each word that passed through Shelby's perfect lips, the sick feeling in my stomach grew.

Shelby, in all of her stunning beauty, seemed so self-important and nasty when she scoffed and said that if he had known she was a critic, she would have gotten better food.

A critic.

The sick feeling in my stomach turned to anger, and all I could see was the asshole who was getting ready to post a bad review of my own wine—not because it was bad wine, but because he had gotten someone else's bottle by mistake.

Lexi asked if Shelby was going to post about it on her blog, *Starving for Southern*, and Shelby just grinned and lifted her glass to her lips. I turned and left without actually finding out her answer.

"She has a blog, too?" Kyle asks.

"Oh yeah, and not a little blog, either. It's a big one." I open my laptop and type in the web address for her blog.

"Well, what is it?" he asks as I move my computer around so he can see the screen.

"*Starving for Southern.*" I watch him carefully as he studies the image of a girl with her hands covering her face. The same girl that has been walking around here for the last twenty-four hours.

"Shut the hell up!" He leans closer to get a better look. Even though her face is hidden, there's no denying it's her. Same hair, same shoulders, just . . . the same. "I can't believe that girl, the one out there, runs *Starving for Southern.*"

"I take it you've heard of it?"

"Of course I have. It's my job to keep a stamp on the who's who of food and wine in the south. This blog has been around for years." He leans back in his chair.

"Yeah, I had heard of it, too. Lexi had mentioned it a few times, at least how much she loved the recipes on it. Needless to say, I was shocked and then pissed when I found out my blind date for the night was the author. I checked repeatedly after that night and searched our name, but nothing ever popped up." Tension builds in my muscles as I think about that night.

Turning the laptop back around, I scroll down through the home page. Most of the posts are recipes and food tips, but every now and then, there's a review.

"Wow, what a small world." Kyle shakes his head.

"Tell me about it." I frown and run my hand over my face.

When Lexi first called and said she had someone she wanted me to meet, I was all for it. How could I say no? Lexi has great taste in friends.

But after what I heard, and then later what I saw, I went out of my way to spend as little time with the girls as I could. I'd run into a few colleagues in the industry, I'd been approached by a few girls, but mostly I kept returning to the bar to try to drown the hours away.

At one point toward the end of the evening Lexi found me standing at a small table. She was fuming and called me an asshole, and although I hated disappointing her, I had my reasons.

No one knew yet about the four wilted grapes review. It was scheduled to go to print a few days later, and until then, I was keeping it to myself. So, I didn't explain.

She pushed her hair over her shoulder, nodded to her friend, who was walking our way, and mumbled, "Whatever."

I knew then I was forgiven.

"Come out soon and see me?" I asked.

"Maybe." She punched me in the arm and then hugged me tight. "See you around, Ten." *Ten*. A stupid nickname she gave me because of my college jersey number.

"See ya, Key Lime." I returned her teasing. Lexi makes pies.

As I walked toward the door, ending the worst blind date ever, my eyes met her friend's. No words needed to be said. We both knew that the likelihood of seeing each other again was slim to none, too bad we don't always get what we want.

"You know what this means," Kyle says.

"Not really. I mean she's a food blogger, critic, whatever. You know how I feel about critics." Saying the word "critic" leaves a bad taste in my mouth.

"I do, but you need to stop thinking of them in a bad way. And really, you're the only one here who doesn't like her. Michelle, the crew, and myself, we all think she's great. So keeping that in mind, also think about how if she's happy here, she might blog about it and/or Instagram the wine. She has like a bazillion followers. And since she's so well known in the southeast, she might be as much of a marketing strategy as the magazine article."

Strategy.

My eyes jerk and lock onto his as the hairs on the back of my neck stand on end—he's right.

Why didn't I think of this sooner? Oh, I know, it's because I've been too caught up verbally sparring with her and trapping her against walls. I shake my head at the imprudence I feel for myself.

"What?" he asks.

"Nothing." He doesn't need to know the war that's going on inside my head.

"We need a plan," he says.

Plan.

I'm good at making plans. I've been making them my entire life. Plans to get me into the college of my choice, plans to get me in the NFL, and plans for the future of this winery. Hell, on a simpler level, I'm best at making game plans. Plans to defeat the other team. There's a reason why I was the top pick for linebackers during the draft, I'm excellent at strategizing and executing a plan.

Most people think the way to win a game falls to the offensive side, but they're wrong. It's the defense that prevents the opposing team from gaining yardage, and best-case scenario is that defense has a turnover and recoups the ball. Although she's a woman, when the same rules are applied how different can it really be?

Rules.

So, when it comes to rules, in defense there are three: run defense, pass defense, and a blitz. If I focus on these three things, I can't lose. She'll leave here in two weeks thinking we are the nicest people she's ever met and our wines the best ever. I personally may not know the ins and outs of her blog, but I had heard of it outside of Lexi, which says something about its popularity and devoted followers. Between the *Food Network Magazine* article and her blog, maybe we can eradicate more of the negativity attached to our name.

So, rule number one: run defense. This is when we add more players to the line of scrimmage to get to the guy handling the ball more quickly. I can do that, but I'll need some help. I know Kyle is in. He sees my wheels turning, and he is smiling so widely, it's almost comical. I'll have him talk to Michelle, and maybe I'll even call in a few of our devoted locals that will just happen to be at the tasting bar at the same time she is. We'll surround her, suck her in, and make her feel so welcome she'll think she was born here.

Rule number two: pass defense. This is one-on-one, man-to-man coverage of the guy carrying the ball—like the wide receiver—or it can be coverage of an area. The objective is to take the ball away. I am going to follow her around as much as possible, and study the ins and outs of her blog to learn all of her favorite things. Every time she turns a corner, I'm going to be there. She doesn't know it yet, but we're going to become best friends, and by the end of the two weeks, any doubt she had because of me will be eliminated and she'll think she's a silent partner of the business.

A shiver runs through me. Being forced to spend time with her is not part of the deal, but unfortunately, there's no getting around this one. It's my winery, my family's name, I have to suck it up and do it.

Rule number three: blitz. This is when the defensive players charge the line of scrimmage in an attempt to tackle the quarterback before he has a chance to pass or hand off the ball to someone else.

Tackle. The. Quarterback.

The feeling of having Shelby flush against me while having her backed against the wall heats through me. Just thinking of her curves and her lips has my blood pumping a little faster. Nothing happened, but damn if that wasn't hot. For a split second, the idea of tackling her doesn't sound so bad, but then I remember who she is.

Switching tactics, I decide I'm going to tackle her brain. I'm good at reading people, so this shouldn't be too hard. I will ask indirect questions to figure out her thought process when it comes to writing her posts and then play right into her moves.

I need to beat her at her own game.

I have to be in control.

I can't let her walk out of here in two weeks without the most stellar impression of us.

I can do this.

I never lose.

Kyle leans forward and places his arms on my desk. "Tell me, boss, what's the plan?"

Excitement courses through my veins. This is the first time in a long time where I've felt like myself. Maybe this is what we've needed all along—a plan. And now that we have one, I can almost taste the victory.

Chuckling to myself, I remember how yesterday I said I'd do anything just short of selling my soul to the devil, well as it turns out, my soul is about to get real friendly with the devil—a she-devil that is.

Ingredients:

1 1/2 cups crumbled gingersnap cookies
1 cup sweetened flaked coconut
1/4 cup unsalted butter, melted
1 (14-ounce) can sweetened condensed milk
½ cup Key lime juice
1 teaspoon lime zest
4 egg yolks
Whipped cream
Toasted sweetened flaked coconut

How to make:

Preheat oven to 350 degrees.

Pulse the cookies in a food processor until finely ground. Add coconut and pulse to mix. Add the butter and pulse to mix. Press over the bottom and up the side of a 9-inch pie plate. Bake for 8 to 10 minutes or until golden brown. Cool on a wire rack. Maintain the oven temperature. For a nuttier flavor, toast the coconut.

In a large bowl combine and beat together the condensed milk, lime juice, lime zest and egg yolks. Pour into the cooled crust. Bake for 8 to 10 minutes or until set.

Let stand until cool.

Top each slice with whipped cream and toasted coconut flakes.

Chapter 7

let's start over

Shelby

"You don't understand, Meg. He's a complete pompous ass."

She giggles, which only makes me even angrier.

After picking up the hand towel lying next to the sink, I begin drying the last of this morning's dishes. Not even a minute after Zach stormed out of the cellar, I snuck out a side exit and bee-lined toward one of the empty golf carts they keep parked under the tree. I drove it straight back to the cottage, where I stayed the rest of yesterday and so far today.

"Why are you laughing?" I yell at her.

"Because it's funny, that's why." In the background, I hear the familiar sound of her chopping. Knowing Meg, she's been at the restaurant prepping for four hours already, and it's only ten in the morning.

"You think it's funny that I'm here and everyone hates me." I return the bowl I had been drying to its place in the cabinet and toss the towel down.

"They don't hate you," she drawls. She only uses this voice when she thinks I'm being irrational about something, but she has no idea. There were no subtleties yesterday. No, he has been very vocal about how I am his problem and my being here is a problem, although, I still don't understand why.

"Oh, yes they do. Their ringleader has made his opinion of me clear to everyone within a ten-mile radius."

She laughs again. She thinks I'm exaggerating, but yesterday ranks as one of my most awkward days, ever.

"It can't be that bad. You haven't done anything."

"It is! And no, I haven't done anything that I can think of, which makes all this so much worse. I can't believe Lexi is friends with someone like him. I can't believe I have to stay here for two weeks!"

"Why is that? Can't you be done with the tasting by tomorrow?"

"I probably could be done with it today, especially if they gave me a few bottles. But, the magazine rented this place for two weeks and has a photographer here onsite. They want to build this article for their online magazine and the special issue. Make it more than just a few photos by adding in video clips, one-on-one interviews, Zach and the staff trying the food I make, things like that. There's an exit interview at the end and then I'll be home."

"I think it sounds like fun."

"You wouldn't think that if you were the one he had pushed up against the wall. Oh, and then he almost kissed me!" I flop down on the couch and cover my face with my arm. I'm not sure who I'm hiding from, maybe myself. I exacerbated the situation yesterday by letting him carry on as long as I did, and I'm thoroughly embarrassed.

"What? Oh, this story keeps getting better and better. I thought he hated you," she giggles.

"He does! And he's so angry all the time." Moving my arm, I stare at the white ceiling and picture his face. I shouldn't have so many details memorized, but it seems I do.

"You're not making any sense. People don't almost kiss people they hate. Maybe he has childhood playground syndrome."

"What?"

"You know, maybe his behavior is like that of a boy on the playground. The one who pushes the girl down and calls her names, but secretly, he likes her."

"Meg, trust me when I say nothing about him is like a boy on the playground. He's all man, and he doesn't like me."

"Did you look him up on the Internet? Maybe you can find out something about him that y'all have in common. If you can play nice for two weeks, I'm sure he can, too."

"I did look him up right after I got here, and I didn't find out *anything* new. There are a ton of pictures of him with different girls, playing football, and a few here at the winery with his parents. As for the articles, I scrolled through them, but all that was there were old TMZ articles about who he was and wasn't dating, the drama of his last girlfriend, a ton of articles about his football career and the injury that ended it, and a few from when he took over the winery. When I searched by most recent, the four wilted grapes review popped up as the most prominent, but nothing about any hobbies, foundations, et cetera."

"What about social media?"

"His Facebook page is set to private, there isn't a fan page, twitter is mostly wine and sports tweets, and Instagram is all pictures from around here. Nothing of any use to me. He—" The doorbell rings, and my eyes dart to the door. "Hey, Meg, someone's here, I have to go." I'm already off the couch and halfway to the door before she answers.

"All right, but remember, you've got this. This is your assignment and it's going to make you shine. Forget the guy, forget the people, remember your rules, come up with some badass food and call me later."

"I will." A pang of longing for my friend hits my heart. I miss her, and I miss our restaurant. "And thanks. I needed that."

"Of course! Don't do anything I wouldn't do . . . well, unless Mr. Hottie Ex-Football Player again decides to push you—"

"Stop! Stop right there."

She laughs and that longing evaporates. So, I do what any best friend would do, I hang up on her.

Zach is standing on the other side of the door. My entire body seizes with an unwanted attraction as I watch him through the crack in the curtain as he runs his hand over his face and around to the back of his neck. This isn't the first time I've seen him do this, and it isn't the first time I thought it was hot. He's hot. Unfairly so. People shouldn't look as pretty as he does.

While I debate whether I should open the door or pretend I'm not here, he takes a step closer to the door and knocks again. Not expecting it to be so loud, I jump.

"What do you want?" I call through the door. I'm not in the mood to deal with this guy today. We saw each other yesterday—can't we be done for a while?

"I thought I'd take you around and show you the property." He pulls his cell phone out of his back pocket, looks at something, and then shoves it back in. He's fidgeting.

"Why?" I ask, taking the opportunity to look him over. He didn't shave today and there's a scruff across his face that takes him from being just a hot guy to a hot guy with an edge. He's wearing a baseball hat low on his forehead and a light blue T-shirt that hugs his chest and arms perfectly. I have a thing for guy's arms, and his are well defined and rock solid. If he were anyone else, I'd be trying to touch them.

"Because you're going to be here for two weeks and should probably know your way around," he answers.

"Can't Michelle show me?"

"No, she can't. She has to work today. Do you have a problem with me showing you?" He steps to the right and pulls a stem of lavender off the bush next to the front door. He brings it to his nose, sniffs it, and then rubs the purple petals through his fingers, sending each petal fluttering to the ground. I hate that he broke the stem, but I love that he thought enough of the plant to stop and smell it. I love the smell of lavender.

"Is that a trick question?" I ask him.

He tosses the stem off to the side and leans against the frame of the door. "Stop being a pain in the ass and let's go." His voice rises and the irritation becomes more evident.

"Me?" I throw open the door and glare at him. "I'm not the one here who's the ass." He's standing so much closer than I thought, and the smell of sage with a hint of lavender floats my way.

He jerks upright and his features smooth as his eyes run over the length of me. He does this every time he sees me, and once again, I hate it and I love it.

"Shelby." His voice is thick as his blue eyes, which always leave me a little bit breathless, climb back to mine. Damn him.

"Zach," I answer, returning his stare. Neither one of us moves, and I'm certainly not going to be the one who falters first.

Letting out a sigh, his shoulders relax and he presses his lips together into a straight line. Pulling off his baseball hat, he runs his fingers through his hair, and then shoves it back on his head. A myriad of emotions passes over his face. It's as if he can't decide which one he wants to throw at me, and this flusters me.

In the end, he clears his throat and looks around at the outside of the building instead of looking at me. "Did Michelle explain the history of the cottage?"

"She did." I keep my answer short and lean against the opposite side of the doorframe, frowning at him. Every warning flag I have is raised and flying. What is he really doing here? What's his angle? He's out of character this morning.

"Good." He nods his head and then moves past me—without an invitation—and walks straight toward the kitchen, taking in all of my things that I have lying around.

"I actually prefer the cottage over the main house." He runs his hand along the back of the loveseat as he makes his way to the breakfast bar. "If it weren't such a great source of revenue for us, I'd move into it."

Visions of sharing the space with him suddenly make the cozy cottage feel about half as big as it is, and it isn't lost on me that this is the first thing he's told me about himself since I arrived.

"I love this cottage." Since he's making an attempt at civility, I smile and add, "And I can't thank you again for putting me in it."

My eyes move around the room, and I smile to myself at all the little touches that make it so inviting, especially the vintage bee decorations.

"Well, better here than the manor," he says dryly, matter-of-factly.

My eyes snap to his. I'm insulted by that comment, but I can't argue with it. Here in the cottage is definitely better. He watches me as I move to stand across the kitchen island from him, putting a barrier between us.

"What's this for?" His eyes flick to the pie dish in front of him.

"The other night when I drank the chardonnay, I was brainstorming ideas to go with it. Everyone knows that white wines and fish go well together, but chardonnays are full-bodied and go great with summer vegetables as well. I improvised and made a vegetable frittata this morning with what I found in the refrigerator and out back in the porch garden. Frittatas are great for brunch and pair well with a salad."

"Hmm. Always working, aren't you?" His eyes narrow briefly at me as he takes the knife lying in the dish, cuts himself a sliver, and drops it into his mouth. I wait as he chews, expecting some snide remark, but his eyes light up and find mine. "It's good . . . really good."

His approval makes me smile, and instantly, I wish I could take it back. I shouldn't care what he thinks, but unfortunately, I do. He's the other half of the assignment, and I bloom inside at the compliment.

"Yes, I am always working, because I love what I do. And thank you. I love frittatas. As a kid, it was one of the first things I learned to cook. They're crustless, can be cheeseless, and filled with pretty much whatever vegetables or meats are in the refrigerator."

His brows raise. "You made this as a kid? How old?"

"Thirteen." My age when my parents divorced and I became a latch key kid. Instead of watching dumb Disney shows, I watched cooking shows hoping that if I made things for my mother she would smile.

"Hmm," he responds, part due to skepticism and the other part awe. "You should use this recipe. I like it." He gives me a closed mouthed smile. This is also the first time he's attempted to smile at me, even if it's forced.

"Okay, I will." I agree with him. It's obvious he's extending some kind of olive branch, and I want whatever truce he's offering. It will make the two weeks go by much faster.

He picks up my water glass on the counter and takes a sip. His ease at sharing my things is a little unnerving, and suddenly, I'm anxious. This Zach is calmer and nicer, and I don't know what to think of this new side of him.

Stepping to the left, he looks around the island and down my legs to my feet, which are bare, and then back up. "Leave the heels, we'll be doing some walking." He cuts off another bite and eats it while staring at me.

He's noticed I wear heels? I look at his feet, and he's wearing a pair of Brooks tennis shoes, but I don't comment. I also don't mention that I didn't actually agree to go anywhere with him, but anything is better than hanging out here staring at the ceiling. So, I walk to the front door and slip on the rubber boots I brought. They're a lot cuter than tennis shoes, and I don't mind getting these dirty.

"What are those?" he asks, finishing the glass of water as I grab a sun hat. His eyes are trained on my boots.

"What do you mean?" I look at my feet and then back at him.

His eyebrows furrow into a scowl. "Nothing. Let's go," he says while walking past me and out the door.

I follow him, and that's when I spot the truck. "You drive a white truck?" This strikes me funny, and I giggle. White is supposed to be for the good guys, black for the assholes.

"Yeah, why?" He's curt and his tone once again annoys me.

"No reason . . . just seems like black would be more your color."

I shrug.

He shoots me a disapproving glare but doesn't rebut my comment. Instead, he pulls a pair of aviator sunglasses out of a pocket in the driver's side door and slips them on.

"We'll take the golf cart," he grumbles through his teeth as he storms off.

Maybe that olive branch resembles more of a short twig, and now I'm second-guessing whether I should go with him today.

"Stop overthinking this, Shelby. You're gonna like what I have to show you." He seems a little subdued and his mood shift confuses me. He pats the seat next to him and gestures for me to climb in.

I sit as far away from him as possible. He notices the move and his hands grip onto the steering wheel. "Hang on," he grumbles, and without looking at me, he puts the cart in drive.

We begin to weave our way up and down the rows of vines. With one hand holding onto my hat, I let my fingers brush against the vine leaves as we fly past. I don't think he's ignoring me, I have to admit it's nice he hasn't yelled at me, but I don't get it.

"What's wrong with you today?" I blurt out.

"What do you mean?" he glances at me.

"Seriously? All right, fine. You've all but told me you hated me, so why the change of heart? Why are you being nice? It goes against your character."

The golf cart comes to a stop, and he angles his body to face me. "I *am* a nice person."

I raise my eyebrows at him, and he lets out a sigh.

"Look, I'll admit that I haven't been the most hospitable, but that's on me—not you. I know the last few days have been a bit uncomfortable, so, for lack of a better expression, how about we start over?"

Start over?

"I don't understand." I blink at him, wishing I could see his eyes through his dark sunglasses.

"I don't want to fight with you, Shelby. I want you to enjoy your time here, and not only because of the project but also because this winery is my most favorite place on the earth."

His words stretch between us, and while I love what he said, I still don't understand why he disliked me so much from the moment he met me. I guess I could ask him, but what good would it do? Plus, I don't really care as long as he can be civil for the next eleven days.

Letting out a strained breath, he tears his gaze from mine, and eases down on the gas pedal. The cart slowly begins to roll forward and then takes off.

Well at least he's finally admitted he's the problem here. I guess that's as good of an apology as I'm going to get, so I'll take it.

"Okay." My voice comes out slightly uneasy.

"Okay?" His eyebrows rise above the sunglasses and push near the brim of his hat.

I nod my head and leave it at that as we continue to ride away from the cottage.

Sweeping left, he takes us to the bottom of the hill and pauses so I can look up over the vineyard.

"My great, great grandfather was a Hungarian immigrant. He was brought over to the States around the turn of the century to help establish a large vineyard in northern Georgia and to make wine. During prohibition, most of the wineries were abandoned by their owners, including this one. They told him if he stayed, the land was his. Having nowhere to go, his friends decided to join him and farm the land for fresh peaches and pecans since they had nowhere else to go. Within a few years, they became one of the largest distributers up the East Coast. Secretly, they still made the wine, maturing the soil and the vines through the generations, and by the seventies, commercial wine production was back in business, and so were we."

"Wow, your family's been here a long time." I peer out and admire the beautiful layout of the farm. Rows and rows of manicured vines sweep and roll with the rise and fall of the hillside, surrounded by peach, apple, and pecan trees. With the manor up at the top of the hill, and a large barn off to the right, the vision before me is postcard worthy. It's breathtaking.

"We have." His voice is a little softer, and the love and respect he feels for not only his family but also the farm is evident.

"So, you're Hungarian?" I honestly have no idea what a Hungarian looks like, but looking at him with his muscular build, trim waist, and long legs, I might become a fan.

"Not really." There goes that thought. "I would say I'm more of an American mutt—a little bit of everything." He grins at me.

Oh, look who's being funny. "Me, too."

He starts the cart again, and we're off.

"How big is the farm?" I think about the wineries from Napa as he starts down the trail again. Some of them are huge and have additional crops in other appellations.

"Wolff owns roughly one hundred and twelve acres, but not all of it is cultivated. The vines cover about eighty-five."

"How many wines do you make here?" It occurs to me I should already know this, but I don't.

"Current is eleven: four red, three white, and four sparkling, but usually it's nine. It really depends on the production of the crops, how long some have been aging in the cave, and different blends we want to experiment with."

"You have a cave?" When I looked up the winery online and scanned over the pages, it didn't mention a cave.

"I do, and we're headed that way." He points toward the east side of his property.

"To make these wines, how many different kinds of grapes do you grow?"

"It really depends on our goals for that year, or the few after. We've had as many as sixteen varietals growing at one time. Some are for our current blends, some are to mature the vines for later use, and some are experimental. Look there at the bottom of the row, each row is labeled, and back up at the manor I have a log of all the vines, where they came from, when they were planted, harvest quantity, and so on."

"They look so beautiful and healthy." The leaves blow around from the wind of the cart as we pass by. "It's really amazing."

His head turns. I can feel him looking at me, but I pretend I don't notice and just enjoy the ride.

Zach parks the golf cart under another tree and climbs out before gesturing for me to follow him.

Together, we wind down a path to an entrance that's built into the side of the hill. The cave. On the left, there's a wooden door, and on the right, wooden garage doors with a wide path that wraps down around the hill. He leads me inside and down a short, dark hallway that opens up into a long, wide tunnel. Zach flips a switch and wall sconces light up the cave.

When my eyes adjust, I'm stunned speechless. "Zach, this is seriously cool." I feel his eyes on me, but mine trail along the walls, which are covered with white stones similar to the manor, and over the curved archway entrances to the two rooms in front of us.

"Yeah, the cave stays around fifty-eight degrees." Zach smirks and then walks toward the room on the right. The left room is full of stacked barrels.

"I didn't mean the temperature, ass, but it is pleasant. I meant the cave in general. I've never been in a wine cave and didn't know they really existed like this."

"A lot of wineries have moved to building caves. It's more energy efficient, and it's easier to maintain a cooler temperature without having to run a cooling unit. Also, the hills trap in the humidity needed."

Zach moves through the room and checks the gauges of several tanks.

"How long has the cave been here?" I ask, watching him do his thing and trying hard not to watch how nicely his shirt pulls across the back of his shoulders.

"As far as we know, the caves were here when they started the vineyard."

"Wow. I'm thoroughly awed right now." Who knew that all of this was sitting under the hillside.

"Thanks. My father had each room in the cave widened in the eighties after the wines took off, and then he had them modernized twenty years later. When I was a kid, I hated coming down here. It smelled weird, the machines were loud, and it was dark."

He's right, the pungent smell of fermenting grapes lingers thick and sweet in the air. We pass large vertical steel tanks full of grapes that are slowly turning into wine. My fingers drift across the barrels, and I'm humbled by this age-old process. On the other side of the room, it's stacked with thousands of bottles of sparkling wine.

"Who helps you with all of this?" I ask, taking it all in.

"I have a crew of four that helps me with anything and everything wine related, especially the bottling. Our operation here is too large for hand picking, so during the harvest, the machines do most of the work. Besides those four, we probably have a dozen other employees that work with Michelle behind the tasting bar, in the manor, or around the grounds."

"The bottling, where's that done at?" I turn and look around the cave for another door.

"We passed it on the way here, the large barn." He moves to lean against the tank next to me.

"What? You bottle in a barn?"

He chuckles at my confusion. "It looks like a barn, but is built more like a warehouse. There isn't enough space down here, and during any given vintage, we can crate between five thousand and six thousand cases of wine."

"Holy moly, that's a lot of wine."

"It is and it isn't. But, down here, we want this as undisturbed as possible. Opening the door, bringing in groups of people, it would just be intrusive and mess with the overall temperature. So, very rarely do we show it off. Mostly, the tour includes the cellar, they can watch the bottling, and wander around the public rooms of the manor while tasting the wine."

"Well, thank you for bringing me down here." I look up at the huge ornate chandelier hanging from the ceiling. "This is seriously one of the neatest things I've ever seen."

Zach purses his lips together and gives me a nod.

"Here, come try this." He walks out of the room, grabs two glasses off a long wall table, and then stops in front of a barrel. I'm fascinated as he turns the spout, fills the two glasses, and then hands me one. I watch as he sniffs, swirls the wine, and then sips it.

"What is it?" I ask, doing exactly what he did. Bursts of flavors such as cherries, black currants, and a smokiness like found in a cigar box fill my mouth.

"It's an eighty/twenty cabernet merlot blend. It's been aging for about eighteen months."

"It's delicious. When will it be done?" I ask, taking another sip.

"We'll pull it sometime within the next month or two, bottle it, and allow it to age a little more. We've been sitting on this one, and I'm excited because I think it will be well received." He sniffs it again and rolls it around in the glass, watching as the wine rolls down the sides. "This one will be better once it's decanted."

"Well, I think it's good now. Can I have some more?" I hold out my now empty glass to him.

His lips quirk, and he takes it to top it off.

When he hands it back to me, our fingers barely graze, the contact is warm and unexpected. Pulling my hand away too fast, I spill the wine, but I'm too surprised by the small flicker of interest the brief graze of skin against skin ignited to apologize. Zach, however, takes a step back and gives me a curious but guarded look.

Did he feel that?

Every muscle in me tightens, and I silently beg him to touch me again, only that would be really bad. Other than the last hour, which has left me incredibly confused, he's been terrible to me. He isn't the guy for me, not even to have a little fun with, no matter how hot he is, so I douse my inner flame with a mixture of reality and a large gulp of wine. It burns a little going down and seconds pass as we stare at each other.

His lips drop to a scowl. Yep, he felt it.

Here we go.

Nice Zach is gone and mean Zach is back as he moves a little farther away and shoves his hand into his pocket. Just when I think I'm about to get a snide comment about my clumsiness or be chided for my lack of manners, he shrugs and smiles.

"So, this is it," he says on an exhale as his eyes move away from me and sweep around the room.

"It really is quite impressive," I mumble, trying not to poke the bear. As I walk back to the entrance to the cave, I finish my glass of wine and copy him by setting it in a used glass rack where there are a few others.

Zach, who has been walking two steps ahead of me, clears his throat. "All of the magazine crew, except for the photographer, left this morning. If you decide you want to go check out the bottling in the barn, text him, and he can go with you. Those shots might be nice, this down here, we like to keep to ourselves."

"I understand," I say, as he turns to face me.

"And when you decide to taste the wines we stock at the manor, Michelle knows to give him a call so he can come and take a few photos of you then, too."

"Yikes! Thanks for telling me. I'd hate for him to show up after I've been for a run or after I'd cooked all day." I briefly glance down at my outfit and then at his. Both hands are now stuffed in his pockets, and they're dragging his jeans down his hips. A chill runs through me from the temperature of the room, and I have an insane urge to slide my hands under the bottom of his T-shirt to feel the warmth of his skin around his waist.

"No worries." His voice brings my eyes back to his. The light in the cave is already muted, but because of his hat and the shadow it casts across his face, I have no indication of what he's really thinking or feeling. "Might be best to spread out the tasting over three separate nights, too: whites, reds, and sparklings."

"Sounds good to me. It'll give me a day or two in between each tasting to play around with corresponding food pairings as well." I start walking toward the exit, and he follows.

"Well, if the food tastes anything like what you made this morning, let me know. I'd be happy to taste test it for you." His voice is all business but casual.

"Okay." I give him a small smile as he flips off the light.

My eyes squint against the brightness of the sun, and I pull down the sun hat and take in the fresh air. The day turned out to be beautiful and right this moment, I'm happy that he brought me here versus Michelle. I'm still not too sure about this "let's start over" Zach. I feel like I've witnessed firsthand a true Dr. Jekyll and Mr. Hyde, but I'm going to take what I can get and continue taking this one day at a time.

Ingredients:

3 Tablespoons of olive oil
Assortment of vegetables
8 eggs
1/2 cup of milk
1/4 teaspoon of black pepper
1/4 teaspoon of cayenne pepper
1/2 teaspoon of salt
1/2 cup of cheese if adding

How to make:

Preheat the broiler to high.

In an oven-safe skillet, I prefer a 10-inch cast iron skillet, cook meat and remove to drain. Add vegetables and cook until tender. If not adding meat, heat olive oil and cook vegetables until tender.

In a bowl, whisk together eggs, milk, and seasonings. Pour the mixture into the skillet with meat and vegetables. Once the edge of the frittata is half-way set, the middle is still runny, sprinkle cheese if adding, and move to under the broiler. Cook for another 2-3 minutes.

Cool and slice.

Chapter 8

lightning will strike

Zach

All day today, I've thought about Shelby. What's she doing? Is she slaying someone's dream? Is she working on the twenty-five recommendations article? Is she cooking more delicious food? Did she wander around the estate? Has she tried more of our wines? Did she *really* enjoy the tour of the cave? Mainly, my thoughts revolve around wondering what she's wearing. Yep, stupid, I know, but I can't help myself.

When I showed up to the cottage yesterday, I expected her to be dressed casually. I didn't realize she would wear it so well, especially in those little shorts. From pants on day one, to a dress on day two, to those shorts on day three, I swear every time I see this girl, she's showing more skin than the last time, purposely trying to drive me crazy. Then, she put on those damn boots. Boots that made her look adorable when we all know it's a ruse because she's really just a wolf in sheep's clothing. I mean who wears fancy rain boots when it isn't raining?

Kyle asked me how our time went together yesterday, and all I had to tell him was, "fine." He regarded me skeptically, as if he were expecting me to say more, but really once I got her to retract her claws at the cottage, the day moved along smooth enough. She didn't say anything that made me want to leave her in the middle of the vineyard by herself, and I appreciated how much she wanted to know about my family and the winery. None of yesterday changes how I ultimately feel about her, but finishing out the two weeks may not be so bad after all. If I stick to the plan, that is.

When Kyle and I walk into the tasting room, I find her sitting at the back bar talking to Michelle, who's standing across from her. They're leaning toward each other as if they've known each other for years instead of days. This should make me happy, but it does the opposite, causing me to glower. I understand the expression keep your friends close and your enemies closer, but having her fit in and get along so well with my staff is messing with my head. Together, Kyle and I make our way over to them, acknowledging a few regulars on our way.

Michelle and Shelby are still laughing—hard, like to the point of tears. I glance over to Kyle, and he winks at me. He's thinking what I'm thinking and this is his way of letting me know he and Michelle had that talk.

Michelle looks up, spots Kyle, and the smile on her face gets impossibly bigger. I smirk at him as he tightens his facial features to keep from responding. Poor guy, it's easy to see that he wants to.

At Michelle's reaction, Shelby turns on her stool to see who she's looking at, and I'm met with sparkling blue eyes. Her smile drops a little and her eyes turn wary, but her overall disposition is welcoming, so I know I did something right yesterday.

Sucking in a deep breath, my eyes fall to the bare skin of her arms and legs. She's wearing a red sundress and another pair of impossible shoes. If she were anyone else, I'd say she's a welcome sight for my tired eyes, but really she's just another problem in my long list of them.

"What are you two looking at?" Kyle asks, taking a seat in front of Michelle and to the right of Shelby.

"Funny movie clips on YouTube." She grins at him.

"Why?" I ask as I take the seat to the left of Shelby. All three of them turn to look at me. That came out a little harsher than intended.

"Why not?" Michelle answers, shooting me a "cool it" look. "Turns out Shelby and I both have a love for dry humor." She smiles at Shelby and then holds out her phone. "Take Napoleon Dynamite for example." She hits play, and there's the dude with the curly hair walking out of his house and toward the pasture.

"Tina, you fat lard. Come and get some DINNER . . ." The llama grunts at him as he holds out a spoon and says, "Tina, eat. Food. Eat some FOOD!" Then he flings the casserole on the ground.

Both girls squeal with laughter, and I find myself chuckling with them. Damn, that really is a funny movie.

"How'd it go? All fixed?" Michelle asks, her look bouncing between the two of us.

"Yeah, we think so," Kyle answers before leaning over the bar to grab a basket of crackers. "We just need to watch the pH levels over the next couple of days and add some more nutrients to the soil."

Kyle's voice fades as my eyes lock on Shelby's. Slowly, hers drop as she takes in my appearance. I know we're filthy, but I don't care, and I prop a dusty work boot on the footrest of her stool.

In front of her are four glasses, three for the current white flight—although they aren't tasting glasses, they're full size—and one for Michelle. In front of me, there are three empty tasting glasses.

"Who was sitting here?" I turn and ask her.

"The photographer."

"Right." An unwanted and unexpected wave of jealousy courses through me. It never occurred to me he would spend time with her. He should be taking the photos, not drinking the wine and laughing with her.

Wait.

Why do I care who drinks wine with her?

I don't.

"What were you doing?" she asks me, following my gaze to the wine glasses. "I thought you might join us." She pushes the photographer's away and then slides one of hers in front of me.

"We had a problem with the draining tiles at the bottom of the hill." I pick up the glass and take a sip. It's cold, familiar, and tastes exceptional.

"What happened to them?" She shifts in her seat, uncrosses her legs, and then crosses them again so she's angled in my direction. The skirt of her dress slides up her thigh a little. That's it; that's all I needed. After seeing her in the shorts yesterday and this dress today, I'm not just drawn to her legs, I'm officially obsessed with them. I clear my throat to answer her.

"Well, it's been a pretty wet spring so far. There was some erosion around a few of the joints, extra sediment build-up, that kind of stuff. We fixed it, but the soil was too wet for the vine roots, which is what he meant about having to rebalance the soil."

She picks up the glass of wine in front of her, which is the sauvignon blanc. I can tell based on the color, or I should say lack of color, it's so light and gives off a pale yellow tint. She brings it to her mouth, and I sit enraptured as her glossy lips touch the rim of the glass. She takes a sip and my stomach tightens with an unwanted desire. A very unwanted desire.

"So, you actually do work around here?" Her voice pulls me away from her mouth, and I cringe inwardly at being caught. She's still smirking at me when her words sink in. Isn't that just like a true critic? Someone who makes general assumptions and doesn't care to know the truth. My irritation over loving her legs quickly shifts to an overall irritation with her.

"I'm sorry, did you suddenly forget whose name is on that bottle of wine you're drinking?"

Her playful face falls and then goes blank, shutting me out. She blinks at me a few times and then sets the glass back. "I was just kidding." Her voice is soft but her eyes narrow slightly. "No need to be so sensitive about everything all the time." She tilts her head to the side. "Oh, wait. Are your true colors coming back out?" With that, she rolls her eyes and turns her body away from me and back toward Michelle. Michelle frowns and just noticeably shakes her head.

Kyle, who can see I'm about to lose my shit, holds out his hands behind her back so she can't see, and subtly tells me to calm down. He's right. I'm angry over a comment that, if it had come from anyone else, I would have laughed at.

Taking in a deep breath, I run my hand across the back of my neck and decide I have to let it go. I did provoke her, which is something I need to stop doing. *Remember the plan* I chant to myself.

"Here, earlier I made these for y'all." Michelle reaches into a cooler and pulls two chicken salad sandwiches wrapped in plastic and places them on the bar before pouring two glasses of sweet tea. My stomach growls as I unwrap mine.

"Ah, you're the best. Thank you," Kyle mumbles as he dives in. She smiles at him and they share a somewhat intimate look. I don't know why I never thought about the two of them together before. It makes complete sense.

Next to me, Shelby picks up her glass.

"So, what do you think?" I point to the wine in her hand, trying to diffuse the tension between us.

She licks her lips and takes another slow sip while watching me. It's incredibly seductive, and my mind wanders to what else she could do with those lips, until she giggles. My eyes snap away from her mouth and back to my plate. Damn, she did that on purpose.

"I think it's delicious. I prefer drier wines and this hits the spot." She looks at the glass, twirls the stem between her fingers, and then sets it back on the bar.

"Do you have a preference over red or white?" I ask between bites of the sandwich.

"Nope. I'm not picky. I'll drink whatever is offered."

Yes. And then you'll voice your opinion about it to anyone that will listen if you don't like it. Anger pushes its way up under my skin, and I breathe through my nose to try to calm down.

Keep the conversation going, Zach.

Make her feel welcome.

Remember the plan.

"What did you do today?" I ask her before a gulp of the sweet tea.

"I went over to the barn and helped the guys with the bottling." Her expression is tentative, and she's waiting to see if I'm going to have a retort to her wandering around the property today.

"Really, what did they have you do?" It seems as if I'm not the only one who likes to get my hands dirty. I finish the sandwich and push the plate away.

"Well, there really wasn't much for me to do. The equipment does most of it, but they answered some questions I had, and they let me help crate the bottles once they were labeled.

Kyle bumps my shoulder and hands me his phone.

"Sorry, just a second," I tell her and angle the phone so she can't see the screen.

"No worries, I get it . . . duty calls." She turns to Michelle and they start talking about someone called Fat Amy.

I flash them a smile and then look at the screen. On it is the winery's Instagram account, and under the profile of *Starving for Southern,* there's a photo of our bottles lined up on the assembly line out in the barn. My heart contracts sharply in my chest when I look at the fifty-two thousand likes under the photo, and see under the illuminated heart over seven thousand new followers. And that was after just one post. My eyes meet Kyle's, and we share a knowing look. The plan is already working.

I hand him his phone and turn back to Shelby with a smile, suddenly feeling a fresh sense of purpose with this girl. "Are there any questions I can answer for you?"

"No, I think I have a good grasp on the operation around here. Michelle did tell me about your wine club, I think it's a great idea."

"Ah, the wine club . . ." I glance to Michelle, who gives me a sympathetic smile.

Shortly after taking over the winery, we implemented the wine club and sales went up. Being in the club means that once a month patrons can come in, do a full tasting for two, and leave with two bottles of wine. We automatically charge them on the first of each month for those two bottles, and it doesn't matter when they make it in, they'll be waiting for them. The locals love it. We are also partnered with a bakery in town to add some finger foods to the mix.

"A lot of smaller family-run wineries have adopted a club. We've had some good and bad experiences with it. More good than not." I smile at her because I don't want to plant any negative thoughts in her mind.

"How many members does it have?" She finishes the sauvignon blanc and picks up the next glass.

"Close to eighty," I say, proudly.

"That's great! I love the idea that you're guaranteed monthly sales."

"Us, too."

Michelle leans over and tosses a few frozen grapes in Shelby's glass before filling it. The grapes help keep the wine cold without diluting it. She turns the bottle my way, but I hold my hand out, covering the top. It's been a really long day in the sun and I don't need any excuse for one of my headaches to kick in.

"Water, please."

She nods and pulls out a fresh cold bottle.

"You tasted all the whites tonight?" I ask, turning back to Shelby.

"I did."

Just to see if she's been paying attention, I ask her, "Which one are you drinking now?"

She brings it to her face, smells it, and then sips it. Her eyes sparkle at me, she knows.

"The pinot gris."

"Correct." I grin at her.

"What's the difference between pinot gris and pinot grigio?" she asks.

"The gris is more full-bodied, spicier, less floral, and has great durability when it comes to being stored in the cellar. I appreciate wines that age well and hold their own."

"I can imagine having a weak wine with a short life span is not ideal."

"No, not really. It creates more of sense of urgency to get it sold."

"I see." She nods her head in understanding.

"So, what's on the agenda for tomorrow?" Kyle asks her, as I unscrew the water cap and guzzle it.

"I think I'm going to run out, get some food, and start planning the pairings for the other whites. Come up with a few different possibilities." She turns to Michelle to include her in the conversation. "I made a frittata yesterday morning and Zach approved, so match made. Do either of you have any favorite dishes that come to mind?"

"Oh, I know. Zach's mother makes the best fried chicken." Kyle smiles at me. "When she isn't away vacationing, she cooks a giant Sunday dinner for the staff, and we all sit together and eat."

Those dinners were my favorite growing up. It was the only time my dad slowed down enough to sit and talk with us.

"That sounds really nice," she responds, smiling along with him.

"It is. If you're ever out this way when they're back you should come, I'm sure she'd love to meet you," he says.

Shelby glances at me, and when she doesn't get a reaction out of me, she shrugs. Neither one of us has any interest in continuing this forced arrangement after she leaves. I think this might be the first thing that we both agree on, but in the meantime . . . stick to the plan.

"I think I'll go with you tomorrow. What time were you thinking?" I ask her.

She blinks a few times and her forehead wrinkles a bit before a sly grin that I don't understand flits across her face, "How about nine thirty?"

"Sure. I'll be ready." I return her grin with a cautious one and say, "I'm looking forward to seeing what you come up with."

"I have some ideas already, but I need to see what's available at the farmers' market first. Lightning will strike and the creativity will rain down, I know it."

Lightning.

There's only one thing, well one place that comes to mind; I hesitate and think, *why not.*

"I want to show you something," my voice trails off, as I almost regret asking, but the invite is out now. "Were you wanting to head to the cottage after this or are you good to go for a ride?"

She glances at Michelle, and the two of them trade a look of surprise and curiosity. "A ride sounds fun." Her voice is cautious, so I give her a reassuring smile. This girl never backs down from a challenge.

Reaching over the bar, I grab the bottle of sauvignon blanc and two glasses. I can feel Kyle and Michelle looking at me suspiciously, and for some reason I suddenly feel guilty. I shouldn't. They know what the plan is, and it's not as if I'm trying to get under her dress, I just think she'll like where I want to take her.

She follows close behind as I lead her out of the manor, the soft click of her heels on the floor keeping time with the muted thud of my work boots. I head toward the golf carts, and pack the bottle and glasses in a bag that's hooked on the back of the closest one. She climbs into the passenger side and tucks the sides of her skirt under her legs.

The air is cool tonight, but not cold. The humidity has held off, and I think I'm going to time this perfectly. Five minutes later, we pull up to the cave. Again, Shelby follows me as I start walking up the dirt path in the opposite direction of the cave.

"Where are we going?" she calls out from behind me.

"You'll see." I smile to myself, eager to see her reaction.

The path isn't too long, maybe a tenth of a mile or so, but it is uphill, and it suddenly occurs to me she isn't wearing the best shoes for this.

"Are you doing okay?" I turn around and point to her shoes just as she wobbles. Reaching out I grab her hand to steady her, and she smiles at me in appreciation.

Damn smile. I'm not supposed to like it either, or her.

"I am, but I think I'll take them off. I don't want the heels to get ruined." She doesn't let go of my hand as she slips her shoes from her feet and then dangles them loosely from her fingertips. She shrinks a good four inches, and now I feel like I'm towering over her.

"All right, let's go. It looks like the sun is going to set soon, and I want to see what it is you're trying to show me," she says, pulling on my hand. Leave it to this girl to hike up a hill barefoot in a dress. I shake my head at her and at myself for finding her charming.

Side by side, we finish the trail and step out onto a rock overhang that gives us a spectacular view of the winery as well as a few others. I'm still holding her hand, and she's still holding mine. I don't know why, I just know I'm not ready to let it go.

"Wow, it's so beautiful." The wonder in her voice wraps around us along with the wind leaving its mark on my skin. I'm elated by the inspired and awestruck look on her face. Her hand tightens around mine, and I watch as she breathes in the earthy clean smell of the air. I want to respond that it is, but deep down, I know I wouldn't be talking about the view in front of us.

For some reason, up here, by ourselves and away from the world, it feels different, she suddenly feels different. It's like she's someone else, or maybe it's just me.

"My father first brought me here on my tenth birthday. I was so proud that he wanted to spend time with me to show me something he loved. He said until then, he thought I was too young and worried that I would fall over the edge, but at ten, he trusted me. I've never forgotten that day, and I don't know why I just told you that, but this is my favorite spot. I've come here a lot over the years."

"Are you close with your parents?" she asks.

"More so with my mother. My father, he ah, he worked a lot. How about you?"

"No, I'm not," she whispers, and then closes the subject. "Thank you for bringing me," she mumbles, her gaze still enchanted by the view.

I watch her face as she stares out toward the horizon. The sun is about to dip down below the peaks of the hills and everything around us is bathed in a golden light.

"I wasn't sure if I was going to or not," I confess, wondering if I should keep this tidbit to myself.

"Why not?" She turns to look at me and our eyes meet.

"Because . . . I've never brought anyone here before, it's my place." My eyes scan her face, and I hate how my stomach tightens. Why is it that when we're in front of other people I want to strangle her, but when we're alone, I forget what she does and who she is, and I kind of enjoy her company?

"Really?" Her eyebrows rise in question. If I would have brought someone, it would have been Elaine, but she was always way more interested in our city life than coming here to the farm.

"Nope. But when you mentioned lightning, I thought of it. In the summer, on the horizon there's a lot of heat lightning. I've always liked to watch the storms off in the distance."

"Sounds beautiful and I love it here." She breaks eye contact and nods toward the bag I brought. "What's in there? Did you pack us a snack?"

"No." I chuckle. "The golf cart we took is mine. The bag stays on the back and holds things that occasionally I need."

Letting go of her hand, I put the bag down and pull out a blanket.

"You need a blanket?" She watches me as I throw it out for us to sit on.

"You'd be surprised how much time I spend up here." I gesture for her to sit, and she moves onto the blanket.

"What do you do up here?" She looks at me as I sit next to her, stretch out my legs, cross them at the ankle, and lean back onto my hands.

"Think."

After the last injury, I knew my football career was done. I woke up in the hospital to the familiar sounds of the machines, and I kept my eyes shut to allow the reality of my situation to sink in. It was there in that bed that I brought myself here and stayed. Even after I got home, I came up here, pitched a tent, and grieved for the loss of something I loved.

Sensing I need a topic change, Shelby reaches over and pulls the wine and two glasses out of the bag. She pours for us and hands one to me.

"What do you think of this sauvignon blanc?" I ask her as she takes a sip.

"I like it. I think it's tart, green apple tart." She holds the glass up and looks at the wine. The sun reflecting through it gives it more of a golden color, and then she smiles at me before taking another sip.

"I wasn't sure what to expect from the person the magazine was sending. They mentioned a chef, but not whether that person would be versed in wines or not. You don't know a lot about wine, do you?"

"No, but I know enough," she says, lowering her glass. "Also, my palate is refined enough to be able to denote the different flavors and nuances, and I greatly appreciate the work that goes into each bottle."

Shifting, she crosses her legs and folds them under the skirt of her dress. I like watching her, maybe a little too much.

"So, which of your wines is your favorite?" she asks me.

"By taste, or in general?" I get asked this question a lot, but this is the first time I've asked someone to clarify.

She tilts her head as she mulls over my question. "I guess in general, which is kind of broad, so maybe favorite grape."

This answer is easy.

"It would have to be the cabernet. The grape has thick skin, so it's durable to most of the elements and can be grown pretty much anywhere. I appreciate strength in all things."

"You said that earlier, too, about the pinot gris." I think back to our conversation and she's right.

"I'm not a fan of weakness." And that's when it dawns on me that Shelby isn't weak. She's strong, independent, and has her shit together. She isn't relying on anyone to make her dreams come true, she's doing it on her own. A fissure of admiration disrupts the shell of usual dislike I have for this girl, and I'm not sure I like it.

"I can't imagine what it would be like to grow up here. Do you have any siblings?" Her attention is again fixed on the horizon as she asks.

"Nope, it's just me, and it was amazing." It really was. Most assume that because I am an only child I was bored often or lonely, but that was never the case. I loved it here.

Silence settles over us as we gaze out at the sun, watching it slowly sink and disappear behind the hills. Above us, the sprinkling of the stars begins to emerge as the orange glow of daylight fades.

"Can we stay here a little bit longer?" she whispers, scooting a little closer to me until her thigh lightly presses against mine. I don't even think she realizes how close we are, and I should shift away from her, but I don't.

"Sure."

I don't have it in me to tell her no.

Ingredients:

2 cups of chicken, chopped
2 stalks of celery, chopped
1 cup of grapes, sliced in quarters
1/2 cup of pecans, chopped
1/2 cup of mayonnaise
1/2 teaspoon black pepper
1/4 teaspoon salt
4 large croissants

How to make:

In a large mixing bowl, combine chicken, celery, grapes, pecans, mayonnaise, pepper, and salt.

Slice the croissants in half, or use bread of choice.

Serves 4.

Chapter 9

whatever floats your boat

Shelby

Zach is standing in the doorway looking at his phone when I pull up to the manor. Like the day I arrived, he's wearing another winery T-shirt with a pair of jeans, flip-flops, a baseball hat, and a pair of black Ray-ban sunglasses. He looks good, too good.

He hears the car, and his head pops up to watch me drive around the circular driveway. With that confident swagger of his, he strolls down the stairs, over to my car and climbs in.

Just him being in my space causes my heart rate to pick up, and I'm surrounded by the smell of him: warm sun, sage, and something earthy that's manly and completely him.

"Hey," he says, turning and stretching his arm out across the back of my seat. His fingers graze the hair on the back of my neck and goose bumps break out across my skin, causing an involuntary shiver. He notices but doesn't say anything, and even though his sunglasses block his eyes, I can feel them as they take in my every detail right down to the blush burning my cheeks. For someone who's just accommodating me, he sure seems to look at me a lot.

"Hey," I answer him, not knowing what else to say. I'm tongue-tied by his presence, and after how sweet he was last night, I'm having a hard time trying to remind myself why I shouldn't like him or really even care. I'm here for the assignment and the exposure it's going to bring me.

Focus, Shelby. Focus.

He clears his throat and turns to look straight out the windshield as I take off down the driveway.

"Where are we headed?" he asks as he tries to stretch his legs a bit more.

"A restaurant called Tupelo Honey." I bite the inside of my lip to keep from smiling.

"I've heard of it. Wait—" His head whips toward me. "Isn't that in Asheville?" His eyebrows rise above the glasses.

"Yep, have you eaten there?" I grin to myself. I knew last night I wanted to drive there this morning, but if I had told him, he might not have come. I really wanted him to—not because I'm interested in him but because I find him interesting. Kind of like a human-interest piece. The way he talks about his family and the winery, I can tell his background is definitely different than where I come from, his lifetime of football, and I'm curious to know why he's such good friends with Lexi.

He pinches his lips into a thin line and shifts in his seat. "No. So, we're going to Asheville?" His voice is a little growly.

"Yes, but we have one stop to make first." When I glance his way, his jaw is tight and the hand on his lap is balled into a fist.

"How long do you plan on being gone today?" he asks, shifting to pull his phone out of his back pocket and looking at what I assume is his calendar.

"Just through lunch, and then we'll drive back. Why, do you need to stay?" I ask innocently, already knowing he won't back out.

"No, it's fine, I can go. But if we're going for that long of a drive, we're taking my truck."

I look over at him, and his face is stern. There'll be no negotiation.

"Fine by me." I turn the car around and head back to the manor. I don't mind driving, but if he's offering, that's even better. Plus, his truck puts more space between us.

"So, why are we going to Tupelo Honey?" he asks once we set off again.

"Meg and I first stumbled upon it years ago and the food was really good. They've expanded and opened a few more locations across the south, and I think it'll be a great addition to the recommendations article that I'm also writing for the magazine."

"If you've already been there, why are we going now?"

"Well, I have to make sure that it's still just as good. Sometimes the smallest things can change the quality of the food from a vendor, to a chef, or new buying manager. I can't endorse something on a past experience, it needs to be current."

His hands tighten around the base of the steering wheel. "You sound like a critic," he says without glancing at me. I'm slightly alarmed by how forceful his words came out and angle in my seat to get a better look at him.

"Do you have a problem with critics?" I'm suddenly nervous about his answer. The blog is such a huge part of who I am, and the thought of having someone disapprove leaves me feeling awkward and uncomfortable.

Does he know I'm a critic? Did Lexi tell him? I mean, I know over the years *Starving for Southern* has become well known, but anyone who's been to the blog, and read it, knows that the summaries of places I give are just my viewpoint on things.

His eyes quickly shift my way behind the glasses, his lips press together, and he wastes no time thinking about his answer. "Yes."

Huh.

My heart sinks a little bit. Maybe this reaction is because of the review he received last fall. I don't know, but now I feel anxious and let out a deep breath hoping that takes with it my disappointment.

"Well, no worries, there's no critiquing today. Just shopping, eating, and having a nice lunch."

"Shopping?" he glances at me.

"Oh yeah." I grin back and then help myself to punching the address into his GPS. He doesn't say anything. He just readjusts his hat and gives me his signature scowl.

The two and a half hour ride to Asheville is strangely peaceful. I quickly learn that Zach can't stand clutter, which is why the inside of his truck is spotless, and he loves country music. With the windows down and a little Will Ashton band on the radio, Zach is beginning to feel more like an acquaintance than an enemy.

"What made you want to own a restaurant?" he asks out of nowhere.

"Technically, OBA is Meg's restaurant, but I do own a small percentage of it. When we graduated from culinary school, her aunt handed her a check and said, "Go make me proud." I chipped in the little savings that I had to help her, but she knows that my ultimate end goal is to work for Food Network."

He pauses as he considers my response.

"So, she doesn't mind when you take off like this?"

"No. Our arrangement works out pretty well. I help her when

I'm in town and not off writing, and any money I get from the freelance jobs, I turn around and put straight back into the restaurant. Steadily, it's been growing, and Meg has really put herself on the map."

"Hmm," he mutters, obviously lost in thought. I wish I knew what he was thinking, but then again, maybe I don't.

A few minutes later, we pull off the expressway and into our first stop.

"What are we doing here?" He looks at me confused.

"Shopping." I'm grinning from ear to ear and feel like a kid who's about to be unleashed in a candy shop.

"Here?" He turns around and looks at the buildings.

"Yes. Come on, Wolff, get out of the truck, or don't . . . I'm going in." I grab my bag and hop out of the truck.

The Western North Carolina Farmers' Market is one of the best farmers' markets in the southeast. The atmosphere, the variety of local vendors for consumers, and the overall freshness of the produce is something that brings me back here every time I'm up this way. I'm giddy with excitement, and hearing Zach's truck door slam, I smile to myself, knowing he's following me.

"What are we doing here again?" he grumbles as he steps next to me and takes in the market.

"You'll see." I grab his arm and drag him between two of the buildings to the entrance. Hanging a left, I find my favorite place, throw my arms out in a look-at-all-this-good-stuff gesture, and grin at him.

His eyes scan over the hundreds of jars of pickled vegetables, jellies, jams, and honey. He doesn't seem impressed. Undeterred, I grab a tasting stick, stick it into the first open jar I see, and then taste the delicious flavor. So good.

"All of this is over honey?" He's standing there, statue still, with his arms crossed over his chest and clear irritation in his voice.

"Not just *any* honey. This place has the best honey for miles and miles around." I twirl around, and my skirt flairs out.

Zach's face is priceless. I can't tell if he's annoyed or intrigued, and I don't really care. I'm that happy being here.

"Years ago, when Meg and I first had the idea of opening a restaurant together, we were standing on Orange Blossom Avenue and that's how it got its name. It really was that simple, and it just so happens that we also love orange blossom honey. Well, any honey actually, but orange blossom honey and lavender honey are two of my favorites. Keeping with the honey theme, we have a bookshelf full of honey for guests to pick and choose from when they come in to dine."

He pulls his hat off, runs his hand through his blond hair, and then fits it back into place. The ends curl out from under the edge, and the look is downright sexy.

"Funny it never occurred to me to ask what OBA stands for, I've just called it that," he says as he picks up a jar of honey to read the label.

"Most do. It's easier to say, and we've had the initials enlarged as a monogram on all of our marketing materials, too."

Spotting the lavender honey, he stops in front of it and grows quiet. His face is thoughtful before he turns to look at me. "So, you like lavender?"

"Like it? I love it! And I was crazy excited to see how much of it you have planted and growing around the winery. Don't be angry if you find some missing when I leave, I do plan to take some clippings back with me."

"My mother likes lavender, she planted them," he says fondly.

"Your mother has good taste." I smile at him.

"Yes, she does." He smiles back, and it's a warm smile. The affection for his mother evident.

"Come on." I bump my hip against his. "Taste the honey with me. I'm going to buy some to take back to the restaurant."

"I'm not tasting the honey." He groans, shoving his hands into his pockets.

"Yes, you are." I find an open jar and dip in another sample stick. "Here."

Begrudgingly, he takes the stick and drops it into his mouth. Looking at me, his eyes narrow and he swallows before confidently saying, "Sourwood."

I glance at the jar, and he's right. My eyes widen in shock and I look at his smug face. "How did you know that?"

"You're not the first woman in my life to like honey."

I'm not sure how I feel about this comment. Is it because he called me a woman in his life, or that he's referencing others, but I decide to brush it off.

For the next half hour, Zach and I taste a dozen different honeys and buy almost as many. We wander through the market, stopping to purchase some fruits and vegetables for a few recipes I have in mind, and not surprisingly, we argue over what tastes better.

Fifteen minutes after we leave the farmers' market, we reach downtown Asheville. Zach finds a parking spot about a block away from the restaurant, and I laugh at him as his stomach growls.

"What? It's lunchtime." He shrugs as we get out of the truck.

"Well, let's go then." I flash him a smile, and dart across the street. I'm halfway to the other side when a gust of wind blows my skirt up. It isn't much, but it is enough for me to throw my hands back and smooth it down. It is also enough for me to realize that I flashed Zach. Looking back, I find him wearing a slightly guilty, slightly pleased smile. Ass.

"Hi, welcome to Tupelo Honey," says a very chipper hostess as we walk in, her eyes skipping from me to Zach and staying there. "Just the two of you today?"

"Yes, please," I answer her, understanding the effect he has on her. After all, he has the same effect on me—until he opens his mouth.

"All right, if you'll follow me this way." She grabs two menus, and we walk behind her to a small table near the front window. This place is exactly like I remembered it, and I'm so excited.

"Your server will be right with you." She blushes as she glances at Zach one more time.

"Thank you." His deep Southern voice causes her eyes to stumble just a bit before she walks away. I shake my head.

Both of us sit, and I can't help but take in every detail. I think there are very few people who enjoy eating out as much as I do.

Feeling Zach watching me, I drag my eyes away from the dining room and to him. He's pulled his sunglasses off and this is the first time I've seen his eyes today. Blue . . . so blue. Butterflies flutter and then take flight in my stomach. I know we're not on a date, but sitting at this small table with him, it sure feels like it.

Since inviting him on this little trip with me, I've toyed with the idea of telling him about my blog. I know he doesn't like critics, but I don't think I'm an average one. I don't usually tell anyone, I like the anonymity as much as possible, but we are working on this project together and I have nothing to hide. Additionally, I don't want to keep secrets from him, even if this is a short-term project. It's a part of me, and I'm proud of it.

Sucking in a deep breath, I decide to go for it.

"So, working as a chef isn't the only thing that I do." His eyes narrow, but he leans forward to hear me better. "Aside from the restaurant with Meg, I also have a food blog I love. It's how Food Network found me."

Like most people, when you're passionate about something and want to talk about it, you get excited. I'm excited. But as he sits back in his chair and grinds his teeth together, anger quickly rolls in over his features and then rolls out, leaving his expression empty. My enthusiasm wavers, and I become self-conscious. Lowering my eyes, I grab my silverware, unroll the napkin, and place it on my lap.

"Have I heard of it?" His voice lacks inflection, and the blue in his eyes have sharpened and become icy. Once again, his mood shift confuses me, and I wish I understood better why he reacts this way.

"I doubt it." I shake my head at him. It does have a lot of followers, but I can't think of a reason why he would know of it, but then again maybe he has. It's been around for a while.

"What's the name of it?" I can't tell if he's interested in hearing about this or not, but it's clear that he isn't happy.

"*Starving for Southern*."

His hands slide off the top of the table, grip the edge, and his eyes narrow. A strange feeling dips into my stomach . . . was he expecting me not to tell him or lie?

"Good afternoon, I'm Kelsey and I'll be your waitress today. What can I get y'all to drink?"

"Tea," Zach and I both say at the same time, still staring at each other. No need to clarify what kind of tea, we're in the South—it'll be sweet.

"I'll be right back." And she skips off, leaving the two of us in a face off.

"I've heard of it," he says in a flat tone. "What made you start it?" He picks up his sunglasses and tucks them into the neck of his T-shirt before folding his arms across his chest. His arms bulge under the sleeves, and I have a strange urge to reach out and squeeze them.

"Meg and I were never into the party scene. Fun for us was finding new and exciting places to eat. We visited so many different restaurants, I decided to write about all of our favorite ones. It was easy to find something amazing at almost every place we went, so we posted a lot and I think that was the main reason why the blog did so well. Also, I rarely posted anything negative."

"And you don't write about places anymore?" He tilts his head to the side studying me.

"Not so much; only every now and then. Since opening OBA, our adventures have slowed down significantly, but that's okay, we're in a different place in life now. Instead, we've grown it substantially in developing fun new recipes. We've been approached about a cookbook."

"All righty, here we go." The waitress sets down the two teas. "Did y'all decide what you'd like?" She opens her notepad and pulls a pen out of the ponytail.

"She'll order for us," Zach says, charming her with his smile. "This outing was her idea." The waitress blinks at him and then turns to me expectantly.

Quickly, I scan the menu, barely seeing the words since I already know what I want to order. He didn't even look at it. Is he making assumptions about me for having the blog or because I've eaten here before?

"We'll have the farmers' market pickled plate, the fried green tomatoes, and the fried chicken sandwich."

"Okie dokie, are y'all going to split it all?"

"That's the plan," he says flatly, and she falters again with her pen.

"I'll get that going, and it'll be out shortly." She gives us both a small smile, takes the menus, and leaves.

His attention swings back to me, and I wish it hadn't. Part of me feels like shrinking and the other part of me wants to punch him in the throat. And now that I know he doesn't like critics, I'm almost scared to find out which version of Zach I'm going to have to spend the rest of the afternoon with.

"So let me get this straight, you write a blog, you're somewhat of a critic, you freelance for Food Network, you co-own a restaurant, and you're working on a cookbook?" His face is blank but his voice drips with disdain.

"Yes. It sounds like a lot more than what it is, but I love my career and all the different sides to it. I would do more if I could."

He frowns as the thinks about my answer and then surprises me when he asks, "Have you ever written about this place?"

"I have. But, like I said, it was a while ago."

"What did you say about it?" This isn't the direction I thought the conversation was going to go. Honestly, I don't really remember what I wrote, but I do remember how this place made me feel the first time I walked into it, so I start there.

"Take a look around and tell me what you see."

His eyes narrow in defiance, so I urge him along. "Humor me."

After a huff, he gives in, and pauses before he slowly looks around the dining room. "I see people, lots of them, and in a small space. I see large plates of food, and a shop in the back to buy stuff."

"Boring . . ." I fake like I'm yawning.

He snorts at me and shifts in his chair.

Leaning closer to him, I ask, "Do you feel the energy of this place?"

His eyes wander around the room, and his frown deepens. "I suppose, it just seems crowded to me."

"But that's the point. Sometimes the draw to a place is more than just the food."

The people at the table next to us start laughing, and I can't help but to smile with them.

"Here's the thing about being a critic, I know you said you don't like them, but everyone is one. It's a subjective opinion that one can agree with or not. Most critics are known for immediately walking into a place and looking for errors, but I think that's the wrong way to do it. I love to look for the good. To me, it's about more than the food. It's people laughing, families eating together, celebrations, memories, and traditions. I love to feel the energy and the sense of belonging. It's a time when people talk to one another and that time becomes sacred. Everything that happens around the table is sacred. Who knows, maybe that is why so many people subscribe to my blog, maybe they're looking for the same thing . . . something good."

He leans back in his chair, picks up his glass, and takes a swallow of the tea. "Well, whatever floats your boat, I guess. That's definitely a different approach to it."

"Maybe, but it's my approach, and that's all that matters." I hate that he's making me feel defensive.

"Do you ever get criticized for not telling the truth?"

"I am telling the truth. What I write about is all true to me. Every experience is *my* experience." My voice rises just a bit, and the people at the table next to us glance our way.

"What about people who disagree with your truth? Do you ever give them an opportunity to change your opinion? Seems to me like a blog like yours has influence."

"No one has ever asked for me to reconsider my opinion. I'm a straightforward person. I leave my reviews open for the readers to decide, but skeptically I guess I would if the situation arose."

"Why do you say you are skeptical?" He crosses his arms over his chest and his brows furrow, which I find annoying. Why is he looking at me as if he's silently judging me, and why does he want to know these things?

"Why is anyone the way they are? Individual life experiences, I guess." I shrug my shoulders, finger the napkin in my lap, and look down at the table as I think about my parents. More than anyone realizes, except for Meg, I'm an extremely skeptical person. People are always fueled by motive, and most of the time it's glaringly obvious.

He takes another sip of his drink and my eyes find his. The blue has softened, removing the edge from them, and his gaze becomes thoughtful as he considers me.

"How did you meet Meg?" he asks, changing the subject.

"We met the weekend before our freshman year of college. We were standing in line at Starbucks, and there was one blueberry muffin left behind the counter. Both of us wanted it, and in the end, we agreed to split it. We've been best friends ever since." I remember that day as if it were yesterday.

"And Lexi? How did you meet her?" He tilts his head.

"In culinary school. She sat down next to Meg and me, and the rest is history. Second semester she moved in with us, and for two years, the three of us were inseparable."

He pauses and bites down on his lower lip.

A waitress swoops by and drops off a plate.

"Biscuits. Yum." Snatching one, I drop the subject, slather on some butter and blackberry jam, and then put half on a plate for me and the other half on a plate for him. I push it toward his side of the table. He looks at me as if I'm crazy but pulls it in front of him. With each bite he takes, I can feel a little more of the previous tension melt away.

"You win, that's tasty." He licks his fingers, and I'm suddenly mesmerized by his hands. "Do you have a biscuit recipe you could use for us?"

Us.

I pause before answering him, and he looks at me funny.

"As a matter of fact, I do. I also spotted some strawberries out behind the cottage that are ready to be picked, so I'll make a jam for them."

"Can we make this tomorrow?" He cracks a lopsided grin at me.

"I don't see why not," I say and then lick my lips. I can still taste the jam and butter from my own biscuit. Zach's eyes drop to my mouth as he watches me and then they cut left to something over my shoulder. I swear this guy gives me whiplash.

"So, how did you become friends with Lexi?" I ask.

"I played football with her brother in college." He answers between bites.

"I know that, but she didn't go to college with him, and from what I know, she barely made it to any of his games."

"No, she only came to two that I know of, but everyone knew who Lexi was, he talked about her all the time. I invited him up for a visit one summer, and she tagged along. We've been friends ever since."

Eventually our food comes, and most of our conversation halts. The food is as good as I remembered it, and Zach agrees with me that this restaurant is a good choice for the recommendation section of the article. We purchase a Tupelo Honey cookbook, and with our stomachs full, we head back to the truck.

"So, are you glad you came with me?" I ask, looking for an opportunity to gloat and rub it in that the drive was worth it.

Zach, who doesn't appear to have heard me, sways in front of me and grabs the back of his neck.

"Are you okay?" I ask him.

He again doesn't answer, but glances my way as I catch up to him and his steps slow down.

"You do that a lot," I say as we walk to the passenger side of the truck.

He leans against the door, takes off his sunglasses, and looks at me—his crushingly beautiful blue eyes are slightly glazed. "Do what?"

"Rub your neck." Concern begins to set in as I watch this large, incredibly masculine guy begin to fade and withdraw right in front of me. Somewhere in the background, I hear a horn honk and people laugh, but all I see is him. His skin turns pale, his lips dry out, and it's like instant bruising forms under his eyes.

For the first time since I met him, he's looking at me, I'm looking at him, and neither one of us knows what to do or say next.

Fearing that he may fall over, I take a step toward him at the same time as he reaches for me—one hand on the truck and one hand on my arm. My hands land on his hips to steady him as he looks down at me helplessly.

"Suppose I do." He swallows. "I get headaches pretty easily, sometimes quickly, and one just set in." Not even hesitating, he leans forward, pulls off his hat, rests his forehead on my shoulder, and rubs his stomach. "Shit," he mumbles.

I'm stunned by not only his nearness but also how he's folded into me for support. *Me*. This person he's tolerating but doesn't really like. This isn't just out of character for him—this is alarming.

"Why?" I ask quietly, holding on to him.

He turns his head so his cheek is resting on me, and he breathes right into my neck. The warmth of the air dissolves into my skin, my heart rate involuntarily picks up, and chills race over my body. "I don't know what brings them on. I'm susceptible to getting them, and lately, I've been trying to figure out if there's a trigger for them, but I can't seem to find any connections."

Triggers. I think back over our meal. It wasn't loaded with sugar and the caffeine in the tea is supposed to help headaches not cause them.

"Did you know it was coming? We could have left sooner?"

"No, this one just hit me. Blindsided." He groans and rubs his forehead back and forth across my shoulder and massages the back of his neck.

"Is there anything I can do for you?" I rub my hand across his lower back, and he leans farther into me, his weight pressing me down.

Minutes pass as he takes one breath after another, a few getting caught in his throat. Eventually, he pulls away but still grabs on to my arm for balance. "Drive fast?" He digs in his pocket and holds out his hand with his keys in it, the pain so evident on his handsome face I feel nauseous for him.

"Wow, I didn't think guys liked to have their trucks driven," I say softly, trying to lighten the mood while hitting the unlock button and opening the door for him.

"I don't, but I don't have a choice. This one is messing with my vision." He climbs into the truck and moans as he places his head on the dashboard.

Running around to the driver's side, I climb in, adjust the seat, and start the truck.

"Do you have any medicine you can take?" I'm anxious and worried to the point that I'm tempted to dig through the center console and the glove box for anything that might help him.

"It's on my desk in my office." He groans again as his eyes shut and squeeze tight.

"Should we stop and buy something?"

"No. Won't help, unfortunately."

"All right, hang tight. We'll be home before you know it." I shift into reverse and back out of the spot.

Home.

Somehow, over the last couple of days, the winery has begun to feel a little bit more like a home and less like a vacation spot. While I still don't understand his mood swings or why he initially disliked me so much, I keep reminding myself that if he's friends with Lexi, there must be something about him.

The truck goes over an uneven bump in the road, and he moans next me as I turn the corner.

I've had migraines here and there over the years, but none of them have been as debilitating as this. It's as if it's morphed him into someone else. That spark and fire he constantly breathes out onto everyone is gone.

A few minutes later, I hop on the interstate, and we're on our way. Without thinking, I reach over so I can thread my fingers through his hair and begin to rub his scalp. He lets out a sigh at the sensation, and I don't even think he realizes he did it. A few minutes later, he slumps my way over the center console, tucks his arms under him, and hangs his head toward my lap. As much as my opinion of him has wavered over the last couple of days, my heart aches at the apparent pain he's in. Keeping the radio down, I press on and hope not to get pulled over.

We're an hour into the drive before I reach down by my feet and dig my hand in my purse to find my cell phone. I know he isn't sleeping, he's moaned a few times keeping his eyes shut, and it crosses my mind that maybe I should take him to the hospital or an urgent care or something. Very carefully, I shoot Michelle a text.

Me: Hey, Zach has a really bad headache, what do I do?

Michelle: Where are you?

Her text comes in almost immediately.

Me: A little over an hour north, just turned onto sixty-four at Sylvia. We're on our way back from Asheville.

Michelle: Did he take anything for it?

Me: No. He says it's on his desk.

Michelle: Oh, no. Okay, just get back safe and Kyle will get him when you get here.

Me: Does this happen a lot?

Michelle: Yes. See you soon.

Ingredients:

3-4 green tomatoes
1 cup of flour
1/2 cup of cornmeal
1/2 cup of breadcrumbs
3/4 cup of buttermilk
1 egg
1 teaspoon of paprika
1 teaspoon of salt
Vegetable oil

How to make:

Three bowls: In the first bowl, combine the egg and buttermilk. In the second bowl, put the flour. In the third bowl, combine the cornmeal, breadcrumbs, paprika, and salt.

Cover the bottom of a large cast-iron skillet with vegetable oil, about half an inch. Heat on medium, no higher than 375 degrees.

Slice the tomatoes quarter inch thick. Dredge in flour, dip in egg mixture, dredge in cornmeal mixture.

Drop each slice into oil and cook for one and a half to two minutes on each side, or until golden brown. Remove from oil and place on a paper towel.

Sprinkle hot tomatoes with salt and serve.

Chapter 10

don't bite the hand that feeds you

Zach

No one likes to show their weak side . . . and that's exactly what happened. She already knows how I feel about weakness, and now she knows mine. Fucking migraine hit, and I folded into her like a deck of cards. I didn't even think twice about it.

Most people don't know about the migraines. It isn't something that I talk about publicly, but after yesterday, there'll be no way to evade her questions. Not that I blame her. She was scared shitless, I saw it all over her face, but she held it together and took care of me. Thank God I wasn't out by myself somewhere. I never would have made it home. Even today, I've spent most of it flat on my back. Kyle checked in a few times, but when these episodes happen, nurse Michelle takes over.

The thing about being laid up and bored is that it allows for a lot of time to think and reflect. Both of which I did today.

I've replayed what I saw and the conversation I heard at the Feeding America event over and over in my head. I know I didn't get it wrong, she said, "If he had known I was a critic, I would have gotten better food. How he stays in business, I will never know."

How bad could the food have possibly been?

But then I hear her talking about how she loves to find new places and looks for the magic in each one, and I don't understand. Yesterday, she said it wasn't always about the food, that it was about the total experience. Something doesn't add up, and the more I try to figure it out and remind myself that in the end she's still a critic, the more unsettled I feel.

Just thinking that I might have pegged her all wrong causes uneasiness to creep its way in. The way I've talked to her, the way I've made her feel, even the plan we derived to win her over . . .

I find myself questioning *everything*.

And then to make it worse, I keep hearing the excitement in Lexi's voice when she talked about introducing us. She's Lexi's friend, and Lexi is a very good judge of character. Then again, someone being a critic isn't a character flaw to her, but it is to me, that and she's a workaholic. Not that what Shelby thinks of me as a person really matters. She's been here for almost a week and only has one to go. Who knows if or when I'll ever see her again. Not that I intend to. I only need her to write a glowing article, and a stellar blog post. A blog that she does for fun, because one job isn't enough for her, she needs to give up all her time.

Shaking my head, I pull myself out of bed, take a quick shower, grab some stuff, and lock my door behind me. I remind myself to stick to the plan and head down to the cottage to spend the evening with Shelby and keep things low-key.

When I reach the cottage, I let myself in. I know it's probably rude, but technically, it's my house, and other than me, who is coming down here to see her? Still, I make it a point to close the door loudly and make noise as I walk inside.

"Hey," she calls out from the kitchen when she sees me. "How are you feeling?" She wipes her hands across an apron tied around her waist and smiles at me. Her eyes are bright but filled with concern, and my heart thuds against my chest unexpectedly. Her and that damn smile. I hate that I have this involuntary reaction to her.

"Better. I'm really sorry about yesterday. I'm sure having to take care of me wasn't on your list of things to do. I appreciate it, so thank you." I place the bag I brought down on the island and sit on a stool across from her.

There's a sincerity in her expression as she studies my face. I know she's looking for lingering traces of the migraine, and it makes me feel exposed and cared for at the same time.

"Michelle says it happens a lot." She moves to the cabinet, grabs a glass, and fills it with water before setting it in front of me. Her thoughtfulness in gestures like this doesn't go unnoticed, and again I'm reminded that it's reasons like this she's friends with Lexi.

Taking a swallow, I soak in her appearance. She's got her hair all tied up and messy on top of her head, her face is makeup free, and she's wearing a T-shirt that reads: Will write for food.

Shit.

Her adorability factor is rising, and I really need to stop noticing these things.

"More like comes and goes, but lately it feels like a lot," I tell her honestly.

She frowns. It's the same frown she wore yesterday when I walked away from her.

Kyle was at the side door of the manor waiting for us as she tore down the driveway. He handed me a pill before I even got out of the truck, which I swallowed dry before I started the mental countdown I knew it took for the medicine to kick in. Kyle slung an arm around my shoulder and helped me up the steps to the west wing. I heard Shelby ask if she could do anything to help, but Michelle told her no and that she and Kyle would take it from there. For a split second, I wanted to argue with her and tell her it was fine, but the energy required to talk was more than I had in me, and it was taking every bit of power I had not to lose my lunch all over the ground. Collapsing in my bed, I missed the smell of honey and her fingers in my hair. No one has ever rubbed my head like that, and I wanted more.

Looking around the kitchen, I chuckle at the mess she's made. "Wow, you've cooked a lot today." There are large platters of food that look as if they could feed a dozen people lined along the top of the island. "And you made the biscuits." My mouth starts watering.

She grins and wipes the counter down in front of her. "I told you I would, and I did make a lot. I needed to make sure I had the correct measurements. A few of them I made more than once to see which version I liked better."

Next to me there are three bowls of macaroni-and-cheese. "What are you going to do with all this food?"

"I thought I would take it to Michelle to see if she wants to put it out at the bar to let the tasters try. Is that all right with you?" Her eyes widen as she waits for the answer, and again I find myself in a situation where I can't tell her no. Not that I would, this food looks amazing.

"I think it's a great idea, and I'll help you here in a bit, but first, I brought the reds down. I thought we could taste them here. It's quieter and there's no audience."

"Don't we need to call the photographer?" She pulls the strings of the apron and it slips off her waist, leaving her in a pair of gray leggings that show off their shape and hug her perfectly.

"Nah, he can meet us another time and get a picture of us drinking the reds then."

"Should you be drinking these after that headache?" Her face is full of concern.

"I'll be fine. We really aren't drinking much, just tasting, and interestingly I haven't found the wines to be much of a trigger."

She looks at me hesitantly, shrugs her shoulders and then smiles. "Okay, well let's see what you brought."

Opening the bag, I pull out our four bottles of red wine, four tasting glasses, and a wine key.

"Will you grab us another glass of water. Palate cleanse between each one."

"Sure." Shelby turns around, giving me an awesome view of her ass, and grabs the extra glass.

"When most people come in to do the wine tasting, it's just that—a tasting. They sip the wines, laugh with their friends, and then move on. But to truly taste a wine, it takes a little more than that and has to involve the other senses."

After opening my wine key, I grab each bottle in turn, keeping the labels faced toward me, and open them with practiced precision. After each one, I set the bottle next to me making sure to keep the label away from Shelby.

"Meg and I have gone to tastings before, and I freely admit to falling into the in-and-out category like the masses." She's watching my hands as I move between the bottles, and I hate to admit it, but I like it.

"And that's quite all right with us. The majority of people who come in are no different, but to those who've made wine tasting a hobby, it's more involved than that."

"So teach me, oh great one." She folds her arms in front of her on the island and leans toward me.

A smile splits across my face, and I shake my head at her. She smiles back, and the air in my lungs freezes. Damn, she's beautiful.

I pour each wine into a glass and set the four glasses next to its respective bottle.

"First is sight and then smell. They say you eat with your eyes first, right? Well, drinking wine is no different. A lot of the time, people make an immediate assumption based on the color or clarity. If it's light it must be weak, watered down, or flat, but if it's dark and thick, it's sweet like grape juice, et cetera. But don't let the way something looks fool you."

"Like don't judge a book by its cover?" She grins at me.

"Something like that." I push the first glass in front of her and continue, "But I'll admit, I do. I'm guilty of keeping or passing on a book based on its cover."

"Tsk-tsk, Mr. Wolff. You should take your own advice." My eyes find hers and there's a playfulness in them. Is she usually like this? Until yesterday, she's been guarded and all business. The first time I saw this side of her was when she spun in a circle and forced me to eat honey. The slips in her armor seem to be coming more frequently, and I find myself becoming more confused and intrigued by what I see—a woman who doesn't fit the image of a dream killer like I've created in my mind.

"Maybe. Here, take a good look at this and then smell it." She picks up the glass, swirls the wine, and tentatively brings it to her nose to sniff it.

"What do you think?" I lean into the island to get closer to her.

"I think its color is a deep red, looks almost like blood, and it smells like pepper." She looks at me for an affirmation.

"Do you smell anything else?" I nod to the glass, and she picks it up again.

"Maybe a little clove and licorice?" she asks questioningly.

"Very good." I smile at her.

"Okay, now taste it."

She smells it again before shifting the rim to her lips, lips I'm suddenly fascinated by. With her eyes on me, she takes a sip of the wine. Her nose scrunches and her lips pucker together.

"It's good, it's just not for me." She licks her lips and swallows again before sliding the glass in my direction.

Reaching for the glass, she freely gives it to me, and I taste the wine, too. I like the peppery undertones, always have. So, I take another sip before sliding the glass back to her.

"Taste it again. Just like eating some candy, say Sour Patch Kids. Your mouth needs time to adjust."

She sips it again and then reaches for the water. "Well, that time it was a little better, but I think I'll pass."

"Why?"

"I like dry, bold wines that are more smooth. This one is way too spicy." She shakes her head and frowns.

"Swirl the glass again." I slide it back across the island to her. She complies, and as she swirls, I continue, "Do you see the streaks running down the sides? Those are called legs. Loose legs usually indicate the wine is light to medium with a lower alcohol content, and thick legs tell us that it's a more full-bodied wine with a high alcohol content."

Her eyes light up. "That's a great tip."

"Yeah, if you plan on drinking for a while, it's a mental reminder to either have at it or take it slow. This wine is a syrah." I turn the bottle around so she can see the label, pick up the glass, and swallow the rest of the wine in one swallow, enjoying the subtle kick it leaves behind. Delicious.

Reaching for my water, she mimics me, and we both cleanse the palate to start over.

She nods her head in understanding and picks up the next glass. "And let's do it again, swirl this one a few times and deeply inhale it."

She swirls, sniffs, and starts laughing. Her eyes are bright and her laugh is infectious. I grin along with her as a spot in my chest warms. Damn, I really like the sound of her laugh. "I know this is part of it, and a lot of people do it, but they look dumb and I feel stupid."

"I actually agree with you. Some people take the nose sniffing way too seriously, but . . . if wine is your thing, then it's a must." I shrug my shoulders, still smiling at her.

"What's your thing?" she asks, holding the glass out in front of her, twisting her wrist to roll the wine. Some people make the action looked forced, as if they're trying to be something they're not, and others it looks so natural. Like it does on her.

Folding my arms in front of me on the counter, I lean into them and closer to her. "Well, for almost thirty years, it was football. Since I've settled in here at the winery, it's making sure it grows and keeping it successful."

She lifts the glass, sniffs it again, and then tastes it as she regards me.

"Are the headaches why you stopped playing?"

Stopped playing. This makes me frown, and a longing for my former life hits me. I loved playing football. Some play it because they're good at it and it's their ticket to a better life, but I played to play. Everyone thinks their sport is the greatest, but to me, nothing compares to football.

"Not really, but they seem to be a residual side effect that I can't get rid of." Just thinking about the headaches causes me to tense. A normal headache people pop two aspirin and it goes away, not me. I'm down for the count.

"I'm sorry," she says sympathetically.

"Why?" I don't want her to feel sorry for me. Everyone felt sorry for me, but it is what it is.

"Because. If I had to give up food, that would suck, and I imagine it did for you. Makes me feel bad for you."

From what I know, her whole world is food. So, hearing her compare something that I love to something she loves makes that ache for the grass, heat and the sweat. Swallowing, I push down the emotion and remind myself how lucky I was to have another life already waiting for me.

"Don't. I've always known I was headed here next. I love this, too." I nod to her glass, asking, "What do you think of this one?"

"This one's tasty, takes over your whole mouth." She takes another sip, hands me the glass, and moves around to my side of the island to sit on the chair next to me. I shift in my seat and twist the bottles so she can't see the labels.

I taste the wine, and after I swallow, it pulls my cheeks in. I hand her back the glass, and she drinks some more. "Do you feel like you have cotton mouth?"

"I do."

"Those are the tannins from the skins and seeds of the grapes. Tannins are the backbone of red wines, giving them texture and different levels of complexity."

She passes the glass back, I pour a little more for us.

"What flavors did you taste?"

She swirls and sips. "This one has the cherry flavors like the wine in the cave, and it tastes earthy."

"You would be right; this is a cabernet. Very similar to the one in the cave." I turn the bottle around so she can see it, and her face lights up.

"In general, cabernets have been nicknamed 'the big boy' wine—big in flavor, big in body, and big in alcohol content. Cabernets will get you the most bang for your buck."

"That one was luscious." She licks her lips.

"Yes, it is." I finish the glass in one swallow, and her eyes zero in on my mouth. Warmth runs through my chest and stomach. As I set the glass down, she breaks her gaze and looks over at the bottles. Her cheeks turn pink. God, what I wouldn't give to be in her mind right this second.

Clearing my throat, I push the third glass toward her.

She picks it up, swirls it, smells it, and tastes it.

Watching her drink my wines and having her enjoy them is like chasing a wide receiver down the sideline and tackling him after a fifty-five-yard pass. It's an adrenaline rush and a complete turn on. I'm aching to touch her, so I shift in my seat, placing my knee against hers as I wait.

"The color is lighter than the cabernet. It swirls around the glass quicker. It smells like pie: berries, jam, vanilla, cinnamon. And it tastes fruity, and it's smoother, softer. I like it."

"Do you like this one or the cabernet more?"

"I think it depends on what we're eating and maybe the time of the year. I feel like the cabernet is perfect for a cold winter day and this one I could drink into the summer."

"Hmm." I take the glass from her, smell the pie—I'll never be able to think of this wine in any other way now—and take a sip.

"Do you like it?" she asks me.

"I do. I prefer the cabernets, but I wouldn't say no to this. Then again, I don't think I would say no to any of them."

She smiles at me and reaches for the glass. "I like it."

Turning the bottle around she sees the label for merlot.

"Speaking of jam." She jumps off her chair, sets the glass down, and moves through the kitchen. "I made a strawberry fig jam to go with the biscuits. Ask and you shall receive, right?" She smiles at me, and I smile back.

"I did ask for them."

Grabbing a basket filled with homemade biscuits, a plate with room temperature butter on it, and a jar of the jam, she sets it on the island in front of me. She sits back on her stool facing me, and this time, one of her legs slides between mine so she can prop a foot on my footrest. Tingles race straight to my groin. And just like at the restaurant, she fixes mine for me and passes it over on a small plate.

"You don't have to do that, you know," I say, shoving half of one side into my mouth.

"Do what?" She sits back but doesn't move her leg.

"Fix my food."

Her face turns beet red. "Sorry. Honestly, I didn't even think twice about it. Meg and I both have our quirky routines and fixing snacks is mine."

I laugh and shake my head a bit. "It's fine. I'm not complaining, just mentioning that you don't have to. What're Meg's quirks?"

"Oh, she has quite a few, but her biggest one is cleanliness. While I'm fixing, she's cleaning around me."

"Someone else who does the cleaning, sign me up." I'm smiling as I pick up the biscuit and take another bite. Damn, this girl can cook. I remember arguing with Kyle about how I assumed all chefs were overweight, when in reality, it's probably the spouses and family members that suffer. I'm not sure if I could ever let any of her food go to waste.

Finishing the biscuit, I stare at my plate wishing there was more.

"Tasty, huh," she mumbles through her bites.

"Very."

"Just like this wine." She holds up the glass and takes another swallow.

"Right. So, merlot grapes are small and dark blue on the vine. They're easy to spot, easy to grow, and have thin skins so they ripen fast. The juice is lighter, smoother, softer, and it's considered a drink-it-now wine. Aging doesn't do much for it."

"Merlot is my go-to wine when we're out for dinner."

"It is for most. It's the number one ordered glass of wine in the United States because it's an easy pick. But if you ask any winemaker about it, and they will tell you that in the tasting room the merlot is one of the least profitable."

"Wow, I wouldn't have thought that," she mumbles with her mouth full.

"It's viewed as boring."

She swallows and gulps down some water before responding. "I don't think it's boring."

"I don't either, but when people come here, they feel adventurous and usually pick something new and different."

"That's interesting." She pushes her plate back, and I swipe the bite she didn't eat. See—I have to eat it.

"All right, are you ready for the last one?"

She sits up higher on her stool and wiggles as if she's having fun, which I hope is the case.

"Bring it on." She licks her lips, making them shine and my stomach clenches as I push the glass her way.

"This is our flagship wine. It's our biggest seller and the one most people come here to taste."

She goes through the motions, and I can't wait. "What do you think?"

She looks down at the deep red wine, thoughtful, and swirls it in the glass. "I think it's dry and not as sweet as the others: earthy, coffee, chocolate, maybe cherries. I want to say it has a bit of spice to it like the syrah, but then I don't know. It has a zing to it also, similar to the whites. What's it called?"

I turn the bottle around, and she whispers, "Norton."

"I've heard of this wine." She looks at me for confirmation.

"Yeah?" I raise my eyebrows to her.

"Over the last couple years, it's popped up more in articles and magazines."

"This wine is definitely making its comeback." Pulling the glass from her, my fingers brush against hers, and another longing sets in. What would it feel like to have her hands on me? Her warm fingertips running across my shoulders and down my back. I take a sip of the wine, shaking off the equally wanted and unwanted thought. The wine is very dry, smooth, and has a kick at the backend.

"Tell me about it." She picks up the bottle and pours more into the glass for us to share.

"The Norton grape is America's oldest grape. It was bred here and, at one point, was the most widely grown grape in the States, predominantly on the East Coast and in the Midwest. It's what my ancestors were brought over to grow and harvest."

"What happened?" She places her elbow on the island and leans into it.

"The Prohibition. Any wine vine that was found, they ripped out. Somehow, they never found ours; I don't know how they hid them, but those vines are generational and have been going strong now for over a hundred years. The Norton wines, at one time, rivaled the Old World wines."

"That's crazy."

"I know. Either people love this wine or they hate it. I love it, not only for its strength, but also for its ability to stay for such a long time. It's a huge part of our family."

"It's my favorite of the reds." She reaches for the glass, and a piece of her hair slips from behind her ear as she takes a sip. I don't stop myself from leaning forward or tucking it back in place. She freezes, and when I realize just how close we are, I force myself to lean away from her again.

She chews on the inside of her lip. I affect her. Good.

"It's great for blending, too. You'll have to come back once the Norton-Claret we have aging in the cave is ready." Wait. What? Why did I say that? She's not coming back here.

"Or, I can mail you a bottle." I retract the invitation.

Her face falls a little. The move is slight, but I see it, and it makes me feel horrible.

"So, that's it. Those are our reds." I need to wrap this up before I say something else.

"I think they're amazing. Other than the first one, I would buy the other three any time."

"Shh, don't say that too loudly, you'll hurt the syrah's feelings," I mock scold her.

She giggles, and I realize it's time for me to go. We tasted the wines, and there's no reason for me to be here.

"I'll leave these here, and we can finish them another time."

"Okay," she says quietly.

"What are you doing tonight?" It crosses my mind to invite her to the tasting room, but for what? It isn't as if I need to spend more time with her. I'm already starting to want what I can't have, well . . . shouldn't have, and less time together will definitely be better.

She looks around the cottage and lets out a sigh. "I haven't decided yet. I might stay here tonight and work on the other article since I need to send it off soon. I appreciate your coming down here for this, saves me the trouble of having to get dressed up for the camera." She smiles and then slides off the stool and starts moving things to the sink.

Following her lead, I stand and help her clean the mess she made of the kitchen.

"All right, well if you change your mind, Michelle is almost always behind the bar, and I'll be in my office playing catch-up from yesterday and today." My inbox is exploding.

"Sounds good. And thanks for taking all of this up there." She tilts her head toward the food as she washes one of the wine glasses.

I chuckle. "I don't think there will be any complaints." I walk to the far end of the island and pick up what looks like barbeque brisket, which makes my mouth water. Then I scan the rest of the food and realize something.

"All of this is perfect for white wines." I don't know why I'm so moved by all of it, but I am. She made this for us, for Wolff wines, and it looks amazing.

"Yep, I have a few more things to test over the next week, but I'm super happy with how this stuff turned out. Let me know what you think of the barbeque sauce. I can tweak it so that it's more your taste, since this is your place." She wipes her hands off on a towel.

"I'm sure it's great. My mother always says don't look a gift horse in the mouth, so I can't imagine I won't like it." I look over at her and have this sudden urge to take her in my arms and hold her. Seriously, between her fingers in my hair, those legs, and now this food I'm losing my ability to rationalize.

She smiles, it's so genuine my insides clench.

Why does she have to be a critic, a workaholic? If she were anyone else . . . doing anything else . . .

Together we grab the dishes, take them out to the cart, and load them into the back. Once we're finished, she turns away, and I drag my eyes over the length of her. Even in flip-flops, her legs stretch on for days. Like a lost puppy, I follow her.

Spinning around, she catches me staring at her ass and shakes her head at me.

"What?" I shrug my shoulders and grin at her.

"You are something else." She shakes her head and then keeps walking, heading for the door. Even though her lips are pinched together, her cheeks are red and she's fighting a smile.

I turn and follow her, noticing her movements are smoother, fluid. The little she-devil likes being watched.

"Do you want me to deny it, because I won't. I very much enjoy looking at you as often as possible."

"Wha—" She spins around, collides with my chest, and doesn't step away. Instead, her fingers wrap around my arm for balance, and I pull her in closer. She doesn't move, and neither do I.

"Easy there," I mutter, brushing her hair over and off her shoulder. "And you're not even wearing any of your ridiculous shoes."

"Hey, I like my shoes." She raises an eyebrow and tilts her chin. I suppose the gesture is supposed to show indignation, but instead, it looks inviting.

"I never said I didn't like them, but the farm might not be the best place for them."

She opens her mouth to reply, and my eyes drop to her full lips. As she hesitates, I wonder what she would do if I kissed her.

"Whatever, they make me happy." She pulls out of my hold and walks toward the door.

I want to reply that she's making me happy, but that's crazy. She's still the same person she was when she pulled up to the vineyard—someone I would never see myself with. Only, I can't seem to stay away from her, and there isn't anything right now that's stopping me.

"I think you should eavesdrop and get us some feedback on what everyone likes and what they don't like." She throws over her shoulder.

"How could they not like any of it, it all looks amazing."

"Well, you never know." She pauses right outside the door and turns to face me. Of course, I followed her, I couldn't stop myself.

"Forget something?" Her eyes are large and filled with an equal mix of apprehension and anticipation. She clasps her hands in front of her and bites down on the inside of her lip. My eyes again drop to her mouth, and I take in a slow deep breath. I don't know why it hasn't dawned on me sooner, but she does this when she's nervous.

"Yeah, I think I did." I move closer, and her head tips back so she can look into my eyes. I know I shouldn't be doing this, but what's one kiss? The constant temptation, pull, and curiosity will end, I'll get this out of my system, and we can all move on.

Slowly, I raise my hand to cup her chin, and my thumb drags over her bottom lip, freeing it from between her teeth. The inside of it is stained red from the wine and there are tiny marks from her teeth. The fire in me grows hotter with each passing second.

This girl, oh, what she does to me.

I want her.

I want her very much.

Sliding my hand around to the back of her neck, I let my fingers tangle in the silkiness of her hair. She lets out a little noise, almost as if she's going to resist, but then her eyelids drift shut and the rise and fall of her chest increases.

She should be stopping me, but she isn't. She's leaning into my hand, and I soak up every little detail of her face. From the way her hair hangs across her forehead, her long dark blonde eyelashes fan over her cheekbones, the freckles across the bridge of her nose, and the shape of her chin . . . her face is gorgeous.

Then I lean down, letting the heat of her skin hit me first, and I kiss her cheek. Except for the time in the cellar, this is the closest we've been, and I'm about to incinerate that memory with this one. She lets out a breath as I tilt her head to the side, slide my lips to the edge of her mouth, and kiss the corner of her lips.

One little kiss.

She trembles in my arms. This moment is just as overwhelming for her as it is for me.

Being this close to her skin, the flavor of honey overtakes me, sweetening my senses. I loved honey before, but now, I could eat it every day for the rest of my life and find myself never being fully satisfied. There's something about this girl that overrides reason, and it leaves me desperate to get more.

Her lips part, and I don't know what I'm waiting for. Easing back a little, my eyes find hers, and they're no longer a light blue, they're darker. They're full of emotion and longing. A longing that's just for me, and it sends a wave of awareness over every nerve in my body. She wants this more than she doesn't, and I hope she doesn't regret it.

Her hand lightly slides up my arm as she presses to her tiptoes, and my breath catches as her lips pause in front of mine. That little movement from her is enough to give me the green light, and I take it. My lips fall onto hers, and she-devil be damned, I want this.

I need this.

Wrapping my other arm around her waist, I pull her body against mine and slowly tighten my grip on the back of her head to guide her exactly where I want her. No one has ever tasted this good.

I am kissing Shelby.

Shelby is kissing me.

Her lips are on mine, her tongue is caressing mine, and right this moment she tastes like mine.

All. Mine.

I walk her backward until her back hits the front door and she gasps. Dragging my lips down her jaw, I suck on the skin under her ear. She lets out a low moan, which I catch by claiming her lips again and dipping my tongue back into her mouth.

Dropping my hands, I reach around and grab onto her ass. Her breath catches, but that doesn't stop me from pulling her hips into mine. I want to feel every curve of hers, so I do. Sliding my hands up her ribcage, I stop just short of her breasts and trace the bottom swells with my thumbs.

She sighs at the touch and pushes farther into me.

Damn, she feels incredible.

I made fun of her during the interview when I implied she was a lush, when maybe it's me that needs to be worried, because right now—tasting her, touching her, breathing her in—I'm drunk on the smell and feel of her body pressed perfectly against mine. No kiss has ever been like this.

Time stands still.

The world could go up in flames around us, and it wouldn't matter. All I see and all I feel is her and her hands roaming underneath my shirt across the bare skin of my back. Her hands sliding up the sides of my neck. Her fingers as they thread into my hair and grab on. There's an intensity to her, an ardor that borders on desperate, and she's taking everything she can because she knows this kiss is fleeting. Just a moment. A moment that has to end.

Pulling back, I lay my forehead against hers, swallow, and try to pull myself together before opening my eyes and looking at her. I can't let her know what she's done to me or how much she's affected me. It'll encourage her to ask for more, and I don't think I can do that.

Feeling her release me, I take a step back and open my eyes. She looks more breathtaking now with her hair mussed and her lips swollen than she did a few minutes ago, and I take a mental picture of the beautiful girl on the front porch of my cottage, hoping to remember it indefinitely.

"Thanks for the tasting and for taking the food up." She blinks at me and blushes.

The emotions are so thick in my throat I can't respond, so I nod my head and give her a small smile.

She twists to open the door, and I take another step back, shoving my hands in my pockets. I feel my pants dip down, and her eyes drop to my waist, noticing the movement, too. Damn, her hands or her eyes, everything about her feels good.

"Good night," I finally choke out . . . and then she's gone.

Silence settles over me as I stand and stare at the closed door.

What just happened? Or better yet, what just happened to me? My heart is racing, my chest feels tight, and I feel panicked.

Kissing her was supposed to be a means to an end. It was supposed to feel good, satisfying. But I don't feel any of those things. I feel confused, altered. I think that kiss changed me.

Reality washes over me like a bucket of ice-cold water. She isn't some random girl. This is Shelby.

I shake my head at how pathetic I am. It's almost twilight, and I'm still standing here like a complete ass. For the first time since I came up with the plan, I'm starting to wonder if it was the wrong one.

Guilt creeps in, and I squeeze my eyes closed.

Shit.

Being nice to her to try to win her over is one thing, but messing with her physically is another. It takes mixing business with pleasure to a whole new level and crosses a line—one I can't explore no matter how great it felt. I feel slimy and deceitful, but that feels wrong, too, because that kiss was something else. It was incredible. I'm so confused.

I should have known that one kiss with her wouldn't be enough, but for her sake and my sanity, it has to be.

Seriously, what was I thinking?

Ingredients:

4 cups of fresh strawberries, tops removed
4 cups of figs, stems removed
1 package of fruit pectin
1/2 cup lemon juice
1/2 teaspoon butter
4 cups of sugar

How to make:

In small batches, put fruit into a large 8-quart heavy pot and mash fresh fruit until you have 5 cups of crushed fruit.

Stir in the pectin and butter. Bring mixture to a boil, stirring constantly. Stir in sugar, stirring constantly. Once all of the sugar is dissolved, bring the mixture to a rolling boil for 1-2 minutes, stirring constantly. Remove from the heat and quickly skim off the foam on top of the mixture.

Ladle hot jam into 8 hot sterilized half-pint canning jars, leaving about 1/4 inch empty on the top. Wipe down the rims to ensure they are clean, adjust lids, and screw on top bands.

Depending on canning method, immediately flip jars upside down or proceed to a boiling water canner for 5 minutes. Remove from canner and cool.

Occasionally, check to make sure all of the lids have sealed and dont pop up and down.

Chapter 11

oh my heavens

Shelby

Zach kissed me.

He *kissed* me.

And I kissed him.

Since the second I closed the door last night, I have been in a Zach-induced fog. Oh my God. It's easy to assume by his looks that he's probably given his fair share of kisses, but that was by far, hands down without comparison, the best kiss of my life.

Over the last couple of days, the struggle has been real, and we've definitely been building up to that moment. Stolen glances, crazy chemistry, and I'd be lying if I said I hadn't thought about it quite a few times since that afternoon in the cellar. Yet, no amount of daydreaming could have prepared me for the feel and taste that is Zach Wolff.

I'll never forget the moment his hesitation and uncertainty left, and his face—his gorgeous face—was stamped with undeterred determination. He'd finally decided to kiss me, I decided to overlook my rule about not mixing business with pleasure, and the butterflies in my stomach could have burst out with sweet anticipation.

The warmth and fullness of his lips, *that* corner kiss, which was a tease and a silent promise, made it seem as if fireworks were going off when he finally sealed us together. I surrendered to the onslaught of erratic flutters, nerves, and want. It was indescribable, nothing has ever come close.

When the kiss ended and Zach rested his forehead against mine, my hand slid out of his hair and down his neck. He might've been trying to show that he was somewhat calm and collected, but his heartbeat thundered under my hand. Then, when his eyes finally met mine, they weren't clear with excitement, they were clouded with unnamed emotions. Good emotions, I can only hope.

And as I stepped away, I fought so hard against wanting to smile and lean back in for another. It was that good. Still, even the next day, I am wondering if a second kiss would be just as good as the first.

Wow.

My heart stutters and skips, squeezes and expands, and then fills with uncertain anxiety about what—if anything—will happen next.

The sound of laughter and men's voices drift through the windows as I finish working on this morning's recipe. After cooking it twice to make sure I had the correct measurements, I wrapped it up.

Michelle called earlier this morning raving about all of the food Zach took with him last night. She wanted to know what I was making today and when would I have more. I'm pleased that everything I've made so far has been a hit. I do think they all complement the white wines well.

Slipping my flip-flops onto my feet, I gather the dishes, load them onto the golf cart, and head for the manor.

Zipping around the path, the voices get louder as I round the turn and spot three guys plus Zach and Kyle tossing the football around.

Shirts off.

All of them.

Muscles everywhere.

Holy hotness.

Oh, my heavens, I won the lottery.

As they hear my approach, they turn, and the guy closest to me breaks out in a huge, welcoming smile.

"Well, well, well, who do we have here?" He walks over to me as I slow and stop the cart. Wiping the sweat off his face, he leans against the golf cart, and I smile back at his ease and apparent playfulness.

The stranger and I both glance to Zach, who has a deep frown on his lips, which deepens as his eyes lock with mine.

"Hey." I give him a small smile, and my stomach tightens as I wait for his response and let my eyes trail over his tan skin and defined muscles.

And wait.

No smile. No words. No nothing.

I don't know what I thought today was going to be like or how he would react to seeing me after last night, but I didn't expect this. For some reason, I thought we crossed into a different level of friendship, but apparently, we hadn't.

Embarrassment washes over me, forcing me to drop my gaze from him to the ground. A lump crawls up my throat and I swallow several times to push it down. How did I perceive last night so differently from what he did? We had a great night. I know I didn't make that up. When I gather enough determination to glance back at him, his scowl is back, and so is his other personality. My heart sinks at the realization that the best kiss of my life meant nothing to the person that gave it to me. I feel so stupid and desperately want to get out of here.

Taking a deep breath, I suck up my humiliation and turn to the stranger, who's still leaning against the cart. His smile has dropped into a crooked grin, and unlike Dr. Jekyll over there, he seems friendly and happy.

"Hi, I'm Shelby." My voice is a little rough. He doesn't notice, but Zach does, and out of the corner of my eye, I see him shift his weight. I hold my hand out for him to shake, which the guy does, wrapping both of his large ones around mine. Sweat rolls down his neck and across his shoulder, I focus on it to keep my eyes from drifting to where they're not wanted.

"James. Nice to meet you." His eyes trail over me, and I look to see what I'm wearing: sparkly flip-flops, white shorts, and a light blue button-down, which is untucked and rolled up at the sleeves. James's eyes crinkle in the corners as they meet mine, and his smile gets bigger.

It's flattering after the blow to my ego that Zach just delivered. Even though I feel mortified by my situation with Zach, this guy James makes me breathe a little easier and feel more comfortable.

"That's Jack." James points to the sandy blond haired guy, who winks back at me. "That's Bryan." He waves his hand toward the guy with light brown hair. "And I guess you already know Zach and Kyle."

My eyes lock again with Zach's, and surprise, surprise, he just scowls harder.

Ass.

I'm officially done. I'm done trying, I'm done "starting over," and I'm done giving him the benefit of the doubt. I came here for the assignment, an assignment that's going to give me an edge up on others, and one I can't afford to get distracted from. I'm not weak, I don't pine after guys, and certainly not guys like him. Less than a week to go, so no more. Done. Just done.

"Yup." The sound of the *p* pops off my lips, irritation evident in my tone.

All three of the new guys chuckle as Bryan, Jack, and Zach move closer to the golf cart. James makes his way over to Zach and claps him on the back before turning back to me. "Better be careful there, darlin, our boy isn't used to not being gawked over. You might be crushing his delicate feelings."

All the guys—all except for Zach, that is—burst out in laughter.

"I doubt that. Given my limited time with him, I'd argue that he doesn't have feelings." I eye him warily, knowing that I'm intentionally pushing his buttons, but he needs to know that I've reached my limit and I'm fed up.

"Ohhh," they ring out in chorus.

"Too bad Lexi isn't here, she'd love this girl." James looks over to Bryan and grins.

"Wait! You know Lexi?" My heart skips a beat at the mention of my sweet friend. We haven't had a chance to get together since that fiasco at the Feeding America event, and I'd be lying if I said I wasn't missing her like crazy.

"Know her? I'm related to her. She's my sister. You know Lexi?" He looks at me questioningly.

"Oh my God! You're her James?" I slide out of the golf cart and walk around the front of it toward him. "Such a small world to find you here. I'm Shelby Leigh. As in Lexi, Shelby, and Meg."

His eyes widen. "No way! I've been dying to meet you for like years! All she talks about is you and Meg." James wraps his arms around me, sweeping me off my feet and into a crushing hug. "Zach, you didn't tell me the third leg to the tripod was here!"

"I'm not really sure what you're talking about so, no, I didn't." His voice is flat, and his face has darkened with annoyance and a hint of jealousy. James picks up on his tone, smirks at him, and holds me a tad bit longer than necessary.

Slowly letting me down, his eyes drop over me again, only this time his look is different. It isn't flirtatious so much as endearing, and I feel like I've found a long-lost friend.

"Lexi told us you were overseas." I take him in and look for any signs of injury or illness.

"I am. I'm on leave right now."

"That's awesome. Do you plan to see her while you're here? Wait! You better plan to see her." I shove his chest, smiling up at him.

He chuckles and wraps an arm around my shoulders. "Yeah, she was going to come here this weekend, but she has a large order she needs to fill. So, I'm headed to her on Monday."

"You guys are staying the weekend?" I ask, glancing at each of them and stopping on Zach.

"Yup," he answers, mimicking the way I said the word moments ago without breaking eye contact—not even to blink. His stare makes me even more uncomfortable and heats me at same time. This seems to be the trend between us: hates me, likes me, hates me, likes me. I remind myself that I'm done with all his back and forth and push out a deep sigh as I turn back to James.

"I should have recognized you right away. I've seen your photo no less than a hundred times, and y'all look so similar." I look over the features of his face—blond hair, dark eyes, golden skin, high cheekbones, and full lips.

"It's the hair, or lack of." He rubs his hand back and forth over the standard military buzz.

"No, I still should have seen it. How do y'all know each other?" I wave my finger between him, Zach, and the other guys.

"Bryan and I have known each other for forever. Zach, Bryan, and I played college ball together, and Bryan and Jack play for Tampa." I glance at each of them, and Jack winks at me.

"Football, got it."

Out of the corner of my eye, Jack moves, slips behind Zach, and steals the ball. All hell breaks loose, and the four of them start running, leaving James with me.

"So . . . you and Zach, huh?" He glances down at me questioningly, eyebrows raised.

My eyes find Zach across the yard. I can hear him laughing at something one of the other guys said, but when he turns so I can see his face, his expression is blank. Historically, he's been very vocal about his opinion of me, but this time he's been pretty quiet.

"Ah, no. I'm here working on a project with Zach; food pairings to go with his wines."

"Sounds interesting." I can feel James studying me.

"It has been." My eyes travel away from Zach, across the acres of the winery, and then back to James. "I'm actually on my way to drop off the food I cooked this morning for Michelle. She offers it up to the tasters who come in and then gives me feedback."

He looks past me to the back of the golf cart and groans.

"I don't suppose you're cooking dinner tonight, are you? Please say yes, please say yes."

A laugh bursts out of me, and Zach turns to look at us before he begins to make his way back over. I hadn't considered cooking a meal and having people over at the cottage, but the idea of it does sound nice. "I can if that's what you want."

"Seriously, my mouth is already watering at the thought. A home-cooked meal. It's been so long, I can't say thanks enough in advance." He rubs his belly as if he's starving and grins at me.

"A home-cooked meal it is then." I smile at James and then turn a glare to Zach, who stopped just shy of where James and I are standing. "I can't wait to call Lexi and tell her what I'm doing tonight, and I happen to know there's some decent wine lying around this place, too."

Zach rolls his eyes.

That's just like him

I know I shouldn't take Zach's reaction this morning personally, because I truly don't think I've done anything wrong, but I can't help it. This one-eighty he's done has affected not only my psyche, but it's left me confused. How do you act like you're into someone, kiss them like it's the first and last kiss you'll ever have, and then twelve hours later pretend they don't exist? It's hurtful and again reminds me why I never let guys stick around long enough to get under my skin.

Whatever.

I need to stop thinking about him, think more about the food pairings, and maybe spend the evening seeing if I can get to know James more. He's friendly, gorgeous, one of my best friend's brother, and he'll be heading back to his job soon enough. Also, he hasn't made me feel bad about myself.

"What are you thinking about?" Michelle asks me as she looks down at the poor chives I've chopped to death.

"Nothing much. Recipes." I smile at her and lie. "I called Lexi earlier to tell her that I met James, and she screamed through the phone." She knew he was coming and wanted to surprise me. Just thinking of the phone call takes some of the weight I feel surrounding Zach off me.

"I think it's crazy y'all hadn't met before." She glances out the French doors where the guys are standing, and I follow, my eyes landing on James. He laughs, and his eyes skip inside and find me.

Both of us pause, neither one breaking the stare as we both quite possibly seek something different from each other.

"He's staring at you," Michelle whispers.

"I know." The familiarity surrounding James's appearance makes me feel like we've been friends for years. It's comforting and much needed. Actually, what I need is for this assignment to be over. I'm ready to go home.

"Not him. Zach."

"Oh." Heat floods my cheeks, and it takes everything in me to continue ignoring him. I have most of the afternoon, which wasn't hard considering he ignored me, too.

"You know, I've never seen him like this," she says, while shaking her head in disbelief.

"Like what?" I turn to look at her. "And you said that on the day I arrived, too."

"I did?" Her brows furrow as she tries to replay our conversations from a week ago.

"Yes. Although, I don't understand why. Every time I see him, he acts the same way."

"That's just it, you're the only girl I've ever seen him act this way around . . ." The expression on her face shifts to one of understanding, when I don't understand anything.

"And what way is that? Like an asshole?" I say this more to myself, but she hears me and cringes. I understand he's her friend, but really, he isn't mine.

"No," she draws out, thinking about how to choose her next few words. "I would say more uneasy. Zach is incredibly laid back and happy. He's dedicated to this winery, his family, and friends, and I swear he doesn't have one enemy. But with you, it's as if he's unsure of everything. He doesn't know which way is coming or going."

"That is not my fault." I walk to the sink and put the knife in it before continuing, "I haven't done anything."

"I know, and I'm not saying you have. I just think there's more going on in his head than he's letting on."

Hearing her say his head makes me think of his mouth and what it felt like to have it on mine. An ache falls to the bottom of my stomach. That ache represents everything I feel about him and that kiss. It's filled with longing, wonder, confusion, and disappointment. Disappointment because it seems no matter what I do or how much time has passed, things never change.

Involuntarily, I glance outside and see that Zach has moved to stand next to James. Both of them are facing the inside now, and both of them are looking at me. Although the wariness that had initially clouded Zach's eyes the first couple of days is gone after he claimed he wanted to be friends, there's still a lingering emotion in them. I can almost feel it when he's watching me, and it makes me nervous instead of relaxed.

"Well, he can keep it there." I mumble as I turn my back to the guys. “I’m only here another week, and he can keep his cryptic signals to himself. Soon enough, this will be over.”

She frowns at me, and suddenly, I realize that she and I will be over, too. Everyday Michelle has gone out of her way to see me. I had wanted a friend here, and I found one in her.

“I’m sorry, that came out sounding really bad.”

“Don’t worry about it.” She cracks a smile and pushes her braid over her shoulder. “I understand.” Her gaze shifts to Kyle and then back to me. She shrugs and walks over to the French doors to tell the guys that the appetizers are ready.

Kyle, James, Bryan, and Jack come inside to join us. They always say the fastest way to a man’s heart is through his stomach, and as each of them taste the different styled deviled eggs I set out in the living room, their eyes flash and they smile.

“Zach ran back to the manor to grab some more wine, he’ll be right back,” James says as he comes to stand next to me. Spicy cologne floats around him. It smells really good, different. Over the last week, I’ve become accustomed to a more earthy scent.

“Oh, that’s great. I didn’t realize we were running low.” I look at him, and his big brown eyes. He looks so much like Lexi, it’s uncanny.

“Yeah, well . . . look at us, we can put down a lot.” He chuckles and pats his stomach.

“I suppose you can.” I grin at him.

“Thanks for cooking us dinner. Zach said you are an incredible cook.”

“Did he now?”

“He did.” I know James is watching my face and my reaction to him talking about Zach. I know he’s trying to figure out if I’m into his friend or not, and while I understand his scrutiny, it still makes me uncomfortable.

"Well, he's tasted the same as Michelle, and I know she's enjoying the food, too. So, that makes me happy to hear."

A beat of silence passes between us, and then he looks around the kitchen and back at me.

"Can I help you with anything?"

"Nope, Michelle and I have everything under control. I appreciate you offering, though. Besides, you're on vacation, you should go hang out with your friends." His friends, who've made themselves comfortable on the couch, and are currently watching baseball on the television. Guys and their sports—it doesn't matter what it is as long as it's on.

"All right, well, holler if you do." He winks at me and then wanders back to his friends.

The three of them plus Kyle joke and laugh together in a way that shows years of friendship. I can't help but to occasionally linger near them to soak up their ease, it's magnetic. As if I subconsciously want to be part of a group that is that closely knit. It makes me realize just how much I miss Meg and the restaurant. I have this kind of friendship with her.

The front door opens, closes, and Zach cuts across the room in long strides. Placing four bottles of wine on the counter, his arm brushes against mine as he comes to stand next to me. The four bottles remind me of the night before, and I step away from him. He burns me with a frustrated look that races straight down to my toes.

"What?" I snap at him.

His eyes narrow and then run over my face. It feels too personal to be perused this way, but I won't turn away.

Ingredients:

6 large eggs
2 tablespoons of mayonnaise
1–1.5 teaspoons of Chow-Chow (sweet & spicy pickled relish)
1 teaspoon of yellow mustard
dash of salt & pepper to taste
sprinkle of paprika to garnish
1 jalapeño (optional)

How to make:

Place eggs in a pot and cover with water. Bring to a boil. Put on a tight lid and turn off burner. Let eggs sit for 10 minutes.

Drain pot of hot water and run eggs under cold water. One egg at a time, tap on the counter to crack shell. Roll it to crackle all over and then peel under running cold water.

Once eggs are peeled, slice long ways and scoop out yolk. In a bowl combine yolk, mayonnaise, Chow-Chow, mustard, salt and pepper. Spoon mixture back into each egg and sprinkle with paprika.

(For an extra kick, I thinly sliced a jalapeño for the top)

Serve immediately.

Chapter 12

Nothing like eating crow

Zach

I forgot the guys were coming this weekend, even though I had it on the calendar. We talked about it almost a month ago when James called and said he was coming home for a break, and at the time, I told him no worries. That was before the opportunity with the magazine came up. And of course, over the last week or so, I've been too wrapped up in her to pay attention to my life and my responsibilities.

"Are you just going to stand in here and sulk all night or are you going to go talk to her?" Kyle asks, shoving a leftover piece of cornbread in his mouth.

I'm not sulking . . . well, maybe I am.

Almost all night, Shelby and James have been glued together. When we got here, he lingered by her while she cooked, offering to help. When it was time to eat dinner, he sat next to her and kept her laughing. And afterward, he helped clean the dishes. I see the way he looks at her. It's the way I catch myself looking at her when I forget who she is and what she does. I understand their connection because of Lexi makes their situation unique, Shelby is his sister's best friend, and that story is as cliché as it gets. Yet, with every smile, every giggle, every casual touch, I feel like I'm losing my damn mind. I don't like it. At. All.

The echo of her laughter carries through the French doors and into the cottage. I turn to look at them, but they're covered in darkness. It's better this way, the less I see, the easier it will be to let him sweep her off her feet and get her out of my hair. So then, why does the thought of this leave me unsettled?

There's no need to pretend as if I don't know who Kyle is talking about, so instead, I try to close the conversation down.

"I don't want to talk to her. I think it's great that he's here. He's entertaining her so I don't have to." I move to sit on the couch, pull out my phone to check my e-mails, and because I know it will rile him up, I say, "Jack seems to be taking care of Michelle, too, so hey, it's a win for both of them."

"What?" His attention whips to the back patio, only to find her sitting in the chair next to Jack. At that exact moment, Jack leans over to her, whispers something, and she laughs. Kyle's hands tighten into fists before he storms outside to join the group. He sits down on the other side of Michelle, and she smiles sweetly at him.

He has it bad for her, and as much as I hate to admit it to myself, I have it bad for Shelby, too.

Shelby.

The image of her face this morning when she said hello to me and I didn't say it back, the disappointment and embarrassment, I don't know how to fix the damage I caused in that moment. I told her I wanted us to be friends, I've treated her like a friend. Hell, after last night, I made her more than just a friend. Then, at the first opportunity I had to show her that I'm not the person I was when she got here, I blew it. In a way, I'm still decompressing from our time together last night, and seeing James's reaction to her elicited emotions from me I wasn't expecting.

I also made the mistake of telling Kyle that I kissed her.

He laughed, but I could see the wheels turning in his head the more he thought about it, and the laugh slipped off his face. He then proceeded to lecture me about the plan, a plan that's working and will be over soon enough. The plan that's left me feeling duplicitous.

When Shelby walks in from the patio, she doesn't notice me sitting in the living room, and I watch as she rinses her wine glass, sets it on the counter, and walks to her bedroom. She's changed from this morning, putting on a top with a little skirt . . . a little skirt that shows off her endless smooth legs.

I get up to follow her, shut the door behind us, and lean against it with my arms folded across my chest.

Her head snaps around and wide eyes lock onto mine. "What are you doing?"

Instead of answering her, I stare at her and feel the temperature of the room rise.

Huffing at me in frustration, she slowly bends over and slips off her shoes. "Whatever," she mumbles without breaking eye contact with me.

"Are you having fun tonight talking to my friends?" My voice is rough, deeper than usual. I swear this girl twists me so badly I can't even speak normally around her.

She stands straight, and her face falls but quickly recovers. The feistiness that I've come to admire in her flashes as she lifts her chin and her stare becomes a glare. "I am. Thanks for asking."

I watch as she moves to the closet and pulls a sweater off a hanger, slips it on, and then crosses the room to stand directly in front of me. Looking me up and down, she twists her lips to the side as if she's contemplating something before a slow, sly smile forms on her lips. "Wait. Are you jealous?"

"No." I snort as if the thought repulses me, but I am. "I am curious. Looks like James is pretty caught up in your spell." I lean forward a little, forcing her tilt her head back if she wants to keep looking at me.

"There's no spell. What you see is what you get; haven't you figured that out by now? And what's so wrong with someone being interested in me? You sure were last night."

"I didn't say there was anything wrong with it." My jaw tightens, and my eyes narrow.

"You are such an asshole sometimes." She tries to push me out of the way to get to the door, but I don't budge and pull her back in front of me.

"You do bring out the best in me," I say sarcastically, when I should be saying she brings out the worst. God, I hate the person I am with her. I'm never deceitful or snappy or short tempered. I was taught to always be honest and kind, and I've tried to live my life this way.

"How so? What have I ever done to you, anyway?" Her face flushes red, she's angry and it makes her look a little wild and a lot irresistible. "I mean really, how do you have so many friends? I don't understand. Do you treat them the same way you treat me and they tolerate it? Because quite frankly this"—she waves her finger back and forth between the two of us—"is a lot of work."

She brushes her hair off her shoulder and shakes her head to settle it on her back as she tilts her head. My eyes run over the curve of her jaw, travel over the long lines of her neck, and land back on her mouth. Part of me is screaming to step away from her and that this is wrong, but the other part of me that's drawn to her says it isn't. The latter is stronger, which is what put me in this situation to begin with.

"He isn't the right guy for you." My blood pumps a little faster through my veins at the thought of another guy's hands on her.

Her jaw drops, her eyes narrow, and she lets out an exacerbated huff. "And how would you possibly know what type of guy is right for me?" She takes a few steps back to put some space between us.

"There's a reason why Lexi set us up, and she's never introduced the two of you."

Why am I saying this? I've made it very clear that I'm not interested in her, which is a lie in and of itself since I kissed her last night and want to kiss her again right now. Not even reminding myself that she's a critic or an insatiable workaholic can help me shake the need.

"Really? You want to go there now? After how you consistently treat me?" Her glare turns sharp and murderous; I have the sudden urge to protect myself.

"It's true and you know it." I take a step toward her, shrinking the distance.

"Yeah, a lot of good that did me. Hands down the worst blind date ever." A flush races up her neck and into her cheeks. She's so angry.

"I'll admit I was not myself that night. For what it's worth . . . I'm sorry." Nothing like eating a huge heaping of crow.

Her eyes grow large. "That night? What about the day I got here, the day of the photo shoot, or this morning . . . were you not yourself those times, either? Because I've been here for a week, and it seems being a dick to me is what's most natural."

I cringe at her words. She's right, and I hate it.

"I didn't mean for this morning to go down like it did. I wasn't intentionally trying to ignore you. One minute we were playing football, and then the next you were there and . . ." I turn my head away from her.

"And what?" she asks, annoyed.

My eyes lock back on hers. "I saw the way James looked at you."

"How did he look me?" She tilts her head, eyebrows raised.

"Interested." The word slithers out through my teeth.

She rolls her eyes and shakes her head as if this answer isn't enough for her. Not for the first time, I wish I knew what she was thinking. I started this conversation, but now, I just want it to be over.

Taking a deep breath, I rub my hand over my face and through my hair. Her eyes track my movements as I rub the back of my neck.

"I told you, the issues I have are mine, not yours . . . and believe it or not, I am trying. I'm sorry about this morning."

Her mouth tips up at the corner. "Say it again." Her eyes blaze in victory, and the tension around her face and shoulders wanes as she takes a step forward.

Inches separate us. We're so close but not close enough, and her nearness is making me ache in places I didn't know could.

Licking my lips, her eyes drop to my mouth and mine do the same. I'm obsessed with how full, soft, and sweet hers taste against mine. Seconds tick by as the tension around us grows thicker and heavier. My stare slowly crawls back up her face and a rush of air leaves me at the depth of fire in her eyes.

"I'm sorry," I finally say, giving her what she wants before taking what I need as my mouth slams down on hers.

Instantly the turmoil I've been feeling all day subsides. Why I've let this girl dig her way so far under my skin, I don't know, but being locked to her, I feel like I can breathe for the first time since last night.

Angling my head to get even more, she matches me move for move. Damn, she tastes so good, and this kiss . . . it's deep, wet, and there's an uncontrolled urgency fueling us. I can't get enough of her, and she can't get enough of me.

I bend, slide my hands around the back of her thighs, and pick her up. Her legs wrap around my waist and squeeze, bringing us flush together as her arms drape over my shoulders.

Warmth, honey, and her heartbeat hit me all at once. I can feel it pound through her chest and into mine, and it forces mine to match hers beat for beat. I'm addicted to this feeling, I'm pretty sure I've become addicted to her.

Walking us over to the bed, I lay her down and lean over, keeping her mouth fused to mine. Damn she feels even better underneath me than she tastes.

Rocking her hips against mine, she slides her hands down my back and grabs on to my waist, fingers slipping underneath my shirt and onto my skin. Her touch feels incredible and electric; it sends tremors straight through me.

Needing to be closer—to feel more—one hand slides up the back of her thigh and under her tiny little skirt to rest on her hipbone. The other falls next to her head as I pull back to hold myself up. My heart crashes into my chest and at least a minute goes by, while neither of us says anything. We're each watching to see what the other is going to do—the sound of our breathing the only disturbance between us.

Leaning forward, I kiss the corner of her mouth and drag my lips across hers, drawing the swell of her bottom lip between my teeth. She sucks in air, and I cover her mouth with mine to take it away from her. Her fingers dig into my back, and her tongue dances with mine.

"I shouldn't want this," she says as my lips move from her mouth to her neck, licking the sweetness from her skin. I shouldn't want this, either, but damn if I do. Her back arches, and her chest pushes into me. My hand slips over the smoothness of her hipbone and around to her ass. Tilting her, I angle her to better align the fit of me against her. She moans into my shoulder as I push against her, and I groan from the heat that's wrapping around me.

"Why do you drive me so crazy?" I whisper, my words leaving a trail of goose bumps on her skin. Her hair is spread out across the bed, her lips are plump from the assault they were given, and her cheeks are flushed with desire. My heart trips in my chest.

Sliding my hand back around her hip, my thumb slips under her lace panties and traces the edge between her legs. She's smooth and perfect. Every muscle in my stomach tightens in anticipation and want. This girl is the sweetest torture.

Somewhere in the house, a door slams, and Shelby tenses. I had forgotten anyone else was here.

"We should go back out there," she says, pushing on me to move as her eyes skip to the door and back to mine.

"Yeah, I think you're probably right." My hand slides back around to her ass and squeezes. Her eyes widen a little. The moment is over, but it's too late for her to be shy about my hand on her ass.

Slowly, I stand and take a step back from her, smoothing down her skirt as I go. God, I want this girl.

Her eyes trail the length of me and pause as I adjust myself. I smirk at her and the flood of color rising on her cheeks.

"Whatever." She rolls her eyes, and flips her hair over her shoulder as she gets up off the bed, pushes by me, and walks into the bathroom. I can't argue her attitude here. My mixed signals over the last week have been confusing even to me, but the last five minutes should have proven that I undoubtedly want her.

Heading out first to the kitchen. Kyle catches my eye and shakes his head disapprovingly. A twinge of guilt inches its way in, but I can't think about that, I only want to think about how she makes me feel. And right now, I feel good.

Ingredients:

2 cups of white self-rising cornmeal mix
1/2 cup of sugar
1 cup of milk
2 large eggs
1/2 cup of softened butter

How to make:

Preheat over to 400 degrees.

Grease a 9×9 dish, cake pan, or glass pie dish.

In a large bowl, beat butter and sugar together using a mixer until fluffy. Next blend in milk and eggs. Lastly, add in cornmeal until mixture runs smooth.

Pour into dish and bake for 22-25 minutes, or until a toothpick runs clean.

Let cool for a few minutes. Slice, add butter and serve.

Serves 6-8.

Chapter 13

oh my stars

Shelby

"What's going on with you and Kyle?" I ask Michelle as she walks behind the bar to grab glasses for a new customer. She skipped out last night, closely after Kyle, and I didn't get a chance to say goodbye or thank her for helping me.

"Nothing much, why?" She doesn't make eye contact with me.

"Oh, come on. I've been here for a week, and it's obvious even to me there's something there."

She pushes her braid off her shoulder and glances at me—her expression full of dejection.

"I thought so, too. Was even hopeful for it. But more and more time has passed and nothing ever changed . . . well, maybe it did last night. I don't know."

"What happened last night?" I lean forward, placing my elbows on the bar.

"Nothing really. It just felt like it used to. But then again, I'm probably making it more than it is." Disappointment laces through her words.

"I don't understand. What do you mean 'like it used to'?" I've seen the way he looks at her, and I've seen the up-front way he acts with Zach. I can't imagine him not going after what he wants.

She shrugs and says, "When I first started working here, he would come in at the end of my shift and we'd sit around and talk into the night. I loved it, but little by little the time would cut shorter, until eventually he stopped coming."

"That's strange. He's so flirtatious around you." Thinking back over the last couple of days, I've seen him wink at her at least a half dozen times.

"I know, right? Well, I'm glad you see it, too. I was starting to wonder if I was reading more into it than there was."

"I don't think so, and last night, he all but made it clear you were his." Kyle's expression when he joined us outside was not only territorial but also determined. Once he sat next to Michelle, he stole all her attention.

"But I'm not."

"Are you sure about that?" The question lingers around us as we stare at each other.

Another couple comes in and she moves down the bar to greet them placing fresh glasses in front of everyone. She smiles warmly and instantly has them feeling relaxed and welcome; that's part of her allure. Michelle is beautiful, kind, and smart, I really don't see what the problem is.

"So, tell me about last night?" I ask when she comes back to refill my wine glass for me.

She lets out a sigh and leans over the bar so she's a bit closer to me. "He heard me leave right after him and offered to drive me back to the manor to get my car. We talked for a little bit on the drive, and then he said good night."

"That's it?"

"Yep." She pinches her lips together.

"That's so strange." I shake my head. "It doesn't make any sense. Why haven't you made the first move?"

She pauses to think about her answer. "I don't know, he's older than me."

"So?" My eyebrows rise in question.

"So, I guess I'm a little bit old fashioned." She squares off her shoulders and stands a little taller. "If he wanted to ask me out, he would have. I shouldn't have to chase a guy to get him to show interest in me. It should be organic and mutual."

"I agree with that, but there has to be more to it."

"Or maybe it's the opposite and there's nothing, which is why he never made a move."

I don't understand how she could possibly think there is nothing there. It's so clear to everyone around them, even Zach watches them. She pulls two bottles from the cooler and starts walking away.

"Michelle, I've seen the way he looks at you, the way he watches you, and after the way he behaved last night when he thought Jack was into you, I'm telling you, there's something there."

She stiffens and pauses as she thinks about what I've said. Quietly, she turns back to face me. "I could say the same to you." Neither of us says anything, and then she shrugs as she moves back to the new customers to pour the next wine in the tasting flight.

I suppose she could.

Zach surprised me last night when he told me he was sorry. Then again, he surprises me every time I see him. He's up, he's down. He's happy, he's angry. He's loud, he's reserved . . . I have no idea what to expect, and it seems I need to add jealous to the list. Jealousy radiated off him each time he saw James talking to me, even after he kissed me senseless in my room. But he still left with the guys at the end of the night, only giving me a nod, a mumbled thanks for the dinner, and a promise to text me tomorrow about a time to meet. Which is why I'm here now, waiting for him.

Taking in a deep breath, I remind myself it's only a few more days. Six to be exact, which is why I need to push all of these mixed emotions over a guy aside, a guy who I have no intention of seeing past this week, and focus on the assignment—and my future.

Feeling a motivated sense of focused purpose, I sit a little taller and take a sip of my delicious wine, and that's when I notice the air at my back has heated. An earthy clean smell floats around me, and my eyelids drift shut as I soak it in. I really do love the way he smells.

Looking over my shoulder, I find Zach standing next to me with a wary expression on his face. Crossing my legs, I remind myself that I'm only here for six more days and twist on the chair to face him, wondering which version I'll have tonight.

"How long have you been sitting here?" he asks me, shoving his hands into his pockets.

"Not too long." I eye him suspiciously. "How long have you been standing there?"

He chuckles. "Long enough."

Moving to stand next to me and lean against the bar, the tension in his shoulders lightens as he takes his time to drink me in with those electric blue eyes of his. So much for my pep talk. Sixty seconds, that's all it took for me to lose my sense of balance, while he remains completely calm and sure of himself. It's as if he's immune to the charged air between us. My heart rate picks up, butterflies have scattered, and I curse myself for having this crazy reaction to him.

Breaking the connection, I grab my glass, take a huge swallow of wine, and clear my throat. "I was ready and bored, so I came here a little early to hang out with Michelle." I glance down the bar, she's washing glasses, and still frowning. My heart frowns with her.

Zach makes a humming noise, pulling my eyes back to him. He looks at my glass and at the mostly empty bottle in front of me.

"Did you eat?" He sounds slightly irritated, and a giggle bursts out of me.

"Did you really just ask me that?" I shake my head at him. "Don't you know that a chef never misses a meal?"

The muscles in his face relax and one side of his mouth tips into a grin.

"So, are we Dr. Jekyll or Mr. Hyde today?" I ask him while leaning back in my seat, and smoothing my skirt down over my legs.

"What do you mean?" He crosses his arms over his chest, and the muscles bulge against the fabric, momentarily distracting me.

"Just want to be prepared for whatever kind of mood you're in before we get started."

He contemplates what I've said as a scowl drops into place. "It isn't like that."

"Oh, yes, it is." I laugh back at him.

He sighs and runs his hand through his hair. It's then I realize his hair is styled . . . and so are his clothes. He has on a pair of navy dress slacks, a pale blue long-sleeve button down with the sleeves rolled up, and a camel-colored belt with matching shoes. He looks delectable and insanely irresistible.

"You look nice," I say, trying to remain composed and keep the peace. His lips mash together and then his eyes sweep down over me again.

"You do, too. But you always do," he says softly, numbing me with the sincerity and warmth in his eyes. I manage to keep the fact that the dress and shoes I'm wearing were chosen with his reaction in mind.

"Thank you," I whisper, the sparked tension between us veering more toward that of a yearning.

Shifting in my chair, the strap on my left shoulder slips out of place, and his eyes follow it. Taking a step closer to me, putting him right in my personal space, he raises a hand and runs his finger up my arm—from my wrist to collarbone. I watch goose bumps chase after him, and he pushes the strap back in place. His hand lingers on my shoulder—searing me with the warmth of his touch.

Trailing my eyes up his chest, the top button on his shirt is undone, and I have the strongest urge to reach out and touch the bottom of his throat. He swallows and I continue my assent, admiring the tiny details that others wouldn't notice—the scar right above his top lip, the bump on his nose where at one point it must have been broken, and the way his eyes crinkle in the corner when he laughs and smiles—I find it all incredibly tempting and sexy.

His hand tightens on my shoulder, and his thumb slips back under the strap and traces the edge as if he now wants to take it off. Without thinking, I lean in toward him, and he does the same, his eyes latching onto my mouth. The air thickens, heats . . . electrifies. This guy is my kryptonite, and when he looks at me as if he wants me, I feel completely at his mercy. If he were to kiss me right now, here in front of his employees and these people, I would let him.

Glass shatters behind us, and we jerk away from each other.

So much for keeping strong and focused on the assignment.

Zach lets out a deep sigh, regards me with uncertain eyes, and then moves behind the bar to put some distance between us. I don't know if he does this for me, him, or because the photographer is sitting there watching us, but either way, I'm glad he does and I hate it all at the same time.

He lines three bottles in front of me. "So, here at Wolff, we bottle four sparkling wines. Our two signature sparklings are the Queen Bee, which is a sparkling lavender honey wine, and the Farkas, a sparkling brut wine. Our other two—a sparkling brut rosé wine, and a sparkling peach wine." He places his hands on top of the rosé and peach. "So, which do you want to start with?" he asks, looking from me to the bottles.

"Let's start with the rosé." I scoot forward in my seat wanting to close some of the distance between us.

His blue eyes flash to mine. "You did tell me you preferred dry wines, so this is a good place to start, but I'll save the best for last." He smiles, and my heart clenches as he unwraps the foil from the first bottle.

"Are you going to pop the cork?" I bat my eyes at him, pretending as if that comment could have come across as something less than innocent.

A devious grin takes over and his eyes fall half-mast, almost hooded.

"No, Shelby, I'm not going to pop the cork, I prefer to ease it out to release that whisper of smoke at the mouth of the bottle. I think it's sexier . . . and less dangerous. Don't you think?" He tilts his head, and his grin turns into a full-blown smile.

Oh my stars. My breath hitches, and I stare at him. "I guess so."

"Most will tell you that sparkling wines should be kept between forty-one to forty-seven degrees, but I think a few degrees warmer is better. The colder the wine is, the more concealed the flavors are. The opposite goes for as it sits in your glass and warms, the flavors and aromas change."

"I guess I've never really thought about temperature affecting flavor before. Either that, or I drink it faster than it warms." He smiles, clearly amused.

Angling the bottle away from us, he wiggles the cork until it slides out with a hiss. The bottle smokes, and he was right, it is sexy. Still holding the cork, he twists to grab two glasses in the same hand between his free fingers, and he holds them as he pours the sparkling wine.

"Mousse is the foam on top, the bubbly." A light pink layer of foam rises to the rim of the glass and stops. The perfect pour.

"I love the bubbles. I love when I can feel them against my lips."

He chuckles, hands me mine, and watches my mouth as I lift the glass to take a sip.

"Mmm, it's good." I lick my lips, and he lets out a breath as he tears his eyes away and takes a sip from his own glass.

Holding the glass up to the light, he examines the color and then grabs a white towel behind the bar to use as a backdrop. He tilts the glass to the side, examines the bubbles, and then sets it back on the bar.

"Instead of using one grape, we actually blend a red and a white to get the pink color. The Farkas is made with the Champagne method, which means it is put through a second fermentation in the bottle where the bubbles are naturally produced until it is opened. The brut rosé and the lavender honey wine are made by the

Charmat method, where the second fermentation is done in a tank, and the peach sparkling has the carbonation injected."

"Sounds fancy," I say, taking another sip.

He shrugs. "Not really. I would prefer them all to be done the traditional way, but time and production factors in."

Traditional.

In many ways, this description fits him perfectly. I know there are a lot of newer techniques he could be experimenting with here on the farm, but the expression, "If it ain't broke, don't fix it," seems to apply to him. From the fields to the cave, to the fermenting and the bottling, he sticks with what's always worked, and I think that says a lot about the quality of his wines.

"I feel very girly drinking this." I hold the glass out in front of me and twirl it, watching the bubbles race to the top.

"In general, mostly women do drink this one. It's why it sells the best during the holidays and around Valentine's. What do you think?" He folds his arms and lays them on the bar so he can lean toward me.

"My overall impression is that it's dry but leaves a berry aftertaste. It isn't super sweet, and it would pair very well with salty Southern snacks and spicy foods."

"Salty *Southern* snacks?" He laughs. "Don't you mean deep fried?" The sound of his laugh rolls over me and penetrates my skin.

"I was thinking canapés, but fried vegetables like okra sound delicious, too." I grin back.

"I volunteer, just say when." His expression is hopeful. Warmth that has nothing to do with alcohol floods through me.

"You haven't tired of my food yet?" I tease.

"No," he says very matter of fact.

"How about later this week then? I'll invite Kyle and Michelle, too."

If I hadn't been watching him as closely as I was, I would have missed the flash of disappointment in his eyes at my suggestion. Then he drums his fingertips against the bar a few times while he ponders something, and then nods his head. "Okay, that sounds like a great idea."

See. I knew I wasn't crazy. He thinks there's something between them as well. I glance over to Michelle, who's laughing with the customers. Maybe my time here will be about more than just the article. I smile to myself.

Zach grabs the next bottle, and opens it quickly and efficiently as I swallow the rest of the rosé. I would drink this one again.

"Now try this one. It's a sparkling peach muscadine." He sets the glass in front of me and removes both rosé glasses.

I sniff it, finding it very aromatic. My mouth is flooded with peaches and mangos as I take my first sip. "Whoa, this one is sweet." My face scrunches, and I shake my head in reaction to the taste.

"It is. It's more of a dessert wine. We use the juice from the two fruits—grapes and peaches—and still add a little sugar." Yeah, it's way too sweet for me.

"This one probably makes a great sangria." I push the glass back to him, and he moves it behind the bar. One sip is enough for me.

"It does. During tourist season over the summer, like the Fourth of July, we'll make batches of sangria for the people wandering in during the afternoon hours. It adds to the whole 'Georgia' experience."

"Well, I happen to like sangria, so I bet I'd be a fan of that. This by itself . . . not so much. Sorry." I grimace again at the memory of the flavor.

"Why are you apologizing? I don't expect you to like them all. If you did, I would wonder about the finesse of your palate." I scowl at the bottle, he chuckles, and moves it behind the bar next to my glass.

"My palate *is* pretty accurate," I remind him, leaning in a little closer to him. The strap on my dress slips again, he stops moving as he glances at it, and I slowly push it back in place, thoroughly enjoying the flashed heated look he gives me.

"So you've said," he mumbles and reaches for the next bottle, which is the lavender honey. I have high expectations for this one. Again, he goes through the motions of opening the bottle, and I watch him, ignoring the little voice in my head that appreciates the deftness of his fingers. The flash that was there seconds ago has turned to a spark. A spark that, if given the opportunity, would burst into flames.

I swallow, and he lets out a sigh before reaching for two new glasses.

"I can't believe you have a sparkling lavender honey wine. Not gonna lie, I've been waiting for days to try this." When we tasted the whites, I looked over their tasting menu that had been lying on the bar and spotted this sparkling. It's taken great restraint not to dive right in. I reach for the glass, but he pulls back at the last second to tease me. My eyes narrow at him, and he grins before handing it over.

"You kill me. You know you could have opened a bottle at any time," he says, pouring his own glass.

"I know, but to keep with the spirit of the assignment, I stuck to the plan. So, is this a sparkling mead wine?" I examine the golden color of the drink.

"No, but we have produced mead wines before. This one is a cuvée, a blend of several different varietals, and we infuse the lavender honey just before we bottle it."

"Is it sweet?" I raise the glass to look at the golden color.

"Not when it hits the palate, but you'll be able to taste the honey notes on the back end."

He tips his own glass toward mine, and we clink them together.

"Cheers," he says. "Here's to a wildly successful outcome from the magazine article."

"Cheers to that!" I smile brightly at him. Whereas I'm certain he's looking for a surge in sales, I'm adding another bullet point to my resume that hopefully pushes me more through the door of Food Network.

A flash from the photographer comes from my right. Zach didn't notice, he's too busy watching me over the rim of his glass.

Taking a sip, I'm rewarded with the perfect combination of a dry white wine and the distinct dash of honey. I really do love honey, and this sparkling wine excites me more than I can express.

"What do you think?" He's still watching me.

"I think it's delicious. I've never tasted anything like it." *I've never tasted anything like you either.*

He's pleased at my response and as if he can read my mind, a lazy sensual smile graces his perfect lips.

"I'm glad you like it. I was hoping you would. When you leave in a few days, take a case with you."

"I don't need a whole case, but thank you." I'm somewhat surprised by the generous offer, and a light blush warms my cheeks.

"Well, then, half and fill the other half with the sauvignon blanc. You seem to like that one, too."

"I do." He's been paying attention.

Lowering my glass to the bar, my hands flatten over the base to hold it in place. Slowly, Zach reaches across and lays one of his hands on top of mine. His warm fingers slide between mine, linking us together as his thumb swipes back and forth.

His hand is so much larger than my own. The strength it possesses and the gentleness of the gesture blurs the lines I keep trying to draw between us.

Trailing my eyes from our hands to his face, I'm met with a heat that speaks to every cell in my body. His eyes show a complete contrast to the gentleness in his hands, and this is a need I understand . . . this need I want.

Reluctantly, I glance toward the photographer sitting off in the corner with his camera pointed right at us. Zach's eyes follow, pause for a second, and then return to mine. When his brows drop with annoyance, I realize he'd forgotten that we have an audience.

"The last one we need is in the cellar. Walk down with me, and we'll drink it there." He gestures to the door, and I nod in agreement before moving to the door to watch him. He says something to Michelle, which makes her and the guests close enough to hear smile. If I had to guess, they're all about to get some free drinks thanks to the open bottles sitting on the bar. Then he moves to the photographer, who's sitting a few feet away from where I stand. "We're all done, but feel free to stick around or take off, it's up to you."

His face lights up. "Really? That's great. I think I'll take off, so thanks." He grabs his bag and starts packing his gear. Zach gives him a pat on the shoulder and then slips his hand into mine. Leading me through the right wing, we pass the library and head for the cellar stairs.

The buzz and the sounds from the tasting room begin to drift away, while the echo of our steps bounce around the hall. As we descend down into the cellar, the temperature drops, and suddenly I'm wishing for a sweater and not this tiny dress.

Zach turns a knob, and the muted glow from the chandeliers brightens the room.

"I'm not sure if I told you this before, but it's beautiful down here." I trail my eyes over the photos that line one wall and show the history of the vineyard. There are several with Zach as a kid, he was good-looking then, too. I'm not surprised.

He chuckles and heads into a side alcove where large coolers are built into the wall to grab the brut.

"Thanks, although, I can't take credit for it. My mother does all of the decorating around here."

As he walks back toward me, my eyes drift down over the length of him, admiring the way his clothes are perfectly tailored to his body. His steps never falter, but his free hand curls into a fist—at my blatant perusal.

"Well, she did an amazing job."

"Yeah, she did." His voice is a little deeper, and inwardly, I smile at the effect my eyes are having on him.

When he gets close enough, he sets the bottle on the high-top table next to me and opens it, the hiss lingering in the air. Once again, he pours the perfect amount into the glass—a single crystal flute glass—before he hands it to me, and his fingers brush against mine. His eyes flare, and a thrill runs up my arm at the contact. Why do I love it so much when he touches me?

Pulling away, I bring the glass to my lips and pause. His eyes roam over my face, glance at my mouth, and then he breaks away, running his hand through his hair and around to his neck. The blue in his eyes is darker down here; I want them to be darker because of me.

The wine has effervescence and a lightness that wasn't in the three upstairs. This wine is completely different, sensational, and in a league all on its own.

"Wow, this is incredible," I say between sips.

He gives me a closed-mouth smile and nods his head. He knows it's good.

Picking up the bottle, I look at the label and then him: Farkas, brut, blanc de blanc. It's dry with no hint of sweetness, even though a touch of sugar is added, and it's made entirely of white grapes.

"Farkas means 'wolf' in Hungarian," he answers the question before I ask it.

"That's your ancestor's name?"

He nods his head. "When the wine industry took off again, my grandfather thought it would be better if we changed our name to a more recognizable one. My father agreed, so they filed the paperwork. This was about a year before he met my mother.

"So, this is fairly new change?" I drink a little more, and he tops off my glass.

"I guess you could say that."

I look him over from head to toe, and he shifts his weight to lean against the table. "You don't look like a Farkas."

He chuckles. "Zachary Farkas?" He taps his chin for a few seconds as if he's thinking about it. "Yeah, no."

A laugh busts out of me, and he smiles in response.

"I like it when you laugh." His dark eyes fall to my mouth. "I like it a lot," he whispers.

My smile slips, and my breath catches as he steps closer. My head tilts back to look at him and every muscle freezes. We're close enough to be touching, but we're not, and my fingers tighten around my glass. He notices and gently lifts the glass away.

I can't breathe.

I can't blink.

All my back-and-forth indecision falls away, and now my reasons for staying away from him seem so insignificant. I know the difference between right and wrong, and what I should and shouldn't do . . . but right here, right now in this moment, under his smoldering gaze, I don't care.

Everything about this guy screams out to me: from the color of his hair and eyes, to the way he confidently carries himself, to his mind and how knowledgeable he is about the wine business—his business. The attraction I feel for him is so strong that the only thing I want to do is give in to it. Give in to him.

He needs to touch me, and he needs to touch me now.

Reaching a hand out, he lightly runs it down my arm until it lands on my hip. Warm fingertips sink through the fabric, squeeze me, and then push so I step backward and bump into the large table in the center of the room. Grabbing on to my waist, he picks me up and puts me on the table. The strap on my dress falls again, only this time instead of correcting it, he slips the other one off too and drags his warm fingertips across the skin of my chest.

"You are so beautiful," he says, stepping between my legs.

A few pieces of his hair fall across his forehead, and slowly and gently, I brush them away and then trace the line of his face and down his jaw.

Dipping his head, his cheek rubs against mine as my hands slowly travel up his hard chest. Such a sharp contrast to the softness of his lips as he places them on my neck.

The warmth of his body, the clean earthy smell of his skin, I'm surrounded and drowning in that feeling that only comes from a man—this man. This man who now seems to be fighting the same battle I am.

Do we, or don't we?

Pressing his hips into mine, he groans at the way we fit together, and I moan at the contact of him against me. My legs pull him closer, and I grab on to his waist as his hands slide in my hair, and fist so tightly I gasp.

Forcing my head back, he stares down at my lips. "God, you drive me insane with that mouth of yours, from the things you say to the way you drink my wines. Why do I find your lips wrapped around one of my wine glasses so incredibly sexy?"

My lips part and a slow breath leaves me.

He groans again, and I feel it against my chest. "All night . . . no, all week I've been infatuated with these," he leans forward, bites my bottom lip and sucks it gently before letting it go. "And knowing what you taste like, it's been driving me crazy."

"Is this why you brought us down here?" My words are breathless and evident of desire.

His eyes find mine, blue eyes that are even darker than before, and there's no hesitation. "Yes." Closing the distance, his lips collide with mine.

Honey, warm honey, that's what he tastes like as his tongue dances with mine—over and over, around and around.

Shutting off the questions and the confusion of our situation, I give in to all of my senses that are demanding I allow this to happen, and I let go. I throw myself into this kiss, his kiss, the hottest kiss I've ever been given.

His teeth clamp down just like the muscles in my stomach as they repeatedly bite and hold on, wanting to mark me. His warm, full lips elicit shivers as they drag across my cheek, under my ear, and down my neck. He wastes no time exploring me with his mouth, and all I can do is hold on for the ride.

Dragging his hands around my neck and to my chest, he pushes until I'm lying on the table in front of him with my legs wrapped around his hips. His eyes drink me in as want pours off him and he runs a hand down my chest between my breasts, over my stomach, and to my waist. I pull him closer with my legs, and he leans over me. He feels so good pressed into me that every pulse point in my body thumps hard with excitement.

His fingers on one hand sink back into my hair, and tilting my head he runs his tongue down my neck and across my chest to the edge of my dress. His blue eyes flash to mine once before his mouth returns to my skin, tasting it, devouring it, while his other hand moves up my thigh and dips under my dress to where I'm most anxious for it.

He pauses, hot air rushing out against my skin as his fingers wrap around and grasp my underwear.

"Don't stop," I whisper in his ear, teasing him and pleading at the same time.

I hear him inhale sharply, and the gaze I'm met with as he lifts his head and his eyes find mine, steals my next breath. That spark from earlier bursts into flames. The hottest part of the flame is blue, just like his eyes, the place of complete combustion. I gasp at the heat he's searing me with.

Challenge accepted.

He steps back, forcing me to unhook my ankles as one hand drags down my body feeling each curve, and the other pulls the small scrap of lace from under my dress and drops it onto the floor. Feeling an urgency to not waste any time, I sit up, unbuckle his belt, and make quick work of his pants. They slide down his legs as my thumbs dip inside his boxer briefs and drag them down his thighs to join his pants.

We both know where this is headed and we both want it. He moves back between my legs, hovers over me, and my heart speeds up. His hands cage in my head as he looks at me and I look at him. I see determination and drive. I see lust, pure unadulterated lust mixed with a little awe. I see him. A man who was my enemy and is now about to be my lover.

"Zach . . ." I whisper, sliding my hands up under his shirt wanting and needing to feel more.

"Shelby . . ." he whispers, huskily, and my hands tremble against him. With that his mouth slams down on mine, and I arch up to get as close as I can, giving him everything I have. His hand finds me as I find him and together we pause at the sensation of being touched by someone else. He tucks his head into my neck and groans as I run my hand up and down the length of him. He feels so hot compared to the air in this room, and I want this, I want him.

Gently, I pull and guide him until he removes his fingers and brushes against me.

"Pill?" he whispers as he drags his lips across my face and back to my lips.

"Yes." It's barely a breath as I exhale, but he catches it and kisses me for what feels like an eternity.

Resting his forehead against mine, his fingertips move to my hips and squeeze to almost the point of pain, to hold me in place and then he fully enters me in one move. The force of his hips, the fullness, the weight of his body all hit me at once, and I drown in the sensations.

Slowly, he pulls back out. My breath catches, and my body arches underneath him, chasing after his.

"Is this what you want?" he asks, moving his lips down my neck and to the swell of my breasts peeking out from under the edge of my dress.

"Yes." A moan slips through my lips as he pushes back in, taking us both to a place of complete bliss. Wrapping my legs tighter around his waist, I want to close all the space between us and feel every inch of him—from head to toe.

He moves his hips into mine, alternating between hard and fast to slow and deep. Never have I completely given over all of me like I am to him in this moment. And I want it. I want it all. Anything and everything he can give me, I'm going to take it.

Threading my fingers through his hair, his lips work their way across my collarbone, back up my neck and to my mouth. His tongue explores every inch of my mouth and moves in time with his body. I am completely consumed by him and my legs start to shake.

Standing up, Zach's hands run from my shoulders over my breasts and down my thighs. Pushing the skirt of my dress up higher, he watches as he moves in and out of me and repositions my legs so they aren't around his back but tucked up under each arm.

Just seeing the way his hair falls across his forehead, the color high on his cheeks, his half-lidded eyes, and his swollen lips, sensations begin to prick down my spine. The sound of his labored breathing, the way his hips fit into mine, and the feeling of him losing his self-control has me climbing and climbing. The last week and a half, the attraction, the buildup, and the urgency to have one another carries me to the top of the cliff. Teetering on the edge, my eyelids slip shut as I mentally spread my arms wide, and together we welcome the free fall. Heart soaring, adrenaline racing, indescribable pleasure.

Panting, Zach falls forward and braces his forearms on the table on either side of my head before tucking his face into the crook of my neck. Sweat from his forehead makes my skin damp, and his lips part as he breathes heavily. Running my hand through his hair, I wait as he slowly relaxes his weight against me. I realize I could lie like this with him for an endless amount of time, but as our heartbeats slow, the coolness in the air descends. I shiver underneath him, and he stiffens as if he's suddenly lying on a bed of nails instead of me.

Propping himself up with one hand, he stares down. Blue eyes are still dark. Only instead of the heated flame, they are stormy and cold as they travel all over my face, taking in detail after detail. In many ways, this direct stare feels more intimate than what we just did. He's searching for something, I don't know what, and I don't think he does, either, but I don't feel that tender connection that should come after a person so freely gives themselves to another. I feel agitation and affliction. Uneasiness slips in, and I close my eyes so he can't see how he's making me feel.

Vulnerable.

He slips from my hold and yanks his pants, which are still gathered around his ankles, up as I fix my dress. The walls he's thrown up to close off his emotions make me feel self-conscious, and instead of basking in the afterglow and this new place we've found ourselves in, I feel foolish.

"Shit. What was I thinking?" His voice is low, monotone, and cool.

What?

Embarrassment. Humiliation. Horror. There isn't a single word to describe how he just made me feel, all of them crash down on me.

I hop off the table and smooth down my dress. "You weren't. Just like me."

He flinches and his eyes jerk to mine. "I didn't mean to say that aloud." But yet he doesn't apologize or retract it. Instead, he takes another step back, putting a distance between us that I thought had been removed.

I feel like this was a one-night stand with a stranger, and I don't like it or understand it. We went from this incredibly intimate moment to him shutting me out. Staring at him, another unwanted feeling takes over and I feel used—something I swore I'd never let happen to me—but a larger part of me is confused. It takes two to make these moments happen, and I know I wasn't in it alone.

Quietly, he watches me as he tucks his shirt back into his pants, zips, buttons them, and fastens his belt. Heat blooms against my chest and up my neck. I now know what's under his clothes, how he tastes and moves, and it's going to make this even harder for me. I know this isn't going anywhere, but I allowed my heart to invest even when I knew better. So, watching his mood and words turn icy is crushing.

Tearing my eyes away from his belt, I find my underwear on the floor and grab them, fisting them into a tight ball in my hand. Zach runs his hand through his hair and lets out a deep breath before pinning me with his remorseful eyes.

"Shelby."

"Don't, Zach." I put up a hand to stop him. I can't handle it if he makes another passive comment like *this shouldn't have happened* or *this was a mistake*. "It's fine." I mean, he did bring us down here. He admitted that he knew what was going to happen, or at least what I guess he was hoping would happen.

His brows pull low over his eyes as he regards me, and he tucks his hands into his pockets.

I never thought we were going to ride off into the sunset together, but I did think we'd moved past the split personalities. Just like that, he switched on me again, and my heart feels bruised. This reaction from him hurts, and my arms instinctively wrap around me. But then again, this is my fault. There's a reason why I have my rules and instead of following them, I broke two of them. I mixed business with pleasure and opened my heart.

"Thanks for the tasting." With that, I turn to head for the door before he sees through the mask of indifference I've put on.

"Shelby . . ." he says again, there's concern in his voice, but I shake my head and force myself to walk calmly up the steps. Nothing good will come from whatever I forced him to leave unsaid.

Ingredients:

1 bottle of pinot grigio
1 bottle of sparkling white wine (I used Prosecco)
1 cup of peach schnapps
1/2 cup of brandy
1/2 cup of simple syrup
2 large peaches sliced
1 large apple sliced

How to make:

Combine all ingredients in a large pitcher. Chill and serve over ice.

Chapter 14

let the chips fall

Zach

My feet pound a steady rhythm into the dirt keeping pace with not only the even in and out of my breaths, but the beat of my heart.

My heart.

In my chest and burning along with my muscles.

Running is my escape. My dad made me do it when I had too much energy built up, every coach made me do it to improve endurance and stamina, and now I make myself do it to stay in shape and relieve stress. It's free therapy, only this time it isn't working. Everything about this run was meant to clear my head and distract me from the mess I've found myself in, but it isn't helping. My mind keeps rewinding itself like a home movie and replaying all of the moments we had together.

Pushing myself harder, I lean forward as I sprint up the hill on the western side of the farm. Sweat is pouring off of me, I'm dying for some water, and all I can think about is her: the sounds she makes as my teeth bite down on her bottom lip, her chest as she arches into me to get closer, her feet as they run down the backs of my thighs to push me harder and faster.

Damn it.

I knew we'd be good together, but I didn't know we'd be *that* good.

Stopping in front of the manor, I bend over to catch my breath. The pulse of my blood is thundering through my body, and I hate that it might not be from the run but more because of her.

Her.

Shelby's face as she jumped off the table flashes behind my eyes, and my heart constricts. I'm disgusted with myself that I was so consumed with my own struggles and how I felt in that moment that I hurt her. I closed off to decompress my thoughts, and she misread me. Girls are easy, and girls are fun. I always enjoy my time with them, but I've never hesitated like I did with her. But then again, I shouldn't be surprised she evoked a different reaction from me, she always brings out the worst in me.

"Did it work?" Kyle startles me.

He's leaning in the doorway of the side entrance with his arms folded across his chest.

"Did what work?" I shake out my legs while wiping the sweat off my face.

Kyle looks at me as if I'm stupid. "You've been running for about an hour and a half, you've looped the property three times, that's twelve miles."

Shit, I didn't even realize. I was lost in my head and just kept running. Irritation leaks in—of course he's keeping track of me and knows exactly how long I've been gone.

"I haven't been out recently, and I needed to get it in," I say as I pass him and head for the stairs to go up to my side of the manor.

"Right," he draws out.

Stopping halfway up the flight, I turn and look at him. His expression is mixed with concern and annoyance. I understand why, I could royally screw this up for us, but this thing between her and me has nothing to do with the assignment. Therefore, none of it is his business.

"Don't you have some work to do?" I know I sound like a dick, but I have enough of my own shit going on in my head without having to listen to him.

"Sure do, boss." He scowls at me as he stalks off.

Taking the steps two at a time, I slam my bedroom door behind me, walk straight for the shower, and blast the water as hot as I can stand it.

I can't lie to myself and say that I never wanted it to happen, because deep down I did . . . and I knew it would. I think what I'm confused about is the lingering sensation of how good it felt, how good she felt, and how right it felt. I thought that if I had her, this crazy pull and want for her would subside. But, nope, five minutes after we were done, I was ready to go again. Still, even the next day, here I am, craving her even more.

Why couldn't I have stuck to the plan? That was all I needed to do. For two weeks. Piece of cake, but no, I couldn't even control myself for fourteen damn days. Now, I've hurt her feelings, and I don't know how to fix this.

Hot water pours down, relaxing my muscles, and the heat reminds me of the warmth from her body, her skin under my fingers, and the sound of her voice as she quietly pleaded for more.

Instead of finding some clarity, I'm flooded with memories, which add to my inability to focus, so I flip the water to cold to wash it away.

Why is this so hard? She's a girl. A girl who I kind of like, well maybe more than a little like, but I'm still not sure of at the same time. The only thing worse than hating her, would be falling in love with her.

Letting out a sigh, I think about the mountain of work I've let build up, and I find I'm pissed off. Pissed off at this situation, pissed off at her, and pissed off at myself.

I'm also pissed because there's no way I'll ever be able to walk by that table in the cellar and not think of her.

As I swallow a mouthful of scotch, I welcome the burn as it slides down my throat. It's almost distracting enough to calm the war inside my head. *Almost.*

"So, what's happening between you and Shelby?" James asks as he deals the next round of cards.

All afternoon, the guys and I have been playing poker in the library, and I've caught both Kyle and James randomly staring at me. I know the topic of Shelby is the elephant in the room, but I can't explain anything to them when I don't know myself. I haven't talked to her today, nor do I plan to. I have no idea what she did when she left me last night or what she's been doing since. I am pretty sure I'm the last person she wants to hear from, and this adds another layer to how I feel like shit for the way things ended. I'm not even sure what to say. "I'm sorry," doesn't seem strong enough . . . I don't know. I'm not ready.

"Nothing." I lie, refilling my glass.

"Come on, who do you think you're talking to?" he says, condescendingly. "I've known you for years, and I've never seen you so sour. This girl is under your skin, and you can't stand it."

The guys fall silent, and I glance over to Kyle, who's watching me. I know he agrees with James.

"She's here to do the assignment, and that's it. There's nothing going on, and she leaves in a few days." The topic of her makes me uncomfortable, and I want it to end.

"Well, I happen to think she's awesome. Gorgeous, too," he says, leaning back in his chair and throwing his arms behind his head.

"She's a she-devil," I mumble to myself, staring at my cards but not really looking at them.

"A what?" he asks.

"Never mind. Look, if you're worried about some unspoken bro-code, stop. She's all yours. I'm not interested." Another lie.

"Whatever you say," he drawls out and then grabs a praline, inhaling it in one bite.

All four of them start chuckling. I've officially heard enough.

Throwing down my cards, I push my chair back. "Today was a long day. I'm beat and I'm gonna turn in." I look at each of them.

"All right." James says around a mouthful of food as he stands and holds out his hand. "We're going to head out before the sun is up tomorrow, thanks for letting us crash for a few days." Guilt slips in a little as I clap him on the back. I know I'm being a bit of dick, I just can't deal.

"Anytime, man, you know it's always good to see you. Tell Lexi she better get her ass up here soon." He grins at me, and I move around the table to give Bryan and Jack a handshake and a back slap, too.

"Goes both ways," he says. "Feel free to get your ass down there to check on my sister." He pins me with a look of seriousness, and I return it. I know how much she means to him, and I'll always look out for her.

"I will, don't you worry. Just take care of yourself and come home soon."

"Always." He chuckles, winking at me.

Walking back into the tasting room, I put the scotch behind the bar where I keep a secret stash and set my glass in the sink. Michelle is watching me. Everyone is watching me. I wish they'd cut it out.

Needing some space to breathe, I decide to head to the cliff. When I pull up, the golf cart that I gave Shelby to use is already parked under the tree, and the irritation I was already feeling intensifies.

What is she doing here?

Not willing to let her have my spot, I climb out and hike the trail. At the top, I find her sitting near the edge with her knees pulled up to her chest. Her hair is blowing in the breeze, and even though her back is to me, she looks small and vulnerable. The anger I felt at her intrusion dissolves, and another emotion slips in. One I'm not ready to think about or recognize.

"Did you follow me?" She doesn't even turn around when she says it, but there is an edge to her tone.

"What? No." I retort as I take a seat next to her.

"Are you sure about that?"

"Shelby, you really need to get over yourself. This is my spot, remember? I showed it to you."

"Right." She drops her chin to her knees and stares out straight in front of her.

Leaning back on my elbows, I kick my legs out and cross them at the ankle. The sun has already set and there's only the remainder of the faint glow behind the western hills.

"What are you doing up here?" I ask her.

"Thinking," she answers quietly.

A breeze blows and her hair swirls around her head. I should ask her what she's thinking about, but something holds me back. Sitting next to her is an empty sauvignon blanc bottle and an empty glass, and I know this is my fault.

"About what?" I ask tentatively.

"About how I broke my rules and I'm trying to reconcile with myself."

I'm not sure what she means by rules, but I'm pretty certain they pertain to me.

"How much have you had to drink?"

Her eyes shift down to the bottle. "Not too much, but it was really good."

"'Was' being the operative word there." I tease her, but she frowns at the insinuation and turns to look at me.

"Do you regret what happened last night?" she asks, straight to the point.

"Of course not," I answer honestly. Regret definitely wouldn't be the word I'd use. Hell, it doesn't even come close to making the list, but what do make the list are: confusion, guilt, adoration. "I'm sorry that you left feeling like I did."

Biting the bottom of her lip, she wrinkles her forehead in thought. I'm not sure if she believes me or not, and not that I would blame her if she didn't, but I think she wants to.

"I don't understand you . . . at all." She exhales, sounding defeated.

When she spots the bottle of cabernet I'm holding, she takes it from my hands, pulls the cork, pours herself a very full glass and hands the bottle back.

"I know you don't. I'm sorry."

"Don't be sorry, tell me what your problem is." She pauses to take a sip of her wine and then continues without looking at me. "I don't understand what I did to make you not like me."

"Come on, you're being ridiculous. You know I like you."

"Do you?" The expression on her face is sad, and she looks so disappointed.

"Shelby, I said this before, and I'll say it again." Using my finger, I guide her chin so she sees me, the real me. "It's on me, not you." I nod my head once, hoping she'll agree with me.

"It isn't nice. Just make up your mind already. Either we're friends or we're not. Either you want me or you don't. This back and forth with your split personalities is giving me whiplash, and it makes me not trust you."

"You shouldn't trust me," I whisper.

She looks at me funnily, pulls her chin away, and then takes another sip of wine.

"But why not? I keep asking myself this. You haven't lied to me. In fact, I think you've been pretty up front with how you feel about me."

I shake my head at her, wishing I could change the conversation.

"I thought you were a player, and maybe you are, which is fine. I'm a big girl and I can handle it. Just tell me, are you playing me, Zach? Is this a game to you? Am I a game?"

Isn't that the million-dollar question? Part of me wonders if this has anything to do with me, but I can't look past my own feelings to even ask her about hers. Her words have shot arrows into me and a heavily weighted guilt slips in. No, I haven't flat out lied to her. I did, however, start this whole "relationship" with her on a rouse. Have I been playing her? In a way, I have been, but that game ended the second I pushed her up against the cottage door. Now, even more so after last night, it's all very real to me.

"No, Shelby. This is not a game to me. Nothing about what's happened between you and me is a game." I may have set up the plan strategically like a game, but when it comes to this winery and the success of it, I take everything seriously. My plan was for her to like the winery and write a good review. Not once did tricking her into sleeping with me come into play.

"Good, because I would hate to leave here hating you, Zach, especially when I just started liking you." She peeks over and gives me a small smile.

She likes me.

I never thought that she didn't, but hearing her say it loosens a knot that had been twisting tighter and tighter inside my chest all day.

Pushing away our career choices, pushing away the insecurities and guilt, pushing away our differences and the plan, it's here and now with her by my side that I decide I'm in.

Let the chips fall where they may.

Wrapping my arm around her shoulders, I pull her close and tuck her in next to me. She lets out a contented sigh and lays her head on my shoulder. Her hair tickles my face, and somewhere in the depth of me, the word "mine" sneaks in. I squeeze her tighter.

Calm settles over me as I come to this decision, and for the first time since she arrived, I let myself acknowledge how right she feels—how right *we* feel. The rational part of me says, "What are you doing?" But the part of me that feels connected to her? It says, "Consequences be damned." And besides, the plan worked. She loves the winery, she loves the wines—I can't see her saying anything bad about us, and she'll never know about it.

Ingredients:

1/2 cup of salted butter (1 stick)
1 1/2 cup light brown sugar
1/2 cup half and half
1 tablespoon vanilla
1 1/2 cup toasted pecans
parchment paper

How to make:

In a large ungreased skillet, heat pecans until toasted (they'll let off a delicious smell). Remove from heat.

In a large pot, stir and heat butter, sugar, half and half, and vanilla until a candy thermometer reads 240 degrees.

Remove from heat and let the liquid sit for five minutes. Add pecans, stir to make sure all pecans are coated.

Spoon out the pecan mixture onto parchment paper.

Let cool and serve.

Chapter 15

bees hate bananas

Shelby

"Hey."

I turn to see Zach slowing from a run to a walk as he comes up the driveway to the front of the cottage.

Pushing my sun hat back, I squint from the brightness of the mid-morning to see his face. There's a small smile that almost borders on shy. Timidness is not a trait I thought I'd ever see in him, but there it is. But then again, after the way he behaved the other night, approaching me with caution is probably in his best interest.

"How're you feeling today?" he asks, sucking in deep breaths, resting his hands on his hips.

The sun is shining off the dampness of his skin, causing it to glisten and my mouth to go dry. "Not too bad. Drank some juice, ate some toast, fixed me right up." I smile back as I stand and brush the dirt off me.

Last night, something shifted. I don't know what, but I know it did. The usual tension he carries around me slipped away when he wrapped his arm around me, making it feel as if a blanket of calmness descended upon us.

"Thanks for bringing me home, I'm sure I would have eventually found my way . . . but you know how it is." Warmth spreads up my cheeks as I think about how he'd held my hand again on the ride back and the kiss he left me with at my front door. His lips are addictive, I'm going to miss them when I'm gone.

"I do." He crosses his arms over his chest, and the muscles from his biceps to his trapezius tighten and bulge. His clothes are clinging nicely to him, which makes me want to peel them off and run my hands over his skin.

Waving a finger up and down his body, my smile turns into a laugh. "I see you're faring well this morning."

He looks down at his shirt, runs a hand across his chest, the other through his damp hair, and then looks back at me with an amused expression and vivid, clear eyes.

"Years of practice and strangely, I have a high tolerance for wine." He grins. It's nice to see him smiling and not scowling.

"I guess so." The light brushing of a hundred wings stir deep inside me at the possibility of having a great day with him today.

"What are you doing?" He looks at my gloved hands, the bush clippings, and at the basket sitting next to my feet.

"There are so many lavender bushes all around the property. I'm stealing some to take home with me in a few days, but don't tell the owner." I bat my eyelashes at him and he chuckles.

"What are you going to do with it?" he picks up the basket, pushes a few pieces around, and then rubs his fingers together before smelling them.

"Oh, I'm going to do all kinds of things: dry and hang some for decoration, make a satchel, tea bags, ice cream. I have big plans."

He looks around the cottage at the bushes lined up one after another. "Well, there's plenty here, so take as much as you want. The owner will never notice. From what I hear, he rarely comes down here anyway." He winks at me.

"Thanks, I appreciate that." My smile widens at his playfulness just as a breeze blows, lifting my hat. Grabbing a hold of it, I laugh.

"Let's go. I have a surprise for you," Zach says, taking the clippers from my hand and then removing my gloves for me. He sets them by the front door and then turns to make sure I'm following, which I am.

Taking my hand, he leads me around the cottage to the parked golf cart. We climb in and off we go. Squealing, I grab my hat and move it to my lap.

"Why do you always drive these things like they're on fire?"

"I have no idea what you're talking about." His eyes cut my way. They're mischievous, and one side of his mouth tips up. Stretching an arm across the back of the seat, his hand falls under my ponytail and on my neck. Warm fingers squeeze me gently, and I relish in the feel of him touching me.

"So, where are we going?"

"You'll see. I'm pretty sure you've seen most of the winery already, but this is something that we keep just for us."

"Oh, a secret place." I grin.

"You could say that." He smiles, and my heart squeezes at his handsome face.

It takes us ten minutes to reach the far northwestern corner of the property. The sun is warm, and the wind that whips by us as we head down the hill feels pleasant and welcome. I'm comfortable sitting here next to him, so comfortable a pang of sadness hits me at the thought of leaving in a few days. When we pull through several rows of apple, peach, and pecan trees, I spot the six bee houses, the sadness melts away, forgotten.

"You have an apiary?" I gasp as I take in the large cedar boxes that have hundreds of bees swarming around them.

"We do. And although I'm sure there's a bit of a mixture of some wildflower nectar in them, they are primarily filled with lavender honey."

"Lavender," I say on an exhale. "I love honey," I say more to myself, but Zach chuckles next to me.

"I know you do. You told me *repeatedly* the day we went to Asheville."

He's smiling and studying my very pleased reaction to this impromptu visit.

"After we opened OBA, Lexi bought a few hives for the orange trees on her property, but I haven't been down to see them yet."

"I know that, too." He shifts in his seat so he's angled toward me and then props his foot on the miniature dashboard. "She called and talked to my mother after she set up shop."

My eyebrows shoot straight up. "These bees are your mothers?"

He nods his head. "My mother loves these bees. She's had these hives for as long as I can remember. She harvests the honey herself three times a season and has made quite a little business of it. Tourists who've come in for a tasting and had a sample of the honey reach out to her year-round, requesting to purchase a jar."

"That's amazing. Where does she jar the honey?" Along with the lavender, I need to take some of this home, too.

"There's a separate kitchen in the back of the warehouse where we bottle wine. My father built it for her years ago." A look of pride graces his face. It's easy to see how much he loves his parents. He's lucky. Such a different childhood than my own.

I picture the barn when we walked through it, but nothing comes to mind. "Oh, I didn't notice it."

"I know. I didn't show it to you." He teases me, pulling on my ponytail.

"Why not?"

"I don't know. My parents are my people. I've learned over the years, the less I talk about them, the more they are mine. If I keep them out of the press, I get to keep them all to myself. It makes our relationship feel like it's more. It's mine, and the things that are most important to me, I don't like to share." His last few words slow as he looks at me.

I think about who my people are, and although I have Lexi, it's Meg who fits that role. She's my family and I didn't realize how lonely I was until the moment I met her.

"So, how do you know it's lavender honey?" I glance back to the bee boxes.

"I just do. Bees will travel up to six miles for nectar, and if you look at the lavender bushes all around the property, they are healthy with honey bees."

"Ha, yes, I did feel like I was competing with the bees for my clippings this morning."

His grin stretches, tipping up one side of his mouth. "Another way to tell is the color. Wildflower honey is typically darker because the nectar is taken from a wide variety of flowers, and the color can change based on what's blooming that year. Lavender honey is called a 'single flower' honey, it's lighter, and year after year the color doesn't really change."

Zach steps from the golf cart and rounds to the back before grabbing a duffel bag that's been sitting in the back. Unzipping the bag, he pulls out equipment needed to harvest honey, and understanding dawns on me what he's about to do. Running his hand through his hair, he pushes it off his face, and then picks up a white bee jumpsuit that has an attached hood veil.

"Have you ever been stung?" I'm a little nervous for him. I get that he knows what he's doing, but still . . . bees hurt.

He steps into it, slides his arms through the sleeves, and zips it up.

"Plenty of times." He laughs. "The trick is to scrape off the stinger, if you try to grab it you'll actually insert more venom into your body, and that is not good. Did you know that the venom has a banana like scent to it? Bees hate bananas, it's like their cue for attack. In fact, if you plan to come out here, don't eat a banana first, you're asking for trouble."

My face blanches. "Noted. No bananas."

Pulling the veil over his head, he smiles at me as he slips on a pair of long gloves.

"Don't they get angry when you take the honey?" I glance over, and suddenly, I don't feel like there are hundreds of bees. I feel like there are thousands. My heart rate picks up in concern for him.

"Nah, these bees are nice. I'm going to smoke them first so I can get to the honey, but you still can't be quick or jerky around them, you have to move slowly and calmly, otherwise you'll excite them. In general, I've never seen them be aggressive. If anything, I think they are grateful for all of the lavender. Unlike other lavender farms, we don't cut it all down for commercial use, we leave a lot wild just for them. Don't get me wrong, as I kid I was terrified of them, but I would lay over there under those trees and watch my mom work with them."

I look toward where he's pointing and find several apple trees that have had their lower branches cut off.

"Hang tight, I'll *be*, right back." He grabs some equipment, turns to walk off, and then spins back around grinning at me. "Pun intended."

I grin with him. Who is this funny guy and what happened to the scowling ass I met back at the Feeding America event?

Zach puffs the smoker and aims it at and around each beehive before setting it on the ground. I watch in fascination as he pulls the lid to the one closest to me and uses a large flat scraping device to cut me off a piece of the honeycomb and drop it into a bowl. After putting the lid back on, he grabs the smoker and starts walking toward me, smiling from ear to ear. If I hadn't had been falling for him before, the moment he hands me the bowl of beautiful golden honey would have done it for me.

"See, not that hard, and not one sting." He smiles as he strips off the gear.

"Well done, Mr. Wolff, and I have the perfect idea of snack to make with this, are you hungry?"

"As a matter of fact, I am," he says climbing in next to me.

Turning on the golf cart, he zips us back through the trees and heads for the cottage.

"I can't believe you just whipped this up," Zach says before taking another bite of his salad topped with grilled prosciutto wrapped peaches and a honey mustard vinaigrette. Most of lunch, we sat in silence as he devoured the food on his plate. His face was one of contented bliss.

"It really wasn't that hard, I only used one pan." I tease him. Just like the night he came over for the red wine tasting, we're back to sitting next to each other at the kitchen island.

"I know, but who thinks like this?" He looks at the grill pan behind me on the stove and then down to his salad.

"You should come to Charleston and taste the stuff Meg and I come up with. She's brilliant when it comes to perfecting the recipes." I tear off a piece of bread and smear some homemade honey butter on it.

His brows raise as his eyes collide with mine, and his chewing slows.

Cheese and crackers! I just invited him to Charleston!

I wasn't even thinking. The conversation has been so easy with him today that I'm talking to him as I would one of my friends. Yes, we slept together. Yes, he apologized for being a jerk. Yes, we have had an amazing morning together. But friends at the end of this? I'm not so sure.

Feeling a bit awkward, I drop my eyes from his and move to reach for my glass, but his hand grabs mine. His thumb gently swipes across the inside of my arm, and I freeze, knowing he's trying to get me to look at him, which I eventually do.

"Well, I happen to be a fan of your cooking." He gives me a reassuring smile, and my heart clenches at his willingness to smooth the awkwardness I'd created.

"Thank you," I whisper.

The compliment was heartfelt, but it doesn't go unnoticed that he didn't agree or disagree to visiting us in Charleston. Last night while we were sitting on the cliff edge, a part of me wondered if we would see each other after I went back to Charleston, if I even wanted us to, and well, I guess I got my answer. I know this is just an assignment and hook-ups happen all the time, but despite his split personalities, I do like him.

Hopping out of my chair, I scoop up the plates and then drop them into the sink. Zach moves over to the couch and settles in.

Brushing away the unwanted discomfiture, I change the conversation. "How did your winery get picked for this assignment?" I move to sit in the chair adjacent to the couch. He shifts and leans in my direction.

"I think there are several reasons. The main one being, one of the editors visited and loved our wines. Plus, we use only grapes that are grown here on the farm, a lot of wineries outsource, so that keeps us local and Southern for their special farm to table issue. Our property is beautiful, one of the larger ones in the area, and we keep it 'visitor ready' year-round. We also offer more in the way of private events, and open the manor and the cottage to overnight visitors."

There's pride in his voice as he talks about his winery. It's easy to see that running this place isn't something he does because it belonged to his family. He genuinely loves it.

"That makes sense to me. I love it here." I look around the quaint cottage and then out the French doors. Rows of grapevines bump up against the porch garden, and it's so pretty.

"And our wines are exceptional." He grins, pointing to my glass.

"Yes, they are." I raise it to him and then take a sip. His eyes fall to my mouth the same way they did two nights ago, and a heat swirls and burns from my chest through my legs.

"When do your parents get back?" I set the glass on the coffee table in front of us.

"August first. They will have officially been gone for one year." He leans forward, picks up my glass, and takes a sip. Why do I love it so much when he does this?

"That's a long time." I know he grew up here and worked the vineyard since he was a kid, but it's still kind of crazy to me that they just up and left right after he took over.

He puts the glass down, leans back, and props his right ankle on his left knee. "Went by quicker than you would think."

"Okay, my turn. Since you took me out and shared something with me today, and it's kind of relevant, I have one for you. Growing up, my nickname was Bee."

His brows raise. "Really?"

"Yep. Get it? Shel-bee. Not sure who first started calling me that, maybe my parents always planned for it to be my nickname, but I dropped it when my parents divorced." My father was the one who called me Bee the most. Just thinking about him has my back straightening and my fingers curling into fists.

Zach tilts his head as he studies me. "Sorry to hear about your parents, but that's a great nickname." He gives me a lopsided smile, effectively melting away most of my tension.

"It happens." I shrug.

"Still, divorce sucks." He lets out a breath and then runs his hand over his face and through his hair.

"Yes, it does." Or maybe it doesn't. Somewhere along the way, I started to believe that the actual divorce wasn't so much a big deal—just two people breaking up—it was everything that went along with it. Those things don't just happen, they ruin and destroy.

Out of nowhere, the brightness in his eyes dulls and shadows dip into his skin under his eyes. He drops his head forward and rubs the back of his neck.

"You just got a headache?" It comes across as a question, but I meant it more as a statement.

"Yeah, that's how quick they can set in." He lets out a sigh, stands and looks at me while shaking his head. "I'm sorry I can't stay longer, but I need to go."

I stand with him.

"I understand." I don't think there was anything in the food that could have triggered it, maybe he is dehydrated after his run.

"Thank you for lunch, Shelby. It was delicious," he says, pulling me against him before dropping his forehead into the crook of my neck. It's the same position he put himself in when we were in Asheville. Only this time, I don't feel awkward.

"Should I drive you back up?"

"No, thanks though. I'll be fine with the golf cart. It's only a few minutes." His arms slide fully around me, and warmth and sage washes over me as he hugs me tight.

"Dinner tomorrow night?" I ask him, suddenly sad that I won't see him until then.

"Yes, that sounds great. I'll bring the wine," he mumbles against my skin before shifting to brush his lips against to corner of mine. It's silly how cherished that one little move makes me feel.

Returning his forehead to rest against mine, I feel him squeeze his eyes shut as the muscles in his face contract and there's a slight shake to his head.

"All right, go. Get out of here," I push him away playfully and toward the door, feeling the loss of him immediately. "Thank you for sharing the bees with me."

He stops and turns to look at me. His eyes lock onto mine and an emotion passes through them. He blinks several times, nods his head, and then he's gone.

Ingredients:

1/4 cup of honey
1/4 cup of Apple Cider Vinegar
1 Tablespoon Dijon Mustard
1/2 cup of extra virgin olive oil
salt and pepper

How to make:

In a jar mix first four ingredients. Add salt and pepper to taste. Makes about one cup and is best served at room temperature.

Chapter 16

four wilted grapes

Zach

I've been sitting at my desk for hours catching up on work that I've put off over the last week and a half. My eyes are starting to blur and maybe I should take a break.

The intercom in my office buzzes, and I hit the button. "Yes, Michelle?"

She giggles at my tone. Between her and Kyle, I don't know what I would do if one of them decided to move on. They are the best employees.

"Thought you'd like to know that Shelby just left."

Out the window I find her heading toward the golf carts. Just the sight of her does something to me. The headaches, the article, our sales, my parents coming home, so much of it has been piling on, and ever since I decided to give in to this crazy attraction to her, all this work seems like not so much. It feels manageable, and I really like that feeling.

"Thanks," I mutter as I jump out of my chair and head for the private exit off my office.

"Shelby!" I yell as I jog toward her. She hears me, turns around, and a smile lights up her beautiful face.

Damn, gut clenching.

"Hey." In typical Shelby fashion, she has on little shorts and heels. Her hair is pulled into a ponytail, and her feet wobble as she walks across the circular drive. This time, I find it endearing instead of annoying, and I drink in every inch of her sexy as hell legs.

"You'd think that you would've learned by now," I say, pointing to her shoes.

"I know, but these are made of cork, and I couldn't help myself." She kicks one up to give me a closer look and smiles. Damn if she doesn't take my breath away. "How's the headache?" Her brow lowers and little wrinkles form as she studies my face.

Scrubbing my hand over my face and through my hair, my fingertips run over the usual suspects and there's no trace of any tenderness. "Gone, which is a good thing. I had a ton of paperwork and e-mails to catch up on today."

"Well, that's good to hear." Her face relaxes, and her smile returns. "I just invited Michelle to dinner, so she and Kyle will be there around six. Are you still coming?" She twists one foot back and forth in the dirt. She's nervous, and I think she's adorable.

"Of course. You're cooking, so I wouldn't miss it."

Hell, I don't even need the food. If she wants me there, just tell me when and where. At this point, I'm hanging on to every second I can get, because in a couple of days she'll go back to her life and I'll still be here in mine.

She blushes and lets out a pleased breath. "Good."

A bee flies by and she jumps closer to me, squealing. With her eyes bright, she laughs and tucks her hair behind her ear. My lungs constrict at the sight.

Damn.

"Would you like to come in?" I blurt out, pointing over my shoulder.

She glances toward the west wing door and curiosity lights up her face. "Sure. I haven't seen this side of the manor yet."

I can't help but chuckle at her enthusiasm as I reach for her hand and lace my fingers through hers.

"It's nothing special, I promise. This wing is mostly offices, and upstairs is my apartment."

"Your apartment?" She laughs. Stepping inside the hallway her eyes sweep over the photographs and articles framed on the walls. "You live in this giant, gorgeous castle/manor, and you call it an apartment."

"Well, it is." I give her hand a light squeeze. "You'll see, it's two bedrooms, two bathrooms, a kitchen, and a laundry room. Everything you would expect from an apartment."

"Hmm," she mumbles as we walk into my office. "Have you ever wanted to live anywhere else?" she asks as she passes by me and scans over every inch.

Looking around my office, I try to see what she's seeing. It looks pretty standard to me. Cherry wood furniture, one wall lined with built-in bookshelves, a fireplace with a flat-screen television over it, and a sitting area. I hate disorganization so it's kept clean.

Yep, this is me.

"Technically, I did. I lived off campus in college and then I had—well, have—a condo down in Tampa." She turns and faces me as I grab a football off my desk and lean against it.

"Oh, right. I forgot about you playing."

It's interesting to hear her say this. There are very few people who know me just as, "the wine guy." Everyone else associates me with football first and wine as a close second, even those in the wine industry. Given the status of our name associated with the winery, that I was a professional athlete in the public eye and who I kept company with, the media loved me. They followed me around for years reporting on every detail of my life, including my break up with Elaine, and had just started to ease up when that review posted last fall. Just thinking about that review makes me want to grit my teeth.

"What's this?" Shelby asks. I turn to see her pointing to the whiteboard on the wall.

"It's our homemade version of a seasonal tracker. We record daily starting and ending temperatures, weather patterns, rainfall inches, any problems that occur, et cetera. It helps us gauge how to the wines are growing from season to season, about when they'll be the perfect ripeness for picking, and what type of flavors we can expect to get."

"Wow, that's interesting. You don't put this into a spreadsheet or something?" She looks at me questioningly, and I laugh.

"I do, but during the season this larger, in-your-face view is best for all of us."

"Gotcha. Tell me more." She walks closer to the board and examines what we've filled in.

"The most important part of the wine is knowing the exact moment to pick the grapes, and tracking the weather affords us a preview of the harvest. For example, the hotter the season, the more shriveled the grapes, which makes the flavors stronger. On the flip side, if there's too much rain, the grapes will swell and the juice will be diluted."

"Has this ever happened to you?" She turns to face me.

"Yes, both have and knowing these things also helps us decide which varietals to blend."

She regards me silently and then picks up the board marker and draws a bee up in the corner.

"There, I've now contributed to the board." She smiles proudly to herself while putting the marker back.

I'm never washing it off.

Continuing her perusal, she inspects everything before stopping to look at my favorite framed awards. Behind the bar, we keep a portfolio of all the articles we can find where our winery or wines are reviewed. I call it my brag book, but really, it's a visual reminder to all of us that what we're working toward here is something great. Our wines have touched people enough that they felt the need to write about them, and ultimately that's what anyone who takes pride in their work wants. Recognition.

She stops again when she spots the magazine that is framed, propped up on a bookshelf, and has been my sole motivation for the last seven months.

"Tell me what happened for you to receive four wilted grapes. Your wines are so good I don't understand." She moves to sit in a chair in front of my desk, and I sit in the other next to her, stretching my legs out.

"After my parents left, Kyle and I decided to launch the wine club membership. I told you about it before." She nods. "Once it was kicked off, more and more locals in the area joined, and after a few months, we started brainstorming with ideas that would make returning each month fun."

"I think that's a great idea."

"We did, too. So, what we came up with first was for our

regulars to do a blind taste test. We bought some off the shelf mass-produced table wines and scrubbed off the label. During the tasting, we put up three glasses, and if the patron can guess which wine is not ours, they get to pick out two dessert truffles. The wine is so different from ours, people never guessed wrong."

"When you say different, you really mean bad, don't you?"

"Yeah, basic table wine is never really good, but it's done on purpose. We don't look to compare, we just want it to be fun.

"So, it was a busy night, Michelle and I were behind the bar, and I'm not sure how it happened, but there was a guy and girl who came in, had one glass of wine between the two of them, and left. They couldn't have been there longer than ten minutes. As I was clearing the glasses, I noticed the color of the wine and realized we'd given them the bad wine. It was a stupid error and one we couldn't fix because they left. Forty-eight hours later, I received a call from my father telling me about the review. Seems the magazine editor thought he deserved notification first, instead of me, and that set off a chain of bad events. This was the night before the Feeding America event. The review went live two weeks later, and I quote, 'How Mr. Wolff can with good conscious serve this wine to the general public, I'll never know. All it took was one taste, one horrible taste, to know I didn't need another.'"

"I read that review," she says sheepishly.

"My father reached out to the guy to explain what had happened, but the damage had been done. Our local business was still thriving, but the traffic flow from vacationers significantly dropped off. This last year our sales were the worst they've been in over a decade."

Unexpected things happen in business all the time. That's reality. Not every year can be perfect, and I don't expect every year to have high profitability. Still, that year was my first year—the year I wanted to prove to my family, myself, hell the world, that I wasn't just a football player. And now, explaining the article, I suddenly find that I care what she thinks, too.

"I take it your father wasn't too pleased." Her tone is softer, as if she knows she's broaching a subject she shouldn't.

"You could say that." Uncomfortableness is rolling off me, and I hate that she can see it. Feeling the need to cut the connection between us, I move over to the window. I don't want her to feel sorry for me. It is what it is, and I've spent the last seven months doing what needs to be done to repair the damage and move on.

"Zach." Warm hands land on my shoulders and lightly run down my arms, causing a slow burn to spread out of my chest. Her hands slip under my arms, wrap around my stomach, and she hugs me from behind.

The heat of her body presses against mine, and I let out a deep sigh. I know it's a stupid thought, but other than Kyle slapping me on the shoulder and telling me that we'll get through this, I haven't had anyone stop and have a moment with me. Not that I necessarily need a moment, and I certainly don't need a "therapy type session" where I unload how shitty it's been dealing with all of this, but I'm surprised how freeing it feels. And of all the people to give this to me, it's her, this girl who I was a complete asshole to, mistrusted, and now she's hugging me because she understands how hard this has been. I don't deserve this from her, but I realize my need to share just a little bit of the frustration I've felt outweighs the other ten-fold.

"Shelby," I whisper, her name sliding through me like a balm as it soothes places I didn't know were sore. Her arms loosen a little, and I turn to face her. Large blue eyes find mine and in this moment they feel like complete solace.

Her hands drop to my waist, and my stomach muscles clench at the contact. I love her hands on me and can't resist running my fingers up her arm to her shoulders.

Reaching the neckline of her shirt, I slip underneath it and push the sleeve off her shoulder, exposing just enough skin to make my mouth water. My fingers thread through her hair on the back of her head and her eyes flutter shut.

Damn, I love her skin, too.

Needing to taste her, my lips fall on the dip just above her collarbone. A barely audible sound rolls through her throat as she tips her head to the side to give me more access. I tighten my grip, locking her in place and link the fingers of my free hand through hers.

Needing to savor every inch of this girl, I kiss up her neck, over her jaw, and linger just at her lips. She leans further into my chest as she tries to get closer.

"You are so beautiful," I mumble against her lips. Her eyelashes sweep against my skin as she lowers them and her fingers curl in the fabric of my shirt.

Sliding my lips across hers, I kiss the corner of her mouth. She lets out a sigh, and I inhale it as my own with every nerve ending standing and waiting with great anticipation of my next move. This girl lights me up like no one has before. I don't understand it, but I'm embracing it.

"Why do I like kissing you so much?" Her voice vibrates against me, and I kiss her again instead of answering. The feeling is very mutual.

Warmth. Cinnamon rolls. Coffee. Delicious.

The flavor of her mouth reminds me of a lazy Saturday morning, and I want to fall into bed with her and get lost under the sheets. I want to sink every part of me into every part of her and stay there indefinitely. From my fingers into the smoothness of her skin, my mouth into the familiar warmth of hers, and I want to bury myself so deep into her there's no beginning and there's no end. I want to make her mine. All. Mine. And I want to do it now.

"Wanna go tour the upstairs?" My hand releases hers, slides across her hip, over her ass, and I pull her against me.

"Yes." Her voice is a whisper, but there's no hesitation. She's with me one hundred percent.

The door whips open and Kyle strides in. "So, I just got off the phone with—" Shelby squeals and jumps away from me.

Kyle freezes.

"Ah, sorry." He looks from me to her and then back to me, but he never retreats the way he came.

"No worries," I grind out, hoping he'll catch on to my tone and leave, but he doesn't.

Silence falls around the three of us, and it's Shelby who breaks it.

"Okay, right, I'll just go now." She sputters the words out as she runs her hands down her shirt and shorts to smooth them out. Her eyes flick to mine as she walks past Kyle, and a small smile tips the corner of her mouth.

Following her, I stop in the doorway and reach to hook my fingers over top the doorframe. Leaning forward, I take in the sight of her in my hallway and her long legs with those high-heeled shoes. It takes everything in me not to follow her and stay here with him.

"Hey, Shelby," I call out just before she reaches the west wing door.

"Yeah?" She spins around and walks backward.

My heart stutters at how impossibly beautiful she is.

I need more time with her.

This is a new feeling for me, one that I'm not ready to put any great thought into, I just know I need more. More of her.

"I'm really looking forward to seeing you later."

Ingredients:

1 tablespoon active dry yeast
1/2 cup of warm water
4 1/2 cups of all-purpose flour
4 large eggs
1/4 cup sugar
1 1/4 cup or 2.25 sticks of salted butter, softened
3/4 cup brown sugar, packed
2 tablespoons of cinnamon
4 ounces of cream cheese, softened
1 1/2 cups of confectioners sugar
1/2 teaspoon vanilla
1-2 tablespoons of milk

How to make:

Using a stand mixer (if you have one–if not then a large mixing bowl), combine warm water and yeast. Then add in only a half cup of the flour. Cover with plastic wrap and let stand in a warm place for about thirty minutes.

Next, add in the eggs, sugar, 1/2 cup of softened butter, salt, and remaining four cups of flour. Knead on medium speed, or by hand until smooth. Add more flour as needed to reduce the stickiness.

Turn the dough out onto a floured surface. Continue to knead if not completely smooth. In a greased bowl, place the dough, cover with plastic wrap or a towel, return it to the warm place, and let sit until it has doubled in size. Roughly 1.5 – 2 hours.

Once ready, put the dough back on the floured surface and roll out to a 12-inch by 18-inch rectangle. Melt 1/2 butter and brush over the entire surface of the dough. Mix together brown sugar and cinnamon and spread on top of the melted butter.

Roll up the dough. Using a very sharp knife or dental floss, slice the roll in half, then into quarters, and continue slicing until you have 12 equal size pieces. Place the rolls flat side down into a buttered 9 x 13 baking dish. Cover with plastic wrap and let it refrigerate overnight.

In the morning, remove and place on the counter for an hour to return to room temperature. Rolls will rise.

Preheat oven to 350 degrees. Bake for 30 minutes or until tops have browned.

To make the glaze, whip together cream cheese and butter until light and fluffy. Add confectioners sugar, vanilla, and just enough milk to make the mixture a glaze.

Once the rolls have cooled slightly, glaze and serve.

Chapter 17

this hit the spot

Shelby

It's just after five thirty when I lift the lid of the old cast iron Dutch oven I found in a cabinet and release the steam along with the delicious scent of chicken and herbs. Michelle had asked me to surprise her with a traditional Southern dish, which of course is chicken and dumplings. This was the first dish I taught myself how to make from old recorded Paula Dean show, and although I've tweaked the recipe some over the years to make it my own, it's still one of my favorites.

All afternoon the time has ticked by as slow as molasses, and I can't wait for six to get here. I didn't expect to run into Zach this morning, but from the moment I left him standing in his office, I've missed him. Knowing that I'm leaving in a few days makes me apprehensive; I'd like to spend as much time with him as I can, which makes me more annoyed that we got interrupted earlier in his office.

It was actually surprising to see how many framed football

articles, awards, and photos of him in football gear were around the room. I'm sure some were left behind by his father, but the space spoke to his years of love and dedication to football as much as it did for the winery.

I had never known anyone who played football on the level he did. Yes, Lexi's brother played in college, but the NFL is different. So many dream of making it to the professional level, but only the best of the best do. I know an injury ended his career, but didn't know what happened. When I searched him, I scrolled through the images and scanned article titles without opening any of them.

Putting the lid back on the pot, I pour myself a glass of wine, grab my laptop, and narrow the search to "Zach Wolff", "football", and "injury". Thousands of results pop up on the screen. I know all of these articles about him are public knowledge, but in a way, I feel like I'm eavesdropping into his life. It's like reading someone's diary and learning about their past without asking them first.

Clicking over to the images, I take in every detail of him in his football prime. When I looked him up last week, I hated the sight of him, but now, these photos get my blood pumping in an entirely different way. It's like a chronicle of his life from college through his time in the NFL. Practices, game days, draft day, events, they're all there for people to view.

In most of the photos, his look is serious, severe, but in the few of him smiling, it's breathtaking.

Flipping through the images, I stop on one of him on the field being loaded onto a stretcher. My breath catches because the scene looks frightening, and I imagine it's every player's worst fear. There are at least fifteen people around him, and the ambulance is parked next to him on the field. The fans in the background are standing, and every face is frozen in horror.

What happened to you?

Switching back to the web, the title to the third listing reads: Crazy collision results in a career-ending concussion for Tampa's defensive linebacker Zachary Wolff.

My stomach starts to ache as I scan the article, and even though I know he's alive and well, it doesn't stop the anxiety from sneaking in and swirling through me. I knew he stopped playing because of an injury, but after reading this, the cause of the constant headaches make sense.

Hovering over the link, I debate on watching the YouTube clip or not. Seeing someone you care for get hurt is hard enough, but knowing that it's going to be life changing makes it that much more excruciating. Feeling the need to understand him more, I click play. The entire clip is only twenty-five seconds, but that's all it takes.

The quarterback lines up for Seattle, he calls the play, and then steps back to fire the ball. The players set into motion, each doing their part, and Zach takes off after an opposing player running down the sideline. Right before he reaches him a second player from Seattle dives through the air to tackle him, grabbing one foot causing him to trip just as the other turns to catch the ball. As the opposing player comes down the momentum of Zach and the other player becomes detrimental. A helmet-to-helmet crash which results in both players being flat on their back.

As the instant replay fires up on the Jumbotron, the gasp that comes from the sixty-thousand stadium is so loud, it's as if they could have sucked the air right out. The Skycam is almost directly over the tackle, making everyone feel as if they were a part of it. The crack of their heads is so loud it echoes through my computer speakers.

Tears swell in my eyes, and my heart races as I hit play and watch it again. I want it to last longer so I can keep watching. What happens next? Does the other player get up? Is there any movement from Zach at all? Not knowing has left me panicky, and I close my eyes to try to block the computer and calm down. At least he turned out all right . . . mostly.

Two knocks hit the front door and then it flies open. Zach strolls in, kicks the door shut behind him, and smiles when he sees me. Relief washes over me, and I let out a sigh. Running my eyes over the length of him, I look for anything that might be wrong, but he looks fine.

"What's wrong?" he asks, the smile dropping from his face. I don't say anything, and his attention shifts from me to the computer screen in front of me. He tenses.

"Why are you watching this?" His eyes still on the screen, his voice deep and laced with emotion.

"I thought it would be fun to look you up on the Internet, I didn't know I'd be finding something like this." My voice is quiet, and I'm certain he hears the guilt in it. Guilt because I invaded his privacy and guilt because one glance at the screen and he's reliving this horrible moment in his mind.

"Well, now you know." Slowly, he reaches past me and closes the lid of my laptop. His crystal blue eyes find mine, grief lingering on the edges.

"Not really, will you tell me?" I scoot over and pat the spot on the couch next to me, but he doesn't sit, he just shrugs.

"Not much to tell, but sure . . . later. Kyle and Michelle aren't far behind me and should be here soon."

"Okay."

He moves into the kitchen, steps around the island, and puts down a couple bottles of wine and a lavender plant.

"What's the plant for?" I pull it in front of me and breathe in the calming fresh scent.

"It's for you. I know you want to take some lavender home, so this is my way of giving you flowers tonight."

"Wow, Mr. Wolff, I'm impressed. Thank you."

He shoves his hands into the pockets of his jeans and gives me a small smile.

I'm pretty sure Zach will always have this air of confident authority surrounding him, he can't help it, it's who he is. Then, there are these scattered moments where he cuts pieces of honey out of a bee house and brings me a flowering plant that shows another side to him. It's the loyal and thoughtful side that I'm certain only those close to him see. It's a side of him that's so different from the one he originally gave me, that in many ways I feel like I'm with someone else.

Moving over to the pot he lifts the lid and peeks inside. "Whatever you are cooking smells amazing."

"Thanks, it should be ready in another thirty minutes. How about you help me put out some appetizers?"

He returns the lid and throws me a crooked grin. "If by put out you mean 'eat it all', then yes, I'd love to help you."

Laughing, he reaches for me and wraps me up in his arms. Without heels on, my head slides right under his chin—the perfect fit.

"I'm glad you came a few minutes early," I murmur into his shirt while inhaling fresh laundry and the outdoors.

"Me, too." His arms tighten around me. "I haven't stopped thinking about you all day."

Heat creeps into my cheeks, and when I tilt my head back to look at him. He smiles and my heart trips over itself as his blue eyes sparkle at me adoringly. Lowering his head, he kisses the corner of my mouth with his warm lips. It's such a simple move, but it feels so right.

Another knock comes from the door, and both of us turn to look at it. Zach lets out a sigh and brushes his lips against my forehead before he releases me.

I give my plate a tiny nudge away from me and lean back in my chair. The meal turned out to be perfect, and I couldn't have asked for a better night.

Originally, I planned for us to eat at the kitchen table, but once we opened the French doors to the back patio, there was no way we could stay inside. The sun had lowered behind the western side of the cottage leaving us shaded and under the most gorgeous clear sky. There wasn't a trace of humidity in the air, just the scent of the vines that surround us.

"Shelby, hats off to you. This was one of the best meals I've had in so long," Kyle says as he stretches his legs out and rubs his hand over his stomach.

"I agree." Michelle nods at Kyle and then turns back to me. "When I asked you to make a classic, this hit the spot, all the way down to the pole beans."

I glance at the now empty dish that had held the pole beans and then lean forward and whisper excitedly.

"This little garden back here has surprised me more than once. I can't believe you actually have pole beans growing back here. I felt like I struck gold when I saw them last week."

Zach grins at me after taking another sip of his wine. "Only seems appropriate we have beans that grow on a vine versus a bush, don't you agree?"

"I do, and I couldn't have said it better. I grew up eating slow-cooked pole beans, so that's why I made them tonight." I also baked cornbread. That dish is empty as well.

Crossing my legs, my foot bumps into the back of Zach's calf under the table, and he reaches for it to hold it in place. He doesn't outwardly acknowledge that I'm touching him, but his fingers trace over the arch of my foot and the anklebone. Tingles race up my leg, and I love it.

"Michelle, I hate to break it to you, but your job responsibilities are going to be expanding when she leaves." Kyle shoots her a mischievous grin.

My heart sinks and Zach's fingers stop their slow circle. Not once have we mentioned my leaving.

"What do you mean?" She shifts in her chair to face him, and he crosses his arms over his chest.

"You're going to have to cook more," he says, matter-of-factly.

Zach and I both laugh, but Michelle glares at him as if he's lost his mind.

"It's funny, I have no idea what we ate before you got here," Zach says to me as he releases my foot, leans back, and stretches his arm until it rests across the back of my chair. The movement doesn't go unnoticed by the two of them, and a blush creeps up into my cheeks. Zach lightly pulls my hair and winks at me.

"I can tell you what we ate—steak and chicken off the grill. I cook for the two of you at least five nights a week."

Zach starts chuckling. "Oh yeah, that's right! Maybe *your* job responsibilities are changing then."

Kyle huffs but smiles back.

"What I can't tear my eyes off is that dessert over there. Did you get some ice cream, too?" Michelle asks.

All four of us glance at the pie.

"I might have, but it isn't needed for this one."

"Banana pudding is hands down one of my favorites," Zach chimes in.

"You should try Lexi's pecan pie, it's to die for. Meg and I don't even attempt to make it, we buy them from her and stock them at the restaurant."

"She ships pies?" he asks, his fingers falling under the weight of my hair and onto the back of my neck.

"Oh, yeah. How do you not know this? She's world famous for her pies."

"I know she is the for fillings, I guess I've never thought about her shipping whole pies. We'll have to stock them here, too."

"What's so good about them?" Michelle asks, watching us.

"Oh, just about everything. Her pecan pie is lick-the-plate-in-public worthy."

Everyone laughs, and I blink quickly, trying to take in as many details that I can.

"Do you like owning a restaurant?" This comes from Michelle, but the both guys look at me, waiting for my answer.

"I do, but it's really my best friend Meg's. She owns the majority of it and pours endless amounts of blood, sweat, and tears into making it what it is today. All I've ever wanted is to work for Food Network." Zach's fingers dip under the edge of my shirt at my neck, I love that he's found some way all night to be touching me.

"Isn't that what you're doing now?" she asks, tilting her head.

"Yes, I guess so. This is more of a one-time assignment. Currently, I'm a freelance writer for them, but in the perfect world, where dreams come true, I'd like to work for them permanently.

I've always wanted my own show." Hesitating, I look away from them and drain my glass. Other than Meg and Lexi, no one else knows about these dreams or what I've been doing to make them happen. "Actually, I recently interviewed for a host position on a new show. Obviously it's not my own, but it would be one foot in the door and one step closer to that dream. I'm a candidate in the final round and waiting to hear from them."

Michelle claps her hands together. "You would be perfect on television!"

"Thank you." I grin at her.

"Is this job in Charleston?" Zach asks.

I turn to face him and instead of finding his expression curious or excited for me, he's frowning. "No, it's in New York City."

"So, you'd be moving there?" His hand slides off my neck, leaving traces of an imprint, and he returns it to his lap.

"Yes, if I got the job."

The table falls silent, all three of us staring at Zach. Reaching for his glass, he takes a swallow, clears his throat and smiles at me. "Well, good luck then."

Why is it that his good luck feels more like he's saying goodbye? And why does this leave this me feeling oddly unsettled? This would be a huge step toward my dream job, one that no one is getting in the way of.

Plastering on my fakest smile, I tell him thanks and turn to Michelle. "What about you? What dreams do you have?"

Taking a deep breath, she glances over to Zach, Kyle, and then back to me.

"Well, since Zach took over, I've learned a lot more about the wines and what it takes to make them. I don't see myself ever leaving the area, and I love it here, so I'd like to become a winemaker. I've found different colleges and organizations that offer online classes in enology and viticulture, and I'm registered to start in the fall."

Zach sits straight, and pulls his hand from the glass to his lap. "Michelle, that's fantastic," he praises, making her visibly relax. Not only is it easy to see how she wants his approval and support but also it's easy to see he's pleased and proud of her. "I didn't know this was something you wanted to do."

"I like it here, and I want to be more than just the girl who pours wine," she says earnestly.

Leaning forward, Zach puts his elbows on the table. "Come talk to me next Monday, once this magazine project is over. We can brainstorm about a career path for you and how I can help."

"I'd appreciate that, a lot. Thank you." She reaches for her wine glass to try to hide her enthusiasm, but she's so happy, she's glowing.

"Wait!" Kyle waves his hands in the air. "You once told me that you dreamed of living somewhere different. Moving to a big city." Whereas Zach is excited over Michelle's confession, Kyle is clearly confused.

"Yeah, I do have that dream, but doesn't everyone?" She looks to me for confirmation, and I shrug.

"I'd love to live in a big city: New York City, Seattle, or even Chicago." I've always said this. Doesn't mean I will, but cities are amazing.

"See," she says, challenging him.

"But . . ." He pinches his lips and looks around the table at the three of us before slouching back in his chair and running his hand through his hair.

"But what?" she asks.

He lets out a deep sigh and lifts his eyes to hers.

"All this time." He shakes his head, and the two of them share a moment filled with a heaviness of misunderstanding and opportunity.

Time stalls as Zach watches them and I watch Zach, who has a small, satisfied smile on his face. Seems I was right, he suspected their hidden interest in each other, too.

Lifting my wine glass, I take a sip. Kyle sees the movement and he lets out a deep breath.

"I think . . ." He looks between each of us before directing the rest of his statement to Michelle. "We need to go." Abruptly, he stands and reaches for Michelle's hand to pull her with him. "Thank you, Shelby, for dinner. It was delicious."

"You're welcome, I'm glad you guys enjoyed it."

Michelle gives me a small wave and an apologetic smile over her shoulder as she scrambles to keep up with Kyle. Without a word, they head out the side gate and disappear into the night.

Ingredients:

1 whole chicken, cut up
1 cup of flour
1 egg
1 stalk of celery, sliced
1 medium sized onion, diced
2 tablespoons of salt
Parsley

How to make:

Stew chicken three hours until shreds a part by putting it in a dutch oven and covering it with water. Add salt to the water, onion, and celery. Add one tablespoon of chopped parsley to the broth.

Remove chicken from broth and allow to cool. Debone meat.

To make the dumplings, in a bowl mix the egg and the flour, add drops of water until dough forms a ball. On a well-floured surface, roll out the dough and cut into squares. Drop the squares into the broth and cook for approximately 30 minutes.

When dumplings are done, add chicken and serve.

(Optional, sliced carrots are a nice addition, too.)

Chapter 18

bastard called an audible

Zach

Once again, Shelby outdid herself. I would never tell my mother this, but Shelby's food is some of the best I've ever eaten. And that banana pudding pie, wow, I don't even think she realizes how good her food is.

"Thank you for helping me clean up," she says, loading the last of the dishes in the dishwasher.

"Of course. You cook; I clean. Those were my mother's rules, and they kind of stuck." I shut off the faucet to the sink and wipe my hands dry.

She smiles appreciatively and then holds up another bottle. "Do you want some more?"

"Sure." I pull two new glasses and watch as she pulls the cork and pours the wine before we move to the couch. I wait for her to sit first, and after she's tucked into the corner by the armrest, I take a seat right next to her. After pulling her feet onto my lap, I unfasten the tiny buckle on the cork heels she likes so much. Her shoes drop to the floor, she wiggles her toes, and groans as I begin massaging the cramps out of them.

"Have you been wearing these all day?" There are strap lines indented in her skin.

"Yep. Before I saw you at the manor this morning I ran to the grocery store to get a few things I needed for dinner. All I did was change clothes before everyone got here."

"I don't know how you do it, there's no way I could walk around in shoes like these for eight to ten hours a day."

She giggles. "Meg, Lexi, and I once ran a stiletto run in New York City."

"Why?" Just the thought is appalling, then again, I look at and admire her spectacular legs. Rocking heels all day has left them toned and solid.

"Why not? The race raises money for ovarian cancer, and we made it a girl's weekend."

"At least it was for a good cause." I grin at her.

Dragging my thumb across the arch of her foot, she sinks farther into the couch. As I continue to press into her feet and up her calves, her head falls to my shoulder, and she lets out a low hum every so often on a tender spot.

"When I leave here, I'm gonna have to go on a diet. I'm so full." She rubs her stomach, looking as if she wants to curl up and go to sleep.

My mind sticks on her words *leave here,* I didn't know she was looking to move away from Charleston, but then again, I guess I don't really know much about her at all.

"How do you do a diet working in the food industry? You cook food all day long." I tickle the bottom of one foot, which makes her giggle and jerk her leg, giving me the perfect view up the skirt of her dress.

"Not nice." Her blue eyes shine at me knowingly, but she slowly returns her leg to my lap. Much to my pleasure, her dress stays pushed back. It's too tempting not to touch, so I run my hand up and down her leg once. She doesn't stop me, and she doesn't take her eyes from mine.

"We do cook all day, but I'm not eating it. Sure we taste as we go, but we don't eat big meals, and we never have food lying around like I've had here."

"Well, I second that. We usually don't have food like yours lying around, either. We've really enjoyed it."

"Thank you, that means a lot," she whispers.

I nod and look at her feet, admiring her pink painted toenails.

"Tell me about the video. What happened to you that day?" She props her elbow up on the back of the couch and leans her head against her hand to watch me.

"Most of the game was played under the shadow of the clouds, and the clock was ticking down on the third quarter. The quarterback from the other team lined up behind his center and shifted to lean on his left leg and wiggle his fingers. He scanned the defensive line, and his eyes narrowed at how we were aligned with his team, and he called out, 'Set!' It was the way he said it, there was a slight dip in his voice, and if I hadn't been paying attention, I would have missed it because it was that quick. His linemen dropped into their stances, and all of his teammates gave a slight turn of their head to hear the call—a call they should have already known from the huddle. That was when I knew. The bastard was calling an audible.

"Everyone has a tell, and I'm good at recognizing them. Hell, the guys have been joking around with me for years that I should head to Vegas and clean house, but gambling isn't my thing.

Anyway, I knew what was happening, so I kept my eyes on their quarterback, and I watched every breath he took, and every twitch he made.

"'Green twenty-two,' he called out, shifting his weight over and slightly back to the left leg, freeing his anchor foot. 'Green sixteen,' his elbows lifted out from his rib cage opening his frame. When he remained tight, they ran the ball up the middle. When he was loose, he was planning for a first down pass. But this, the open frame, it only means one thing and adrenaline spiked through me. 'Hut hut,' he called, rocked forward on his toes, and quickly reached for the ball. He was going to sprint backward and pass the ball. And not just any pass . . . Hail Mary style."

"Isn't that risky?"

"It is, but they didn't really have another choice at that point. Prior to this play, he'd attempted four other passes to the same running back, but they were desperate to put some points on the board."

"So, you guys were winning?"

"We were."

"What happened next?"

"I watched him and went after the guy I figured he would most likely pass to. I took off, and just as I was closing in on him, he turned and looked for the ball. I remember feeling the guy coming up behind me, but that's it. What you see in the video, I don't remember. I woke in the hospital nine days later."

A sharp inhale comes from Shelby, and I leave the game in my head and focus on her. Wide eyes meet mine, and I briefly wonder what it would have been like to wake from that coma to her beautiful face.

"The theory is that I already had a slight concussion going into the play, making this one amplified times ten."

"You didn't know you had a concussion?" She frowns at me, concern etched across her face.

"I suspected, but when you're in the game, headaches can come from a lot of things, and there's just no time to think about them. Plus, we're conditioned to suck it up and play through it. The phrase, 'Are you injured, or are you hurt?' is thrown around a lot, and when you're being paid to perform, this is the law when it comes to pain. On average, there are one and a half concussions per NFL game. They happen, we deal with them."

"Really? I'm not sure how I feel about that. Aren't there long-term problems with concussions?" She frowns.

"There are, and unfortunately, a lot of players are suffering long-term consequences because of them. The league has tightened its view on concussions, and they are taken a lot more seriously now than they were even five years ago. I'm still experiencing what they call Post-Concussion Syndrome, which is nothing compared to what some other ex-players deal with. The severity of the injury could have been much worse considering the impact. I do have some attention difficulties, but mostly I suffer from migraines. They told me that the symptoms would be gone by now, but they aren't. I haven't figured out what sets them off, but damn if they aren't debilitating."

"How often do you get them?" She pushes her hair off her face and then stretches her arm out reaching for my hand.

"At least once a week, sometimes twice. You've seen two since you've been here, plus I had one the day you arrived." I weave my fingers in between hers and rub the inside palm of her hand with my thumb.

Her frown deepens. "I'm sorry."

"Thanks, I thought I'd have a much longer career than I did. I really love the game." And I do. People play for a lot of different reasons, but me, I loved everything about it: from being a part of a team, the strategy, even the travel. And there's nothing like winning.

"But you love this, too, right?" she asks, curling her fingers around mine.

"I do. And I was always set on buying my dad out and taking over, but what guy doesn't have dreams about winning the Super Bowl and the hall of fame? Especially when you get as far into the game as I did."

She gives me a small smile and nods her head in understanding.

"What about you, has your dream always been to cook?"

"Yes, but a little bit more than that. I told you when I was a kid that I watched a lot of the Food Network Channel, but like I mentioned at dinner, my dream has always been to have my own show." She breaks eye contact with me like this admission is hard to say.

"So, you really want to be on television?" I don't know why this surprises me, it shouldn't. She's gorgeous, everyone loves her, and she makes amazing food. Maybe it's the thought of having to share her with the world, but that would be dumb because she isn't mine to share.

"Yes, but not just any television, I've always wanted to be a part of the Food Network family. More than you can even imagine. I was a communications major in college and then I went to culinary school. I've set myself on this path to build a strong case for myself. That's why this project is just as important to me as it is to you. It's just one more thing that puts me one step closer."

I didn't think it was possible for her to get any sexier, but I was wrong. Part of me is torn loathing the idea of her being a workaholic, but the other part of me admires her dedication to what she ultimately wants. Listening to her and hearing the drive in her voice . . . such a huge turn on.

"Tell me about where you came from. Tell me about your parents."

She pulls her hand from mine and shifts so she's sitting a little taller. Walls just went up around her, as she tries to throw off an air of indifference.

"There isn't much to tell," she shrugs, but I can tell there is.. "I grew up in a small town in South Carolina where traditions and stereotypes seem to be one in the same."

"What do you mean?" I resume rubbing her feet, and her shoulders drop just a little.

"Well, every Sunday, we showed our faces at church like the happy little family, but Monday through Saturday the whole town knew my father was having an affair with my mother's best friend. Who, by the way, would also attend Sunday service and kiss my mother on the cheek in greeting."

"You're joking?" I frown. "Didn't your mother know?"

"I don't know. She claimed she didn't, but looking back, I don't see how that's possible. She had to have known. But where my mom turned a blind eye, the husband of the woman didn't approve. The whole mess got pretty ugly, and in the end, my father claimed he only married my mother to get closer to my grandfather, who was the town mayor, and that he never wanted kids."

I try to imagine what it would be like to hear my own father say this, and I can't. Maybe this drive in her comes from a deeper place than I thought.

"What an asshole." Fury slides into my veins at the life she was raised in.

"Yep. My grandfather didn't take too lightly to the situation, either. He fired my father, who was the police chief, and ruined any possibility of a political career for him. My father divorced my mother, my mother's perfect little Southern stepford life imploded, and she ended up having to find a job. Needless to say, we were never the same."

"How old were you?"

"Thirteen." She looks away from me and reaches for her wine glass, clearly trying to shut down the conversation.

"I'm sorry." It's all I really know to say.

"Don't be. It's shaped me into who I am, but I don't think that's a bad thing. What I've learned and what I value above all in people are character and honesty. She was fake, he was fake, they used each other, and he lied. I have no place in my life—ever—for any of that."

Unease rushes under my skin, and a cold sweat breaks out on my back. I should tell her, now would be the perfect time to clear the air and admit to what we've been doing, but I don't think she'll respond kindly to it. It doesn't matter that I've told her and shown her more than I ever have another woman, she'll still see 'our plan' as betrayal. Just knowing that I have the potential to hurt her, I feel like I've betrayed myself.

Pushing her feet off my lap, I get up and grab our glasses to refill them. Oblivious to my internal panic, she smiles at me and then follows me into the kitchen. I drag my hand over my face before I squeeze the back of my neck and shake off the guilt.

Three days.

Three days until her stay here is over, and then maybe one day, we can look back on this and laugh about my stupid plan.

Handing over her wine glass, I scan her from head to toe as she walks over to the window and looks out at the night sky. She's shorter without the shoes on, her hair is slightly messy from running her hand through it, and she looks like a fantasy come true in this dress.

"Why do you wear dresses all the time?" I ask, stepping up behind her. This dress looks like a men's dress shirt, and I let my mind believe it's one of mine.

"Why not?" She glances over her shoulder at me and smiles.

My fingers slip under the edge and graze up the outsides of her thighs. Goosebumps trail across her skin. I love that she continually reacts this way to me.

"Don't act like you don't love them. I know you do, more than once I've caught you staring."

"Not denying that, I really do," I say, sweeping her hair back off her shoulder and then taking the wine glass from her hand. I set both of the glasses down and wrap my arms around her so I can run my nose up the column of her neck. Her head tilts to the side, and she lets out a sigh as my lips pepper kisses over her skin, tasting, sucking, memorizing. Dragging my teeth along her jaw, I turn her chin and sink into the warmth of her mouth.

What is it about kissing her that makes me delirious?

Twisting in my arms, she steps closer, and I tangle one hand in her hair and rest the other on her lower back, pulling so there's no room between us. Fervor burns through my veins. She's a perfect fit against me, and I devour her mouth as if it's the last time I'll ever get to taste it. Shelby matches my intensity, and her fingers manage to become restless as she finds the top button on my shirt.

I pull back—not to stop her because heaven knows I don't want to stop. It's the urge to see her eyes full of the heat I know . . . *hope* will be there.

I'm not disappointed. Her eyes are slightly glazed and wild and her chest is rising up against the fabric of her dress, and I ache to see her flawless skin. Pushing her back against the wall, I'm enthralled with the way the moonlight makes her glow.

When I slip my finger around the top button of her dress, she doesn't stop me. I pop it open and then slowly trail one finger down her skin to the next. She shivers even though her skin is warm, and I love that I know she tastes like vanilla and honey. One by one, the buttons open until I reach the bottom, revealing a sliver of her skin peeking out straight down the middle. Softly, my hand flattens across her chest and slides down the middle, between her breasts, over her stomach, and grazes the top edge of her panties before sliding over her hipbone and up the bumps of her spine. When I reach the clasp to her bra, I snap it open and am reminded why I love that she wears strapless bras, too.

With her standing before me like a goddess of the night, her lips swollen, her hair wild, and sexy, any willpower that I had left against her is eviscerated. No one has ever left me feeling like this. I'm always the one in control. I have always set the pace, giving and taking exactly the way I want to. Yet, here with her, I feel completely out of my element. It isn't that my confidence is gone, it's that she makes me want to drop to my knees and beg.

"Zach." Hearing my name whispered from her lips causes my chest to constrict and everything south of my waist to tighten.

My eyes find hers, they're dark and sultry and my heart rate picks up. "Yeah?"

"More." She breathes out with an assertiveness that has me slipping my hands inside the dress. They slide up her stomach and palm her breasts. Her head tips back and hits the wall as she arches her back, pushing into me and letting out a low moan. Moving my hands outward, I slide her dress off her shoulders and then dip my head back to her skin.

My tongue runs over the swell of her breasts and finally, when she lets out an impatient noise, I latch on while massaging the other. I could taste her from head to toe every day for the rest of my life and it would never be enough. Feeling her hands on my shirt, she resumes unbuttoning it as my fingers dip under the edge of lace resting on her hipbone.

Cold air hits my skin as she drags my shirt off, and I slip my hands around the backs of her thighs and lift her against me. When her legs wrap around my hips, I almost stumble from how good she feels surrounding me. Her warm hands glide across my shoulders, and sink into the back of my hair as I pin her against the wall and crash my mouth against hers.

"Stay with me tonight," she mumbles against my lips, and I chuckle.

"I wasn't planning on leaving." I press my hips against her and tighten my grip on her ass so she knows exactly how I want this night to go.

"Good." She lets out a soft groan.

Damn this girl.

Without breaking the kiss, I turn and carry her to her bedroom and then drop her on the bed. She lands and looks a little wild with bright eyes, her hair messed up, and her lips swollen and damp from our kisses. I watch her as I toe off my shoes and remove the rest of my clothes before crawling onto the bed after her. She scoots away from me with a come-and-get-me smile. When I wrap my fingers under the piece of lace that's hiding what I most desperately want, she stops playing games and lets me pull the fabric down her legs.

Never in my life have I seen anything as perfect as she is. I knew she had an awesome body, and for almost two weeks, I've imagined what she would look like bare, but nothing prepared me for this.

"You're so beautiful." I run my palm up her leg, needing to touch her. The muscles in her stomach tighten, and her fingers curl into the sheets, but she never breaks eye contact with me.

"You're not so bad yourself," she teases. "Come here." She pulls on my arm.

Instead of moving up her body, I move down, wanting to take my time exploring every dip, and every curve, everywhere.

Hours pass as Shelby and I forget about who we are, what we're doing, when she's leaving, and what this might mean. We lose ourselves in the feel of each of other, and I block the emotions that make me feel as if I'm losing myself to her. I focus on how, with each exhale, her breath rushes out, and my name is whispered past her lips and against my skin. It's the sexiest sound I've ever heard.

Ingredients:

1 box of instant vanilla pudding
1 can of sweetened condensed milk
2 cups of cold milk
1 tablespoon of vanilla
4 bananas sliced
1 large container of frozen whipped topping, thawed
1 box of vanilla wafers

How to make:

In a large mixing bowl, combine and beat together pudding and milk. Once smooth add in the sweetened condensed milk, vanilla, and half of whipped topping.

In a glass bowl or 9x13 dish layer wafers and bananas, then pour pudding mixture on top. Let dessert sit for five minutes, then spread on the remaining whipped topping.

Chill until serving.

Chapter 19

sweet tea and sunshine

Shelby

A muted light dips into the room as the sun slowly makes its appearance. It's early, too early to be awake after the night we had, but I don't mind.

Stretching my leg out, it runs down beside his, and I feel him stir. I didn't mean to wake him; I just want to be touching him.

He adjusts his head on his pillow, slips his arm around my waist, and pulls me until I'm flush against him. Tingles spread through my limbs as his warm muscles blanket over me, his heartbeat pounds steadily against my back, and a sense of belonging washes over me. A belonging that is foreign and if I'm honest, scary.

"You smell good," he says, his voice raspy and full of sleep. Dipping his head, he buries it in my neck, and breathes me in.

"I probably smell like you."

"Hmm," he murmurs as his hand tightens against my stomach.

My eyes drift shut to the steady rhythm of his heart. Neither of us is lulled back to sleep, but neither of us makes a move to get up, either.

Slowly, the light blooms, brightening the room. Zach rolls over onto his back and lets out a contented sigh. I miss the feel of him already.

"Are you staying for breakfast?" I turn to face him. His eyes are closed, his hair is sticking up everywhere, and his lips look puffy and inviting. I swear he's never looked better.

His drowsy eyes find mine, and his fingertips slide across the space between us in search of my hand. "I wish I could, but I need to get some work done."

"Work, shmerk."

He chuckles at my evident pout and rolls to face me.

Tucking a strand of hair behind my ear, he trails his thumb across my cheek, tracing every feature on my face before pressing down on my bottom lip.

"So beautiful," he says, shifting us both so that I'm tucked under him and he's braced on his elbows.

"I made a coffee cake yesterday, it's on the counter if you want to take it."

He smiles, and I feel it straight down to my toes. "Don't you want some of it?"

"No, I made it for you."

He pulls back and the heated way he looks at me makes me want to melt. "I don't know why, but I find it incredibly sexy that you cook for me."

"Well, maybe if you're lucky, I'll cook you something for dinner tonight, too." I add a little sultry tone to my words.

He slides off me and stretches as he stands; I swear he does it on purpose. So much skin and so many muscles that I can hardly think.

"Something tells me I have a little luck on my side." He grins, enjoying my perusal of his gorgeous body.

"You might be right." I smile back.

He pulls on his clothing. I want to beg him to stay, but I know he can't, so I keep my mouth shut as he leans over and gives me a kiss goodbye. I listen to him as he moves through the house, grabs the coffee cake off the counter, and then shuts the front door softly behind him.

Sliding my foot across the sheets to his side of the bed, it's still warm, and a piece of me falls even more for him. I know I'm really in trouble when I trade out my pillow for his and snuggle down. I just can't help myself.

It's mid morning before I drag myself out of the bed, brew a pot of coffee, and sit to do some work. I look over the different recipes we've selected, meal plans I've put together, and the pairings to go with each. For the most part, I feel like I'm done with the assignment. I'm pleased with how it's all come together, and I think they will be, too. Sometime before the final interview, I'll sit down with Zach and Kyle to see if they have any last-minute changes they'd like to make. I think I'll even invite the photographer.

Done with work, I pack a small bag, throw on my boots, grab my sun hat, and wander over to the barn. I could've taken the golf cart, but there's something about today, something in the air that makes me want to move a little slower, memorize more of the details.

I think about Zach growing up here, and how different his family is from my dysfunctional one. He has roots here. There isn't one inch of this property that hasn't been touched by Zach in some way, and I've never had anything like that. He's a part of the vineyard as much as the vines are, and my heart longs for this, too. Even if it's just a tiny piece.

"Hi, how are y'all doing today?" I ask to a couple that's walking out of the barn. I know I'm not a part of the Wolff Winery staff, but I can't help but feel pride as if I am.

"We're great, thanks," an older gentleman says. "It's just so beautiful here."

"Thank you, that means a lot to us." I smile at the couple. "I hope you enjoy your time here, and don't forget to taste The Queen Bee, it's delicious."

They nod their heads, and I give them a wave and walk into the barn.

"You know, if you ever decide on a career change and want to give up your fancy restaurant in Charleston, I might be able to squeeze you in as a staff member." Kyle is grinning at me from his spot by the label machine.

"Such a generous offer," I drawl, smiling back.

"How's your morning?" he asks, abandoning what he's working on and coming to stand next to me.

A blush creeps into my cheeks as I think about Zach, and Kyle smirks knowingly when he spots it.

"It's good. Two days left, and I realized that I don't have many pictures of my own, so I'm snapping a few." I also plan to use some of them with the blog post, but he doesn't need to know that. It'll just open the door for questioning on the content of the post, and I need to do this without influence from someone else.

"Two days. Yeah, Michelle mentioned that last night. Two weeks sure flew by. She's going to miss you. She's really enjoyed not being the only girl around here."

The thought of leaving sends an unwanted pang to my chest.

"I bet. It's a serious business having to put up with you two all the time." I tease and Kyle laughs.

"Is there anything else I can show you? Any questions?" he asks, genuinely.

"Nope, I think I've seen it all and I'm question free."

"Well, all right then, I'll let you get back to it." Kyle's Southern charm shines through with every word.

"Thanks."

He gives me a wink, and I sneak past him to the kitchen. Zach mentioned this was where his mother jarred the honey, and sure enough, as I open the cabinets there are several jars just sitting there for the taking.

Jackpot.

Each jar has a piece of lavender-colored fabric wrapped over the top and a piece of twine tied in a bow around the lid. I snap a quick picture and grab a jar for myself before I head out the back and across the property toward the bees. It's time to write the blog post and that's the perfect place to do it.

All of the posts I write for the blog come from the heart. Whether it is about something I love or something I hate . . . they are all still me. And this post is no different, except I know that by posting it, I will be exposing myself.

In general, the food industry is relatively tight. Anyone who is serious about their career as a chef, who's trying to make a name for themself, stays up-to-date and informed about what is going on around them and who they need to know. I'm certain my blog is followed because of the comments on the reviews, and I know those same people will also read the regional issue of the magazine to see who was mentioned and who wasn't. Putting two and two together won't be difficult. The question is: am I ready to step out and be accountable to my peers? The answer is yes. My career is changing, I feel it, and so does Meg. This assignment was just the push I needed to firmly stand behind my name and my work in the culinary world.

Last year when I gave them the recommendations, my name was just printed along with other contributors to the magazine. This year, my name and my face will be attached to the article. I'm proud of that. Between the online stories of my time here and the print magazine, this is an incredible opportunity, and I'm not going to let it pass by.

I find a spot under Zach's apple trees, unpack my blanket and laptop, and then set to writing . . .

Two weeks ago, if you had asked me about wine country in the United States, my mind would have gravitated to the West Coast. Stretching from Napa Valley and Sonoma north to Willamette Valley in Oregon, I would have named one vineyard after another. But if asked about the East Coast, I may have said, "Oh yeah, there are supposed to be some amazing wineries on Long Island and in Virginia." However, Dave Matthews' wines in Charlottesville being the only specific one to come to mind.

Given the opportunity for a freelance editorial assignment, I found myself staying at a vineyard in northern Georgia, Wolff Winery, and being thrown into the world of vinification and food pairing. Openly, I admit to knowing little about the process of winemaking, but being tucked away at the base of the Blue Ridge Mountains, I fell in love with not only the ambiance and friendly staff of the winery but also the award-winning wines, too.

It's easy to see why there are so many wineries around the world. There's a certain magic to cultivating, growing, harvesting, fermenting, and bottling wine, and anyone who makes wine will tell you the most important step comes from the heart. It takes passion, patience, and more knowledge than can come from just a harvest or two. Sure, if you water a plant and give it sunlight, it will grow, but growing grapes—the science behind creating the perfect clusters—is truly fascinating.

What I discovered is, in many ways, making wine is like cooking with different spices. Too much of this or too much of that and it can throw the taste off, but where they differ is cooking problems can be easily fixed, usually on the spot, but there's only one harvest per year and only one chance to get it right.

Wolff Winery, from what I've tasted, never gets it wrong. This is why it was the chosen vineyard for this assignment, and I've loved creating and pairing some amazing dishes to accompany their wines. From reds to whites, and of course sparklings, they are delicious, high-quality wines that are comparable to some of the most sought after flavors around the world. They're affordable, great for any occasion, and need to be tasted by all.

Be on the lookout in a few weeks, I'll post the assignment once it releases. You'll be able to read all about my experiences at the winery, get an inside look at how wonderful the Wolff Winery family and staff are, and see what has made this hidden gem at the base of the Smokies such an incredible find. And if in the meantime, you run across one of the Wolff wines while out dining or in a retail store, make sure you grab it and see for yourself why wine with food is . . . the perfect pairing.

Ingredients:

3 cups of flour
1 1/2 cups of brown sugar, packed
1 cup of vegetable oil
1 cup of milk
1 cup of sugar
1/2 cup of salted butter, melted
2 large eggs
1 tablespoon of cinnamon
3 teaspoons of baking powder
1 teaspoon vanilla

How to make:

Preheat oven to 350 degrees.

In a large bowl, mix together milk, oil, eggs, and vanilla. In a medium bowl, blend together flour, white sugar, baking powder, and salt. Combine the two mixtures until smooth. Pour half of the batter into a greased 9 x 13 dish.

In a medium bowl, blend brown sugar and cinnamon. Sprinkle half of the streusel mixture on top of the batter.

Top with the remaining cake batter and sprinkle the other half of the streusel mixture on top. Drizzle with melted butter.

Bake for 25-30 minutes.

Can be made the night before, or served warm.

Sprinkle with powdered sugar.

Chapter 20

be stil my heart

Zach

I hated leaving her this morning. Never have I wanted so badly to stay with a girl like I did with her, but knowing I had work to get done this morning and needing to put a bit of space between us, it was best that I left. All morning my mind has been consumed with blonde hair that was spread all across her pillow and mine, soft skin, and a sleepy content smile that damn near cracked my chest in half. This girl is under my skin, and I'm afraid to look and see how deep.

Minutes pass and agonizingly accumulate into hours. The space I thought I needed from her came and went and the longing I have for her has grown into an excruciating ache under my ribs. I feel like a loaded gun about to go off. I know Kyle is itching to sit and discuss how we're going to play out her last few days here, but I can't. Knowing that while I'm up here working she's down there and we're losing time is killing me. I can't take it anymore. She'll be gone before we know it, and then it'll be business as usual, but for now, she's here, and I can't wait any longer.

"Where are you going?" Kyle calls out from his office, which is next to mine, as I jog past his doorway and down the hall toward the back door.

"To find Shelby," I throw over my shoulder.

"Wait!" He emerges, and his face drops a little, giving away that he's worried. He's also holding one of Shelby's biscuits, and I'm insanely jealous that he's eating something of hers. Irrational, I know, but I want her and everything about her all to myself.

Kyle's watched us closely over the last couple of days, and he knows I've deviated from the plan and we've grown closer. Hell, everyone who works here probably does, but I don't care.

"Are you sure that's a good idea?" he asks, mumbling through another bite of the biscuit.

"Don't worry, Kyle. It'll be fine. The winery's good, we're good, and I'm good."

He crosses his arms over his chest. "Well, I do worry, and as your friend, I'm warning you to be careful."

I hear what he is saying, but I don't agree. There is no reason that I can't indulge in something good for a few days. The plan was to woo her enough that she would feel the need to write a kick-ass post for her blog, but what if she doesn't write the post? We have always assumed that she would, but maybe she's only writing an article for the magazine. If she doesn't write it, then things are no worse or better than they were before. We could move forward with the marketing of the magazine article, and the whole plan can be forgotten as if it never existed.

"It's all good, trust me." I smile at him, and his eyes narrow with concern before he lets out a huge sigh.

"Last I saw her was at the barn. I think she's wandering around the property today taking pictures."

Pictures.

My heart starts racing with anticipation of seeing her, and I know the place she's ultimately headed.

"Thanks, man. I'll catch up with you later." With that, I'm out the door and running in the direction of the apple trees.

She loves the bees almost as much as she loves the cliff.

Turning down the last row, I spot her sitting under the shade of the trees, and the sight stops me in my tracks and halts the breath in my chest.

"Be still my heart," I whisper to myself and rub the burgeoning ache in my chest.

Shelby is lying on her stomach with her feet kicked up in the air, her blonde hair is pulled up into a messy knot on top of her head, and she's reading a book. She looks so comfortable and so relaxed that part of me doesn't want to bother her. She looks so at home here.

Wow is all I can think.

My heart starts to race, my hands have started to shake, and as a breeze blows the leaves on the vines move in unison like an ocean wave and I know . . .

This is the moment.

The moment people talk about when they say they just knew.

She's perfect.

She's wearing cut-off shorts, a tank top, and those ridiculous rain boots. Her face is pink from the afternoon sun, and she's never looked more beautiful. She takes my breath away.

I try to burn this image of her in my mind. I never want to forget it, not that I think I could.

Walking straight for her, I force my steps slower so I don't startle her, and she looks up as she hears me approach. Big blue eyes shine at me, and her smile lassos my heart.

Everything inside me clenches with want for her. Want for her friendship, want for her heart to be mine, and want for her body. I want to imprint myself so deeply on her that I consume her mind as much as she consumes mine.

My knees hit the dirt next to her blanket, and I soak in every tiny detail of her face.

"Hi," she whispers, watching me with wide eyes. Tiny freckles dot the skin under her eyes and across her nose. I've never thought once about freckles on a girl, but damn on her these are adorable.

Being at a loss for words, all I want to do is drop soft kisses across said freckles and one to her lips. She tosses her book to the side and sits up, resting her weight on her heels and watching me.

What do I say to her? How would I even begin such a conversation and after only two weeks. She would think I'm crazy and, if by some chance she doesn't, how do I ask her to be mine?

Mine.

This girl, this beautiful, easy-going, independent, driven girl is mine. As sure as the sun will set tonight and rise tomorrow, I know in my gut this is a certainty, and I'm so moved by the realization that I cup her face between my palms and bring her lips to mine.

Her lips are full, warm, and easily follow my lead as she kisses me back. Her tongue dances with mine, and I drown in what has now become my favorite flavor . . . her.

This kiss is different.

It's because I am different.

I was so focused on football for so long and then the winery that I didn't even realize I was starving until I met her. I've had a taste of what life is like with her, and there's no going back.

Sliding my lips across hers, I kiss the corner of her mouth and pause to breathe in the air surrounding her. Sweetness fills my nostrils and pieces of her hair tickle my face, but I hold her close never wanting to let her go.

I need to be closer.

Lowering her down to her back, I run my finger down her cheek, over her jaw, and across her lips. Lips that are parted, and flushed red as she breathes heavily.

"What are you doing?" Her eyes caress my face as I brace myself over her.

"I don't know." I answer her honestly, because I really don't. I want to do and say everything, but I don't know how or where to start.

"Everything okay?" she asks, running her hand up my arm and pushing the hair off my forehead.

I nod my head, my eyes briefly slip shut at the feel of her touching me. "How's your morning, what did you do?" I ask her.

"I wrote a post for my blog about your winery." She pauses, looking for a reaction, but I steel my emotions and lock the muscles in my face. I'm afraid that she'll read my anxiety instead of my gratitude, and I don't want that. "I really do love it here," she whispers.

And there it is.

The part of me that naively had been hoping she wouldn't write the post slowly backs away, bowing to the truth. She's a passionate person when it comes to the things that matter most to her, and over the last two weeks, I've watched her fall in love with the winery, the wines, and all the details that make us the brand Wolff.

Pain slams into my chest, and I lower my forehead to rest against hers. I should be more elated but the premise behind getting the post makes me feel dirty.

Maybe I should ask her not to post it?

No.

Then I would have to explain why, and I can't bring myself to explain to her that originally my goal was to lure her in and lie to her through kindness to get the post. She would see this as the ultimate deception.

Squeezing my eyes shut, I frown and shake my head. Shelby feels the movement and pulls back to look at me, her brows lowered over her eyes. Guilt engulfs me, and I feel like the worst kind of person.

"Aren't you worried people will discover who you are after the magazine prints?" She must have thought of this, right? Maybe this is the angle I can use to get her not to post the article. Kyle would be disappointed, but we're smart and resilient. We can find other ways, in addition to the magazine, to get our name out there.

Her hand slides over my shoulder to my arm, and her warm fingertips slip under the edge of my sleeve.

"I thought about that, but I think it's time. I think I'm ready. A lot of work has gone into the blog for a lot of years, and if I'm looking to advance myself professionally, then I need to let others know besides my partner and my editor who I am and how truly committed and in love with this industry I am."

Pulling farther away, I look deep in her eyes and find a confidence that wasn't there when she spoke of the blog in Asheville. Before she liked her anonymity, and now, I can see that she's made this decision and wants to stand behind it. If I weren't already proud of her, this would have done it.

A bee buzzes by her head, and she jerks to the side and starts to laugh. I grin back at her while getting lost in the sound.

"I don't think people will be too surprised when they find out who *Starving for Southern* is. You are amazing, and anyone who's ever met you already knows this, including me."

"Thank you." Her lips tilt into a bigger smile, and her hand moves to settle on my waist.

"Shelby, if I didn't tell you already, I'm really sorry about the way I behaved at the event and when you first got here."

She giggles. "You still haven't told me why, other than giving me the 'it-wasn't-you-but-me' line, but I think we've moved past that, don't you?"

"I hope so," I whisper, finding forgiveness and adoration beaming back at me. There's no trace of suspicion, only trust.

Ducking my head into her neck to hide so she doesn't see the raw emotions on my face, her arm slips around me and pulls me close. My weight falls over her, and my body comes to life. Teasing her skin, I pull the strap of her tank top to the side and trail my lips down her neck and over her collarbone. Tasting her as I go. Her head tilts, giving me more access, and her back arches, pushing her tighter into me.

"I need more of you. I need to be inside you," I mumble as her free hand finds it way into my hair. I'm crazy for this girl, and the need I have is so overwhelming that it almost borders on desperation. I need to take her, claim her, mark her . . . anything that will make her mine.

And ease my guilty conscious.

"Okay," she whispers.

Her hand trails from my waist over my back and finds the hem of my T-shirt. She easily lifts it up and off my body, allowing the sun's rays to warm my back as they slip through the branches of the tree.

All around us, the sounds of the hills float by and not once do I hear the telltale signs of another person. Just the buzzing of the bees, the chirping of birds, and the leaves waving in the passing breeze. We are alone and lost to the world. This moment feels stolen, but as I sit back on my heels, I intend to take it anyway.

Removing her clothes, I start with her boots. It's like unwrapping a present that I've waited my whole life for and as my eyes peruse each newly bared section, her soft ivory skin flushes pink.

"Hmm, where should I start?" I tease her, rubbing my thumb on the inside of her thigh.

"With your clothes," she says, her voice a little labored.

Smiling at her, I strip down, and slowly begin worshiping every inch of her beautiful body. Her sounds, the expressions revealed on her face, and her fingertips as they dig into my hair, shoulders, and back, all of it lets me know she's as lost in the sensations as I am. I could live a thousand years and never tire of touching her.

"Zach," she whispers my name as I trace my tongue over her hipbone and travel up to her breast. "More," she says on an exhale. When I glance up to her face, I find her eyes filled with desire and yearning.

Not needing to be asked twice, I lace my fingers through hers, seal my lips to hers, and push home.

Home.

Her.

Her breath rushes out on a gratified sigh, and I breathe her in as her fingers tighten around mine. My eyelids slip shut as I'm hit with a fervent onslaught of tingles racing from my groin up my spine. Being inside Shelby, being connected to her, it doesn't even come close to comparing to anything ever in my life before. It's a feeling so strong that as I start to move, with each stroke in and out,

I feel like her body is holding on and taking a piece of my soul, and I freely give it.

Time stills as we lose ourselves to the emotional and physical act of making love to each other. Light and shadows dance behind my eyelids, leaves all around us blow in the wind, but all I see, feel, and hear is her. I would give her anything and everything to be able to relive this intense, exquisite, incredibly euphoric feeling every day. That's what this is for me . . . love.

Smiling to myself, I think these are the kinds of moments that artists are constantly chasing. Words aren't needed, but many different sentiments are radiating off us. I know this is new, and I know we got off to an unconventional start, but I can feel the way her heart is drifting in every touch, every kiss, every look. It's the way she stops breathing when I come near, and the way she breathes me in at the same time too.

"Tell me," I whisper some hours later.

Her eyelids flutter open and she blinks against the brightness of the late afternoon sun.

"Tell you what?" she asks, her eyes sleepy and satiated as she rolls to face me. Her lips barely move as she speaks, but they still draw me in as I burn to memory each curve, freckle, and eyelash.

How do I explain to her what I'm asking for? How do I tell her she's what I need? There's so much to say, and so much to do. I want it all. I want . . .

"Everything."

Ingredients:

2 cups of flour
8 tablespoons of salted butter
1 tablespoon of baking powder
1 teaspoon sugar
1 teaspoon salt
1/4 teaspoon baking soda
3/4 cup of buttermilk

How to make:

Preheat the oven to 425 degrees. Grease cookie sheet for baking.

In a large mixing bowl combine flour, sugar, baking powder, salt, and baking soda together. Cut 4 tablespoons of softened butter into the mixture and grate 4 tablespoons of frozen butter with a cheese grater into the mixture. Using a fork, make a well and pour in buttermilk. Knead the dough and add more buttermilk if necessary.

Turn out dough onto a well-floured surface. Continue kneading until the dough consistency is even and roll out to 3/4 inch thickness, or desired thickness. Cut with a 2.5-inch biscuit cutter.

Place cut biscuits onto the cookie sheet and bake for 12 minutes or until golden brown.

Chapter 21

don't get your feathers ruffled

Shelby

Zach stayed with me the rest of the day and all through the night. If we weren't tangled up in each other, we were drinking his wine, eating, and laughing. As serious as he has been and can be, I've never laughed with one person as much as I did with him.

I think what surprised me the most was how tender he was with me. Maybe it was because we moved past that initial must-have desperation, or maybe because we weren't limited on time, but he was different yesterday, and it was noticeable. Not that there is anything wrong with the difference, but I almost wish his movements were still lust filled and less warm, less loving. It all adds to the vision of what I think a life with him might be like, and considering I have one day left here, this makes me long for something that won't be.

Deciding I need to stop thinking about him and start thinking about leaving, I move from room to room through the cottage, picking up the mess we made last night and setting my things off to the side for packing. At some point, I glance outside, and my breath catches because the black crow is back. The world around me blurs as I narrow my gaze on it and my heart rate picks up. It can't be coincidental. It must mean something, and dread slips in under my skin. Closing my eyes, I turn away and do my best to forget about it.

Stopping next to the kitchen island, I run my fingers over the lavender flowers and then lean in to smell the plant. Lavender is supposed to have a calming effect, if only it would work on me and my anxious heart.

The problem is, Zach isn't what I expected, not that I have expectations from him, but there's this gentleness in the way he looks at me and touches me that I'm not used to. As blissful as my heart feels, it's because of this that there's an unwanted nervousness sitting deep within me. A nervousness that seems to be growing the closer we get to the assignment ending. Maybe that's all it is, I'm anxious about saying goodbye and not knowing what happens next, or maybe there's a reason for this gut feeling . . . I haven't figured it out yet.

From across the room, my cell phone starts ringing, and my heart jumps. Thinking that it might be Zach calling, I move across the room, and see that it's Meg. I let out a sigh of relief, she's the person who can calm me down.

"Hey!" I answer on the third ring.

"One day left!" Meg squeals. "I'm so excited for you to get back home. I don't think we've ever gone this long being apart."

I can almost see her bouncing around in the kitchen at OBA, and I can't help but laugh at her enthusiasm. "I miss you, too."

"So, have you and Zach talked at all about what happens after tomorrow?"

Well, there's no beating around the bush with her, straight to the point.

"No." I walk back into the kitchen and sit at the island, hoping that eventually the plant will work its magic on my nerves.

"But you want to see him again, right?"

"I think I do," I say on a sigh.

"Then why don't you sound more excited?"

"I don't know. Everything was great, no it *is* great, but I woke this morning feeling off. All of this is so quick, so unexpected, I feel—"

"Stop right there. I know you, Shelby. Nothing is off, you're anxious because you like this guy. I've seen you do this before, and it's like as soon as things move out of your comfort zone, you're sitting around waiting for the other shoe to drop. Are you listening to me?"

"I am, but Meg, there's a large black crow sitting on the table outside the French doors and it's staring at me through the window." I glance outside and she's still sitting there.

"So?"

"You know what this means, don't you?"

"No, enlighten me, Oh Great One," she says sarcastically.

"Black crows are a sign of a bad omen. I know this feeling I'm having isn't for nothing."

"Have you lost your mind? Seriously? A crow? Now you're looking for trouble when there isn't any. Are you trying to sabotage this good thing that you have going? I mean really, you've cooked food there all week, I'm sure it smelled divine, you eat outside, and the bird is probably looking for a snack."

"Explain to me why I saw one on my first day here, and now on my last."

"It isn't your last day, you have one more, and you didn't see one because you weren't looking for one. You do this when things don't seem to be going your way—you start looking for answers to questions or problems that aren't there. It's the control freak in you, and you need to stop this. Seriously, don't get *your* feathers ruffled over it. Throw the bird a piece of bread, and watch, it'll fly away."

"Maybe you're right."

So, I do as she suggested and toss a chunk of break outside onto the back patio. Sure enough, the bird swoops in, grabs the bread, and flies away.

"Is it gone?" she asks.

"Yes," I say with a sigh. "You were right."

"I usually am."

"Maybe I am overthinking this, and maybe it is because I'm leaving tomorrow. What do you think?"

"I think it's okay to like him. Not every guy out there is a douchecanoe or has a hidden agenda. You've worked hard to get where you are. You're the most beautiful person I know, and I'm certain this guy sees the same amazing qualities that I do."

"I hope so. I really do like him."

"I know you do. So, what you need to do is get your cute butt up to the manor and go tell him good morning. The longer you stay in the cottage, the more you're going to psych yourself out, and time's a ticking. Don't waste it."

"You're right. I think I'll invite him to lunch."

"There's my girl. What are you going to fix him?"

"I was thinking a smoked sausage and black-eyed pea soup." I need to use up the few remaining ingredients I picked up at the farmers' market.

"Sounds perfect. And then after you feed him his lunch he can feed you his—"

"Ahhh, don't say it." I laugh at her.

She giggles back, and I feel infinitely better.

"Go get your man and give me a call tomorrow once you get on the road."

"I will, and thanks, Meg. This was just what I needed."

"I know, because I know you. See you tomorrow!" She hangs up, leaving me smiling and heading to the bedroom to get ready.

I think a lot about who I am and how far I've come. I think I'm kind, giving, and loyal. I love my home and making a home for my friends. I hate it when my friends hurt, and I would do anything for any of them. But, that's where it stops. I only allow this for my friends; I don't allow it for myself. Even though it was over ten years ago, I've let one person have an affect so profound on my life, and I've spent every second possible focused on trying to be successful and proving that I don't need anyone or anything to get me where I want to be in life. But I've realized after coming here that I'm missing some of the best parts of life. The part of life that lets me connect with another person, a person that might just be meant for me.

Is it possible that Zach is that person? Maybe. But I'll never know if I don't put myself out there.

Running back into the kitchen, I grab my phone and shove it into my back pocket. Before I can turn, though, there's a fluttering to my left. The crow is back. I'm met again with the black as night eyes and my stomach plummets. I know Meg has a point that I haven't been looking for bad signs, but not once over the last two weeks have I had a bird land on the darn table. That I would have remembered. Yes, the timing is odd, and no, it isn't as if I have been sitting around doing nothing but looking out the door waiting for a bird. Still, I have to push past the dark thoughts and swallow a huge dose of optimism. Turning away from the bird, which is still staring at me, I head for the door and smile. In a few minutes, I'll get to press my lips to his.

Ingredients:

1 lb or 5 cups of black-eyed peas
1 smoked sausage, sliced
1 8oz package of diced ham
1 small Vidalia onion, chopped
1/2 cup of celery, chopped
8-10 cups of chicken stock
2 cups of white rice (optional)
1 tablespoon minced garlic
1 teaspoon of salt
1 teaspoon pepper
1 teaspoon of thyme
2 bay leaves
fresh parsley (optional)

How to make:

If black-eyed peas are dried prepare per package directions.

In a large pot heat two tablespoons of olive oil and saute garlic, onion, celery, ham, salt, pepper, and thyme. Once onions are translucent add chicken stock, sliced smoked sausage, black-eyed peas, and bay leaves.

Bring soup to a boil and then reduce heat to low. Cook for one and a half hours.

Prepare white rice per package directions. White rice is optional but can be added to the bowl with the soup poured on top, mixed into the soup, or not used at all.

Remove bay leaves.

Parsley to garnish.

Serve warm.

Chapter 22

I reckon so

Zach

Kyle and Michelle are waiting for me in my office when I walk in. They're both glued to an iPad, and I know they're looking at Shelby's blog. Both of them look up and watch in silence as I move around the desk and drop down in my chair. It creaks as I lean back and run my hand over my face and through my hair, which is still wet from my recent shower.

"Did you see the post?" Kyle asks, excitement radiating off him. If only I shared that same excitement, but I don't.

"I did, and I'm taking both of you saw it as well."

Smiles split across their faces. They are so happy they're damn near bursting, and more than anything, I wish they would take their giddiness, grab their stuff, and leave me alone.

I woke this morning to my phone constantly buzzing on the nightstand. Shelby, who had been wrapped in my arms and snuggled against me, had mumbled at some point for me to make it stop, but I just glared at the small black device. I didn't have to look at the texts, I knew, and the knowledge was a boulder that rolled onto my chest and settled in the pit of my stomach.

Eventually, I cracked and grabbed it to silence it, but I ended up scrolling through the activity. Her post had gone viral and had been shared on dozens of industry sites, from top ten places to visit in Georgia to wedding destinations. I had hundreds of notifications waiting for me, and it was only nine in the morning. Feeling guilty and trapped inside myself, I kissed her goodbye and let her know I would see her later.

"I was walking the property this morning when Dan radioed over that the phone was ringing nonstop in the barn with people wanting to know our hours. So, on a hunch, I checked, and sure enough, there it was. I've already shared it across all our social media platforms," Kyle says, flipping between several tabs on the iPad to show me the activity and shares we've had on each one. Looking at these numbers after only a few hours, I understand his enthusiasm. I mean, this is outstanding for the winery, but I can't embrace the excitement like they are.

I feel uneasy, and my conscious is loud, lecturing me that this wasn't a clean win.

I nod my head at him and thank him for being proactive. It was the right business thing to do.

"Online orders have picked up over the last couple of hours, too," Michelle says quietly. Her eyes have softened as she studies me, and her infectious spirit starts to wane as she reads my mood.

"Why aren't you happier about this?" Kyle leans forward, placing his elbows on his knees and scrutinizing my lack of enthusiasm.

I shrug and turn away from the pair of them. From here, I can see the hill off in the distance with the underground cellar. My mind wanders to the overhang and the night Shelby and I watched the sunset. She asked me, "Are you playing me Zach? Is this a game to you? Am I a game?" I told her I wasn't, that it wasn't, but I also told her not to trust me.

Kyle lets out a sigh before pushing to his feet and pacing the room. Every minute or so he looks over at me in frustration, and I can't say I blame him.

"This is crazy. You do realize this, right? So crazy that one person can cause such a ripple." He glances over to Michelle, obviously wanting her to back him up. She doesn't.

"It is crazy. It'll be interesting to see if this is a one-day blast or if there will be a trickledown effect over the summer," I tell them.

"My money's on the trickledown, which will lead into the best season's sales yet." He stops in front of the white board, reads over the data we've collected so far, and then moves back to his seat.

Trickledown through the summer would be amazing.

Shelby's following is much larger than I anticipated. It's easy to see now why the magazine hired her two years in a row. Also, based on some of the remarks I saw on shared posts, her opinion is highly respected in the Southern foodie industry. Shelby is not just a chef from Charleston, she's big time, and I'm so proud of her. She's built this *Starving for Southern* image for herself, and she's right, it's time for her to make herself known.

"Did you know she had written it?" Michelle asks.

"Yes. She told me yesterday, but she didn't say when she was scheduling to post it. Honestly, I thought it would be closer to or after the release of the regional issue. That maybe it would coincide and she'd link it to the online interviews and posts following her stay here. I don't know."

"Well, I'm glad she posted it sooner rather than later. Quarter two numbers are going to go up, and so will quarter three with summer travelers to the area."

"Yeah. Dad already sent me a text, too." I glance at my cell phone. I turned it off before my shower and I haven't turned it back on.

"Of course, he did. His time zone is hours ahead of us, and you know he can't help himself. He may have retired, but he can't shut it off." Kyle grins.

I chuckle, and finally, both Kyle and Michelle relax a little bit.

"I'm going to print the post and have her sign it tomorrow before she leaves," Michelle adds.

"I think that's a great idea, Michelle." I nod, and she relaxes farther back into her chair.

"Dude, why aren't you more excited about this? I'm trying to wrap my brain around this sullen behavior of yours, but it isn't working. This isn't you." He waves his hand up and down in front of me, frowning. "You plan, you execute, and you win. Your general personality is more animated than this, and you're freaking me out. This is the break we've been looking for, working for, and waiting for . . . for months."

"I reckon so, and I am excited. It's been a long two weeks, and I'm tired. Twinges of a headache are trying to move in, and I'm staying calm."

"Well, one more interview, a few pictures, and this is over. She'll go back to Charleston, and things will get back to normal for us."

Over.

Only, I don't want it to be, and I don't know what to do or how to approach the subject with her.

"Yep, one more interview," I say to pacify him, but deep inside it feels more like a finality that causes the dull pressure behind my eyes to throb.

Shit. I rub the back of my neck and open my drawer for some medicine. The stress of this situation along with a lack of sleep is catching up to me and, getting a migraine is the last thing I need.

"Well, I have to say, I honestly didn't think you'd be able to pull this off with as much as you dislike her, but you turned on the charm, and she played right into it. She never saw it coming."

"I don't dislike her, and I don't know if that's exactly how it happened." I pop two pills in my mouth and reach for the sweet tea sitting on my desk.

I hate that this is how he's summarized my relationship with Shelby. Not that we have one, or maybe we could, I don't know. I still need to sit and discuss this with her, both of us have been avoiding the conversation so we didn't ruin the time we have left. But hearing him so nonchalantly talk about her this way makes me feel like shit.

"It is! Zach, we talked about this the day after she got here, last week. Remember: strategy, game plan, execution. Win her over, get the post, and get more business."

My stomach turns sour, and I want to yell at him and tell him not to remind me. She's going to think I used her. And I did.

I hate this. Yes, it started out as a game, but it stopped being that days ago—for all of us. Although, it was never a game to her. She thought I was real, that we were real.

And we were. No, we are.

Everything about this is real. Every touch, every kiss, every glance; it all means something to me.

I should tell her. She wrote the post because she genuinely loves it here. I want to be able to share the success with her without feeling guilty over something that doesn't matter anymore.

The door to my office, which was half closed, slowly opens and all three of us turn to see Shelby in the doorway. Her arms are wrapped around her stomach and she's looking at me with eyes filled with hurt and accusations of betrayal.

No.

No. No. No. No.

Heat flushes straight up my back and into my face. I should stand, move to her, something, but I can't, I'm frozen to the seat. Not one of us is breathing, and I swear I can hear her heart breaking from across the room. Or wait, maybe that's mine.

"Did I hear that right?" she asks in a shaky voice, the sound slashing its way straight through my shoulder to my solar plexus. "You made a plan to have me fall for you so I'd write a blog post about your winery? You tricked me and lied to me for sales?"

My fingers curl into the fabric of my jeans, my blood starts torpedoing through my veins, and my heartbeat pushes harder behind my eyes. Hearing her say it like this, it doesn't matter if I come clean or not about the plan, it sounds wrong. I don't know how to answer her, so I don't.

"Yes." The single word comes from Michelle, and my head whips in her direction. Shock flooding me as my jaw drops open.

"Michelle, no!" I jump up, but her eyes never drift my way, they stay on Shelby. I understand they've become friends and Michelle did the right thing by telling her, but it could have been explained better. I should have been the one to admit to it. I just needed more time to figure out what to say.

"I see," Shelby mumbles after a stalled pause, and I look back to find her staring at the floor, her chest heaving.

"Shelby, please, I can explain." No three words have ever been uttered more when it comes to being busted, caught, and they are pathetic. Her eyes flash to mine, there are a thousand emotions swimming in them. The one that grabs me and squeezes the most is disappointment.

Holding up one hand, she shakes her head just as my mouth opens. I'm not sure what I can say to make this better, but begging is a good start. Her chin trembles, her eyes glaze over, and my heart splinters into an infinite number of pieces.

Slowly, she drags her eyes away from mine and looks over to Michelle, Kyle, and then around my office. It's as if she's seeing us for the first time, and her lips press together. Tears float in her eyes but don't fall as she raises her head higher and nods in understanding. She thinks this was all for business . . . and nothing more.

My heart aches, my chest aches, my head aches, and my hands desperately want to reach out and grab her. But I don't. I can't. Instead, I watch her fingertips find her lips. I don't know if she's trying to physically stop the small quiver there or if she doesn't even know she's done it.

Dropping her hand, she lets out a sigh and takes a step back out of the doorway. The light shifts, revealing just how pale her face is as she straightens her shoulders and turns cold, indifferent eyes back to me.

I've hurt this girl, this beautiful, kind, funny, wickedly talented girl, and I know the damage is irreparable. This one look, this one definitive look, it says it all . . .

I've lost her.

Ingredients:

6 tea bags
2 cups of boiling water
Pinch of baking soda
1.5 - 2 cups of sugar
6 cups of cold water
Lemons and mint, optional

How to make:

This recipe is pretty standard. Steep tea bags for boiling water for 15 minutes. Add a pinch of baking soda and stir in sugar until dissolved. Transfer into a pitcher and add cold water. Refrigerate until serving. Pour over ice and add sliced lemon and mint leaves for garnish and extra flavor.

Chapter 23

shoulda, coulda, woulda

Shelby

I put one foot in front of the other and walk out of Zach's office. The weight of the three of them staring at me falls so heavily on my back, I feel like it's collapsing my ribcage and I can't breathe. Tears blur the hallway in front of me and begin to fall one after the other.

How did I let this happen to me? I've never put myself in a situation where I think someone will take advantage of me, yet that's exactly what I've done. Every mantra I've told myself, every move I've made professionally, and every relationship I've not given myself to, turns out it was all for nothing. Because no matter what, here am I, in the one position I never wanted to be in.

Used.

Hurt.

Picking up the pace, I reach the back exit door and push through to the outside. The brightness from the sun blinds me and I squeeze my eyes shut. Blinking a few times, they adjust but I keep my eyes on the ground in front of me. I don't want to look at the vineyard or be reminded of how beautiful it is.

I fell under the spell of this place, of him, and I'm *so* embarrassed.

I feel manipulated and taken advantage of, but I also feel naive and incredibly stupid, which is all on me.

How had I not seen right through him? He *hated* me when I first arrived, and I was so blinded by the beauty and magic of this place and him—this gorgeous ex-football player turned successful business owner—that I allowed myself to be duped and manipulated. He didn't like me, he *told* me he didn't like me. Then he has a sudden change of heart? No, that doesn't happen, not in real life. He dates actresses, supermodels, high profile women, not small-town chefs. He had a motive, a *plan,* and I played right into it.

Stumbling, I curse under my breath and then pull my heels off. Once I'm out of site of the manor, I run.

I never should have come up here. After seeing the crow, I shouldn't have tempted fate. I could have stayed in my perfect bubble, gone home the day after tomorrow, and taken memories with me that could be remembered fondly for a lifetime.

Instead, everything is now tainted and I allowed the one thing to happen that I swore I never would. He used me, just like my father used my mother.

Memories of being that sad little thirteen-year-old come flooding to the surface, and my father's voice rings out in my ears. "Don't you get it, the fastest way to the top was through you. I needed the connections. I don't love you, I never planned on loving you, and well, as for Shelby, she was a mistake."

A mistake.

Yes, I've grown up, and I do realize there are wonderful people in the world and some not so wonderful people, that is reality. That doesn't mean the indescribable ache that comes with not being wanted and hearing that I was a mistake isn't something that truly ever goes away. It can be buried, because life goes on, but it isn't forgotten, and Zach concisely got out his shovel and dug up the ghosts of a pain I never wanted to feel again.

By the time I reach the cottage I'm out of breath and my feet hurt, but I don't stop—can't stop—until I'm through the door with the lock secured behind me. Hidden from prying eyes, I allow myself a single heartbroken audible sob before I swallow the emotions. I hate crying. There's no point to it. It doesn't make things better, it only makes you weak, vulnerable.

My shoes make a loud thud when they hit the floor and piece by piece my clothes follow as I make my way to the bathroom.

The water is freezing when I step into the shower. I mean, people take cold showers when they are upset, right? Wrong. This is the worst idea ever, and I end up huddled just out of the spray, waiting for the shower to heat up. There, pressed against the frigid tiles, I pick up all the chains that I let drop the day I let Zach in and add a few more—shock, humiliation, gullible, sadness. I hate that they've made me feel less than who I am, like a disposable pawn.

All of my teenage years I felt like a pawn. My father used my mother and I as pieces in his life until he didn't need us anymore, making us disposable; and my mother emotionally used me because she couldn't handle how her life had turned out. I became the parent and she became the child. She became weaker than she already was, and I vowed never to turn out like her. I would never let someone else define who I was. So what she didn't have a lying, cheating man anymore. So what she had to get a job and work like the rest of the world. So what she lost her fake, stepford identity and never found it in herself to get a new one. A genuine one.

It was pathetic. She was pathetic. And I refuse to be her.

Sitting down under the spray, I shiver, hoping to end up numb, but instead the pain staining my skin doesn't wash away and is replaced with anger as the water warms. I'm not even sure what I'm angry at, it could be him, me, or both, all I know is that this assignment is done.

Done.

There's a loud knock on the front door, startling me, and my heart hammers in my chest. I know it's him, but I'll be damned if I'm going to answer it. Still, I turn the water off with more force than necessary, grab a towel, and head into the bedroom.

More knocking, which causes me to pause, and then I hear the creak of the front door as it is being opened and closed.

Of course, he can't just leave like a normal guy would when being ignored, he had to dig out his keys and let himself in where he isn't welcome! I'm fuming over his audacity when he pushes my bedroom door open.

Very cautiously, he steps into the room, and my body jolts with an unwanted natural reaction to him. His hair is sticking up from running his hands through it, and his eyes are wild with worry. His cheeks are flushed from the trip down here, and there's stubble across his chin that I didn't notice earlier. I'm bombarded by the outdoor smell of him, and my breath catches at how it had become something I craved.

"What are you doing here?" I ask sharply. He needs to go.

The sound of my voice has his eyes, which had been doing a slow trek down my body, shooting back to mine. I almost wish they hadn't, because he watches as water drips from my hair over my face and reads every emotion I'm trying to hide. His hands slowly fist at his sides, and his chest moves faster with each breath he takes.

I hate that I'm overly exposed to him right now, physically and emotionally. He shouldn't be here. He doesn't get to see me like this. No one should see me like this.

"Shelby." He takes a step toward me and pauses as I take one back, gripping the towel tighter. His presence is warming my chilled skin. It's quite possible if he comes any closer, I will either strip him or punch him. I don't know which urge would win.

"Get out, Zach." My tone is calm but annoyance is evident.

His eyes narrow as the thoughts in his mind go to war with each other. I spot the shadows under his eyes letting me know one of his migraines is setting in, and I hate that I care. He needs to go, but his steely determination tells me he won't, he can't. For his sake, I hope he took that medicine before he came down here.

"No," he replies with a small shake of his head. "I'll wait for you in the kitchen." Then he walks out of the room.

Why did he come after me? Why can't he just let me be? The assignment is over, we are over, not that there ever truly was a 'we'.

Resigned, I take my time getting dressed, but I can only stall for so long. With a heavy sigh, I put on my big girl panties and make my way to the kitchen to talk to the one person I *really* don't want to talk to.

Zach is sitting with his elbows on the kitchen island, his head lowered, and he's rubbing the back of his neck. As much as I don't want to feel bad for him, I do. Even if he did bring this upon himself.

"What's that?" I spot a pecan pie next to him.

His head lifts, and he follows my gaze to the pie. He lets out a sigh and then turns to look at me, blue eyes darker than normal. "I called Lexi and had her ship it for you. You said it was your favorite, and I thought you might like it."

"You thought I might like it . . . or was this part of *your plan*?"

He flinches. Good.

"I honestly don't know what to think," I say walking to the opposite side of the island so I'm not standing so close to him. "I'm sure you meant well, nice gesture and all . . ." My eyes narrow. "Or maybe you didn't, maybe it was all part of your win-her-over plan by calling my friend to have her help you with this little duplicitous charade of yours. Kind of pathetic, don't you think?" I cross my arms over my chest and briefly look away from him. He doesn't need to see how much this thought hurts me.

He lets out another sigh, runs his hand across his face, and again through his hair before pinning me with an unreadable look. Maybe he doesn't have anything to say for himself, so I save him the trouble of asking and tell him what he wants to hear.

"If you're here to make sure I don't take down your coveted blog post, I won't. It's already out there, so what would be the point?"

"I'm not here for that." He shakes his head, imploring me to understand. Understand what?

"Then why are you here?" I yell at him, and he flinches again.

"I needed to see you. I need you to let me explain." His hands slide across the island palm down, as if he's reaching for me.

"There's nothing to explain." I take a step back and lean against the oven. "You said it yourself, winning is everything to you. I should have known . . . I should have seen it coming from a mile away, and I definitely should have seen straight through your, 'let's start over' bullshit. The hatred you had for me at the event and when I first arrived was too strong to be swept under the rug. Why I thought you'd suddenly changed your mind about me, I don't know. God, I feel so stupid." I turn away from him and walk toward the French doors.

"Stop. Right there." His voice is firm, and I slowly spin to face him, anger flaring.

He's only a few paces away, but before he can open his mouth to say anything, I lay into him. "Even though I still have no idea what I did for you to dislike me so much, the truth is, someone like you was never going to like someone like me, and that's fine with me, I get it. But I know who I am. I'm smart, I think I'm beautiful, I'm successful, and I hate that until I met you, no one's opinion of me mattered but my own."

I saw the pictures of him and his ex-girlfriend on line. Hell, I saw all the photos of him with other girls, and none of them look like me.

"Shelby, you *are* beautiful and you are smart." He gets up and moves around the island taking a few steps toward me, his hands flexing like he wants to touch me. "And you're right, no one's opinion should matter but your own."

So, why did I allow yours to?

The sincerity of his words resonates deep within me, and my heart aches for the moments we had and will never have again. I liked him. I *really* liked him.

How did we get here?

How did I get here?

He hears the questions with each breath I take and sees the hurt as it trembles on my lips. With my eyes again burning, I spin around and put my back to him. Wrapping my arms around my middle, I look out the window and wish that I were anywhere but here with him. This assignment was supposed to be fun, and I had hoped it would be a two-week getaway on a vineyard where I got to cook and drink great wine. Instead, I broke my number one rule: never get involved with someone in my industry. I should have stayed clear of him, and none of this would be happening.

In front of the window the crow flies by. I turn to again find it again sitting on the back table, staring at me with its tiny black mocking eyes. The bird told me, I should have listened.

"I hate critics," he spits out with an edge to his tone that slices my heart. Whereas I had hoped he was going to apologize, I was wrong, he's only made me feel worse. My lips dip into a frown as he again hits me with another direct insult.

"So, you've said," I say dryly, not wanting to allow him insight to anymore of my thoughts. He doesn't need to know that sadness cloaks over me and pools at my feet.

As a critic, I've become immune to people's assessment of my work, but I let him in, and all it took was two weeks for him to tear me down. Not even two weeks.

"This all started because of one."

I know he's talking about the review from last fall, and I whirl around, bringing us face to face. "Not this one"—I point to myself, voice raised—"someone else!"

Brushing past him, I head back toward the bedroom. I can't stand here and talk to him. I need to get ready to leave. I need him to leave. The sooner the better.

Pulling open the first drawer, I yank all of my clothes out of it, and toss them into the suitcase that's open on the floor.

Zach, who didn't take the hint to leave, leans on the doorframe and watches me.

"Shelby, I told you about the review and the four wilted grapes. You have no idea the negative impact it had on our winery, and we didn't do anything wrong. It's critics and bloggers, people like you, who for whatever reason feel entitled to put their words out into the world as if they're gold. You don't suffer the repercussions of those words, we do, the owners."

"People like me!" My mouth drops, and I feel slapped. "That's really rich coming from you, I mean do you even hear yourself? You're such a hypocrite! You spent the last two weeks manipulating me with your words so I would write a good review for your winery, and now you want to slander my profession? It's funny how when the reviews are all shiny and perfect, like mine was this morning, you love them and what they do for your business. You encourage others to write more of them and flash them as often as possible. But when one comes your way you don't like, you pass judgment, hold a grudge, and holler for a penalty."

His eyes narrow, and his back straightens as he comes to his full height. His shirt stretches across his chest, through his shoulders. He looks pissed, but I don't care. He's a big boy and should be able to handle being shown his own hypocrisy.

"Oh, we're trading football analogies now, are we?" The tips of his ears redden. "Well, at least in football when a coach thinks something is called incorrectly he's allowed to dispute it! The play is reviewed and then the final call is made. I should have been allowed a review that night. He should have given me a second chance to correct the mistake and these last few months never should have happened." He turns around, walks out of the doorway, and then walks straight back in. "And for the record," he says, towering over me, "I heard you in Atlanta. I was standing behind you and Lexi, excited to meet you actually, even though I knew that review was coming. I heard you laughing about a bad review you had just posted. As I stood there being slammed with disappointment, I couldn't help but wonder if the guy who wrote our review stood around and laughed about us, too."

Somewhere in the middle of his tirade, I'd stopped packing and was acutely listening to him. He overheard my conversation with Lexi in Atlanta? Is that what this is all about? That's the real reason he never liked me?

Oh my God!

"I don't feel entitled when it comes to my reviews. They are my thoughts on my own blog. They are not published anywhere else. I told you in Asheville what writing those reviews meant to me. And, what you heard in Atlanta at the event was a completely different situation than yours. I gave them a chance to correct the error! I was served burnt food, and when I asked to have it recooked, the chef came out and served me raw food. He purposely went out of his way to be an asshole to a customer because I sent his food back. He caused a scene in the restaurant, was unapologetic about it, and then made me pay for inedible food. How would you have written that up?"

"I wouldn't have written anything at all," he says so matter-of-factly it makes me want to scream.

"That is not the point!" We stare at each other. "So, basically you're saying if the other team shows unnecessary roughness while you have the ball, it should be overlooked and you don't get the fifteen yards and first down?"

He pauses and licks his lips before lowering his head and pinching the bridge of his nose. I wait as he takes a few deep breaths and then drops his hand.

"Look, you don't have to agree with me, it doesn't matter anymore. The reviews I write aren't like the one you received with the four wilted grapes. That isn't what *Starving for Southern* is about, at least not for me. The people I write about, they followed their dreams and opened a restaurant. How can I criticize that? Just because the food wasn't for me, doesn't mean it isn't perfect for someone else. I've always tried to stay true to two things: writing the facts and keeping my opinions subjective."

"Still, a critic is a critic." He huffs.

"No, it isn't! No two critics are the same, just like no two reviews are the same. Zach, the critic and the review, they are one person's opinion and like anything in life, they vary. Take a look at your walls and the binder behind your bar. So many wonderful things said, but you're so focused on the *one* negative as if none of the others matter. What a shame to all those people who wrote something nice."

He pauses and his nostrils flare as his body goes completely stiff. "I saw you hug him."

"What? Who?"

"That night. In Atlanta. He was at the event," he all but snarls at me.

"So, what does that have to do with anything?"

"People surround themselves with like minded people, and if you're like him, then I have zero interest in knowing you. Also, the level of friendliness you shared with someone I perceive as an enemy is another red flag and where I draw the line."

Feeling completely dumbfounded, my jaw drops open as I replay the words he just said. How is this rational?

"So, what you're saying is, in order for us to be friends I have to share all of your same ideals and like all the same people you do and no one else?"

"No, I'm not saying that at all. Be friends with whoever you want, but know this, if someone had treated you badly, I wouldn't have stood for it, not for one second, nor would I want to be associated with them." He walks backward and leans against the wall with his arms crossed over his chest.

"First off, I've never read any of his reviews because they're about wine, so I don't know anything about him professionally. I only know him through mutual friends and events. Secondly, I didn't even know about yours because *it wasn't out yet*! And third, what makes you think I wouldn't have stood up for you had I known? This all goes back to your misconstrued perception of my character. It's funny how I worried about not trusting you, but did anyway, when all this time, you were *never* going to trust me."

I leave him to mull over my words and move to the closet to start pulling my clothes off hangers. A lump forms in my throat as I'm overcome with inadequacy and sadness. I don't know how to deal with him or this situation anymore. What I thought I knew about him and us is wrong, and that hurts more than I thought it would.

With my arms full of clothes, I storm back to my bedroom—where he's still standing—and stop in front of him. He sees unshed tears, and the anger etched on his face dissipates while wrinkles of concern form on his forehead.

"You could have asked me about him and I would have told you that he's no one to me, just an industry acquaintance I see in passing here and there. You should have read over my blog, if not only to read that review for yourself to see why I wrote it, but also to learn more about me. But you never even took the time. Instead, you chose to judge me for months while I was unsuspecting. Who does that? You have no idea what I do every day, but because of this fortunate situation we've found ourselves in, you saw a large following and an opportunity. All the while, you assumed the worst based on one experience that has nothing to do with me, a conversation you partially overheard, and a two minute greeting with someone I barely know. Whatever, Zach. Walk around and talk all you want about how you hate critics, but I didn't do anything wrong. I didn't do anything to you,"—I pause and pin him with a glare that I hope withers his balls—"except fall for you and sleep with you. All this is on you . . . not me. This is about your character, not mine."

A clock chimes in the hallway and the sound echoes through the cottage. Moving away from Zach, I continue packing, and this time I let the hated tears fall.

He crushed me, I'm pissed off, and my resolve is shattered.

"I should have looked more closely at your blog," he says, voice deep with dejection.

"Shoulda, coulda, woulda." I sniffle and hope he doesn't hear it. "I'm thinking you should have done a lot of things."

"Shelby," he whispers, moving to wrap one hand around my elbow and pulling me to him. I let him, but I don't relax as his other hand moves to hold the back of my head and he rests his forehead against mine.

"I'm sorry."

I take his apology for what it is, because I do think he means it, but too little too late.

"Zach, any relationship I go into, be it a short or long one, I go into honestly." I find the strength to pull away from his hold and put some space between us. "Honesty is the most important trait that I value in a person. There is no such thing as too honest. Does it hurt sometimes to hear the truth, yes, but it is always for the best, and it's that truth that allows loyalty. Honesty, truth, loyalty, and kindness are all qualities that I hope to find in someone. Do you want to know why?" I pause just long enough to take a breath before answering the question for him. “Because, that is who I am. This is what I give, and this is what I deserve.”

He runs his hand across his face, looking anxious. “How do I fix this? How do I fix us?”

“You don’t. There is no us.” Although we never discussed anything beyond the two weeks, prior to this morning I was open to the idea, now, I just can’t. “This was supposed to be fun . . . fleeting. It was never going to move past the two weeks. I am sorry it’s ending the way it is, though.”

“I don’t want this to end.” He shakes his head.

I didn’t want it to end, either. But I never lied and he did. I also didn’t use him, but he had no problem positioning me for his own gain. I am the exact person he saw, but turns out he is someone else.

“And I don’t want to be associated with someone like you. What was it you said again about like-minded people?”

He sucks air into his lungs. “You don’t mean that.”

“Yeah, I do. Zach, you used me.” I let those words sink in because he knows they are true. Of all the things he could have done, this is completely unforgivable. “You lied to me, you tricked me, you’ve humiliated me, and you belittled what I do. This is my life, I work hard for it, and I get to decide who is in it and who isn’t. You and me, we’re done.”

“Shelby—”

“Please leave.”

Ingredients:

1 unbaked 9-inch pie crust
4 tablespoons of butter, softened
3/4 cup of light brown sugar, packed
3 large eggs
1 tablespoon of cornstarch
2 teaspoons of vanilla
1/4 cup of dark cane or corn syrup
1 cup chopped pecans
pinch of salt

How to make:

Preheat over to 325 degrees.

Press uncooked pie crust into a pie dish.

In a mixing bowl, whip butter, and brown sugar together until smooth. In a separate bowl, beat eggs with a fork or wire whisk and then blend into sugar butter mixture. Sift cornstarch and salt into the mixture, and stir in vanilla. Blend in syrup and pecan pieces.

When all ingredients are thoroughly mixed, pour into the pie crust.

Bake for 30 minutes. Then lower the heat to 300 degrees and bake for 30 more minutes, or until the center is firm.

Serve warm with vanilla ice cream or whipped topping.

Chapter 24

sweet as a peach

Zach

It's day fourteen.

Her last day here.

Ominous clouds have settled in over northern Georgia, and bleakness across the hills and the vineyard perfectly match how I feel inside. We are meeting with Kelly for the final interview, and after this, the assignment is over. She's going to leave. Hell, if it weren't for this, she would have left already.

Behind me, people are moving about the library, staging it for the photos and video coverage, but I don't have it in me to oversee anything. Kyle took one look at me this morning and winced. I didn't sleep last night, combine that with a tenacious migraine and a bruised heart, and I know I've looked better. He patted me on the back and said he'd take care of everything, so I let him. For the last half hour, I haven't moved from this window.

I think it's safe to say that yesterday Shelby handed me my ass on a silver platter before she kicked me out the door. But then again, if you talked to her, she would probably say silver is too nice for me and I belong in a cast iron skillet—one where she's frying something.

I never meant for things to get as off course the way they did. I should have told Michelle and Kyle that the plan was off the table. They both had to have known that something was happening between Shelby and me, knew my feelings went deeper than business. Did I spell it out for them? No. I figured they would have put it together and figured the plan—that stupid, stupid plan—was done. Busted.

She bewitched me, and she managed to work herself into every part of my life. It's as if her just being here made this place cozier, happier. Of course, she's still a she-devil, but I love her sassy mouth and that she's never backed down to me. She's savvy and full of fire. She gives as good and she gets, and no one gets in her way . . . except for me, that is.

The way her body folded into itself when I told her I hated critics, well, I'm a jackass. The equivalent would be her saying she hated my wines, and that would have broken my heart. I tried to defend my rationale, but I only made it worse. That guy, the guy I was for most of the last two weeks, that is not me, and now I have to deal with the consequences.

I've lost her.

I am paralyzed by disgust with myself.

Looking down at my watch, I see it's noon and turn to watch the door. Shelby walks in, right on time. She isn't a minute early or late, and she looks stunning. Everyone turns to look at her, but she ignores us all as she moves across the room to sit in her original chair on my right.

Her hair is twisted into a knot, exposing the long lines of her neck, and her lips are shiny and pink, but her eyes are dark and her usual glow is dull. She's wearing pearls, a long-sleeved black dress, and gold heels. My eyes are drawn to her legs, and my body tightens as I remember the feel of them being tangled around mine. Warm, smooth, and soft, they were mine, and now they aren't.

Michelle walks over to her and asks if she would like something to drink, but Shelby frowns, shakes her head, and crosses her legs.

Her spark is gone today. The fire that she usually has blazing in her path has been extinguished, and it's all my fault.

"All right everyone, let's do this!" Kelly calls out. As we move to our seats, she leans into my personal space and bats her eyelashes. "You look nice today, by the way."

I can feel Shelby's eyes on us, on me, and my hands clench into fists. Keeping it professional, I nod my head and give her a forced, closed-lipped smile before turning and finding my seat.

I shift closer to Shelby and turn to look at her. Her eyes find mine and neurons fire all over my body. This girl affects me like no other ever has, and she's closed herself off with an impenetrable wall. She gazes at me as if I'm a stranger, and she's completely indifferent. It wrecks me to see how much I've damaged what we had.

Her beautiful deep blue eyes trail over me once and then turn away.

Kelly straightens the list of questions on her lap, clears her throat, and signals to the camera guy. He hits the button, and it begins.

"So, we meet again." Kelly smiles brightly at me. She has this thick ugly red lipstick on, and some of it is on her teeth. I should tell her, but she'd read into the comment that I'm looking at her mouth, and I can't deal with her today. I quickly return her greeting and cut my eyes back to Shelby, who smiles out of courtesy and politeness to both of us. I wish her smile were real, but it never reaches her eyes.

I am such an asshole.

"I have to say, Zach, my brief memory of your winery didn't do it justice. It's even more exquisite here today than it was two weeks ago."

I would have to agree with her, it is more exquisite here today, but that's because of the beautiful girl sitting next to me. She lit this place up in a way that it hasn't been for a long time.

"Thank you, I appreciate that." My voice is thick with emotion.

Turning her attention to Shelby, she pastes on an even bigger, now fake smile. "So, Shelby, tell me, how has it been for you? Two weeks is a long time to be away from home."

"Two weeks is quite a stretch, but I very much enjoyed being here." She relaxes deeper into her seat. "Like you said, it's exquisite, so I soaked up every moment, every taste, and the time flew by."

Hearing her words, they're like arrows straight to my chest.

"What was your favorite part about being here?" Kelly leans forward as if she's hoping to be let in on a secret. Her eyes dance back and forth between me and Shelby, and I know she's watching both of us and hoping for a reaction.

"My favorite part of being here is just that, being here. Zach and his staff took me right in and made me feel at home. Almost immediately, I felt like I was one of them, that I belonged, and that's a great feeling . . . one memory I'll take with me when I leave."

My heart plummets into my stomach. I want her to feel like she belongs, she does belong, but I'm certain after yesterday, she feels anything but. To be forced to stay here, play this charade being surrounded by people who you think were out to deceive you, must be awful for her. And it suddenly occurs to me that this interview could have gone in an entirely different direction. But knowing Shelby, who's always full of grace and class, she would never outright try to sabotage someone.

Just like the posts on her blog.

Damn. Now, I feel even worse when I didn't think that was possible.

A groan escapes me, and both of them turn to look at me. I close my eyes and rub the back of my neck.

"That sounds lovely," Kelly says with a hint of jealousy and curiosity in her tone.

Shelby smiles, and I hear the *click* of a camera behind us.

"What did you think of the wines? The last time I was here, I missed out on the tour, maybe I can sneak in a few tastes this time." She glances at me with a sly smile, and my skin crawls. How does this woman have a job? I can't be the only one who sees how lurid her remarks are.

"I *loved* the wines," Shelby replies, her irritation in this chick's constant behavior evident. "The chardonnay reserve was the first wine I tasted, but the sauvignon blanc stuck as being my favorite; it's delicious. To keep things fair though, we didn't rush the tastings. We spread them out over the two. Full. Weeks. Turns out there wasn't one that I didn't like." She smiles sweetly but tips her chin triumphantly.

I have to bite the inside of my cheek to keep from smiling. Shelby may have come into this interview wanting to get it over with, and to get away from me, but watching her spark flare because she refuses to be a doormat for anyone is amazing.

"Well, my, my. I'll definitely have to sample that one," Kelly says with a tempered gaze and a slight bewilderment.

"Michelle," Shelby turns to find her by the door, "will you please grab Kelly a bottle of the reserve?"

"Of course." Michelle smiles, playing along with Shelby. It seems Shelby is not the only here put off by this woman.

"Perfect!" Shelby slides around to face Kelly again. "She'll have that ready for you when we're done so you can take it home and drink it." Shelby shifts and crosses her legs in the other direction, ignoring the tension that's radiating from Kelly.

"I think that's a great idea," I chime in. Shelby's eyes drift to mine, they've hardened, and although nothing is being said, she's screaming a thousand profanities at me. She hates this interview, she hates having to be here, and she hates that I'm smiling at her. "I love the cabernet, so we'll include a bottle of that as well."

Her eyes narrow.

"How kind of you. I look forward to drinking every last drop." Someone in the room clears their throat, which is enough to snap Kelly back into her role. "Zach, tell me, how did it feel to have *her* here following you around?"

"I wouldn't say *Ms. Leigh* followed me around. She dove into the assignment with an incredible level of professionalism and worked tirelessly on what she was hired to do. I was present for the tour, two of the three tastings—the red and sparkling, and other than that, when given the opportunity, I would say I followed her around, waiting for handouts of the next amazing food item she was creating down in the cottage. She's very talented."

Kyle murmurs in agreement from his spot in the room, and Kelly glances at him in annoyance.

"So, how did the pairings go?" she asks, tilting her head to the side, pushing the interview along.

“Deliciously well. Many of our patrons were able to taste the ideas Shelby created, and everyone had a hand in choosing their favorites. We’ve all agreed that her final selections are the perfect pairings for our wines.”

“Actually,” Shelby interjects before Kelly can jump in with the next question, “I brought one here today for you to taste. It didn’t seem fair that you got to listen to us talk about the food and not taste any.”

Michelle walks over and sets a tray down on the table between the three of us. On it are three bowls of peach cobbler, and the admiration I have for Shelby multiplies.

“You never cease to amaze me,” I say softly, leaning over and placing my hand on her knee. Goose bumps run down her leg, and her eyes flare at the contact. Heartache leaks out from behind her structured wall and damn near knocks the breath out me. I never meant to hurt her.

“Well, look at this! Doesn’t it look tasty and full of calories,” Kelly says snidely as she picks up the bowl and takes a tiny bite.

“Yes, since you were sweet as a peach the last time you were here, I thought this would be perfect. I did consider making the lighter version for you, but all true Southerners know fat equals flavor, and when it comes to cobbler, it’s all or nothing.” Shelby smiles.

Kelly chokes on a half laugh, half shock, and I reach for my bowl to hide my pleasure at the dig. Never a dull moment with the she-devil.

The cobbler melts on my tongue, and I moan in satisfaction. “Shelby, this is delicious, and unexpected. Thank you.” I give her a small smile, but she doesn’t return it. “Eat up, Kelly. We don’t let good food go to waste around here.”

She takes a few more bites, each one less modest than the last.

"Speaking of unexpected, did you uncover any surprises during your stay?" she asks Shelby before setting her bowl down.

"Yes, actually I did." Her eyes sail over me quickly and then fall back to Kelly. "As you may know, my best friend and I own a restaurant back in Charleston called OBA—short for Orange Blossom Avenue. At the restaurant, we have a wall of honey. We love honey, all kinds of honey, and I was surprised to learn that Zach is a beekeeper, too. At the bottom of the hill, the bees are working hard to make the most heavenly lavender honey. It's delicious."

"Honey. Wow, Zach, don't you worry about getting stung?" Kelly picks the bowl back up and takes another bite. I wonder if she realizes she's eating it all. The cobbler is addictive.

"No, we have suits for that. Technically, the bees are my mother's, she loves them." I cut my eyes to Shelby, at least she has the decency to look a little remorseful. She knows the honey is private. "Although, we don't sell the honey, if you look around, you'll see she's subtly used the honey bee as a symbol here at Wolff Winery. The honey bee spends its entire life making the honey, and it never stops to enjoy the sweetness of what it's made. When we see one she wants us to remember that not everything is about work, which we all have a tendency to do, that sometimes we need to slow down and enjoy the sweetness of life."

Silence.

I peer over at Shelby. Her eyes are on me, and even though her face is blank and calm like she's taken on a bit of an introspective look, I can see they've thawed just a little. I'm not surprised that my mother's words might have meant something to her, nor am I surprised that I'm touched by this.

"How . . . sweet." Kelly loudly puts her bowl down and drops the fork so it bounces and bangs against the edge, breaking mine and Shelby's gaze. There's movement from the people behind us, but Kelly's petulance has me seething.

"I think so." The tone in my voice alerts her to my irritation. Her face blanches, as I scowl at her and she leans back in her seat.

"Well, from the sounds of it, you two knocked this assignment out of the park."

"That's baseball," Shelby states flatly.

"Excuse me?" Kelly flips her hair off her shoulder.

"He played football," she responds.

"Yes, I know."

Shelby looks at me and shakes her head. I think we've all officially had enough of this interview.

"Well, Kelly, thank you for coming." Shelby and I both stand with Kelly shuffling to follow. "We appreciate you making the trip back down here and look forward to seeing the interview online."

I shove my hands into my pockets, attempting to ward off a handshake, and step closer to Shelby. She's the only person in this room I want touching me, and based on the look she's giving me, I think she'd rather cut her hands off.

"It was my pleasure, honestly." Kelly adjusts her top so more of her cleavage is exposed and winks at me.

I'm officially uncomfortable, and my face glowers.

"Honesty sure is an underrated quality these days," Shelby says as she glances at me soberly. Without giving me time to respond, she turns, holds her head high, and heads for the door.

"Excuse me," I mumble to Kelly and follow before she has enough time to get in her car and drive away.

Humidity hits me as I run through the front door and catch up to her on the landing at the top of the steps.

"Shelby, please wait," I beg, reaching for her arm and pulling. I'm trying my hardest to stay calm, but all I want is to jerk her into my arms and to hold on to her for as long as I can.

Pausing, she keeps her back to me, and drops her head.

"Why, Zach? The project is over. That horrible interview is over, we are over, and I just want to go home."

Running my free hand through my hair, I look around at anything and everything, praying for something to pop in my head that will make her stay.

"But I don't want you to leave, not like this . . ." And that's when she turns around, and that's when I see it.

The end.

Her eyes are flat, her face is devoid of any emotion, and the only tiny tell that she's giving me to show she isn't completely indifferent is that she's chewing on the inside of her lip.

"Look, I don't know what more you want from me, but I'm done." Her eyes bounce back and forth between mine, and she lets out a slow defeated sigh. "You. Win. Isn't that what this is all about anyway? Winning. Well, guess what . . . you won. Game's over."

A chill sets in, and I'm numbed by the realization that she truly thinks all my actions—every touch and every word whispered to her over the last week were insincere. She believes that I was using her the entire time.

Yes, I wanted the blog post. I should have just asked her for it instead of playing games. And instead of asking her to write one, which she would have because she cares, I continued to let her believe she was doing something nice for us. But that isn't why I kissed her or made love to her.

Suddenly, one of the things I've always said I value most in people, I now have to question about myself—character.

"Shelby—" I try to speak, but my throat's constricting with guilt, and then I feel a pinch and a burning sting in my neck. "Shit." My free hand slaps at the spot, pushing away the bee that stung me. Shelby and I both watch as it falls to the ground. Neither of us move, and neither of us says anything.

How ironic that I get stung by a bee at this exact moment. Between my mother's symbolism, Shelby's love of honey, her nickname . . . I'm at a loss. For two weeks these damn bees have been beloved, and as it all comes to an end, I get stung. Just perfect.

Looking up into my face, Shelby's eyes are large as she takes in what just happened. Slowly blinking twice, she pulls her arm out of my grasp, and then backs away. Reaching the steps, she takes one long last look at me and the manor, turns, and walks away. The only sound I register being the clicking of her heels. Heels that I hated on her in the beginning and now love.

Ingredients:

8 peaches, peeled, pitted and sliced
1 cup sugar
3/4 cup brown sugar, packed
1/2 teaspoon cinnamon
1/4 teaspoon nutmeg
1 teaspoon lemon juice
2 teaspoons of cornstarch
2 cups of all-purpose flour
2 teaspoons baking powder
12 tablespoons of salted butter, chilled and cut into pieces

How to make:

Preheat over to 400 degrees.

In a large bowl, combine peaches, 1/4 cup of sugar, 1/4 cup of brown sugar, cinnamon, nutmeg, lemon juice, and cornstarch. Stir to coat evenly. Pour into an 8-inch glass baking dish. Bake for 10 minutes.

In another large bowl, combine flour, 1/2 cup of sugar, brown sugar, baking powder and salt. Using a mixer add in butter until mixture is crumbly. Add 1 tablespoon of hot water at a time until all combined.

Remove peaches from the oven and spoon on the topping mixture. Sprinkle the remaining sugar over the top. Bake for 30 more minutes or until golden. (Sometimes the cobbler will bubble over, so best to place the dish on a foil lined cookie sheet.)

Serve warm. Optional to top with ice cream or whipped topping.

Chapter 25

lace it with a laxative

Shelby

"Don't look back!"

I chant to myself as I make my way to the car.

"*You know he's watching.*"

"Don't break."

That interview was exactly twenty-four hours after he had left me at the cottage and being in the same room, that close to him, had been complete and utter torture. I couldn't wait for it to be over.

Over.

This is over. It was a fling. Time to go home.

Home.

It's funny how quickly I had started to feel at home here in northern Georgia with Zach, his friends, and his winery. It isn't a place I'd ever seen myself, but I had been becoming more open to the possibility. The possibility that maybe we were starting something worthy of pursuing. Then again, he wanted me to feel that way, so who knows what life here is really like.

The gravel under my heels causes me to wobble. I should have known better by now than to wear these shoes, but I'll be damned if I don't walk out of here at least looking like I got the last word in.

I make it to my car without incident, and as soon as I'm tucked inside with the door locked, I kick off my shoes and start the engine. Any shoe lover, such as myself, will tell you the fastest way to ruin a pair of heels is to drive in them. With the angle of the gas pedal the fabric of the heel will rip, plastic will scuff, wood will scratch, and worst of all, it could break. Just like my heart.

It hurts more today than I thought it would. The shock and adrenaline has worn off, and it has left my heart feeling as if it's been run under a meat tenderizer. I'm sore, I ache, and I feel like I've been flattened. I ache for what I thought I meant to him and for what he meant to me. I fell for him. Hard.

Under all the hurt, I'm angry. I'm angry at him and at myself. How did I let this happen to me? I know better.

Risking one more glance at him, my eyes flicker up to where I left him standing. Only, he isn't standing, he's on his knees. One hand on the ground, the other on his neck, and his face is wrenched up in pain.

What in the world.

Watching him, his arm collapses and his head hits the dirt. Unbridled fear shocks me as he rolls to his side, and with shaking hands I open the door and jump out.

"Zach!"

He doesn't acknowledge me; he just continues panting with dust flying around his face.

I don't remember moving, nor do I feel the bite of the gravel in my feet or knees as I land on the ground next to him.

"What's happening! Talk to me!" I push on his shoulder.

He shifts to his back and I'm assaulted with panic filled blue eyes.

"I can't breathe," he barely gets out, clutching at his chest.

His entire face is flushed red and has started to swell. The skin around his eyes, his lips, and his tongue.

Oh my God.

The bee sting.

Jumping to my feet, I start running for the manor screaming.

"Kyle!"

"Michelle!"

"Anyone!"

"Help!"

My heart is racing. I know I should stay calm, but I can't. He can't breathe and I feel like I can't either. Anxiety is sucking up all of my air and none of it is reaching my lungs.

Kyle meets me in the foyer, rushing straight toward me, and although there are other people behind him, all I see is him. Tears flood my eyes and Kyle's go wild as he grabs me.

"What, what's wrong!"

"Zach." I point out the door. "Bee sting," I say on a rush hoping it makes him move faster.

Quickly he drops me and runs into the tasting room. Michelle bursts past me and out the front door. I follow her as she pulls out her phone and dials 911.

Kneeling next to Zach, the next seven minutes of my life blur.

The winery keeps a bee kit in their first aid kit. Kyle flips off the blue cap to the epinephrine shot, lines the orange cap up with Zach's thigh until it clicks, and he administers the shot straight through his pants. Liquid Benadryl is shoved down his throat and he coughs uncontrollably but somehow manages to swallow most it. Lastly, hydrocortisone cream is rubbed all over his neck where hives have begun to spread.

In the background, I hear Michelle answer every one of the dispatcher's questions: name, symptoms, age, weight, does she know what type of bee it was, when did it happen, has this happened before, what medicines does he take, what he's been given, et cetera. They remain on the phone as the sound of emergency sirens drift through the air becoming louder with each passing second.

A crowd has gathered around us, but when Zach's eyes aren't pinched shut, they're focused on me.

"You're going to be okay," I whisper through the tears, assuring him, holding his hand. He gives me a slight nod and then looks up at the sky, while rubbing his chest and breathing hard.

The ambulance arrives, and the paramedics take his vitals as they load him onto the stretcher and into the truck. Kyle hops in with him, instructs Michelle to hold down the fort, and before I realize it they are gone.

Dust from the tires settles back on the ground, but I can't tear my eyes away from the long driveway. Michelle moves to stand next to me, and not one person says a word, the only evidence that this just happened being my galloping heart.

One by one, murmurs take up behind me as the magazine crew and the guests who had dropped into the tasting room, make their way back inside. Michelle gives my arm a squeeze and she leaves me all alone.

Sitting at the top of the steps, the tears drop faster as I think about how easy and quickly it could have been to lose him. I've never lost someone close to me and I'm shaken by this entire experience.

Part of me wishes I had gone with him, but who am I? I'm no

one. They are his family, I'm—for lack of a better word—just a colleague.

Some time later, Michelle sits down next to me. The sun was high in the sky when he left, but now it's begun its descent west. I'm afraid to ask what time it is, sitting here for so long, it serves no purpose, other than I just couldn't leave yet.

"He's fine. Kyle said the doctor is going to let him go home once the swelling is gone."

"That's good to hear," I answer without looking at her.

"Are you okay?" she asks.

"No."

It's the most honest answer I can give her, because right this moment, I can't filter through all of the emotions I'm feeling. I said goodbye to him and the stubborn part of me didn't want to take that one last look. If I hadn't . . . no, I can't go there. That didn't happen, so I need to focus on what did. I looked, and now he's going to be fine.

"Should I stay until he gets home?" I glance at her and she frowns with heartache.

"That's up to you. I do think he would like to see you." And this just takes me back to our conversation where I told him I was done, that we were done. That being said, there's no reason for me to stay.

"No, I think I'll go ahead and go." I stand and shake the dirt off of my dress. "Please tell him I'm glad to hear everything turned out okay."

"I will. If you're ever back this way, please stop in and say hello."

Giving her a closed lipped smile, I nod my head and make my way back down the steps to my car.

A deep sigh escapes me as I slip on my sunglasses and put the car in drive. The sound of the car, the crunch beneath the tires, and the distance growing between me and the manor has me squeezing the steering wheel, fighting the overwhelming sorrow seeping into my bones.

This was supposed to be only a stupid assignment with the added bonus of a fun getaway fling on the side. And as far as vacation flings go, I can't imagine one being better or more than this.

More.

Is there more than this? It was only a vacation fling, right?

Reaching the end of the driveway, I crack and pull to the side of the road. I certainly don't regret my time here. I'm appreciative of the opportunity to experience something so different from my everyday life.

I turn to look over the property memorizing the details. I spot two stone columns, one on each side of the driveway entrance. The stones match that of the manor, and on each column is a metal plaque that says *Wolff Winery.*

"Huh," I say to myself.

I'm not sure why I didn't think of this before, but Wolff is the perfect name for him and this place. What I know about wolves is that they are intelligent and work together in a pack. They watch their prey and study them for weaknesses, then they chase the mark over long distances, looking for the perfect opportunity to take them down. I hate to think that I have weaknesses, but I guess here I did have some.

The first being a six-foot plus male that exudes strength, raw energy, and undeniable sex appeal. I was attracted to his work ethic, the love for his family's business, and his perfect smile. The second being his attributes made me trust the things he said and did, and the fact that we were working on something together, and that he's Lexi's longtime friend.

My eyes move to her pie sitting on my passenger seat. What I wouldn't give for a fork at this moment. Yesterday, I couldn't eat anything, but today, I want to drown my emotions and my gullibility with food and Southern spiked iced tea.

After one last glance around the sweeping property, I find my favorite playlist and pull away. The gravel disappears as smooth concrete takes over, and just like that, the last two weeks are nothing more than an image in my rearview mirror.

I understand that in life people come and go. It would be so much easier if there were a way to stay emotionally unattached, but I'm certain there's a hidden lesson in all of this. I'm sure eventually I'll figure it out, but getting the CliffNotes version sooner rather than later on how to avoid this ache and emptiness would be much appreciated.

My phone rings through the Bluetooth of my car and Lexi's name pops up on the console. I have zero interest in talking to her after all that just happened, but I still accept the call.

"Hey." Wow, even I can hear the sadness in my voice. How pathetic am I?

"Hey, Zach texted me yesterday and said I should call and check on you this afternoon. What's going on?"

In the background, I hear the screen door slam that leads to her front porch. Lexi has the most beautiful old Florida farm home that sits on acres and acres of land in central Florida.

"Nothing at the moment, assignment's over, and I'm driving home." I contemplate telling her about Zach, but that is his business and he might not want me to, so I don't.

"Oh, then I don't know why he made it sound so urgent. Did

you get the pie? I was shocked when he called and asked me to send it. Such a thoughtful idea," she says all dreamy and cheery.

"Oh, he's Mr. Thoughtful." My words drip with sarcasm and suddenly I'm angry all over again. This episode with the bee sting is so unfortunate I wouldn't wish it upon anyone, but I can't let it detract me any longer from my gut feeling of why I am leaving in the first place.

He lied to me. He used me.

"What's that supposed to mean?"

"Do you remember how he was at the Feeding America event?" He was the perfect image of arrogance: icy blue eyes, a deep scowl, and a better-than-you attitude.

"Yes, don't remind me." She groans. Poor Lexi was so embarrassed that night.

"Well, let's just say I didn't find him to be that different during my stay here." Here he took that arrogance one step further and allowed his own self-importance with his *plan* to overshadow human decency. He wanted what he wanted, and it didn't matter if anyone got in his way.

"Really? I don't understand. When he called and asked for the pie, he sounded so happy. Happier than I've heard him in a long time. What did he do?" She asks the question in a low, hissing tone, as if she already knows she will need to roast him over a fire after I tell her.

Hearing Lexi get worked up on my behalf has a tiny smile making its way onto my lips.

Meg is a man-eater, guys love her and girls are intimidated by her. She's fiercely independent, and infectious with her personality and flare. Lexi, on the other hand, is the exact opposite. Lexi likes to be seen more than heard. She's kind, overly humble, and fiercely private. Her feathers never get ruffled, which makes her reaction just that much more satisfying, and me love her even more.

"Let's just say his motives over the last two weeks haven't been from the kindness of his heart." A heart that I felt beating under the warmth of his skin. Too bad its cold and calculating ways didn't reach the surface to give me a warning.

"I'm going to kill him. Explain."

"I will, but not today." And maybe not ever. For years, I despised my mother because she allowed my father to use her. Whether she knew he was doing it or not, it doesn't matter, all I know is now I don't feel any different. I feel stupid and want to forget about the whole thing.

"Well, you know I'm here for you if you need me."

"I do, and I appreciate it."

"Maybe I should send him a pie, too, but lace it with a laxative."

A laugh bursts out of me, oh my God, who knew Lexi had it in her? Her laugh follows mine, and the heaviness in my chest loosens a little.

"Poor guy, I don't know if he can handle it along with all those migraines."

Come to think of it, there were shadows under his eyes today, and his skin was more pale than usual. Yesterday must have hit him hard, and it must have lasted a good portion of the day. My go to would be *good*, but I think after the sting he's earned a pass.

"He's still getting those?" she asks, concerned.

"Yeah, he had several while I was there."

"That's unfortunate for him," she says sincerely. "Hey! How was my brother? I'm so glad you got to meet him."

My mind drifts back to the guys playing football behind the manor. Every one of them shirtless, sweaty, and looking like they belonged on a damn calendar.

"Your brother is hot!"

"Eww!" she squeals.

"Well he is, and his friends, too."

Silence falls on her end of the line, and this silence speaks louder than she probably intends it to. Hmm.

"Why didn't you come see him?"

"A large order came in, and I couldn't get away." There's sadness in her voice, but I know there is something more. For as long as I have known her, if she has a chance to spend time with her brother, nothing gets in her way.

"Must have been a big order." I'm probing because something about this isn't adding up.

"It was," she mumbles, sounding defeated, and then she changes the subject. "Hey, I have honey for you."

"Orange blossom honey?"

"Yep, lots of it." She sounds proud.

"Oh, Meg will be so happy." We have been toying around with the idea of selling a few brand products at the café, and her honey is one of them. We'll give her the money, like a commission sell, but it will have our name on it.

"I'll ship them to the restaurant later this week."

"How many are you sending?"

"How many do you want?" She giggles.

"All of it!" I laugh back.

"I'll see what I can do."

"Thank you."

"Shelby . . ." The creak of a rocking from her front porch makes its way through the phone to me. I can picture her so well with her shoulder-length light brown hair pulled into a tiny pony tail and bright green eyes, and I wish I were sitting next to her rather than sitting here.

"Yeah?"

"Are you okay?"

"I will be." A lump forms in my throat.

I've never really had a boyfriend, I've never wanted one past a couple of weeks here and there, but to me this feels an awful lot like what a breakup might, and we weren't even together. This sucks.

"For what it's worth, I'm sorry."

"You have nothing to be sorry about. Zach on the other hand—" Just saying his name causes my breath to catch and the ache to increase in my heart.

"I know, but still."

"Still nothing. This isn't on you."

"Maybe, but sometimes I think we don't realize the thing we need until it happens and then it's too late."

"What is it you think I need?" I ask, knowing this statement was meant for Zach, but hoping she can give me something, anything.

"I don't know, you tell me."

I thought I wanted him, but it's this one thing . . . this one unforgivable thing that I'm not sure I'll ever get past.

He used me.

Ingredients:

6 tea bags
2 cups of boiling water
Pinch of baking soda
1 cup of sugar
1 cup of peach nectar
6 cups of cold water
1 cup of whiskey
Sliced peaches, optional

How to make:

Steep tea bags for 15 minutes in 2 cups of boiling water. Add a pinch of baking soda and stir in sugar until dissolved. Transfer to a pitcher and add cold water, peach nectar and whiskey. Refrigerate and chill thoroughly before serving. Serve over ice and add sliced peaches for garnish.

Chapter 26

see the forest for the trees

Zach

I feel like I've changed.

I'm not the same person I was a month ago, and I don't know what to do with myself.

When I glance in the mirror, I still look the same. When I talk to the staff, I still sound the same. But when I stare out over the vineyard from the back porch, I don't feel the same. The colors aren't as bright, the wine isn't as delicious, and I feel out of place.

Fuck me, I miss her.

Shelby drove away a little over two weeks ago, and every day still feels like the first day. I had been hoping she would be at the manor when Kyle and I returned from the hospital, but she wasn't. What a debacle that was. Apparently, having one type of reaction doesn't mean you'll always have the same type reaction when stung, and now I'm extremely susceptible to anaphylaxis going forward. Thank goodness my mother had the foresight to have a bee kit, or that entire situation could have turned out so much worse, and thank goodness Shelby was there.

Shelby.

My heart dips as I think back to the moment of the beesting. I can see her sad eyes, the slight pout of her bottom lip that's lost its smile for me, and the closure she was giving us as she squared her shoulders and turned away. I'm trying to give her some time, but with each passing day, I doubt a little more that she's going to come back. I've sent her a few texts, which have gone unanswered. I've called both her cell phone and the restaurant, but she never responds. It's as if she's disappeared.

Swiveling around in my desk chair, I grab a hot boiled peanut and eat it without tasting it. Michelle made them and brought a bowl in. She's been making my favorite foods and snacks and bringing them to my office. I guess it's her way of apologizing, but it could also be because I haven't left my office much or that she misses Shelby, too.

We all do.

The sky is darkening again. We had near perfect weather the entire time Shelby was here, and ever since she left, it's been one storm after another. Currently, Kyle and I are tracking a storm cell that's coming more from the north than the west. It does seem fitting that the day she left, she took the sun with her, but we could do without the rain. Overcast, yes, it matches my mood and I welcome it, but for the sake of this year's harvest—enough is enough.

The door creaks open, and Kyle walks in. Without saying anything to each other, he sits in his usual spot across from me, grabs a peanut, and we stare at each other.

I don't think he knows what to do with me, either.

"How are the vines?" I ask him.

He glances toward the white board and looks at the overall

rainfall so far this season. We're almost to the halfway mark of what's desired, and there's still three months to go.

"They're fine. Soil is fine, too. At least this is happening now and not six weeks from now." He leans forward in his chair, tosses the shell, and grabs another peanut.

"Agreed." It's all I offer. I know I should care more, this is my livelihood and my reputation, but I can't find it in me today.

Resting his forearms on my desk, he studies me as he sorts through what he wants to say next.

"After this rain moves through, let's do a little crop thinning." His voice is low and calm. "It'll get you out of here and keep you busy."

Busy.

My brows drop down, wrinkling my forehead, and irritation leaks into my bloodstream. Does he not think I've been busy doing shit this entire time?

"Are you handling me now?" I ask through gritted teeth.

"Do I need to?" he fires back.

"No!"

Frustrated, I get up and start pacing around. I know I'm down. I know I could do more outside of my office, be more sociable toward my employees and our regular patrons, and I will, it's just I'm disappointed with myself and confused by the loss of her.

How can one person alter me so drastically? I feel as if I've lost a part of myself. I ache for her, her laughter, smart wit, gracious heart and her shine. Why did I have to fall for her? Of all the girls who've crossed my path, why her?

Before her, my life was simple. It was me and the winery—the way I wanted it. And now, I don't know.

Kyle's expression wanes as he tracks me around the room.

Sitting back in his chair, he crosses one ankle over his knee, and just waits patiently. He knows I'm having a hard time, even he feels the loss of her.

Sitting on the corner of my desk, I shake my head and stare at the floor.

"I keep asking myself, if I could go back and do the two weeks over again, would I do them differently? And I don't think I would. From the night of the Feeding America event to the weeks that followed, I directed endless amounts of hate her way. I needed to be angry at someone, and she unknowingly became the target. I've been pissed off for so long, I didn't even realize I was. The way Elaine ended things, and how that asshole critic and his shitty review left a taste so bad in my mouth I haven't been able to see the forest for the trees. Then as fate would have it, she shows up at our door. I desperately wanted to be proven wrong. I wanted to believe she didn't have that much power to influence the buying habits of so many, like that guy, but I wasn't wrong. Her post affected us just like the four wilted grapes."

"Yes, but it affected us for the better. There are always going to be articles, there will always be reviews. Some will be good and some will be bad, you're never going to please everyone."

"I know that, and I'm fine with it. I know who we are and how good our wines are, but this once, as we got closer to the end of the two weeks, I wanted to be wrong. I wanted to believe that she didn't have the power to do what was done to us to someone else."

"She's not Elaine."

"I know that." My fingers grip the edge of the desk with tension.

"And she isn't like that guy."

"I know that too, but at the time, hearing what she said and seeing her with that guy, it felt too reminiscent of Elaine's social climbing ways, and all critics were the same. Add in the fact that she works *all* the time, and it was the perfect storm."

I release the desk and flex my hands. Hands that love the feel of her skin and hair.

"Then you should have stayed away from her. There's a reason why people say you don't mix business with pleasure."

Pleasure I can handle. I think that's been my track record for most of my adult life. What I felt with her, physically and emotionally, it went way beyond pleasure.

"You're right. I should have stayed away, but I couldn't. She . . . she's just so . . ." I take a breath, trying to find the right words. "It was more than that, *she* was more than that, and you know it."

He nods.

"I don't think you were ever really testing her. The magazine hired her because of her knowledge in Southern foods and her popularity among foodies in the South. She wasn't a random freelance hire. Look at her Instagram account, she has over a million followers. There was no way we weren't going to have kickback from her post. This is why you set the plan in motion in the first place, are you forgetting that?"

"I haven't forgotten, which is why I say I don't think I would have done things differently. But what does that say about me? And I'm ashamed to admit I've looked at *Starving for Southern* and OBA's Instagram pages way too much over the last few weeks. The amazing pictures of her food and the few shots of her at the restaurant, it makes me feel like I haven't eaten in weeks, and I'm starving for it all."

"I think you're being too hard on yourself."

"Am I? Because the only thing I know is I am no better than or different from the critic from last fall. Because she is a critic and words are her profession, I lumped her in with the rest of them. For months, I've been asking anyone and everyone to hear my side of the story, how we served the wrong wine, but at no time did I offer her the same courtesy. It didn't even occur to me to go on to her blog and read what she has to say about the places she's reviewing. In my head, I made her out to be a blood-sucking dream killer, when in reality she is the opposite."

Getting up, I move back around the desk and drop into my chair. There's a football on the floor, so I begin rolling under my foot back and forth.

"Okay, I'm not going to disagree with you there, but you can be different than him. It isn't too late."

I stop rolling the ball and eye him questioningly. How? It certainly feels too late.

Turning my head, I find the spot where she parked her car on day one. The ache and heaviness in my chest continues to grow, and I'm starting to think that maybe I'm one of those people where no matter what I do, or what decision I make, it's going to be the wrong one.

One after another, some small and some large, incidents keep happening. I didn't mean for the mix up in the tasting to occur, but it did and sales suffered. I didn't mean for my plan to be mistaken for some sinister plot, I was trying to focus on what was important—the business. And I certainly didn't mean to break her trust and hurt her, when in the end all I wanted was to love her.

Love her.

Turning to Kyle, I tell him the thing I desperately wish I had told her.

"I am in love with her."

"I know," he says, giving me a small sympathetic smile. "I've known since the day she arrived. Michelle, too. I tried to ignore it, keep my head in the game, but I knew."

"Not true. I hated her then."

"No, you didn't." He actually laughs at me.

"Yeah, I did," I say more sternly.

"Zach, you're one of the most laid-back people I know. It doesn't matter what the situation is, you are known for being the calm, sensible one. You always act on logic and never emotions. That is until you found her standing in the tasting room."

Thinking back to the Feeding America event, when I first saw her I felt like I had been struck with an electric rod. A zap of sorts that burned. Suddenly, I felt as if I wasn't just meeting Lexi's friend, I was meeting someone who was going to be so much more. Maybe I loved her in that first moment, maybe I just didn't know how to recognize it, maybe that's why I was so irrationally mad, but I do agree with Kyle, I have never acted like that before.

"So, how do I fix it?" I ask, hoping he has some advice for me.

"I don't know." He shrugs. "Grovel?"

"Grovel?" I chuckle. It occurs to me that this might be the first one in two weeks.

"Well, I happen to know when you want something bad enough you're great at putting together a plan and executing it." He grins and the tightness consuming me loosens a little.

"Yeah, you might be right."

Ingredients:

2 pounds of green peanuts in the shell
3 jalapenos chopped
1/2 cup of salt
3 tablespoons of Old Bay seasoning
3 tablespoons of Cajun seasoning
1 tablespoon of garlic powder
3 tablespoons of red pepper flakes

How to make:

Rise peanuts in a colander to remove any excess dirt.

Pour peanuts into a large crockpot. Top with sliced jalapenos.

In a bowl, mix together all spices and sprinkle mixture over the top of the peanuts.

Add approximately 10 cups of water.

Slow cook for 18-24 hours. Check periodically to see if water needs to be added.

Drain and serve warm.

Chapter 27

food for thought

Shelby

Cool air bursts into the kitchen as Meg swings open the door from the dining room. It's five fifteen in the morning, it's still dark outside, and the ovens have been running for an hour already.

"Wow, you are up bright and early this morning," she says cheerily as she wanders over to see what I'm working on.

"Yeah, I couldn't sleep, so I thought I'd get in and get a head start. First batch of biscuits are done, and I'm working on a new cornbread recipe for brunch."

"Yum! What's in it?" she asks, sticking her finger in the bowl and then licking it clean.

"I'm thinking a coastal skillet with shrimp and spicy sausage." Lately, we seem to be getting more tourists during the brunch hour, so I've been trying to make it more Southern authentic and less breakfast traditional.

"Sounds like coins in the bank to me." She turns to grab the iced coffee out of the refrigerator. "Want some?" She waves the pitcher at me and I take in her outfit. It's Saturday, so it's going to be a long day, and she's wearing skinny jeans and four inch heels. The girl is amazing, has legs to die for, and it dawns on me that I haven't worn heels very much at all since I've been back.

Looking down, my converse sneakers have seen better days, and suddenly I hate the way I look. When did this happen? No makeup, simple clothes, hair just pulled into a knot—this isn't me. I've always prided myself more on my appearance.

Meg waves the pitcher again looking for my answer.

"Sure, as if I haven't already had two cups this morning." She refills my glass and then makes one for herself before putting the pitcher away and pulling up a stool next to where I'm working. Her perfume floats my way, she smells nice, clean, and I'm pretty sure I don't.

"You ready to talk about what happened yet?"

"Talk about what?" I play dumb and turn away so I don't crumble under her all-knowing stare. I was motivated this morning to make this new dish, but even I know that's a lie. I've been showing up before her, which never used to happen, and I've been cooking like a woman with an army to feed. It's all been a not-so-subtle attempt to distract myself.

"Shelby, don't act like I don't know you, I do. You haven't been sleeping well since you got back, and we've had more new recipes than ever. It's been a month since you left. I've steered clear, hoping you'd work it out of your system and find some sort of decision, but that isn't happening."

"I'm well aware that it's been a month." Walking to the trash can, I pull off the plastic gloves from peeling the shrimp and toss them in. "It's just that he threw me off balance and I feel like I'm still trying to find my footing. I swear it's a never-ending case of vertigo."

Reaching for my drink, I take a sip hoping to swallow down the emotions rising in me.

"I think you're overreacting, and you've overreacted to the entire situation."

I narrow my eyes at her, feeling a bit incredulous that she isn't firmly on my side in this. She just looks at me as if she's said the simplest, most obvious thing in the world.

"What?" She's my best friend, she's always on my side. I don't understand why all of a sudden, she's changing her tune. A few weeks ago, she wanted to burn down his winery, and now she's changed her mind? "How can you say that? You know what happened, you know what he did, and you know what he said."

"I understand that. But given a little time and some separation, I've realized this is different."

"How is it different?" My throat aches, my voice cracks, and my heart races. I take another sip of the coffee.

"For starters, it's been weeks and if it were really nothing, you would have moved past this. Also, if you weren't so stubborn, you might be able to think about this a little more from his point of view, too. And . . . he is not your father."

"S-s-stubborn!" I stutter, moving to set the coffee down. "His point of view!" I shake my head like she's crazy. "Not my father!" I don't even know where to go with this one. "Seriously, Meg, don't patronize me!" I point to myself.

"I'm not." She lowers her voice and holds up her hands in surrender. "All I'm saying is you've been so stuck on what you think he did, you're missing what he actually did. You both were given the assignment, and he was doing what he needed to do to maximize the opportunity and help grow his business. Was he using you, yes, but it had nothing to do with you. It wasn't meant to be personal, and his plan would have been the same no matter who they brought in. And I think if you'd step back and look at this on a broader scale, you'd realize you were doing the same to him."

"What!" I yell and take a step away from her. I would never use someone. My entire life I've been vehemently against even the idea of it. She is wrong. So wrong.

"Shelby . . ." She crosses her legs and leans forward. "I talked to you on your third day there. You told me how much of an ass he was being, but instead of leaving, you chose to suck it up because this article—this opportunity—was worth it, no matter what. You made your own plan to stick it out, period. A plan that had nothing to do with him and everything to do with your goals. The only difference between you and him is that he talked about this with his friends, and if he hadn't shown up to take you on the tour of the property, we would have formulated one, too."

My head becomes cloudy, and I pause to sort through what she's said.

"But he crossed the line." I cross my arms over my chest and glare at her. He made me believe there was something more, something real—he hurt me.

"Did he? What about you?" She picks her coffee up and stirs it with the straw, looking calm and composed. This infuriates me even more.

"That isn't fair! I never hated him. He disliked me from the minute he saw me last fall, judged me for something that I wasn't involved in, and then tricked me. He tricked me into liking him beyond a professional acquaintanceship."

"I don't know if he really ever tricked you. I think he was hopeful you'd write the post, but based on what you've told me, he wasn't suggestive toward it, and if he had been, you could have said no."

"That's the thing, I probably wouldn't have said no. Actually, I'm certain of it, and you know why? Because I thought we had become friends, more than friends, when all the while he was only pretending to be nice to me."

The timer on the oven dings, and I grab the mitts off a hook on the wall so I can take the biscuits out and place the tray in the warmer. Meg is watching me, but everything inside me is screaming.

Returning the mitts, I turn to face her and her determined expression slips a little at the sight of me. Persistent in continuing this talk, she sits up straight.

"Okay, maybe at first, but anyone who spends any amount of time with you sees how amazing you are. Everyone adores you, Shelby. Is it so hard to believe that he might have had a change of heart? Seems to me, he was pretty taken with you by the end."

"Doesn't matter anymore." I shake my head, and the grief I've felt over the finished label I stamped on us returns.

"Why not?" she asks, tilting her head to the side.

"Because. No matter how we ended, I'll never forget how we began."

Knowing she's not getting through to me, she frowns and then lets out a deep sigh.

"So, now what?" she asks.

"Now there's nothing." I move to sit back on the stool next to hers and look down at my hands in my lap. "I promised myself years ago that I wouldn't let anyone, man or woman use me as a stepping stone to get themselves something greater, and that's what he did." I raise my eyes to hers. "That when I found someone, any successes we had would be because we worked independently or together. You know how important character is to me. Kindness, loyalty, honesty . . . Zach lied."

"He also apologized to you, repeatedly. I know this all stems because of your father and your mother, but Zach is not your father. Your father never said he was sorry for what he did, just that he got caught."

"Why are you pushing this so much?"

She leans over and places a hand on my knee. "Because I think he's worth it. Don't you?"

"You don't even know him."

A small smile lifts one side of her mouth, and in a mocking tone, she says, "No, but Lexi does."

"You talked to Lexi about this!" I don't know whether to be shocked or pissed.

"Of course, I did. He called her, and she called me. Seems I'm your gatekeeper since you won't turn on your phone." She glances at it over on the prep station.

"I don't want to turn it on." I've been using it as a clock, it's been in airplane mode for almost two weeks now.

"Why? Are you afraid you'll answer one of his many calls?"

I don't respond because she's right, and I hate it. I want to talk to him, I do, but I don't know what's left to say.

"Shel, you like him. A lot. This is the first guy I have *ever* seen you like. Nobody can fake anything for two weeks. Whatever you saw in him—whatever you found so alluring and wonderful—that's who he is. Hearts speak to hearts, regardless of what comes out of the mouth. What he gave of himself to you and vice versa, there's no pretending, only genuine truth."

Hearts speak to hearts.

Oh, for cryin' out loud, she's right again. His did speak to mine.

I know it did, and that's why this has been so confusing.

"Food for thought," she says. "Maybe you should take one of his calls and hear what he has to say." Her eyebrows rise in challenge and then with her coffee in hand she slips out of the kitchen, leaving me to sort through this mess.

I know I'm going to have to talk to him eventually. I can't avoid him forever.

"And stop working so much, it isn't good for you," she yells from the front of the restaurant.

"Hello, pot meet kettle!" I yell back.

I have been working a lot. I finished the assignment and e-mailed off the pairings, complete with recipes, and my experience at Wolff Winery. I wrote and scheduled several blog posts for the release of the magazine. I created new menus for summer and fall for the restaurant. Also, I've steered clear of anyone and everyone who's come my way.

Feeling suddenly exhausted in a way I didn't know was possible, my eyes slide over to the boxes of honey that Lexi sent. As much as Zach and I talked about bees, and as much as he knows I love honey, I'm surprised he never mentioned the meaning behind his mother's love of the honey bee symbol. It's funny, too, because once he said it, I started remembering all the different places I saw them. Throughout the cottage, in the barn, on the wine labels, everywhere. Not once was there a wolf head, only bees.

Bees.

How disappointing that I'll never be able to look at bees or honey again and not think of him. He's tainted one of my favorite things, which I'm still trying to come to terms with, and he's also made me fear their sting even more.

Ingredients:

1 package of chorizo, sliced and chopped
1 cup of crab meat, chopped
1/2 pound of raw shrimp, chopped
1 small onion, chopped
1 cup of corn
2 tablespoons of seafood seasoning
2 tablespoons of olive oil
2 cups of self-rising corn meal
1 1/2 cup of milk
1/3 cup of vegetable oil
2 large eggs
1 cup of sour cream
1/4 cup of chopped chives
1/4 teaspoon of black pepper

How to make:

Preheat the oven to 425 degrees.

In a large cast-iron skillet or oven proof skillet, heat the olive oil over medium.

Saute together the first four ingredients until onions are translucent and shrimp are pink. Add in the seafood seasoning and corn. Remove from heat.

In a large mixing bowl, combine corn meal, milk, vegetable oil, and eggs until well blended. Pour corn meal batter over sauteed skillet ingredients.

Bake for 30 minutes or until top is golden brown.

In a small bowl, combine sour cream, chives, and black pepper.

Slice and serve. Top with sour cream mixture.

Serves 6-8.

Chapter 28

when you know, you know

Zach

I'm trying to remember the last time I was in Charleston, and I can't. It's been years, and I don't know why. I've always liked this city, the people, the food, the culture, and the architecture. It suits Shelby perfectly, and I can see why she ended up here.

Last night, I reached my breaking point. It's been a little over a month since I've seen her, and I understand her being angry, but at what point does that subside enough for us to have a conversation? What we had, or at least what I thought we had, wasn't something you just walk away from and never look back.

So, I got out of bed and drove half of the night to get here before her and her friend Meg get started for the day. I don't know why I'm here . . . I just know I need to see her.

I'm sitting leaning back against the front door to OBA when laughter floats down the sidewalk, and a surge of adrenaline spikes through me. I'd know that laughter anywhere, but as much as I want—need to see her, there's still a very strong possibility that

I'm not welcome here.

Closing my eyes, I inhale deeply, which smells salty like the sea, to try to calm my nerves. Knowing it's now or never, I open my eyes, stand, and step off the stoop. Through the darkness, I find her, and my heart takes off galloping in my chest.

Shelby's hair is piled into a knot on top of her head, and she's wearing a T-shirt, skin-tight pants, and heels. It's just like her to be walking down the sidewalk at five in the morning in high heels.

Damn, she is so beautiful.

The moment she spots me, her steps falter and she reaches for her friend's arm.

"Zach," she whispers, and the two of them come to a stop several feet away.

I'm assuming the woman standing next to Shelby is Meg, which makes me more nervous than I ever had been on any playoff game day. As the three of us stand there, I'm locked on to Shelby, and her mouth dips down into a small frown.

My heart sinks a tiny bit. I knew that frown was coming, but there was a part of me that had been hopeful she might be a little happy to see me.

Sucking up my manners, I tear my eyes off Shelby and look at her friend.

"Hi, you must be Meg," I say, taking a step forward and holding my hand out.

Meg is tiny. She has dark hair, light eyes, and I think if she possessed any type of superpower it would be laser vision. She would burn me to the ground and sweep away the ashes. Glancing down at my hand, her intimidating stare comes back to mine, and she raises one eyebrow in a you-have-to-be-kidding-me gesture.

"Okay." I chuckle, clearing my throat and feeling slightly

awkward. Her refusal to shake my hand reminds me of the Feeding America event where I did the same to Shelby. Man, I was a dick.

Meg shifts, shoots me a heavily weighted glare, and types in a code on her phone. The front door beeps twice, and she pushes it open before turning and giving me a warning look. I dismiss it since I've already decided I don't give a damn what her friend thinks of me.

"I'll make us some coffee." She swipes her finger around in a circle to let me know I'm included before settling on Shelby. "If you need me, holler," is all she says before the door slams behind her.

Even after she moves inside, I can still feel her stare through the window as I look to Shelby. Her eyes are full of caution, and I desperately want to remove the skepticism.

"Hey," I offer, trying to break the ice. My emotions are going haywire with want, yelling at me to grab her and kiss her when logically, I know I should drop to my knees and beg for her to tell me we can get past this.

Taking a few steps closer, she stops in front of me and takes a deep breath. "What are you doing here?"

"Waiting for you." I shove my hands into the pockets of my jeans to keep from reaching out to her.

"Why?" she asks, the shock mixed with confusion is clear in her tone as she shakes her head.

"Because. You won't answer my calls or texts, and I don't know your home address. Lexi wouldn't give it to me. OBA was the only way I knew how to find you. I want to talk to you. I *need* to talk to you, Shelby. Please."

I'm not past begging. Can she hear the desperation? Does she see it blanketed all over me? I hope so, because I need this resolved between us. I need her.

A light flips on in the back of the restaurant and pushes the shadows off her face. She pinches her lips together, looks off to the side, and lets her bag slide off her shoulder and down to the ground. Tension I didn't know I was holding falls with it.

"Okay, well here I am. Talk." There's fire under her words and skin, I can feel the heat, and I welcome it.

"Why wouldn't you call me back?"

Her face falls a little, but her eyes lift to find mine. "You know why." She stuffs her thumbs in her pockets and shifts her weight from one foot to the other.

"That isn't good enough." I lean toward her a little and her back straightens.

"Well, it has to be. I don't even understand what you want to talk about in the first place."

"Well, for starters," I say a little calmer and softer, "I never got to thank you for the blog post."

Her mouth falls open, and her brows pull down. "You're joking? You hate critics, remember?"

"No, I'm not joking, and it turns out I don't hate *all* critics." My mouth twitches, giving her a glimpse of a grin.

She hears the implication between my words, and her cheeks flush.

"That morning after you left, I locked myself in my apartment and stared at my phone while it buzzed. Plenty of people have written posts about us over the years, but it doesn't mean the same as when it comes from someone who you admire and care for. I was nervous to read it, and I don't know why. But when I finally opened it, I felt a pride like I haven't felt in a long time. Go ahead, take away the business it's brought us, none of that even compares to what your words meant to me. Thank you, Shelby."

"You care for me?" she asks, full of doubt.

"Yes, very much so. I'm sorry you feel the need to clarify that." I'm reminded again that she isn't just mad at us for the plan. She also thinks that *everything* that happened between us was part of said plan. I hate that.

She walks over to the window, leans back against it, and stares at me. "I really do like your wines," she says hesitantly, giving me a small smile.

"Anytime you want some, all you have to do is text me and I'll ship it up. Or, if you'll let me, I'll bring it in person."

She thinks about my offer and chews on the inside of her lip while her gaze drops to my feet. I don't know what she's thinking, but she isn't shooting daggers at me, so I'll take it.

I also take it as an invitation to lean against the window next to her. She doesn't move away. Instead, she tilts her head, looks over to meet my eyes, and takes in a deep breath. "Was it real for you? Did I make it all up in my head?"

"It was real. Very unexpected, but so real." Running my hand through my hair and across my neck, I think about how there are so many things I want to say to her. "Before you left, you told me I won, but you were wrong." My eyes drift over her face and return to her eyes, her beautiful blue eyes. "Don't you see, I lost. I lost the one person who has come to mean so much to me."

As my words sink in, she lets out a long exhale and shakes her head. "I don't know, I mean, how is that even possible? I was only there for two weeks, and most of that time you spent hating me."

"That isn't true, and you know it," I say, matter-of-factly.

"Do I?" Her spark makes an appearance.

"Yes." I lean down into her space to get my point across.

Her gaze scans over my face, and her lips tip down into a frown before she slowly reaches up and lightly runs her fingers across my cheekbone and down the stubble of my jaw.

My eyes momentarily drift shut at the contact, and my face tingles in her wake. Yes, I know I look terrible, and no, I didn't shave, but feeling her touch and this tiny flicker of concern she has for me tells me I did the right thing by coming here.

Realizing what she's done, she yanks her hand back and her expression shifts to a scowl. Pushing away from the window, she walks a few paces down the sidewalk and then back. Her heels click loudly and she squeezes the bun on top of her head before stopping in front of me.

"Zach," she starts, gesturing with her hands. "All of this, it's so hard for me. I don't just feel humiliated—I feel betrayed, too. It's one thing to embarrass myself, I've done that plenty of times in my lifetime, but I opened myself up to you. I bared it all, literally and figuratively. I never had anything to hide. Do I wish I had kept my cards closer? Maybe. But I don't regret my actions. What you see is what you get. But all of you . . . you sucked me in so I would grow to care for each of you, and then I come to find out all of you were conniving against me and lying. Who does that?"

"It wasn't a lie." I shake my head, pushing off the window to stand closer to her.

"But it was." She throws her hands out before they drop.

"Tell me, what can I do or say to you to make you believe differently?" I reach for her, but she steps away.

"There's nothing you can say, and even if there was, I don't know if I have it in me to go there again. Can't we call a spade a spade? We had fun, we finished the assignment, it's time we both move on."

"See, that's the thing. I don't want to move on . . . at least, not without you."

Her eyes widen in disbelief. "Two weeks, Zach. It was only two weeks."

"Who cares! Two weeks, two months, two years . . . whatever. When you know, you know. And I know I want you." My eyes bore into hers, no hesitation, no doubt.

"Why?"

Do I or don't I lay it all out there? Something tells me no. Keep it honest, keep it real, but keep it simple.

"I remember having a conversation once with my mother. It's one of those conversations that really shouldn't have stuck with me, but it did. I think I was thirteen at the time, and we were collecting honey from the bees when she said, 'One day, when you least expect it, you'll get stung, and there's no turning back.' I don't find it a coincidence that she loves bees, you love bees, your name is Shel-bee, and here I am floundering because I've been stung so hard it hurts. It hurts to be with you, it hurts to be without you."

"Zach—"

"No, let me finish. Over the last couple of weeks, I've ached so bad that I don't know what to do with myself. Shelby, I'm sorry. I'm sorry I hurt you, I'm sorry I didn't tell you about our plan sooner, because it did cross my mind to, and I'm sorry I waited so long to come here. I'm just sorry. Sorry for everything. Tell me, how can I make this right? Us right?"

The door opens, and we both turn to look at Meg. Her eyes skip between the two of us as she tries to assess the situation.

"Is he staying?" she asks Shelby.

Shelby turns to look at me, as I run my hand over my head again, waiting.

"No," I tell them.

"Are you sure, there's plenty of work around here that needs to be done." Meg smirks.

"I have to get back. They didn't know I was leaving, but . . ." My eyes trail back to Shelby. "I needed to see you. It's been too long."

"Okay, be right back then." Meg slips inside, leaving us alone on the sidewalk once again.

She isn't going to give me an answer, and she isn't going to tell me what to do. Taking a deep breath, I push away my frustration and bring up the last thing I wanted to talk about.

"Next weekend is the wrap-up party. I can't imagine that you won't come, but I hadn't heard if you were. I really hope that you do. The wines are an afterthought to the work you did for the assignment. This party is really for you."

"I disagree." She pushes a few fallen hairs off her face. "The wines are the showcase, the food is the afterthought."

"I guess we'll have to agree to disagree." I give her a small smile, and her eyes soften. Her beautiful blue eyes.

The door flies open. "Here." Meg hands me a large to-go cup and a bag. "Our iced coffee is to die for, and I packed you some orange blossom madeleines."

Orange blossom, just like their restaurant.

"Thank you, Meg. I appreciate it." The emotion is thick in my voice, which I'm sure they both notice.

She gives me a small smile, turns around, and goes back inside.

The darkness of the night has shifted to more of a midnight blue, sunrise is on its way, but where Shelby's standing with the light of the street and the restaurant, I can see her perfectly. I take another mental picture, hoping—no, praying that this isn't the last time I'm going to see her.

"Shelby—"

"They offered me the job," she says quickly, cutting me off.

My heart skips a beat and pain weaves through every part of me. I had forgotten about the job she interviewed for in New York City and every little bit of hope I had been clinging to snatches free. It's not that I'm not up for long distance, because I am, but the five hours we have now is nothing compared to the sixteen between here and there. Looking at the ground, I need a moment to pull myself together, recognizing the distance already growing between us. This is her dream. This is what she wanted. I need to move past myself and give her what she needs.

Finding her eyes, I smile and see her let out the breath she was holding. "Congratulations. I'm so happy for you."

"Thank you," she whispers.

Silence falls between us. I guess there's nothing else to be said. How do I compete with her goals and dreams? It's not like I can ask her to stay. Hell, I can't even get her to answer my phone call.

Needing some type of connection with her before I go, and before this ends, I step forward and cup her cheek in my hand. She gasps, but that doesn't stop me from leaning down and kissing the corner of her mouth. God, do I miss her mouth.

Her hand wraps around my wrist as I drop my forehead to hers, but she doesn't pull me off. Can she feel my heartbeat? Can she feel how fast it's beating for her?

"Zach," she whispers, my name on her lips almost causing me to shake.

"I know, and I'm going, I just—"

Not wanting this to be goodbye, and being afraid that it is, I pull her body against mine and drop my head down beside hers. She stiffens in surprise, but my arms wrap around her, holding her tight. I need to soak in the feel of her curves and the smell of her hair and skin. I need this moment as much as I need my next breath, after all, this is why I came, right?

When I find the strength to step back, I slide my free hand down her arm to her fingers. Tangling them together, we both watch as I run my thumb over the inside of her wrist and across her palm. The rise and fall of her chest picks up, but I can't tell if it's because she likes me touching her or if she's repulsed by it.

I second-guess leaving here and not telling her exactly how I feel, after all, what do I have to lose, but I don't. There isn't really any one thing holding me back, but here in the dark as she's heading into work, after the silence of the last month and knowing she's moving, this isn't the time or the place. Instead, before I turn, let her hand go, and walk away, I say the other three words that constantly consume me . . .

"I miss you."

Ingredients:

2/3 cup of sugar
3 large eggs
Dash of salt
1 1/2 teaspoon of water
2 Drops of flavoring (I used orange essential oils)
1 cup of all-purpose flour
3/4 cup of unsalted butter, melted, cooled
Powdered sugar

How to make:

In a large bowl, beat together sugar, eggs, and salt. Once whipped, add the flavored water.

Next, mix in flour and butter – alternating.

Refrigerate the batter one hour to thicken.

Preheat oven to 375 degrees.

Grease the Madeline pan and dust with flour. (If you skip this process the cookies will darken.) Using a teaspoon, spoon the batter into the wells. Bake time for a standard cookie size is 12-14 minutes. (Since the cook time is short, I recommend trying just a couple the first time to make sure your spooned portion isn't too large.)

Return unused batter to the refrigerator until it's time for the next round. Repeat.

Remove pan from oven and allow to cool.
Sprinkle with powdered sugar when ready to serve.

Chapter 29

not the end

Shelby

It's been six weeks since we finished the assignment and almost two since Zach came to Charleston. I know most—like Meg and Lexi—thought I was being irrational over this entire situation, but I needed the time. I needed to pack away over a decade of determination and stubbornness that I had allowed to take over, I needed to let go of the misconceptions I had about the role of a partner, and I needed to get myself together enough so I could swallow my pride and face him. And you know why?

Meg is right . . .

Zach is worth it. He's so much more than worth it.

He wasn't the only one who had a plan. I always have a plan, a plan for everything, and Meg pointing that out to me was eye opening.

The thing is, I fell for him. I fell hard. Harder than I ever have, and in such a short amount of time, combined with our unique situation, the speed at which we were traveling was faster than my ability to mentally adjust my plans, my dreams. Emotionally, I was already derailing and then after overhearing them in his office, I crashed into a thousand tiny pieces.

It had to happen. I needed to break in order to put myself back together. And in doing so, I looked at all the different pieces of myself and realized that, although I do love how hard I've worked and who I am, plans don't need to fit together so tightly. I need to be able to make room for the unexpected, forgiveness, and love.

All three of which happen to encompass Zach.

Zach.

Inwardly, I sigh when I think his name. Every time. I was already finding my way back to him, but to have him show up in Charleston and lay himself out there for me, to me, it was all I needed to be able to make this drive today with a renewed purpose.

"I can't believe you spent two weeks here. This is incredible." Meg says with her face glued to the window as I turn into the entrance of the winery. It's as beautiful as I remember, only now the vines are fuller and the hillsides are more lush from being kissed by the summer sun.

I'm also pleased to see that there are cars lining both sides of the driveway. The more people that are here, the more time I'll have to work up the courage to talk to him.

Not that I don't want to talk to him, I do. I just need a few minutes . . . or hours for my nerves to calm down.

When I step from the car, the air clings to my skin as if it's welcoming me. There's a hint of clover and lavender, and as I breathe it in, I breathe this place in. With each inhale, a small piece of my anxiety falls away. I can do this.

Meg pops the trunk, and we pull out four large thermal bags filled with fifty individual peach and blackberry cobblers. After reviewing the end of the assignment interview, the website content editor of the magazine fired Kelly. It seems he also found her behavior inappropriate and assured us that there would be modifications to the video, or if we so chose, we could re-record it. Feeling somewhat vindicated, I offered to make the same cobbler for the party. He was thrilled with the idea.

"Where's the cottage you stayed in?" Meg asks as she turns in a slow, awe-struck circle. I can relate. I felt the same way the first time I fully saw the vineyard, too.

"It's behind the manor and down the hill."

I miss the cottage. I miss this place.

"Well, I'm completely jealous. You call it a manor, but it's a castle and you got to live like a princess."

"Come on, let's get this stuff inside." I laugh and bump my shoulder against hers. The move makes her wobble a bit, and I look down at her feet. "Oh, yeah. Make sure you watch how you're walking, heels aren't the best here."

"Oh, I'm on my toes already." She giggles, gravel kicking up behind us.

Today, I decided to wear a long light pink dress. The color compliments the wine, it has short sleeves in case we end up outside, and has a nice slit to show off my legs when I walk. It's subtly sexy and when paired with a new pair of gorgeous sparkly heels, I may be nervous on the inside, but on the outside—no way.

The front door to the manor is wide open, and the closer we get, the louder the hum of voices gets, which is causing the small slip of calm I had a moment ago to falter. I listen closely to see if I hear his laugh over the others, but I don't.

Zach's called me twice since visiting, neither time I answered, but I did text him back when he asked if I was coming. His only response was, "Good." I worry a little that he might be upset—or by this point indifferent—but I'm hoping that he is at least going to hang on through this party. If I hadn't come, I could see him being fed up and walking away, but I'm here, and I hope it isn't too late.

"You came!" Michelle squeals after she spots us in the doorway and races our way. "Zach said you were coming, but I wasn't sure." She throws her arms around me and squeezes, hanging on a tad longer than normal. "I'm so sorry, Shelby." She lets out in a rush, and I pull back. Her eyes are large and remorseful, the sincerity shining in them.

"We'll talk about it later, okay?" I reassure her, giving her a small smile, which she mirrors.

"Yes, I hope so. Here let me help you with these." She takes the bags and turns to Meg. "Hi, I'm Michelle."

Meg gives her a once over, spots her boots, and smiles brightly. "Meg," she responds, a friendship already forming.

"Shelby, you go mingle, we'll take care of these." She glances at the bags, but I see right through her suggestion. It's her not-so-subtle way of telling me to go find Zach.

Wandering into the tasting room, I pass the first of several large foam board photographs of Zach and me placed on easels all around the room. Yes, there are a few of the winery, other employees, patrons, the dinner party with Zach and his friends, but mostly they are of the two of us tasting the wines. My head tilts to the side when I spot a few I don't remember being taken at all.

In some, we are looking at each other cautiously, curiously, and in others, we are laughing. But seeing these in sequence, the way our expressions and body language changes over time, it's so obvious how deeply we both fell. By the end, Zach's blue eyes aren't piercing and calculating, they're warm, thoughtful, reverent, and mine are tender, affectionate, and in awe.

Zach is right, two weeks, two months, two years, it doesn't matter. When you know, you know, and I know, too.

"Hi."

My ears burn, and my heart skips as his deep voice settles within me. There's a part of me that wonders if he's angry for how I handled the past six weeks, or will he be happy I'm here.

When I turn, my eyes drop to his feet. I need that extra second to compose myself, because seeing him today is different, I am different.

Sliding up the length of him, I find I'm met with crisp blue eyes filled with wariness mixed with adoration. I hate that he feels unsure because of me.

"Hi," I say, giving him a small smile. I'm trying so hard to hide the fact that my heart is galloping like it wants to race out of my chest.

Tension around his eyes and through his jaw slips away and he returns my smile with one of his own that leaves me breathless.

"The pictures turned out great." I point to the few that have been displayed near the back bar, but Zach doesn't look away. His eyes are for only me, his sparkling blue eyes.

"Yeah, they did. Teddy said the videos turned out nice as well. The magazine is really pleased with the footage for their website."

"Good, that makes me really happy to hear."

He smiles, lips closed, but still looks at me with complete adoration.

Hearing Michelle laugh, I glance toward the table filled with food and see her leaning into Kyle with his arm wrapped around her. Both completely caught up in each other and radiating happiness.

"Well, look at the two of them," I say, and this time Zach

manages to drag his eyes away from me.

"They've been inseparable since the dinner at the cottage." There's a fondness to his tone, he's happy for them.

"That's so great," my thoughts echo his.

"Michelle told me they barely made it around the corner of the cottage before he had her pushed up against the wall and was kissing her."

My jaw drops open, and I let out a small laugh. "She told you that?"

"Yeah, she was really happy." He shrugs his shoulders. "I'm glad you decided to come. If you had missed all this because of me, I um—" He shakes his head and flattens his lips into a thin line. Taking a deep breath, he runs one hand through his hair, disheveling the way he had it styled. I desperately want to reach up and smooth it down. He's nervous, and that makes him sexier and even more endearing. "You look beautiful," he says softly, running his hand through his hair again trying to fix the mess he made.

"You don't look so bad yourself." And you smell delicious.

His smile widens, and my breathing picks up as I shift closer to him just a tiny bit.

"No headaches today?" I scan his face, looking for any trace of them, but the looming shadows are nowhere to be found.

"No. Kyle and Michelle sent me back to the doctor, seems everyone thinks I needed to get a better handle on managing stress. I can't imagine why?" He grins, joking, and I smile along with him.

Goodness gracious, what this guy does to my heart.

A throat clears to my right, and I turn to see Meg standing there beaming from ear to ear at us. We didn't even realize she had joined us.

"Sorry!" Zach says as he turns his attention to her and holds out his hand. "We haven't properly met yet. Hi, I'm Zach." He gives her a megawatt smile, and she falters briefly. When he turns on the charm, it's impossible not to swoon.

"Meg. Nice to meet you." She slips her hand in his. "This is quite a place you have here, Zach."

"I think so," he says proudly as he releases her hand.

"Shelby's a lucky girl to get to spend two weeks here. I mean in a castle and a place that has endless amounts of free wine, I can't think of anywhere better." She winks at me, and then she turns back to him with a stunning smile of her own.

Zach laughs, and my heart dances at the sound. Two of my favorite people are conversing, happy, and my cup runneth over.

"Actually, I'm the lucky one," he says affectionately. He pulls his hand out of his pocket and reaches over for one of mine. Warm fingers bring my hand to his mouth and he kisses the back of it. This man melts me and in the best way possible.

"Zach!" From behind, he gets slapped on the shoulder, and we turn to see Jack and Bryan, but no James. "Hey, Shelby," Jack says cheerfully as his eyes drop to our connected hands. He grins and gives Zach an "I told you so" look before turning his attention to Meg.

Neither of them moves or says anything, and I inwardly laugh at their competing appraisals of each other. Jack's more in intrigue, and Meg's more in scrutiny. "And hello, gorgeous," Jack says after the silence between them has already stretched into uncomfortable.

Meg, the girl who isn't normally thrown off by meeting new guys, seems flustered. Her sharp tongue and quick wit are missing in action. Interesting.

"Hey, I'm glad y'all could make it," Zach says, breaking the silence and turning toward Bryan.

"Absolutely!"

"We're glad the timing worked and we could drive up. Wine and some of Shelby's cooking . . ." Jack eyes me hopefully until I nod. "How could we turn it down?"

I laugh and shake my head at Jack. "Meg and I brought the cobbler, but the rest of the food was prepared by others from the recipes for the pairings. Although, I personally didn't cook the food today, I promise you won't be disappointed."

His face falls a little. "I don't know about that." He huffs, and a sense of pride washes over me. I love that Zach's friends like my food. Food is my thing, and to me cooking for friends is an expression of love, so knowing he feels this way means something to me.

"Well, if you like mine, you'll love Meg's even more. Her cooking is way better. You should drop by our place in Charleston next time you're up and have her cook for you," I say conspiratorially.

"Is that so?" He turns and looks at her again as if she's become the answer to all his prayers. He grins, dimples popping out, and inwardly I laugh. Dimples are her weakness.

Meg's glare drops into a scowl. I almost feel bad for Jack. He has no idea what he's getting himself into, and Bryan chuckles next to him.

"Come on, darlin', how about we leave these two to do some work, and you and I can get to know each other better." He holds his hand out to her, but she doesn't take it.

Frowning, she looks at Zach and me as she weighs her options. She knows we need some time to talk, but she isn't sure about his friend.

"Fine." She finally relents, but instead of taking his offered hand, she folds her arms against her chest. But he smiles even bigger, his dimples deepening, and drops his hand.

"Fine starts with an F. Did you know there are only two Fs needed to satisfy a man? Food and fu—"

"Oh my God! Don't even say it," she snaps as the three of them turn and head for the bar. "You do realize we just met?"

He laughs and places his hand on her lower back.

"Should I be worried about her?" I ask Zach, half joking, half not as they disappear into the crowd.

"Nope. From what I experienced of her outside your restaurant, I think she'll be fine," he draws out his words.

"Yeah, you're probably right." My eyes skip to the direction the three of them walked off in, but I don't see them.

"Want to move outside with me? It's a little quieter out there," Zach asks.

"Okay." I give him a small smile and resist telling him that I would go anywhere with him just to be near him.

Walking out onto the terrace, my breath leaves me. I didn't forget how beautiful this view was, but seeing it again, it's so much more than I remember.

I scan across the countryside, taking in each of my favorite places: the overlook, the back orchard where the beehives are, the barn, and lastly my cottage. The memories here feel like a lot more than what occurred over only two weeks, and elation fills me at the thought of more. Many more.

A breeze skims across the terrace lifting my hair, which he gently tucks back behind my ear and out of my face. My skin warms from his touch as he settles in closer to me.

"Did you miss it?" he asks quietly.

When I turn, I find him leaning against the railing watching me. "Yes, but not as much as I missed you."

He releases a breath, which is filled with apprehension and anticipation, and he blinks slowly as he opens his eyes with a calm confidence. Zach isn't the type of man to give up on something that he wants, and I find this determination and drive incredibly attractive.

"How are you?" he asks stepping closer, lightly grasping my fingers with one hand and running his thumb over them.

"I'm good. Better now." My cheeks heat and his eyes brighten at the emotion. "I didn't take the job."

His fingers tighten around mine and his throat moves as he swallows. "Why not? I thought this was your dream?"

"Well, my dream has always been to have my own show. This isn't that. Do I think this is an incredible opportunity, yes. Would it help my career, maybe, but I don't know. What I've realized over the last couple of weeks is that dreams can change, and that's okay. Starting when I was thirteen, I was by myself every night until I left for college. I think a big part of that dream was wanting to escape the life I had. But now, I love the life I have. I'm surrounded by friends that I adore, I'm part owner of a restaurant that is amazing, and I'm not ready to leave that. There will be other opportunities, this one just isn't it."

"I see." His face is unreadable, but the tension in his jaw fades.

What I don't tell him is that a week after he came to Charleston, Meg and I had a heart-to-heart where she broke down and cried. We've always been so supportive of each other's dreams, it never occurred to me how much me leaving would impact her. Truth is, after almost ten years, it would impact me greatly, too.

"Shelby!" I turn to see Mr. Carothers walking our way, smiling as if he's won a prize. "Great news!" He claps a hand on my shoulder as he continues, "I talked to my friend, Dale Lawler, he's a producer for our network channel, and after reviewing the video clips and your two assignments for the magazine, your blog, and the reviews for your restaurant, he's very interested in hearing your pitch ideas for a show."

What?

My eyes dart to Zach, who's looking at me with an innocent expression.

"I'm not sure I understand what you're talking about," I say to him, confused.

He looks from me to Zach and then back to me.

"You didn't tell her?" he asks Zach.

"Nope. I wasn't sure of her upcoming plans and I didn't want to get her hopes up. I figured we'd wait and see."

"Get my hopes up about what?" I ask Mr. Carothers.

"A couple of weeks ago, Zach mentioned that you had on-air aspirations and some great ideas for a new network show. June and July are our pitch months, so if you're interested, now's the time."

My mouth falls open; I can't tear my eyes off of him.

He can't be serious?

I glance to Zach. He smiles at me and nods.

Oh my God! He is serious.

"I'm definitely interested," I squeak out, barely being able to form the words.

"Great! And I also happen to agree with Zach, too, you'd be great on the screen. I'll e-mail you Monday with more details."

I squeeze Zach's hand to keep from reaching out and grabbing him. "Thank you. I appreciate that."

"And I know I've told you both already, but again, well done on the assignment. The food and the wine are superb. And, now that I've found you, talked to you, and congratulated you, I can go eat some more. There's brisket on the table calling my name." He nods his head and turns to leave as quickly as he came.

"Did that just happen?" I turn and ask Zach while pointing my thumb at Mr. Carothers's retreating form.

He laughs at my stunned discomposure. "It did."

"But? Wha— I feel like I should have a dozen questions to ask you, but I don't know where to start." My mind is racing and there are a million thoughts all vying for first in line.

"The night you had Kyle, Michelle, and me over for dinner, you mentioned that you wanted your own show. All I did was mention in passing to Teddy how much their audience would love you, and he agreed. Who knows if your pitch will be picked up, but this'll still put you in front of the executives and other producers. It'll get your name and face out there, and you can begin building direct relationships that can only help you going forward."

"I don't know what to say." No one has ever done anything like this for me before.

He smiles and takes a step closer. The fingers of his free hand slide under the fall of my hair to my neck, and his thumb tenderly brushes along the edge of my jaw. "Shelby, I don't ever want you to think that I'm using you. Never. I want to help make your dreams come true. I want to support you, encourage you, and stand on the sidelines to cheer for you. That's what you do for people you love."

"You love me?"

He chuckles. "I do. I'm pretty sure I've loved you since the first moment I saw you months ago."

"Zach . . ." I step forward, and snuggle into his chest. His arm wraps around my back to pull me flush against him and then, one by one, the rest of my self-induced expectations of my life break free. The weighted chains clatter around my feet and my heart soars. Bending down, his face brushes against mine as he tucks it into my neck with his warm lips resting against my skin. For years I've said "career first, guys later," but what I've realized, with the right guy I can do both. It doesn't have to be one or the other, and I know I've found the person who's meant just for me.

"So, what happens next?" I ask and he pulls back a little to look down at me.

"We go inside and mingle with our guests, drink some wine, and the rest we'll figure out together, later."

"And here I was hoping you'd have a plan," I say playfully.

His lips twitch, and he holds back the smile I know is there. "The only plan I had was do whatever it takes to make you mine."

"Well, I guess that makes you two and oh."

"No, that makes *us* two and oh. Together, remember? If I win, you win. If you win, I win. Going forward, you and me . . . always," he says as if he's never been more convinced of anything in his life.

Tears fill my eyes and linger. He frowns as he notices the change and bends down to kiss my eyelids.

"These better be happy tears," he says, and a laugh bursts out of me.

"They are." I want to crawl inside him and be surrounded by him and his warmth, energy, and thoughtfulness.

His hands cup my face, and his thumbs swipe back and forth along my cheekbones affectionately. Blue eyes shine down at me with happiness and the corners crinkle as he smiles softly at me.

"I love you," I whisper.

"That's good, because I love you, too."

Needing to be closer, I raise up on my toes and his lips lightly brush across mine, before moving to the corner and pressing down more firmly. A rush of heat floods through me and makes me weak in the knees. I don't know if I'll ever get used to him and his delicious corner kisses, not that I'm complaining, I feel like the luckiest girl in the world.

Hearing a *click* to our left, Zach drops his hands to my waist as both of us turn to see the photographer grinning.

He shrugs and slings his camera up on it. "Seems like a nice photo to end the assignment with." He tilts his head toward the tasting room where the others are hanging, and I couldn't agree with him more.

"No." Zach cuts his eyes from the photographer to me.

A lot can be said in a look, and right now, Zach's crystal blue eyes are speaking volumes to me. There's hope in the transparency of his intentions, there's excitement for what's to come, and most of all, there's his love that he has for me and only me.

His heartbeat falls in sync with mine as it beats against his chest. And even though there's a mixture of people talking and laughing all around us, it blurs into a buzz that reminds me of the bees, and right this moment I can't imagine life being any sweeter.

Letting out a slow breath, Zach's smile tips up on one side, and just like that, I know. No matter what he says next, he's going to own me indefinitely, and I think that's the best plan of all.

"No, not the end . . . just the beginning."

The end.

Ingredients:

2 cups of flour
1/4 teaspoon salt
1/2 cup shortening
2 cups of fresh blackberries
1/2 cup sugar
2 tablespoons of cornstarch

How to make:

To make the pastry, in a large bowl sift together the flour and the salt, then add the shortening. One tablespoon at a time add ice water, until the dough forms into a ball. Refrigerate until chilled.

On a floured surface, roll out 2/3 of the pie pastry and press it against the sides of a lightly greased baking dish or cake pan.

In a large saucepan, add berries with two cups of water. Carefully stir in sugar and cornstarch until the mixture starts to thicken.

Pour into the pastry-lined dish.

Roll out the remainder of the pastry and cut into 1/2-inch strips. Lay them crisscross over the top of the cobbler.

Bake for 45 minutes to one hour, or until the top is browned and berries are bubbling.

Serve warm as is, or pour milk or half and half over the top. Also great with vanilla ice cream and/or whipped topping.

Acknowledgments

To my husband and my boys, none of this would be possible without you. Thank you for the endless amounts of love and support you give everyday to help me pursue my dreams. I am the luckiest girl and I love you more than all the words on all the pages, in all the books, in the whole world.

Elle, thank you for always holding my hand and continuing to be my voice of reason.

Megan, line by line you've helped me build this story to what it is today. Thank you for the time you've given and for your friendship, I appreciate you more than you know.

Tribe, they say stick with the people who pull the magic out of you and not the madness, well, the world better watch out, we're so magical we sparkle. I love you hard. Thanks to each of you for being who you are.

To my beta readers: Andee, Maritza, Erin, Brandy, Brenna, Jodie, Julie . . . thank you from the bottom of my heart for reading The Sweetness of Life in all it's phases, for all of your suggestions, and for making the story be the best it can be.

To the team of people who brought this story life: Ashley the grammar guru from Adept Edits, Virginia and Karla my proofreader extrodinaires, Braadyn from ByBraadyn photography for the beautiful cover shoot of Julia and Mike, Julie Burke for the gorgeous cover design and teasers, and CP Smith for the perfect formatting . . . Thank you! Thank you! Thank you!

To the readers, thank you for your patience. I may not be the fastest at releasing stories, but know that one is always headed your way. I hope you enjoyed this first book in the Starving for Southern series, but be on the lookout for book two, Last Slice of Pie. It's coming soon!

As food is love, from me to you, I hope you enjoy the blog. Try a few recipes, I promise you won't be disappointed and remember . . . always slow down and enjoy the sweetness of life.

About the Author

Kathryn Andrews loves stories that end with a happily ever after. She started writing at age seven and never stopped. Kathryn is an Amazon Bestseller for her much loved Hale Brothers Series and is a chi-lit, contemporary romance, and new adult writer.

Kathryn graduated from the University of South Florida with degrees in Biology and Chemistry, and currently lives in Tampa, Florida. She spends her days as a sales director for a medical device company and her nights lost in her love of fictional characters.

When Kathryn is not crafting beautiful worlds that incorporate some of her most favorite real life places, she can be found hanging out with her husband and two young sons, while drinking iced coffee and enjoying the sun. To find out more about Kathryn and her novels, visit:

www.kandrewsauthor.com

Also by Kathryn Andrews

THE HALE BROTHERS SERIES:

Drops of Rain

Starless Nights

Unforgettable Sun

STANDALONE:

Blue Horizons

Made in the USA
San Bernardino, CA
05 June 2019